LIGHT

MW01139222

QUEERS DESTROY SCIENCE FICTION! SPECIAL ISSUE

LIMITED EDITION

ISSUE 61 • JUNE 2015
GUEST EDITED BY SEANAN MCGUIRE

LIGHTSPEED MAGAZINE: Queers Destroy Science Fiction! Special Issue   Issue 61, June 2015

Publisher: John Joseph Adams   Guest Editor: Seanan McGuire

LIGHTSPEED

QUEERS DESTROY SCIENCE FICTION! SPECIAL ISSUE
ISSUE 61, JUNE 2015

FROM THE EDITORS

ORIGINAL SHORT FICTION
edited by Seanan McGuire

ORIGINAL FLASH FICTION
edited by Sigrid Ellis

REPRINT FICTION
selected by Steve Berman

EXCERPT
presented by Open Road Media

AUTHOR SPOTLIGHTS
edited by Sandra Odell

NONFICTION
edited by Mark Oshiro

PERSONAL ESSAYS
edited by Wendy N. Wagner

MISCELLANY

The Queers Destroy Science Fiction! Manifesto

QDSF Editorial Team

Seanan McGuire, Guest Editor

Some things are invisible.

Air. Gravity. Faith. Love. When I was a child, I moved through the world unaware of the invisible things around me; I grew to know them as they impacted my life. I learned that without air, I couldn't breathe. That without gravity, I couldn't walk. I found my faith in the places where it was waiting for me, and I learned about the different kinds of love. What took longer to learn was that I lived in a world where certain kinds of love were considered better, or more valid, than others. Where if I read a book that was full of people who loved each other, whose love I could see in the space between the sentences, I would be told that some of the love I saw didn't exist. Men and women loved. Men and men, or women and women? No. Never.

Science fiction was the genre I turned to when I wanted to be told that things would get better, that we would carry air to the bottom of the ocean and gravity to the depths of space, that our faith in the unknown would never waver. And even there, again and again, I found the denial of most of the invisible force of love.

That's finally changing. This collection, this grouping of stories and essays and personal moments, is a part of that change. Because you can see the air on a foggy day. You can see gravity pulling a stone down. You can even see

1

faith in the way we reach for each other, flinging our hands across the void, confident that someone will be there to catch hold.

It's time that we finally admitted that we can see the love that's everywhere, filial and romantic and platonic and shared by all different types of people, in all different combinations. This is the future. All we have to do is open our eyes, and see.

STEVE BERMAN, REPRINTS EDITOR

Once we told stories to stay alive. Stay sane, stay together, stay special. Around a fire, gesturing at the burning coals, at the men and women huddled together, at the stars. Oh, yes, the stars. The open sky, whether dominated by the single star, so close and majestic, we worshiped for thousands and thousands of years (and still do, to an extent, at Fire Island and Rehoboth Beach in summertime) or at night when tempting jewels stayed out of our reach. The queer ones told stories. We have always been there, from the beginning, and our tales, our songs, our verses comforted the ones that felt different from the rest. Gay and lesbian culture as we know it, gender dysphoria, and the rest of the complicated spectrum of sexual and gender identity may be postmodern constructs, but there have always been men who loved men and women who loved women and folks who felt suppressed by what society told them to wear and act because of what was found between their legs.

When *Lightspeed* publisher John Joseph Adams asked me to be the reprint editor, I was honored. Is there any better feeling than unearthing a treasure, showing it to others, seeing their faces, knowing their imaginations are set on fire by what you share? Most of my choices are from the later decades of the twentieth century—alas, so few queer-identifying authors wrote spec fic before I was born. The Golden Age of SF is a rather heteronormative, pale one. I imagine that transgender readers must feel the same way about years where I first read a gay story by a gay author; and so, for one of the best works of science fiction by a trans author, I looked to recent times, when folk are realizing that binary in SF should remains 0s and 1s and little else.

Geoff Ryman is probably the most well-known of my choices. I wanted to include his massive and genius "A Fall of Angels, or On the Possibility of Life Under Extreme Conditions," but I don't want to break the bank on the paperback of QDSF, so enjoy his "O Happy Day!" and do yourself a favor and buy Ryman's collected stories. He's both a gentle man and a gentleman.

I want to thank everyone who offered suggestions (including the eager authors who wanted to be part of QDSF—your enthusiasm for the project moved me). I double my gratitude to John and Wendy who were not only wonderful parents to QDSF but made me feel special. I was allowed to share stories. I felt alive. Come, stare at the stars with me.

SIGRID ELLIS, FLASH FICTION EDITOR

The term "science fiction" is sometimes metonymy for "the future." We hear people say "it's like science fiction" when they mean "this is what I imagined the future would be." But the two-edged sword of fiction is whether it is descriptive or prescriptive—does it describe some things out of many or does it define the limits of the possible? This is an incredible power. Those of us who produce fiction have a responsibility to wield that power for the greatest good.

I chuckle at the title of this anthology. Queers can't destroy science fiction. No one can. No one can destroy the future. But we can, through malice or complacency or inattention, limit the future. We can so narrowly, so tightly map the possible that we wall ourselves into a cave of our own making. And we queers, we can and will and must destroy that narrowness of scope.

We have always been here. We will always be here. Destroying the familiar, the comforting, the sameness. When we do so, we make the future greater, wider, more open to all. When we destroy science fiction, we must do so with joy and glee.

I found that joy in editing the flash fiction. I found that joy in the humor, anger, hope, and brilliance of the writers you soon will have the pleasure of reading. If we have destroyed anything, it is merely to bring you a shining future.

MARK OSHIRO, NONFICTION EDITOR

I'm always perplexed (and, if I'm being honest, peeved) by the tokenization of queers and LGBT characters within this genre. With few exceptions, there only seems to be room for one of our kind within a work of fiction. No matter the role we play in these stories, our purpose tends to be singular. Our participation limited. Our meaning muted. For all the talk of diversity and representation in this community right now, there seems to be something missing from it: We flock to each other.

While geographical boundaries or intersecting marginalizations may make socialization difficult, I've found that we queers seek each other out. We form communities within communities, as is the case within SF fandom at large. One of the most rewarding aspects of soliciting and editing the pieces for the nonfiction section of QDSF has been because of this phenomenon. I'm a longtime SF/F fan, but relatively new to the community itself, so it's been a pleasure to have the chance to meet and become friends with other queer and

LGBT fans and writers and creators who love the same things I do. I wanted to foster that sense of community with the pieces I chose, even if that meant turning a critical eye on what we consider a community. But that's important to me. Community has never been about assimilation or homogenization; the communities I felt most rewarded by were those that challenged me.

I hope these works challenge you.

Paul Boehmer, Podcast Producer

Working on this project has been extremely fulfilling in ways I hadn't quite realized. I have been a science fiction fan for as long as I can remember. I raced home after school to see afternoon reruns of *Lost In Space* and *Star Trek*. I couldn't read enough of it. I built model space ships and made special effects movies. I was a geek. I was different. I remember the promise of flying cars. I believed.

I never thought for an instant that there would be the sweeping change that we have witnessed in the past ten years. I believe that we are living in future times. This is science fiction fulfilled. We are always marching toward further acceptance in society, and we *continue* to move forward. I believe that one day we will reach full acceptance, and that we will in fact boldly go ... where no one has gone before. This has been an honor.

勢孤取和
(Influence Isolated, Make Peace)

John Chu

Jake acquired his target as soon as he stepped into the cafeteria. For the good of the war, he had passed without a trace through forests and mountains to reconnoiter and assassinate. For the good of the subsequent peace, Jake now needed to have lunch with a random stranger and emulate a human being.

The target sat by himself at a table in the corner, staring at his tablet. His lunch sat untouched, his chopsticks clearly unused. Slices of poached chicken breast lay on a bed of brown rice next to a pile of kimchi. The soy sauce and star anise of the poaching liquid and the spicy salty tang of the kimchi no one else seemed to notice hit Jake from across the room. Far more interesting than four slices of cheese pizza. Grease pooled in tiny orange circles on Jake's slices and soaked through the paper plate onto his hands.

"Excuse me, is this seat taken?" Jake pulled out the seat next to his target as he set his slices of pizza on the table.

The target's gaze flicked up at Jake. "Cyborg."

"Well, that didn't take long."

The mission was to avoid detection. If cyborgs could pass for human here, they could pass anywhere. Everyone on base knew that Jake and the rest of his squad had been ensconced here until DAIS decided their fate. They'd been sold out in the peace treaty. If DAIS could be convinced that cyborgs could successfully blend into society, DAIS might choose not to obey the treaty and decommission—that was the term the treaty used—them.

"The behavior's about right, but you'd look more plausibly human if you lost, say, twenty, thirty pounds of muscle." The target set his tablet down on the table. Text and a diagram of black and white circles on a 19x19 grid, a Go problem, filled the screen.

"So would you." Jake glared at him. "That's why I chose to sit here."

Both Jake and the target were cracked tea eggs, white veins of scar tissue radiating across their skin. The way the target's shirt warped around his torso betrayed the sort of solidity that didn't come from benign neglect.

"Except I *am* human."

"No kidding. Any of us would have solved that puzzle long ago." Jake gestured to the tablet. "From that board layout, if both black and white play optimally, white will win by five stones. See ya. I'll try to fool someone else."

"Wait." The target reached for Jake's forearm. "You play Go?"

Jake rolled his eyes. "No point. Too much like work. I used to. Before."

"Before?" The target picked up a slice of poached chicken breast. "Before DAIS reconstructed you."

Jake discarded the sarcastic remark that headed his list of conversational alternatives. Snarking with every response was a decades-old gambit that anyone on base would recognize. Cyborgs soared through the Turing Test— they still had some human brain function, after all—but composing words was just a sliver of what he needed to do. He couldn't merely pass for human; no one could be allowed to suspect he wasn't.

"I'm too good at it now." Jake shrugged. That sounded arrogant as all hell, but nothing he could do about that. "During the war, I used to joke that the worst thing DAIS had done to me was destroy my love of Go."

"Too good at it?" The target's questioning gaze brushed Jake.

The face that gaze betrayed, the slim hope of seeing it again could have pulled Jake through the war. Jake bit down that unhelpful thought.

"Are you just going to repeat everything I say? Who's the cyborg in this conversation?"

"Tyler." The target offered his hand. "Please, sit. Can you walk me through the answer?"

Jake shook Tyler's hand, pursed his lips, subjected Tyler to a critical gaze, then sat down. Dealing with humans was annoying. He had to do everything off-speed. Dealing with humans who treated him like a glorified computer was especially annoying, even if the human in question had an especially winning smile.

"Sure." Jake pushed away his greasy paper plate and then pulled the tablet to him. "I can be Jake, the analysis engine."

"Oh, I'm sorry." If Tyler's head radiated any more heat, he'd have glowed. "That was really thoughtless of—"

"It's okay." Jake knew how to be polite. "You actually asked."

Being Jake meant he could break down the Go problem and savor the fragrance of Tyler's lunch at the same time. The sweet meshing with the salty crashed into the spice and tang. For a moment, the heat of the gas stove in his parents' kitchen grazed his face. He let that rare fragment of Before drop to the back his mind. The child who experienced that had become something else entirely.

Being Tyler meant Tyler's gaze gravitated to the pizza and darted to the tablet only when he caught himself. If there had ever been a great pizza shortage, Jake would have known about it. Still, Tyler's odd behavior was making him wonder.

"Trade lunches?" If Jake was going to grind through an analysis, Tyler had damn well better pay attention.

Tyler pulled the pizza to him, then slid his own lunch to Jake. Pizza sauce dribbled down his chin when he smashed a slice into his mouth.

"Pro tip." Tyler wiped his chin with a napkin. "If anyone challenges you on the pizza, tell them that today's your cheat day."

Jake tested a slice of Tyler's chicken. Overcooked chicken breast had the taste and consistency of soft wood. During the war, he'd resorted to eating trees more than once. Tyler's chicken still had a hint of pink and a mild flavor that underlay the star anise and soy sauce. Not that surprising. Tyler looked like someone who'd cooked then eaten a lot of poached chicken breasts. Jake wanted to inhale the chicken like Tyler was inhaling the pizza.

"Is today your cheat day?"

"I had one coming." Tyler took the next slice in multiple bites rather than one. "Look, I owe you at least one real conversation. Are you free tonight? The Go club meets at seven. We can go for drinks afterwards. Plenty of unsuspecting humans for you to fool."

"Sure, if you can get me off base."

Tyler's face broke into an amused expression. "You can't sneak away unnoticed any time you want?"

Jake glared back. "We are choosing not to flout the peace treaty for now. Maybe later if we have no other choice."

Jake and his squad were illegal munitions. They'd blend into human society before they'd let DAIS kill them to meet the terms of the treaty. If they simply escaped, though, DAIS would have to search for them, hunt them down.

"So if I get permission to chaperone you out, you'll go?" When Tyler's gaze scanned Jake's face for a reaction, Jake gave him one. "You don't think I can?"

Jake could know everything about Tyler right now if he wanted. Breaking into even DAIS's databases was nowhere near as impossible as they'd represented to DAIS. However, he wanted to be surprised if Tyler could and disappointed when he couldn't.

"If you can, I'll go."

"It's a date, then." Tyler patted Jake's shoulder. Jake enjoyed Tyler's pliant touch, the gentle attempt to squeeze his shoulder more than he'd expected or wanted.

● ● ●

The gate out of the base looked plausibly intimidating. The base hadn't been designed to contain cyborgs; something had needed to be done about this, and what they did to the gate, if nothing else, was something. Barbed wire wove around substantial metal bars, blocking the outside world from view. Their pointed spikes writhed in a chaotic sequence. The gate seemed to ripple behind its implacable guard house and the sturdy soldier who manned it.

Even idling, Tyler's truck rumbled like a feral beast eager to kill, or at least to crash through the gate. Jake displayed his most naïve expression as Tyler and the sturdy soldier exchanged brief glares. The soldier tapped Tyler's badge against the sill of the guard house window as he weighed the situation. Tyler's faint smile dared the soldier to deny him exit.

The gate parted. The barbed wire tightened, choking out the space between the metal bars. The soldier returned the badge and Tyler's truck purred through.

"Requisition managers wield a lot of power." Tyler could not have been more deadpan. "Cross me, and you may never get so much as a pencil from

DAIS again." With that and a smile, Tyler made it clear that how he got permission to take a cyborg off base would remain a mystery.

At least the bit about Tyler being a requisition manager was true. Jake's squad mates had scoured the databases for Tyler as soon as Tyler offered to bring Jake off base. They could sense Jake now looking out the window, just as he could sense them reconfiguring the temporary structure that served as their barracks. He sighed. Their barracks weren't meant to be reconfigurable.

Tall buildings slid by on either side of the truck. Trees canopied sidewalks dotted with pedestrians. Jake didn't plaster his face to the passenger side window. Humans might get away with that; someone trying to avoid attention needed more self-control.

"You've never seen the city before?" Tyler's voice pitched high with surprise.

"Not in person, no."

"Hmm." As though Jake had just unwittingly revealed a vital secret.

The Go club met in the basement of one of the city's many interchangeable office buildings. Florescent lights buzzed from the room's low ceilings. People sat across from each other at long, thin tables huddled over boards already in various states of gameplay. A dozen conversations untangled into separate threads in Jake's head.

In the corner, Tyler taught a class on endgames. Jake leaned against a wall, watching the class and trying to be as unobtrusive as possible. That lasted for about thirty-seven seconds before boredom drove him to graze past the games in progress, sizing up each player, projecting every game to its conclusion.

Eventually, Jake found himself looming over a Go board and his sixteen-year-old opponent, Christie. She'd seen him come in with Tyler and, after dispatching her opponent in short order, she'd asked him to play. Based on what he'd seen, she might, at her best, beat a low-ranked pro. He aimed to lose by exactly three stones.

She pursed her lips as she played, her fingers lingering on the stone when she made key moves. Jake pruned branches from the tree of possible Go games in his head, choosing moves that created interesting situations but punished her misplays. He snapped his stones on the board with the arrogance of a blowhard who kept expecting that his next move would somehow put her away for good.

Tyler finished his lesson and stood behind Christie to watch the game. Chains of black and white stones spread across the board, pushed against each other and, sometimes, were captured. His bemused expression dissolved into concern as the stones solidified each player's claim to territory on the board.

When both players passed, Jake had lost by exactly three stones. Christie frowned.

"You let me win." Christie's quiet voice only amplified her disappointment.

"You won fair and square." Jake deployed his best confused expression. "You stemmed my every attack. I thought I was good, but—"

"If I'd wanted a teaching game, I could have asked Tyler." She began sorting the stones off the board into their respective bowls. "We're going to play again. For real, this time."

Playing for real, of course, would give him away. Given her attitude now, even winning by a mere few stones might. She'd belatedly realized how much he'd controlled the game play.

"I'm Jake's ride, Christie, and I gotta get going." Tyler's pointed stare at Jake vanished when Christie looked back at him. "Let's go, Jake."

"Good playing with you." Jake offered his hand, which Christie took reluctantly. "Look forward to hearing about your inevitable win at the U.S. Championships in a few years."

The bar was down the street from the Go club. Jake and Tyler had gone from one basement filled with people to another basement filled with people. However, the bar was darker, its occupants drunker and their words louder.

Tyler sipped his whiskey. He sat across from Jake and leaned in as he spoke.

"Instead of just pretending to play about as well as Christie, you just couldn't help picking at her weaknesses, could you? You did subtle work. She didn't realize she was playing a teaching game until the end." He gave Jake a sympathetic smile and continued, seemingly unaware of Jake's long-held puzzled gaze. "If you'd simply let yourself win, she might never have. Or, better yet, you might simply have just offered her a teaching game. From how you'd read all several dozen games in the room—What?"

Jake had held his surprise-indicating glare for what felt like days before Tyler got it. In reality, he knew it'd only been three seconds.

"You're debriefing my performance." Jake downed his whiskey in one gulp. Courage in convenient liquid form never hurt, even though his metabolism would burn it up in an instant. "Why?"

Tyler pursed his lips. He stared down at his whiskey, took another sip, then set it down. His fingers tapped against the glass.

"Not a good place to talk about that, but you're a sharp guy. Stick with me a little longer and you'll figure it out for yourself." Tyler matched Jake's gaze. "Jake, no one is ever going to mistake you for a normal human being—"

"But if I own up to that, they'll decide I'm an odd human and carry on. No one thinks 'cyborg' as a default. Understood."

"You're going to hate me for this, but it's for your own good." Tyler drained his whiskey. "We need to engage in sustained small talk."

Jake stifled his sigh. In the back of his mind, he sensed his squad rebuilding the barracks. Even though that hardly endeared to them to DAIS, it was still much more fun.

• • •

Jake's barracks now squatted over the parking lot like a hulking, three-legged beast. The squad doubted DAIS had intended the building to be configurable, but it was a temporary structure and cyborgs were easily bored.

A seeming visual contradiction that shouldn't have been stable, it disoriented anyone who didn't know how to parse it. Tyler had looked a little queasy before he drove off in his truck but the building made perfect sense to Jake.

The asymmetrical panes of the skewed windows were dark. The building made no sound except the faint whir of the air conditioning. The squad had decided they needed to debrief him too, then. They shared memories but constructed their own narratives. Jake leapt up to the door and wasn't surprised when Gray fell onto him as he walked through.

Gray slid him into a half nelson then shoved him to the floor. Jake shoved beds away as he fell.

"Gray, can we have the debrief without the horseplay?" Jake grabbed Gray's arm and rolled. He escaped, then backed away. "I'm not really in the mood for this."

"After all those hours around humans?" Gray threw himself around Jake's torso. "We have to be so damn careful around them." He launched Jake into the air. "Fine, but you need to pair with me."

They were never a gestalt and, by now, the consensus corridor defining their average mental state had shifted. None of them were in spec by pre-war standards and everyone dealt with it differently. Gray, for example, had a habit of pushing his mind even further out of spec. Nothing wrong with that on occasion, Jake supposed, except when you couldn't nudge yourself back into the corridor. Gray's habit was innocuous so long as he remained around sturdily built friends who had direct access to his mind. Anyone else would be crushed by one of his hugs with no way to calm him down. This didn't exactly show DAIS that they could survive long-term among humans without, say, accidentally killing them all.

Jake rolled out of his landing. As Gray reached for him, Jake quickly ran through the series of key exchanges that allowed them access to each other. Gray had gone too far out to adjust his own brain chemistry, but not so far that he'd deny access. Jake nudged Gray's mind into some less slap-happy state.

"You're no fun. You know that?" Gray set the tables and chairs upright again. "Nothing wrong with a little recreational mind hacking."

Gray was too hard, too buff, and too tall all at once to truly look human.

However, no human ever noticed. Blond haired with intense blue eyes and an irrepressible smile, he and his lightly pink, freckled skin invoked the heartland, middle America, and the Things That Made Us Great. Granted, this would be some sort of middle America where everyone changed the tires on their pick-up trucks by lifting them to chest height with one hand while loosening lug nuts with the other. He'd always been the squad's candidate for Cyborg Poster Boy.

Jake paced the room. Staying still was maddeningly hard when cyborg minds were in the corridor. His path weaved between the beds strewn around the room like an asteroid field. Gray weaved his own path. The two swerved past each other as though they were simulating two bodies of a many-body problem.

"Nothing wrong with showing DAIS we can be trusted around civilians either."

"Does that matter? You've done the analysis like the rest of us. The consensus is still that they will likely follow the letter of the treaty. Which brings us to your boyfriend."

"Sure, he behaves like he's interested." Jake laughed. "He's just gathering intel. DAIS knows we won't simply wait for them to decide what to do with us."

"No, he's *also* gathering intel." Gray tapped his fingers against skewed window panes as he strafed the walls. "Getting permission to take you off base? Absolutely mating behavior. He's a peacock showing off his plumage."

What they hadn't learned about Tyler intrigued them more than what they had. No one believed that Tyler was merely a requisitions manager, if he actually was one at all. For a human, staying in Tyler's physical condition was a full-time job. Anyone who could get permission to take a cyborg off base—to make the United States contravene a peace treaty, even in secret—had to be more important than a front-line manager.

"He definitely wants us to know that he's a big deal." Jake rolled his eyes. "DAIS is undoubtedly playing some game where we try to score intel off each other."

"So as long as you're both pumping each other, you might as well pump each other." Gray made obscene gestures with his hands. "Know what I mean? Once we leave, you two'll never see each other again. Might as well have some fun."

Part of Jake knew that they should just escape as planned. However, they might have overlooked something, and Jake wanted DAIS's blessing to leave. Otherwise, they'd be hiding from a massive military organization for the rest of their lives. That always went well.

• • •

The door yielded to Jake on the third try. Its articulated slabs of metal clattered as they slid up rails on each side. Apparently, this gym didn't depend on a lock to keep people out. It depended on practically nobody being strong enough to lift the door. The sort of heavy machinery that could winch the door up would never make it past the base's perimeter security. Until Tyler suggested they come here to work out, Jake had wondered what the building was for. No source of information he could tap into even admitted to the building's existence.

The surprise on Tyler's face as Jake held the door open was worth giving away the limit of Jake's strength. In the past weeks, at Tyler's suggestion, they'd rock climbed, endured several adventure-type obstacle courses, and played Go and duplicate bridge, not to mention several types of chess against strangers. Jake enjoyed clinging to cliff faces and being drenched in mud as much Tyler did. That didn't mean Jake hadn't felt like Tyler was testing him.

Then again, Tyler gave away about as much as he learned. He was worse than even Jake at pretending any of the physical activities had challenged him. The struggling at advanced Go puzzles seemed genuine, though, as did playing only at a near-pro level.

"Oh." Tyler walked into the gym. "You're not supposed to be that strong."

But Tyler was more than that strong—and by a comfortable margin. He had planned on actually entering the gym, after all. Jake might have taken how blatantly Tyler had dropped that fact as an insult, but he didn't want to.

"Specs do get upgraded on occasion." For bonus points, Jake lowered the door smoothly to the floor rather than letting it slam back down. It cut into his reserves more than he liked but showing off a little now might put Tyler off whatever trap he'd planned. "Into the Faraday cage with me."

The door sheared away Jake's remote senses as it sealed off the gym. Losing access always unsettled him. Information stored on every networked computer in the world, live data from countless surveillance devices, and the presence of his mates in his head blinked away. He'd worked on his own plenty of times, but he didn't have to like it.

"Be careful as you enter, Jake." Tyler sat on a thick weight bench. "Gravity is about five times stronger in here."

As was everything else in the room. Benches and racks sported extra and thicker struts. Cables spun from carbon fiber rather than steel ran through the pulleys in various weight machines. The black padded floor felt hard but gave with each with step. For all of that, the room might otherwise have been any other weight room. Mirrors filled every wall, except for two small gaps for doors into other rooms. Weight machines and benches sat in rows in the warehouse-like space. Hefting ridiculously heavy weights over and over again was still the best way to actually get stronger, even if science and technology had obviously increased Tyler's potential strength.

The air felt thick as Jake's lungs pushed against his new weight. He'd humped this much weight before, but never for long. Just being in this room was out of spec for him. That Tyler was stronger suddenly mattered.

"Okay, you've got me at my most vulnerable." Jake sat next to Tyler on the bench. "How long before you kill me?"

Tyler tensed. Fear bound him like an ill-fitting shirt. "你聽懂不聽懂國語?"

Jake stared at Tyler, annoyed that Tyler had asked if he understood Chinese in a way that assumed the answer. They'd discovered while hanging off a cliff face that they were both children of immigrants who opened restaurants when they'd settled in the States. "國語" gave away that Tyler's parents had come from Taiwan. Someone from the mainland would have called Chinese "普通话."

"當然聽懂。 不過十億多人講的語言不比英文安全。"

"Sorry, bad habit." Tyler had the good sense to blush. "You're right, of course. A language spoken by one billion plus people isn't safer than English. I dunno. Since I was a child, I've always thought of it as my secret language."

Jake stood. His thighs burned from the extra weight. It might be good to leave before he was too weak to open the door.

"You didn't bring me here to share your childhood misconceptions about Chinese."

"No, I didn't." He sprang to a stand and then spread his arms, showing Jake his palms. "I need you to break my shoulder."

Well, if Tyler insisted. Even if nothing else, it might even up the odds if they had to fight later. Jake sized Tyler up, then launched himself at him.

Momentum shoved Jake to the floor and, on reflex, Jake made Tyler his crash pad. Tyler's scream hid the crunch of bones. Even in normal gravity, Jake was heavier than he looked. His legs nearly buckled as he picked himself up off the floor. Stomach felt as though it hadn't come up with the rest of him. Killing Tyler would definitely not convince DAIS that cyborgs could be trusted among civilians.

"What the fuck is wrong with you?" Tyler lay supine, his limbs and torso twisted at unnatural angles. "Break my shoulder, not smash my skeleton."

"I thought your bones would be like mine." Increased strength required a tougher skeleton to be useful. "Um, should you be glowing like that?"

Tyler's skeleton shone, highlighting the cracks in his bones. Ripped and bruised muscle sparkled. For the time being, Tyler was a collection of stars twinkling in a human-shaped, fractured, red sky. Crack by crack, his limbs straightened and his torso lined up with his legs.

"No, but I do when I push my heal rate out of spec." Tyler gestured Jake toward him with his head. "In case this doesn't go well, reach into my left front pant pocket."

"Excuse me?" Jake inched towards Tyler. "Is this ... foreplay?"

"How old are you? I have something I need you to pull out—" Tyler's gaze dared Jake to comment. "Microfilm. Take the microfilm from my pocket."

"Microfilm?" Jake stared at the white, palm-sized, slightly cracked reel of film he now had in hand.

"You know, old-fashioned microphotographic—"

"The only libraries more comprehensive than the one in my head are the ones in the heads of other cyborgs. I know what microfilm is. Why are you giving me a reel of it?"

The glowing eventually subsided. Tyler hefted his torso so that he sat on the floor. He shoved himself away from Jake before standing. Like Jake's, his legs seemed to buckle for an instant before recovering.

"Plan A was to be all badass so you'd realize what's on the microfilm is the truth. Spending myself to heal my body has the same effect, I guess." Tyler tottered backwards, his hands warding Jake away. "You control cyborgs by curating their access to information, right? Well, my project was conducted entirely off network. All records strictly on paper. You never even knew it was there to look for."

Jake turned the reel over and over in his hand. It was too delicate for this environment. He'd have to read it later.

"That doesn't actually answer my question." Jake zipped the reel into a pocket of his jacket. "What game are you playing?"

Tyler shuffled through one of the side doors, then returned with a Go board and two bowls of stones. "This, Jake, is the only game I want to play with you. How many handicap stones will you give me?"

Jake stumbled to the door out. Between his own failing strength and help from a spent Tyler, they crawled through the thin gap they opened and escaped onto the street with its normal gravity.

• • •

After words were had, the barracks were restored by the cyborgs to its squat right-angled self. The entrance now hugged the ground and the beds inside sat in a perfect grid. No one felt the need to piss DAIS off, even though Jake was the only cyborg left who had any hope of DAIS giving their blessing to sneak away. The microfilm had crushed that hope in everyone else.

Jake was alone in the barracks getting debriefed again by Gray, this time surrounded by cases of beer. They couldn't get drunk, not exactly. Gray's mind was barely out-of-spec and it'd drift back within the minute. Alcohol was just a pleasurable source of calories, and they were always running low on calories.

"Jake, you do understand why we need to leave now, right?" Gray crouched on a bed and downed a bottle of beer in one swallow. "We're not leaving anyone behind."

"Sure." Jake needed to demonstrate his non-consensus analysis was not a sign of malfunction. "No one replaces the calcium in skeletons with titanium, and then lards those skeletons with synthetic yet, strictly speaking, organic muscle fiber just for grins. Technically speaking, Tyler and all the other Organics are human. They aren't subject to the treaty. They're also stronger and faster than anyone else on the planet and smart enough to take advantage of that. We need to leave before DAIS makes enough of them that we can't leave."

Jake downed his own bottle of beer. He grabbed a new bottle for himself and tossed one to Gray.

"You have to hand it to DAIS." Gray snapped the cap off his bottle. "They knew if someone kept a cyborg curious and occupied, that would keep all of us here until they could get the infrastructure together to kill us. Which bring us, again, back to your boyfriend. You should do something about Tyler before we go. He's certainly not unwilling."

"Tyler gave himself away. He gave DAIS's entire plan away. That has to count for something."

"Yes. It's obvious to everyone except the two of you that you both are—as the kids say—sweet on each other."

"No, even if he were, that's not the reason he gave the plan away. Too smart for that. He has some other reason."

"He *also* has some other reason." Gray pointed his bottle at him. "Put this question to your supercharged mind: DAIS has soldiers who can dismantle us before we can stop them. Of DAIS's many secrets, this is the only secret that they've gone to any length to hide from us, and they've gone to an extraordinary length. Set Tyler aside for a moment. Do you seriously think they're going to give us permission to live within human society?"

"Passing for human is one thing. Hiding from DAIS for the rest of our lives is quite another."

Gray shrugged. "No plan is perfect, not even one of ours."

"No, not when passing is the best case scenario. There's no chance we could ever just be ourselves out there." Jake glanced down for a moment, then met Gray's gaze again. "We don't have a choice, do we …"

"No, we don't."

Jake raised his bottle in a toast. "To as much freedom as possible under the circumstances, then."

Gray raised his bottle in return. "To as much freedom as possible under the circumstances."

• • •

Plan A was for the cyborgs to simply disappear into the night. They'd jump the base's barbed wire walls, pretend to be human as well as they could, and create new lives for themselves. The base wasn't designed to contain them. Infiltration and elusion were why they existed in the first place. No one had built a database yet they couldn't access and alter in secret. Of course, no cyborg expected Plan A to work as stated, not with a squad of Organics guarding the walls every night.

Instead, the cyborgs went for Plan A-Prime. They scattered towards every section of the wall armed with pens and pushpins. Floodlights pinned everyone guarding the wall in pools of light. Jake aimed himself at Tyler, Gray rushing up behind Jake as an unnecessary chaperone.

Tyler's legs gave way. He collapsed to the ground along with the rest of his squad. Jake stood close to Tyler, but not too close. The increase in gravity that pinned Tyler would crush Jake. The high gravity zone they'd created trapped Tyler and his squad, but also fenced the cyborgs in better than any wall. It was a calculated risk.

"Go get it over with. Say goodbye to your boyfriend." Gray stood next to Jake, a pen in each hand, not to mention several in various pockets.

"Boyfriend?" Tyler managed only the one word before his chest collapsed. He shook but only managed shallow breaths.

"Ignore him." Jake gave Gray a dope slap. "He's not my boyfriend."

"I'm not?"

Tyler's face contorted with strain. That had to have more to do with him struggling against the sheer weight of his body than anything else. Jake decided to ignore Tyler's question and press on with what the other cyborgs were telling Organics they faced.

"Tyler, you can't show me a graviton generator without expecting us to figure out how it works." Jake shrugged. "Anyway, we had to reconstruct your gym. Don't worry. We left a write-up so you can undo our changes if you want. But we think you'll like the upgrades. It now has backup power. You can distort the gravity field anywhere on base, so you can create, say, a gravity moat around the perimeter. The upper limit on intensity is now somewhere north of ten times Earth gravity."

"Still. Not. Intense. Enough." With each word, Tyler squirmed away from the wall, inching his way towards normal gravity.

"Please, stop." Jake held out his palms as if the high gravity zone were this thing he could push against. "If you all would just succumb to unconsciousness from the strain of the extra gravity, we could disappear without hurting anyone."

"Have. A. Duty." Tyler continued to work his way towards Jake. Sweat plastered his shirt to his body.

"I need to see you do this, Jake." Gray handed Jake a couple of pens. "If you can't do this to him here, you won't be able to defend yourself against him out there."

"We have biometric data for all of you. Even out there, we'll always recognize you." Jake threw the pens into the air. "Sorry, Tyler. We just want to be left alone."

The pens tipped into the high gravity zone. They sped down towards Tyler, the pens' nibs glowing from the friction. The glow worked its way back until the pens were bright rods deforming in the heat. Tyler screamed as they pierced his stomach and leg. Screams from his fellow Organics echoed across the base. They'd tried to squirm away from the high gravity too.

"Pens?" Tyler stopped moving. "Kill. With. Pens?"

"We improvised." Jake shrugged. "No one notices pens going missing. But we're not trying to kill you, just knock you out so that we can return gravity to normal, then leave."

The flood lights went out. DAIS had cut the power. Even if the cyborgs did nothing, gravity would return to normal by itself when the graviton generator's backup power ran out.

The world re-rendered itself in shades of luminous green. Troops began to muster in the distance. In Jake's night vision, they looked those plastic toy soldiers kids played with. They'd keep their distance for now. Except for the Organics, any weapon that could take cyborg outs were sloppy enough that those troops would take themselves out at the same time. DAIS hadn't come to that yet.

Tyler's stomach and leg glowed. He grunted as he forced himself to sit up. A glowing, bent pen stuck out through the small of his back. He ripped the pens out of his body and screamed. Tears streamed down his face.

Grunts and shouts from the other trapped Organics crisscrossed the base as they all pushed themselves toward the cyborgs. They formed a slowly tightening ring as they plowed ahead only to collapse under their own weight.

The cyborgs linked their minds and caucused. Throwing more pens at the Organics would halt them for sure, or they could let the Organics exhaust themselves. Jake's view held sway. They stood pat and waited. No one had the appetite for war anymore, if they had ever had any.

Instead of lurching through the high gravity zone, all the Organics had to do was lie still until the graviton generator failed. After that, they could have easily overpowered the cyborgs. They were too smart not to see that. They were also too smart not to have planned ahead. They'd been ordered to prevent the escape at all costs. Either they chose to obey the order or they chose to look as if they were.

The Organics lay exhausted on the ground. Only the dull red glow of their bodies convinced anyone that they hadn't worked themselves to death. The cyborgs returned gravity to normal, and then leapt the wall. As he disappeared into the night, Jake hoped the Organics had exhausted themselves on purpose.

• • •

Dressed in a bulky jacket and baggy pants, Jake slid through the sidewalk crowds. People stared at him, of course, but not everyone and not every stare radiated fear or caution. Some were curious and a few were downright appreciative. All of them, fortunately, were fleeting.

The crowds thinned as he reached the outskirts of the city. Tyler didn't live on base. He lived in an apartment not an unrespectable march away. As if he were a normal person.

Jake made sure to arrive at night. He knocked on Tyler's door with a gentleness learned from broken chopsticks and cracked teacups. As his reward, Tyler, stripped to the waist, opened the door.

"Jake?" Tyler's mouth worked soundlessly for a few seconds before he could speak again. "It's impressive how no one has been able to find any trace of you since you escaped, but isn't the point of disappearing to stay gone?"

Tyler stepped aside and Jake entered the apartment. The coffee table and couch hunkered down like the massive beasts they were. Anyone else might have thought Tyler simply had a taste for austere pieces of solid hardwood. Jake suspected Tyler's furniture could survive a full-scale military assault, or at least accidental shows of superhuman strength.

"You want me to visit." Jake shed his jacket. It always cinched his shoulders, making him hunch over. He'd need freedom of motion if it turned out he'd guessed wrong about Tyler.

"You realize I'm more than capable of holding you here until my buddies show up. Once we have physical control over you, we can strip your mind bare, expose the locations of the rest of your squad."

"But you haven't called your buddies, and I don't think you will."

Tyler smiled. "Why not?"

"Because you let us escape. You ate lunch at the cafeteria because you knew eventually one of us would sit at your table. What DAIS did to you and your buddies nicely dodges this peace treaty, but you're all looking ahead to the next one. You're smart, but you're not us. You'll need our help to disappear."

"Yeah, that too." Tyler hung Jake's jacket in a closet.

"And I owe you a game of Go."

"You do, indeed." Tyler gestured for Jake to follow him. "My Go set's in the bedroom."

The bedroom matched the living room's cool, clean style. An unadorned rectangular dresser sat against the pale tan wall. The closet's pocket door lay closed, melting into the surrounding wall. A skeletal cube of hardwood framed a substantial king size bed. Tyler reached into a drawer beneath the bed, then slid out a Go board and two bowls of stones.

"Let's play on the bed." Tyler centered the board on the bed, and placed the bowls on opposite sides. "I have to practice my finesse—"

"I'm aware of the problem." Jake slowly sank before the bowl of white stones.

Tyler did the same before the bowl of black stones. As they played, if either one of them moved too much or too quickly, they'd jostle the stones out of place and ruin the game.

"So how many handicap stones do I get?" Tyler leaned towards Jake, his hand poised over his bowl of black stones.

Jake shrugged. "As many as you'd like."

"Fifteen?" Tyler began laying out a starburst of black stones on the board.

Fifteen handicap stones was enough to allow a competent beginner to beat an accomplished pro some of the time. If Tyler never threw games to avoid attention, he'd be the top amateur in the country, perhaps even good enough to play professionally.

"Sure." Jake nodded slowly. "We can start there. Add more for the next game if you need it."

Tyler gazed expectantly at Jake. A smile spread across Tyler's face. Jake placed his first stone, the lone white stone defiant in the lower left corner against the surrounding swarm of black stones.

~

John Chu is a microprocessor architect by day, a writer, translator, and podcast narrator by night. His fiction has appeared or is forthcoming in *Boston Review, Uncanny, Asimov's Science Fiction, Apex Magazine,* and *Tor.com.* His story "The Water That Falls on You from Nowhere" won the 2014 Hugo Award for Best Short Story.

Emergency Repair

Kate M. Galey

Art by Paige Braddock (colors by Jose Mari Flores)

1. Allow system to cool before servicing.

I work the tip of a flathead screwdriver into the barely visible notch along the sternum and pry up the aluminum polymer casing covering the android's chest. My fingers burn when they make contact with the exposed skeletal components—no time to let it cool down. If I were back in the R&D lab at Hess Industrial, I'd spray the unit with a liquid nitrogen compound to get it down to temperature quickly and use therma flec gloves to handle the carbon-nanotube motors. But the Hess compound, with my lab and its specialized equipment, is all the way across the bay. It might as well be across the Pacific.

The inside of the casing is printed with instructions, complete with diagrams, but I shouldn't even need to look. I wrote them. I wouldn't be able to see them anyway, not in the dim light of the basement, not with my vision blurred by tears. I recite them step by step by memory, an anchor against spiraling despair.

The instructions tell me one certainty: This is one of the originals. One of mine. I wish it wasn't. I won't be able to forgive myself now.

If this works, you will forgive me. You've forgiven me for much worse.

2. Drain and flush the ferrofluid circulation system.

Along the clavicular ridge, I find the port to the circulation. Every system in my original design corresponds to human anatomy, a complex advertisement of the medical applications the technology could have. It's designed to be drained, and even with my improvised IV drip system the silver ferrofluid rushes out when the pressure is released.

What comes next isn't half as easy. It takes all my courage just to turn around, to face your still body on the bloody gurney in the corner. There's an IV line, a real one, running into a vein in your neck, the bag of saline suspended from the exposed PVC plumbing above. Dark deoxygenated blood fills the tubing and seeps into the clear liquid in the bag; without the beating of your heart to pull the saline into your veins, the blood seeps out.

Panic I can't afford surges in me, making my hands tremble and my stomach turn. How long is it since your heart stopped beating? Three minutes? Five? One is a minute too long. Every second I waste on grief, the odds of my success halve. I tear the saline bag from the tubing, replacing it with the silver liquid. Burgundy mixes with silver in the line. I twist a knot in the tubing, sealing it until I need it.

3. Remove the outlet housing and take out the core.

I go back to the android—back in my element—and lift the hatch covering the core. The core is revolutionary, the pinnacle of human technological achievement, the world's most complex chemical computer. It's the unit's brain and heart, all in a cylindrical cartridge that slides out of the center of its chest. It's my life's work. It operates on the same principals as a single massive cell: terrabytes of data are stored in artificial DNA within a nucleus while RNA carries operating commands. Just like a human heart, chemical interactions produce the electricity it needs. In the long term, the technology in my design could have replaced organs, revolutionized renewable energy, mined asteroids for precious resources, terraformed Mars. Instead, it self-replicates like a cancer, consuming whatever it can convert to energy.

The glowing eyes of the unit dim with the core gone. I can't help but savor it. It's meaningless—the androids don't have lives to end—but ripping its heart out feels good after what it did to mine.

I've been trying to avoid thinking about what I have to do next. My doctorates aren't worth half a damn here—I'm not the surgeon, you are. But I can't quit. I can't give up on you. You didn't, not even after everything went wrong and the whole world turned on me.

I run my fingers along your chest. I know every inch of you by touch, and the topography under my hands is all wrong. I can feel where your ribs caved in along the sternum from my failed attempt at CPR. That's where I have to cut. I press my lips against your collarbone, right where I will start the first incision of the Y-cut that will open you up to me. Your skin is still warm against my lips. I wrestle down a sob; you don't have time for sentimentality. I'm armed only with scraps of 201-level anatomy I retained from college and whatever vicarious knowledge you managed to pass to me, but it's not as if I can do any more damage than what's been done. I pick up your scalpel and press the blade to your flesh.

It cuts easily. The blood pools but doesn't surge. I have to remember that the flesh and bone, that's not you. You're in the wetware, in the brain, a chemical computer of such complexity that I couldn't dream of replicating it. The longer I wait, the more of you goes dark. It's all just mechanics at this point, and that's what I'm good at. I pick up the circular bone saw, tearing through the muscle and cartilage to get at the broken component.

It's too messy. The viscera starts to overwhelm me. I'm sawing through meat with no idea what I'm doing, or even what it will look like when I find what I'm looking for. The ribs are keeping me out, caging the vital parts of you that power the part of you I love the most. How is your body this resilient, this strong, but so easily broken?

I find the heart at last, deep in your mangled chest, a smooth muscle between the lungs. It belongs to me, isn't that what you always say? I wonder if it still does, even though it's not beating. I pierce it with the diamond tip of your knife, through the thick tissue to the hollow chambers within, carving an X into your heart.

4. Clean the core mounting surfaces.

I crack open the seal on our last gallon of water, pouring every ounce into your open chest cavity. You always tell me to be careful with it, to ration it. It's what's left of your disaster kit, the one you kept in the trunk of your car just in case. It's kept us alive ever since we fled back into the city I destroyed. You used to joke that with me, you had to be ready for anything. I wonder if you ever suspected the disaster you prepared for would be my fault.

The last of the precious liquid runs red onto the floor. I use a fistful of gauze to blot at what remains, but I can't get everything dry. Five liters, isn't that what you told me? We've all got five liters inside of us, and that's eighty percent of what we are. If two liters of that drains away, that's enough to kill us. The last death total I heard—months ago, back before the feds came hunting for me—was sixteen thousand. That's thirty-two thousand liters of blood spilled, at least. And all of it is on my hands.

Well, metaphorically. It's only your two liters staining me red from elbow to fingertip right now.

5. Insert core into outlet housing, pushing firmly to properly seal the core in the housing (as shown in the diagram).

The diagram is sterile and cartoonish, all arrows and exclamation points. It's so incongruous with the nightmarish viscera around us that I can't stop myself from picturing a grotesque cartoon of my own, a stick figure standing over a body with Xs for eyes, an image showing a cylinder disappearing into a perfectly symmetrical cartoon heart. I could almost laugh. You never liked that sense of humor, the way my mind goes right to the absurdity in tragedy. You'd never laugh at something that hurt another person. I know it bothers you that it doesn't bother me. But with things like they are, with the entire West Coast a no-man's-land and my androids advancing to the east, I can't help myself. What good is empathy against killing machines?

I've got the core, still glowing white from the chemical reactions happening constantly inside, in my left hand. With my right, I reach into your heart, pulling it open with my fingers until the core will fit in the gap. It's exactly the wrong way to do it, at least according to the diagram, which warns with exclamation points and big red slashes not to put my fingers near the housing when I install the core. I wish the diagram had been that emphatic about activating the androids in the first place.

You tried. I know you did. You tried to convince me to take the teaching job at Berkley, to turn down the offer from Hess Industries. You were right— we didn't need the money. We've still got plenty, tucked away in a bank we couldn't get to even if the feds hadn't frozen the account. You hated the idea of Hess and their military contract turning my mind into a weapon. But I'm not like you. The work isn't its own reward, not to me. I wanted the world to see what I could do. I wanted to be the next Einstein, the next Marie Curie. I never thought I'd end up being Oppenheimer instead.

I slide the core into the incision I made. It's too long and juts out of your heart, but that shouldn't matter once it's activated. My masterworks adapt, self-repair, self-replicate. Command codes in their chemistry instruct them to alter their function based on their environment. They could have changed the world. I suppose they did.

If my life's work is worth anything at all, it will save you.

6. Refill ferrofluid circulation system and seal core housing.

I release the silver liquid into your veins. It's heavy enough that gravity starts the work, pushing the blood that's seeped up the tubing back down and chasing after it, but your heart isn't doing its part to carry it along. I have to squeeze the bag, pushing it into your system, until I see silver ooze out around the core in your heart. Without electricity, it's just viscous sludge, but once it's activated, it will move through you on its own. It will mix with your blood and emit electrical signals that will put the rest of your organs back to work like a system-wide pacemaker. In theory, at least.

We never got to perform human trials. That was going to be the next step. Hess's original grant money was intended to fund a prototype heart, an elaborate proof of concept to dazzle the media and lure investors in. But once they grasped the military applications, they wanted more. I wanted more. I gave them weapons, and when I turned them on, they did exactly what I built them to do. How were they to know the difference between friend and foe? They are essentially single-celled organisms, operating on only the base instincts I gave them. They weren't ready.

I never told you about the weaponized experiments. I thought you'd hate me for it. That shows how little faith I had in you—when the worst happened, when the androids breached Hess's attempt at containment and swarmed into the city, you braved the trip on foot from the hospital to the Hess campus to make sure I was safe. You told me what I created didn't matter, that you loved me for myself and not my work. I never understood how you made the distinction. Even after the evacuation, after the media firestorm and the federal manhunt, you stood by me, you defended me. When I fled back into the city to evade justice, you followed me, even knowing what we'd face. I don't deserve any of it.

Tens of thousands of humans have been killed by my computers, but none have ever been treated by one. You'll be the first. I selfishly hope you'll be proud.

I push your ribs back into place, trying to put your split chest back together the best I can. You keep an aerosol can in your medical bag: a spray-on bandage like shaving cream made of adhesive rubber foam. I spray it along your seam, and tan foam blossoms along your sternum. It's supposed to be flesh-colored, but it doesn't match the color of any flesh I've ever seen, certainly not yours. Still, it's your pride and joy, your own invention. It's a lot like you, in a way—simple and practical, understated but effective. You didn't even bother to patent it, so we never saw a dime, but you don't care.

The news channels, when there still were news channels, loved to bring that up. Their hyperbole labeled us the angel and the demon, the hero surgeon and the mad scientist. While my creations darkened the West Coast, your innovations gave hope to my victims. That's pretty much how it's always been with us, isn't it? I make messes, destroy things, hurt people, and you're always right there behind me, trying to make things right.

After all I've put you through, I wonder every day how you still love me.

7. Activate unit with remote electrical impulse.

The AED from your kit is on the floor. There's a crack in the LCD screen where I flung it against the wall after it failed to revive you, but the display lights up when I turn it on. It still works. I replace the old adhesive defibrillation pads and place one on your left shoulder and the other under your right arm. The display says it still has a charge, enough for one more shock. You'll need to charge it after this, but that's why we're in the hospital basement in the first place, isn't it? The old propane generator in the corner would have fed our meager electricity needs for weeks—long enough, maybe, for me to develop my kill switch and be the hero again.

It's just chemicals. All life, even my synthetic facsimile of it, comes down to chemistry. Therein lies the efficacy of my methods, and therein lies the cure. Cells are delicate; it doesn't take much to kill them. I can think of sixty solutions off the top of my head that might prove fatal to my androids. Of course, I built in countermeasures for most of those. The few that remain are impossible to synthesize without certain specialized equipment. Outside of the lab, genius is just a pretty word.

Thank God you're not a genius. You've got a mind for taking problems and finding simple solutions without a second thought. You knew that my core is almost chemically identical to a simple cell, and that was enough. Your answer? Sugar. Dextrose, in a 50% saline solution, injected into the blood stream could save a diabetic's life; injected into the tissue, however, it causes a chain reaction of life-threatening necrosis. Better yet, it's standard issue in any emergency medical kit.

The trial we performed on a salvaged core from the battlefields at Fisherman's Wharf proved it works. The hospital should have given us a base from which to operate, the computing power to spread the word outside the no-man's-land, and the supplies to create the kill switch. The public who waits with torches and pitchforks back in society won't be able to crucify me if I come back a savior. As long as we could restart the generator, our plan gave us a chance. Instead, it gave us this.

My creations are self-sustaining and self-replicating, in theory. They convert solar energy into power the way we convert calories into energy. But growth takes more than light from the sun. Organic or not, they are as dependent on electricity as we are. They've probably been on the same goose chase we've been on since the blackout. I shouldn't have been surprised to find the android there, drinking in the power, barring our way.

You should have run. But you never run. You're too brave. You take risks, you thrive off of adrenaline, you look before you leap. It's what has carried my heart for these long years; of course it would also be what breaks it. If you were just a little more of a coward, we could have beat a tactical retreat, lived to fight another day. If you had let me face my own demons, I might have gotten the syringe through its casing before it got you, and I wouldn't have watched you bleed out in my arms. I begged you not to leave me, but did you listen?

It's okay. I'm not mad. You know I can never be mad at you.

I push the button on the AED and stand clear.

Your back arches, your limbs kick and flail and twitch. The ferrofluid is doing its job, starting an electrical storm in your brain, the same as a seizure. I press my fingers to your carotid artery—I feel it throb under my fingers, and throb, and throb. I'm not Oppenheimer anymore, I'm Frankenstein, I'm Christ raising Lazarus. Your eyes fly open.

Can you see me?

~

Kate M. Galey is a speculative fiction debutante, with Queers Destroy Science Fiction! as her first publication. She migrated from the Colorado mountains to the Californian central coast, where she works at a beautiful zoo and lives among a wonderful menagerie with her oldest sister and her family.

Trickier With Each Translation

Bonnie Jo Stufflebeam

I watch my girlfriend leave me for the second time. Snow whispers through the crack as she opens, shuts the door. *Webber is leaving*, I think, as emotionless as the white walls in the hospital room where I just visited my husband, Logan, with his broken leg, one hour ago and ten years in the future. My hands still wring with the pressure of his grasp.

The first time I watched Webber leave, my chest ached, a heartburn that didn't disappear for months. We'd been together three years, my first love, but it had gone stale. She was the most beautiful woman I knew. I guess she still is, though I no longer know her in the present, not the way I do in the past watching her ice thin figure disappear down the stairs of my apartment. I worry, even knowing what will come of this, that she'll slip on the ice. She doesn't, of course, and even if she did, she could save herself. Superheroes are made to save. She slips inside her car. The engine rumbles, frozen snow cracking as she drives away. It will be a month before I see her again. It will be two years before we fully realize that we are no longer right for one another, a mess of swansongs and false beginning-agains.

I remember the warmth of Logan's skin next to me, the straight slate of his chest upon which I rest my head. His hands, big and red and thick, as they trace the outline of my body in our bed that feels like home. I wonder what will happen to him. As I'm being forced through time, translating, will he miss me, or will he never suspect that I'm gone? Will I see his future? I wish I could stop and explain what's happening to me. That our very best friend, Archer, is still in love with me, that he's pushed me into a loop I don't know how to get out of, that he is not to be trusted. "Logan," I want to say, "don't let Archer near you." But when I try to speak to Logan in the moments we're together, my throat closes up, another one of Archer's tricks.

"I've been a fool," I say to the empty apartment I used to call home. It no longer smells like home, musty and old and slightly sour. I look around at all my young person belongings: a couch ripped to shreds by our cat, a three-legged coffee table, posters featuring all our lesbian icons—Ani, Joan, Ellen. I remember, and feel an even bigger fool for forgetting, The Board. My own superpower: a board upon which I can pin any wish, and it will come true. I can wish to be let free. But rushing into the bedroom, where The Board hangs on my wall, I'm translated again; the scenery folds into itself, walls fall, and a new scene erupts around me. I put my hands on my knees, bend over, breathe deep.

I'm home, back with Logan, where we belong. Home. It never seemed so temporary. In another hour, it'll change again. It's only been three days since Archer's proposition, since he touched me in a way that made my skin crawl and pushed me out of time. Things happen to men, I know this. But I don't know it well. They're still new to me. I'm not yet used to their smell, used to the way their eyes travel a body like a hunter. Archer—a fitting name. I wish I'd gotten the clue.

• • •

It is difficult to tell a story out of time just as it is difficult to live out of time. I try to keep hold of the present, but it's trickier with each translation to know the present, to remember if a scene is new or old. And in a way each moment is new because I look on it with new eyes. The bigger moments are easier to categorize. Webber leaves me for the first time: past. As she walks out the door, I try to remember that she is not, after all, the love of my life. And because I remember Logan so clearly, the knowing is easy. But then another translation and I'm stuck with her in one of her coiled webs of tattered bed sheet and cat hair, and we are warmth against one another's cold, and she has a laugh like hot chocolate, and I'm there again, and she's mine again, and we are perfect, so perfect I can't be sure why we ever weren't.

After those moments, I'm cold with Logan, the way I was with her in our final weeks. He holds me close and begs, *What's the matter?* Slowly, I remember that I love him.

I ache for two hands, his and hers.

At each translation, I try to visit The Board, but as soon as I remember it, the world blurs. Archer has tripped his translations to trigger once I remember, which makes me sure that The Board would fix things. Of course it would; it's fixed so much. I close my eyes and try to force myself to translate back to the high school day I discovered its power, but I can't get there except in my head.

• • •

When I was a high school freshman, my mother bought me a cork board rimmed with a rainbow of costume jewels. When she handed it to me, I stared at the rainbow pattern; did she know, I wondered, about the feelings I'd been having for girls at school, the rainbow bracelet I bought at Claire's like a pea under my mattress? But she smiled so warmly I didn't want to ask. I'd read of the power of visualizing your goals, so I pinned up a picture of a test with a bright red A at the top. At school I got a B on the English test I hadn't studied for. I didn't try again.

Then Mom and Dad came down with The Infection, which doctors had just traced to a bacteria that overwhelmed the human body. They didn't have an antibiotic for it yet. I hadn't caught it, but they were so sick they couldn't move from their bed. I didn't sleep at night for fear of their deaths.

The doctors told us they wouldn't recover unless a cure was found, and fast. I wanted it so bad I could think of nothing else. I found a photo of us, a healthy family, in the shoebox under my bed. I attached it to The Board. The next day, headlines proclaimed that a cure had been found, an antibiotic which would destroy the bacteria and would be available to the public in one week's time, rushed by public need, some two million people ill.

Two weeks later, my parents were back at work.

I pinned more on the board: a Christmas wish list; an expensive meal my father then made, without my asking, for dinner; a haircut the stylist replicated perfectly but which turned out to make me look like a mole. I chalked The Board's power up to voodoo, some mystical power. After all, other people had told me about visualization. There was a popular book about it. But no one I could find online had quite the same success as I did.

Then the news came. The bacteria didn't make everyone ill. In a small number of people, mostly the young and the old, the bacteria made them stronger. Experts linked it with a recent string of hushed-up superheroics. An elderly man in San Francisco could suddenly fly, and a young woman in Dallas could morph into a giant praying mantis. I'd looked at these news stories and laughed. How ridiculous grown-ups could be, falling for these hoaxes again and again. But there was still the problem of that damn board. I decided to test it, for real this time, and glued a pair of wings to a picture of me. The next day I woke to an itch in my back where the wings had poked through, an outline of my body in feathers on my bed.

I took them for a test flight. That was when I saw Webber for the first time.

Remembering The Board, the bacteria that still nestles in my gut, I close my eyes. Can I make myself go where Webber first found me?

When I open them, a dizzying rush of warmth spreads through my body. I fall from the sky, where I've been soaring, where my gaze had just caught another girl's, my age, suspended from the side of the clock tower by a single string of webbing. I'm not used to the wings; it's been ten years since I've worn them. My stomach rises as I plunge toward the ground, flapping the wings like it might save me. But I flail about, jerking from side to side.

Then Webber's arms are around me, and we're sliding down a length of web which looks like it might be made of bits of feather and sunlight. When our feet touch ground, she lets me go.

"I reckon you're one of us," she says.

Her body is as thin as a child's, but she's my age, the acne marks on her face evidence of a passed puberty. She wears black jeans and a black sweater, and as she stands before me with her hands on her hips, I realize her beauty even through the jagged liner around her eyes.

"One of you?" I say, once I find my voice again.

The string of webbing has blown off in the wind, so she pushes her palms together as if praying. The wind shakes. Dust and dirt rush from both sides, from beneath the buildings, from the top layer of dirt in the flowerbeds in the city square. The bottom of my shirt lifts, the threads coming apart and moving toward her, where they meld with the dust and dirt. Before my eyes, an intricate web forms, though it's lopsided, the design like a toddler's snowflake cutting. She gets so much better, I think. One day she surpasses me.

"This is my power," she says. "What's yours?"

Of course. I understand, then, though here, this time, I've known all along. The surprise of revelation folds into the feeling of already knowing. An unbearable déjà vu.

"Those wings?" she asks.

"No," I say. "I can make anything I want happen."

But you, I think. I didn't make you happen.

"I showed you mine…" she says.

But as we walk along the path to my parents' house, my wings having folded themselves back into my skin—The Board's power, as I came to know, did not last, though I would learn to stretch its limits—I start to feel faint. My feet don't feel like my own; I'm inhabiting a body I don't belong in. We reach the door. She pulls me close before I open it and kisses me dead on the mouth, and I'm gone, translated behind the curtain of time, with no idea where I will end up next.

• • •

Somehow, Archer keeps me away from Logan as much as possible. I see earlier, childhood days and those first college days and the days where Archer and I first met, sophomores at the university, but I have yet to relive the experience of meeting Logan or the day we said the L word. The day of our wedding, Archer beside me, my man of honor. He was always more threatened by Logan than he was by any of the women in my life, as if he didn't think of women as competition. I hated that about him. It wasn't until Logan came along that there was ever any trouble between Archer and me at all.

He can't avoid all the Logan memories, however. Each time I stumble into one I'm reminded that Archer's power isn't as well-honed as Webber's came to be. He's weak inside. If only I could catch my breath long enough to exploit that weakness, to reach my hands into his ribcage and rip his power from him. Only of course this is not the way superpowers work, not outside of movies.

The next time I see Logan, we are in bed together, untouching in the tense air. I'm not sure what day it is, but there's a tightness in my chest. I'm upset about something. Beside me, Logan's silent. You fool, I think. There's nothing worth losing Logan for.

Before I can tell him that I forgive him for whatever wrong we've done to one another, to tell him that I too am sorry, I hear his ragged breath begin. This, then, is the first time I heard Logan cry. The ragged breath turns into a sound like hiccups, or a hyena's cry in the dark, the most animal sound I've ever heard. It rattles me.

"Rosalinda," he gasps. "Do you even like me anymore?"

We're two years in, unmarried. We've just moved in together and are adjusting to sharing our lives. I've been thinking I might not love him. Once I hear him cry, I'm sure that I do. I've never been surer of anything.

I wrap my arms around him. He doesn't cry for long; he is steel. I'm not used to such steel. With Webber it was never like this, never solved so easily. Always there was a trust to be regained, a balance to be restored. In the morning, I know, everything here will be stronger than before.

Except I won't be here in the morning. Or I will, but *I* won't be here. My body aches to be part of the past, more than a visitor. Instead, as I hold him, I know that I'll soon disappear and won't see him for days, for weeks, for years.

• • •

"Have you realized what a mistake you've made?" Archer says.

This is not the way it was to begin with. I've faded into a piece of my life I never wanted to remember. I'm in my bedroom, beneath a mound of blankets, the sickest I've ever been: a bacterial infection of the throat. I've tried already to heal myself through The Board, but all it gave me was the money for a doctor's visit, which I found beneath my car's tires, and a doctor's business card left on my windshield. The doctor, when I went, prescribed antibiotics. Being who I am, what I am, I cannot bring myself to take them; they might destroy the bacteria which gave me my abilities. I hid them in my bedside drawer. I will wait it out. It will take a full month to go away.

But Archer wasn't here the first time; he wasn't even part of my life yet. It'd be three more months before we met at my friend's Halloween party.

I cough. It hurts to talk, but I force myself. "I do," I say.

"You do?" he says.

"A huge mistake," I say.

I remember our confrontation. He kissed me without warning. We stood at the door to Logan's and my apartment after an evening of card games and glasses of cheap red wine and when it was time for him to go, time for Logan and me to rehash the night's events with our heads on our pillows and laugh into the night, Archer kissed me. Logan was washing dishes in the kitchen. I pushed Archer away.

"What the fuck?" I said. "Are you drunk?"

"I'm not," Archer said. "I'm still in love with you."

I knew, every time he looked at me with those doe eyes. They made my stomach churn. I thought our friendship was stronger than those eyes.

"You're drunk," I said.

"I'll show you," he said. "You don't love him like I love you. You don't." And he grabbed hold of my arm and didn't let go, not even when I screamed, and as I finally pried his fingers from me, I was struggling through a blankness, thinking I had fainted, thinking I had died.

Then it all stopped, all came into focus, and I was gasping in Webber's arms while she stroked my hair and said, *it's all gonna be all right. Just a dream. Just a nightmare, Rosa. It's over now.*

"I told you," Archer says. "I knew you didn't love him." He sits beside me, wipes the sweat from my forehead. Presses his finger to my lips. "You don't have to tell me. I knew if you couldn't love me, you couldn't love any man."

I open my mouth and chomp down. His blood wells across my tongue. He screams, pulls his finger from my mouth, wraps his hand around it.

"The mistake I made," I say, spitting his blood onto the bed sheet where the red spreads across the fibers, "was trusting you, you fucking coward."

Archer's lips shake the way they did after he kissed me the first time, sophomore year, two weeks after meeting me. I let him then. When the kiss was over, I got into my car and turned on the radio—a song Webber and I used to love, *come back to me, come back*—and bawled until my cheeks and chest throbbed.

"I know you, Rosa, better than anyone in the world. I was there for you when you had no one. And you never gave me a proper chance. Because you were always pining over her, over a woman who didn't deserve you." He paces back and forth at the foot of my bed. I'm not scared of him. He says he knows me, and he does, but I know him too. I've been under his skin for years. He can keep me trapped in his time loop forever, but he won't lay a hand on me. He is, after all, my best friend.

"And then, all of a sudden, you were over her? Fallen for a man, who wasn't even one of us? How can he ever understand you the way I do? I know what you need. You need someone fierce, someone who twists you into knots. Logan's tame. You can't possibly expect to be happy with him forever."

We've been married three years already, I want to say. *Together for five years of our lives.* But then, of course, I've said it all before. Every other year since Logan and I got together, Archer's broken down, told me he loves me, struggled to avoid me, given in. There was always a speech at the end where Archer went on about how he could learn to see me only as a friend. I'm an idiot. But I don't know how to let go of my only real friend. This time he's gone too far, done the one thing we promised we would never do, back when we first bonded over our shared strangeness. He's used his power against me. I won't ever forgive him.

"Just a chance, Rosa, it's all I ask." He stops, wringing his hands together at his chest as if he's any moment about to kneel at my bedside and burst into prayer. "I'm the best man for you."

Rather than answer, I hack a hunk of phlegm at him, but the blob lands at his feet. He stares down into it, then back at my washed-out face.

"Suit yourself."

And I am falling again, holding my stomach to keep from puking.

• • •

"What's the matter, darling?" My mother's hand holds me up. When I'm finally able to stand again, I am startled by a scene I haven't seen in a good, long while; my parents sitting together on the couch, enjoying a movie, though at this moment it's paused. I feel younger than I really am, filled with a nervousness I can't quite guess at the reason for. My stomach is a knot, and I don't know if it's the translating or something else.

"You look like death," my father says, patting the couch beside him. "Have a seat. Whatever it is you wanted to tell us, it can't be all that bad. Just lay it on us."

Mom nods. "We can handle it, whatever it is."

I sink into the couch cushions, peek at the television screen. It's a superhero movie. I laugh, then remember what I'm supposed to tell them here. I've never told them about my ability, about The Board. I never wanted them to think of me any differently; it's the only secret I've ever kept from my parents. And still, I think it would be less painful to admit to than this:

"I've met someone," I say.

"Well, that's great," my dad says.

"Who is she?" My mom smiles, squeezes my knee. "And when do we meet her?"

"His name's Logan," I say. I feel like a fraud. After all these years of claiming I could never love a man, I'm admitting that I was wrong. I know that they, though they accepted my relationships with women readily, do not understand. They can see me as either gay or straight, but I will never be both in their eyes. They will never know me, not really. Now they'll think all those years before were nothing to me. Just like that, a part of me buried in the dust.

It should be easy to tell them otherwise. But in a southern town, in a southern family, words stick in your throat until you give up and swallow them.

"That's great," my dad says. My mother chews her nails. *Men are different creatures*, she will tell me later. *Be careful, Rosalinda.* "We could use another man around."

• • •

After coming out, again, to my parents, after feeling as though I've given a piece of myself away, being translated back to Webber is like a welcoming home.

She cooks for me: blackened chicken and salad globbed with thick ranch dressing and sweet tea to drink. I do her dishes. She lives by herself, having been kicked out of her parents' house when she told them. I was lucky.

When we kiss, and then fall into her bed, I think of resisting. I imagine Logan's body, then hers, then Logan's again. Her sweat is tangy and sweet and her skin smells of sunlight. She clasps her hands together and shuts her eyes, and the fabric of her bed sheets unravels and forms a webbed design of roses above our bodies, pressing us closer.

"I love you," she says.

Because I no longer do, because I wish I still could, because she needs to hear it or the evening will spoil like the milk she left on the counter—later I'll find it hidden behind a pile of clean dishes in a drying rack—I say it back. "I love you too."

It almost feels true.

• • •

The next time the translation wraps back around to Logan I can't kiss him. I rationalize being with Webber, tell myself if I hadn't succumbed, if I hadn't repeated the memory as it was that first time, it would've caused a rift in my past. But I know that time is not quite so fragile. That much I remember from Archer's ramblings, his late-night beer-fueled tirades on the inaccuracy of time travel mythos.

"The big events aren't so easily altered," he would say. "Unless you do something drastic, like kill a man, or burn down a federal building, or do something where you're no longer in control of what happens to you, chances are your future will still iron itself out, that nothing will change."

He's made sure I can't do those things. I only have so long until I translate again, until I'm thrust into another memory.

It's been a long time now since I touched The Board. When I met Logan, I told myself I was going to do everything the natural way. Logan's abilities were limited: normal stuff. He could play the piano. He could carry a tune. He could cook the best tomatillo enchiladas, as authentic as my mom's. And I wanted to be fair to him, with him, so I hid The Board in my upstairs closet. Now I ache for it. If I could just stay with Logan, I could be sure again.

I say his name: Logan. It feels like it's been a lifetime since I've said his name. We're on our honeymoon, a pleasant memory marred by Archer's bullshit, marred by the lingering smell in my nostrils of Webber's coconut shampoo. Logan stands by the window in our hotel room, looking out over a South American city we never thought we would afford to visit; his parents lent us the money. We'll never be able to pay them back. Outside the window, young lovers walk with their arms slung around one another, giddy and drunk and sure of themselves. Logan and I no longer feel the heat of that new lust, and it's good to have a love that is calm and gentle. But I envy them their hot clarity.

"I'm out of time," I say. "Archer tore me out of time."

Logan turns, and the light hits him from outside. Then, in a flash, his face is a skull; his face is the face of Archer.

I scream, fall back onto the bed. He holds out his hand.

"What's wrong?" he asks, frantic. "Babe, what's the matter?"

But it's too late; I'm going. I'm gone.

• • •

Archer has more control than I thought. I can't go to The Board without translating. Can't tell anyone what happened. This leaves me little choice. I don't want to be confused anymore. I don't want to be the person I once was. I want my husband and my life and my best friend back. Only that last bit I now know I'll have to let go.

I met Archer sophomore year. At the Halloween party, I was dressed as Wonder Woman. He was Lex Luthor. We were the only two superhero-themed costumes at the party, drawn to one another across the room crackling with bad pop music and drunken chatter. I think we must have sensed our shared secret. We were two of the few who had chosen to keep the bacteria within us, to keep our ability. Webber wasn't there; we'd been fighting. I can't remember over what.

I'm surprised Archer hasn't made me relive this yet. I'm surprised I haven't seen as much of Archer as I thought I would. I thought he'd trip the loop somehow, make himself a frequent stop. Or intrude again, like he did when I was sick. Maybe that's a limit he can't overcome.

"You're one of us, aren't you?" Archer asked me later as we stood on the balcony, smoking cigarettes. Archer still smoked them; I'd given them up a year after college.

"Us?" I said.

"I haven't found any here yet, not at this school, but there's a huge online presence."

I nodded. "I'm one of you," I said. "My girlfriend, too."

"What's your power?" he asked.

"What's yours?"

That was the first time he touched me, a stroke of his finger down my arm. I shivered. Goosebumps rose. I felt like falling, a confused fog in my brain, a dizziness which overcame me until I realized we were in the midst of frozen time. Behind us, a young man stood with one foot outside the door, one foot in, his mouth open in one of those embarrassing expressions like when you pause a movie while an actor is speaking.

"Come with me," he said. We scaled the patio fence and walked to the apartment pool, empty at that time of night. We went through the unlocked gate. He pushed me into the water. The splash froze in the air. I grabbed his feet and pulled him in after me. My stomach felt light, as if I might could get used to this, this boy thing. But once we got back to the party and time fell back into its familiar rhythm and he kept talking, kept downing bottles of Shiner Bock until his eyelids drooped, I changed my mind, not for the first time. Men weren't for me. Not at this age, at least.

I told him goodnight. We exchanged numbers. After that first awkward kiss when Webber and I broke up the first time, after weeks went by and we still found ourselves talking, after he met Webber once we got back together and they got along in a bickering brother-sister kind of way, after he was able to put his arm around me when we broke up yet again without trying to kiss me, I knew we'd be friends for a good long while.

The next time the loop throws us together, translates into a time before this madness, I wrap my arms around him. We've just returned home from a party; he's broken out his battered tarot cards, a brief hobby of his.

"What do you want me to read for?" he asks, our knees almost touching as we sit cross-legged on the floor.

"Read us," I say. "Read our friendship."

But the moment he turns over the first card—the tower, crumbling to pieces—we're interrupted by a knock on the door.

He never finishes that reading. Webber enters the room, her body jittering with unspent energy.

"Let's go out," she says. The glass lamp on my nightstand rattles. Webber and Archer head out the door. I tell them to go ahead, I'll follow. In the real memory, I go to The Board. I pin a picture of Archer and me onto it, hope that we'll stay friends forever, no matter what. This time I don't. I want to relive this memory, and if I go to The Board it will end.

We go into the night. Archer freezes time, and Webber spins webs from grass and sand and we watch her build them like art across the campus buildings. We sit in the grass, far enough away from her that we are not caught in the crossfire, and we laugh and lie back in the grass and watch the smog drift across the stars. I wish I could love him. I wish I could forget the man at home, could go along with Archer's crazy scheme. It would be easier.

Logan is waiting. Or not waiting, because time has possibly frozen for him, because he has not realized my absence yet. I like to think he can feel me being gone like a limb missing. But maybe it's not like that.

As I watch Webber dart across the grass, such power in those fingers of hers, part of me wishes for her, too. Because we belong together in a way, more than me and Logan. We grew up together, discovered ourselves together. We each hold power in the palm of our hands. But I know if I were with her, I would still miss the part of myself that loves him, loves a man, loves the only man for me.

Once I'm falling again through the loop, it becomes a waiting game. The perfect moment. I'll know it when I'm in it.

• • •

It takes time I cannot quantify. Time means little to me, yanked in and out of the past like this, pushed into my childhood, adolescence, young adulthood. My life rushing by like scenes outside the window of a train.

Then it comes. A minor moment, nothing special. It is after that illness which kept me bedbound for a month. I find myself at my dinner table; my mouth tastes of cheap chicken noodle soup. I laugh into the bowl of runny broth. I have to take this slow. I don't know if it's possible, but I don't want Archer to know I've got something planned.

I stand and place my bowl in a sink overflowing with dishes. When I open the door to my room, I am met with the smell of dirty laundry and stale air. The bottle of antibiotics is where I left it, in the drawer of my bedside table. I slip it into my pocket.

Back in the kitchen, I dump the whole bottle down my throat.

• • •

When I come to, I'm in Logan's and my apartment. An empty bottle of red wine sits on the coffee table. I'm sprawled on the couch. I try to remember the past as I knew it happened, but the memories are gone, nothing more than a story I choose not to tell myself.

I met a man once, at a Halloween party, dressed as Lex Luthor. I was dressed as David Bowie. We had nothing in common. Our conversation was brief. I remember looking at his costume and thinking it was sad. I'd lost my own abilities a month earlier: antibiotics. Webber had been angry, asked me again and again why I'd taken the pills. I didn't have a good answer.

When I met Logan, that part of me, The Board, the superhero shit, was nothing more than a once-I-was story. We were both normal people.

As for Webber, well, we always hang onto our first loves longer than we should. I let her go, but I keep the parts that made me who I am, the parts that have loved a man and women equally.

Logan walks into the room, his hands all wet and wrinkly from dishes. When he touches me, I don't shrink away. I let him rub his wrinkled hands all over. They feel like home again.

~

Bonnie Jo Stufflebeam's fiction has appeared in magazines such as *Clarkesworld*, *Beneath Ceaseless Skies*, and *Interzone*. She lives in Texas with her partner and two literarily-named cats: Gimli and Don Quixote. She holds an MFA in Creative Writing from the University of Southern Maine's Stonecoast program and curates the annual Art & Words Show in Fort Worth, profiled in the March/April 2014 issue of *Poets & Writers*. You can visit her on Twitter @BonnieJoStuffle or on her website bonniejostufflebeam.com.

THE ASTRAKHAN,
THE HOMBURG, AND
THE RED RED COAL

CHAZ BRENCHLEY

Art by C. Bedford

"Paris? Paris is ruined for me, alas. It has become a haven for Americans—or should I say a heaven? When good Americans die, perhaps they really do go to Paris. That would explain the flood."

"What about the others, Mr. Holland? The ones who aren't good?"

"Ah. Have you not heard? I thought that was common knowledge. When bad

Americans die, they go to America. Which, again, would explain its huddled masses. But we were speaking of Paris. It was a good place to pause, to catch my breath. I never could have stayed there. If I had stayed in Paris, I should have died myself. The wallpaper alone would have seen to that."

"And what then, Mr. Holland? Where do good Irishmen go when they die?"

"Hah." He made to fold his hands across a generous belly, as in the days of pomp—and found it not so generous after all, and lost for a moment the practised grace of his self-content. A man can forget the new truths of his own body, after a period of alteration. Truly Paris had a lot to answer for. Paris, and what had come before. What had made it necessary.

"This particular Irishman," he said, "is in hopes of seeing Cassini the crater-city on its lake, and finding his eternal rest in your own San Michele, within the sound of Thunder Fall. If I've only been good enough."

"And if not? Where do bad Irishmen go?"

It was the one question that should never have been asked. It came from the shadows behind our little circle; I disdained to turn around, to see what man had voiced it.

"Well," Mr. Holland said, gazing about him with vivid horror painted expertly across his mobile face, "I seem to have found myself in Marsport. What did I ever do to deserve this?"

There was a common shout of laughter, but it was true all the same. Marsport at its best is not a place to wish upon anyone, virtuous or otherwise; and the Blue Dolphin is not the best of what we have. Far from it. Lying somewhat awkwardly between the honest hotels and the slummish boarding-houses, it was perhaps the place that met his purse halfway. Notoriety is notoriously mean in its rewards. He couldn't conceivably slum, but neither—I was guessing—could he live high on the hog. Even now it wasn't clear quite who had paid his fare to Mars. The one-way voyage is subsidised by Authority, while those who want to go home again must pay through the nose for the privilege—but even so. He would not have travelled steerage, and the cost of a cabin on an aethership is … significant. Prohibitive, I should have said, for a man in exile from his own history, whose once success could only drag behind him now like Marley's chains, nothing but a burden. He might have assumed his children's name for public purposes, but he could not have joined the ship without offering his right one.

No matter. He was here now, with money enough for a room at the Dolphin and hopes of a journey on. We would sit at his feet meanwhile and be the audience he was accustomed to, attentive, admiring, if it would make him happy.

It was possible that nothing now could make him exactly happy. Still: who could treasure him more than we who made our home in a gateway city, an entrepôt, and found our company in the lobby of a cheap hotel?

"Marsport's not so dreadful," the same voice said. "It's the hub of the wheel, not the pit of hell. From here you can go anywhere you choose: by canal, by airship, by camel if you're hardy. Steam-camel, if you're foolhardy. On the face of it, I grant you, there's not much reason to stay—and yet, people do. Our kind."

"Our kind?"

There was a moment's pause, after Mr. Holland had placed the question: so carefully, like a card laid down in invitation, or a token to seal the bet.

"Adventurers," the man said. "Those unafraid to stand where the light spills into darkness: who know that a threshold serves to hold two worlds apart, as much as it allows congress between them."

"Ah. I am afraid my adventuring days are behind me."

"Oh, nonsense, sir! Why, the journey to Mars is an adventure in itself!"

Now there was a voice I did recognise: Parringer, as fatuous a fool as the schools of home were ever likely to produce. He was marginal even here, one of us only by courtesy. And thrusting himself forward, protesting jovially, trying to prove himself at the heart of the affair and showing only how very remote he was.

"Well, perhaps. Perhaps." Mr. Holland could afford to be generous; he didn't have to live with the man. "If so, it has been my last. I am weary, gentlemen. And wounded and heart-sore and unwell, but weary above all. All I ask now is a place to settle. A fireside, a view, a little company: no more than that. No more adventuring."

"Time on Mars may yet restore your health and energy. It is what we are famous for." This was our unknown again, pressing again. "But you are not of an age to want or seek retirement, Mr. ... Holland. Great heavens, man, you can't be fifty yet! Besides, the adventure I propose will hardly tax your reserves. There's no need even to leave the hotel, if you will only shift with me into the conservatory. You may want your overcoats, gentlemen, and another round of drinks. No more than that. I've had a boy in there already to light the stove."

That was presumptuous. Manners inhibited me from twisting around and staring, but no one objects to a little honest subterfuge. I rose, took two paces towards the fire and pressed the bell by the mantelshelf.

"My shout, I think. Mr. Holland, yours I know is gin and French. Gentlemen…?"

No one resists an open invitation; Marsporter gin is excellent, but imported drinks come dear. The boy needed his notebook to take down a swift flurry of orders.

"Thanks, Barley." I tucked half a sovereign into his rear pocket—unthinkable largesse, but we all had reasons to treat kindly with Barley—and turned to face my cohort.

On my feet and playing host, I could reasonably meet them all eye to eye, count them off like call-over at school. Hereth and Maskelyne, who were not friends but nevertheless arrived together and sat together, left together every time. Thomson who rarely spoke, who measured us all through his disguising spectacles and might have been a copper's nark, might have been here to betray us all except that every one of us had reason to know that he was not. Gribbin the engineer and van Heuren the boatman, Poole from the newspaper and the vacuous Parringer of course, and Mr. Holland our guest for the occasion, and—

And our unannounced visitor, the uninvited, the unknown. He was tall even for Mars, where the shortest of us would overtop the average Earthman. Mr. Holland must have been a giant in his own generation, six foot three or thereabouts; here he was no more than commonplace. In his strength, in his pride I thought he would have resented that. Perhaps he still did. Years of detention and disgrace had diminished body and spirit both, but something must survive yet, unbroken, undismayed. He could never have made this journey else. Nor sat with us. Every felled tree holds a memory of the forest.

The stranger was in his middle years, an established man, confident in himself and his position. That he held authority in some kind was not, could not be in question. It was written in the way he stood, the way he waited; the way he had taken charge so effortlessly, making my own display seem feeble, sullen, nugatory.

Mr. Holland apparently saw the same. He said, "I don't believe we were introduced, sir. If I were to venture a guess, I should say you had a look of the Guards about you." Or perhaps he said the guards, and meant something entirely different.

"I don't believe any of us have been introduced," I said, as rudely as I knew how. "You are …?"

Even his smile carried that same settled certainty. "Gregory Durand, late of the King's Own," with a little nod to Mr. Holland: the one true regiment to any man of Mars, Guards in all but name, "and currently of the Colonial Service."

He didn't offer a title, nor even a department. Ordinarily, a civil servant is more punctilious. I tried to pin him down: "Meaning the police, I suppose?" It was a common career move, after the army.

"On occasion," he said. "Not tonight."

If that was meant to be reassuring, it fell short. By some distance. If we were casting about for our coats, half-inclined not to wait for those drinks, it was not because we were urgent to follow him into the conservatory. Rather, our eyes were on the door and the street beyond.

"Gentlemen," he said, "be easy." He was almost laughing at us. "Tonight I dress as you do," anonymous overcoat and hat, as good as a nom de guerre on such a man, an absolute announcement that this was not his real self, "and share everything and nothing, one great secret and nothing personal or private, nothing prejudicial. I will not say "nothing perilous," but the peril is mutual and assured. We stand or fall together, if at all. Will you come? For the Queen Empress, if not for the Empire?"

The Empire had given us little enough reason to love it, which he knew. An appeal to the Widow, though, will always carry weight. There is something irresistible in that blend of decrepit sentimentality and strength beyond measure, endurance beyond imagination. Like all her subjects else, we had cried for her, we would die for her. We were on our feet almost before we knew it. I took that so much for granted, indeed, it needed a moment more for me to realise that Mr. Holland was still struggling to rise. Unless he was simply slower to commit himself, he whose reasons—whose scars—were freshest on his body and raw yet on his soul.

Still. I reached down my hand to help him, and he took it resolutely. And then stepped out staunchly at my side, committed after all. We found ourselves already in chase of the pack; the others filed one by one through a door beside the hearth, that was almost always locked this time of year. Beyond lay the unshielded conservatory, an open invitation to the night.

An invitation that Mr. Holland balked at, and rightly. He said, "You gentlemen are dressed for this, but I have a room here, and had not expected to need my coat tonight."

"You'll freeze without it. Perhaps you should stay in the warm." Perhaps we all should, but it was too late for that. Our company was following Durand like sheep, trusting where they should have been most wary. Tempted where they should have been resistant, yielding where they should have been most strong.

And yet, and yet. Dubious and resentful as I was, I too would give myself over to this man—for the mystery or for the adventure, something. For something to do that was different, original, unforeseen. I was weary of the same faces, the same drinks, the same conversations. We all were. Which was why Mr. Holland had been so welcome, one reason why.

This, though—I thought he of all men should keep out of this. I thought I should keep him out, if I could.

Here came Durand to prevent me: stepping through the door again, reaching for his elbow, light and persuasive and yielding nothing.

"Here's the boy come handily now, just when we need him. I'll take that, lad," lifting Barley's tray of refreshments as though he had been host all along. "You run up to Mr. Holland's room and fetch down his overcoat. And his hat too, we'll need to keep that great head warm. Meanwhile, Mr. Holland, we've a chair for you hard by the stove …"

• • •

The chairs were set out ready in a circle: stern and upright, uncushioned, claimed perhaps from the hotel servants' table. Our companions were milling, choosing, settling, in clouds of their own breath. The conservatory was all glass and lead, roof and walls together; in the dark of a Martian winter, the air was bitter indeed, despite the stove's best efforts. The chill pressed in from every side, as the night pressed against the lamplight. There was no comfort here to be found; there would be no warmth tonight.

On a table to one side stood a machine, a construction of wires and plates in a succession of steel frames with rubber insulation. One cable led out of it, to something that most resembled an inverted umbrella, or the skeleton of such a thing, bones of wind-stripped wire.

"What is that thing?"

"Let me come to that. If you gentlemen would take your seats..."

Whoever laid the chairs out knew our number. There was none for Durand; he stood apart, beside the machine. Once we were settled, drinks in hand—and most of us wishing we had sent for something warmer—he began.

"*Nation shall speak peace unto nation*—and for some of us, it is our task to see it happen. Notoriously, traditionally we go after this by sending in the army first and then the diplomats. Probably we have that backwards, but it's the system that builds empires. It's the system of the world.

"Worlds, I should say. Here on Mars, of course, it's the merlins that we need to hold in conversation. Mr. Holland—"

"I am not a child, sir. Indeed, I have children of my own." Indeed, he travelled now under their name, the name they took at their mother's insistence; he could still acknowledge them, even if they were obliged to disown him. "I have exactly a child's understanding of your merlins: which is to say, what we were taught in my own schooldays. I know that you converse with them as you can, in each of their different stages: by sign language with the youngster, the nymph, and then by bubbling through pipes at the naiad in its depths, and watching the bubbles it spouts back. With the imago, when the creature takes to the air, I do not believe that you can speak at all."

"Just so, sir—and that is precisely the point of our gathering tonight."

In fact the point of our gathering had been ostensibly to celebrate and welcome Mr. Holland, actually to fester in our own rank company while we displayed like bantam cocks before our guest. Durand had co-opted it, and us, entirely. Possibly that was no bad thing. He had our interest, at least, if not our best interests at heart.

"It has long been believed," he said, "that the imagos—"

"—imagines—"

—to our shame, that came as a chorus, essential pedantry—

"—that imagos," he went on firmly, having no truck with ridiculous Greek plurals, "have no language, no way to speak, perhaps no wit to speak with. As though the merlins slump into senescence in their third stage, or infantilism might say it better: as though they lose any rational ability, overwhelmed by the sexual imperative. They live decades, perhaps centuries in their slower stages here below, nymph and naiad; and then they pupate, and then they hatch a second time and the fire of youth overtakes them once more: they fly; they fight; they mate; they die. What need thought, or tongue?

"So our wise men said, at least. Now perhaps we are grown wiser. We believe they do indeed communicate, with each other and perhaps their water-based cousins too. It may be that nymphs or naiads or both have the capacity to hear them. We don't, because they do not use sound as we understand it. Rather, they have an organ in their heads that sends out electromagnetic pulses, closer to Hertzian waves than anything we have previously observed in nature. Hence this apparatus," with a mild gesture towards the table and its machinery. "With this, it is believed that we can not only hear the imagos, but speak back to them."

A moment's considerate pause, before Gribbin asked the obvious question. "And us? Why do you want to involve us?"

"Not want, so much as need. The device has existed for some time; it has been tried, and tried again. It does work, there is no question of that. Something is received, something transmitted."

"—But?"

"But the first man who tried it, its inventor occupies a private room—a locked room—in an asylum now, and may never be fit for release."

"And the second?"

"Was a military captain, the inventor's overseer. He has the room next door." There was no equivocation in this man, nothing but the blunt direct truth.

"And yet you come to us? You surely don't suppose that we are saner, healthier, more to be depended on ...?"

"Nor more willing," Durand said, before one of us could get to it. "I do not. And yet I am here, and I have brought the machine. Will you listen?"

None of us trusted him, I think. Mr. Holland had better reason than any to be wary, yet it was he whose hand sketched a gesture, *I am listening*. The rest of us—well, silence has ever been taken for consent.

"Thank you, gentlemen. What transpired from the tragedy—after a careful reading of the notes and as much interrogation of the victims as proved possible—was that the mind of an imago is simply too strange, too alien, for the mind of a man to encompass. A human brain under that kind of pressure can break, in distressing and irrecoverable ways."

"And yet," I said, "we speak to nymphs, to naiads." I had done it myself, indeed.

I had spoken to nymphs on the great canals when I was younger, nimble-fingered, foolish, and immortal. For all the good it had done me, I might as well have kept my hands in my pockets and my thoughts to myself, but nevertheless. I spoke, they replied; none of us ran mad.

"We do—and a poor shoddy helpless kind of speech it is. Finger-talk or bubble-talk, all we ever really manage to do is misunderstand each other almost entirely. That 'almost' has made the game just about worth the candle, for a hundred years and more—it brought us here and keeps us here in more or less safety; it ferries us back and forth—but this is different. When the imagos speak to each other, they speak mind-to-mind. It's not literally telepathy, but it is the closest thing we know. And when we contact them through this device, we encounter the very shape of their minds, almost from the inside; and our minds—our *individual* minds—cannot encompass that. No one man's intellect can stand up to the strain."

"And yet," again, "here we are. And here you are, and your maddening machine. I say again, why are we here?"

"Because you chose to be"—and it was not at all clear whether his answer meant *in this room* or *in this hotel* or *in this situation*. "I am the only one here under orders. The rest of you are free to leave at any time, though you did at least agree to listen. And I did say 'one man's intellect.' Where one man alone cannot survive it without a kind of mental dislocation—in the wicked sense, a disjointment, his every mental limb pulled each from each—a group of men working together is a different case. It may be that the secret lies in strength, in mutual support; it may lie in flexibility. A group of officers made the endeavour, and none of them was harmed beyond exhaustion and a passing bewilderment, a lingering discomfort with each other. But neither did they make much headway. Enlisted men did better."

He paused, because the moment demanded it: because drama has its natural rhythms and he did after all have Mr. Holland in his audience, the great dramatist of our age. We sat still, uncommitted, listening yet.

"The enlisted men did better, we believe, because their lives are more earthy, less refined. They live cheek by jowl; they sleep all together and bathe together; they share the same women in the same bawdy-houses. That seems to help."

"And so you come to us? To *us*?" Ah, Parringer. "Because you find us indistinguishable from common bloody Tommies?"

"No, because you are most precisely distinguishable. The Tommies were no great success either, but they pointed us a way to go. The more comfortable the men are with each other, physically and mentally, the better hope we have. Officers inhabit a bonded hierarchy, isolated from one another as they are from their men, like pockets of water in an Archimedes' screw. Cadets might have done better, but we went straight to the barracks. With, as I say, some success—but enlisted men are unsophisticated. Hence we turn to you, gentlemen. It is a bow drawn at a venture, no more: but you are familiar with, intimate with the bodies of other men, and we do believe that will help enormously; and yet you are educated beyond the aspiration of any Tommy Atkins—some of you beyond the aspiration of any mere soldier, up to and including the generals of my acquaintance—and that too can only prove to the good. With the one thing and the other, these two strengths in parallel, in harmony, we stand in high hopes of a successful outcome. At least, gentlemen, I can promise you that you won't be bored. Come, now: will you play?"

"Is that as much as you can promise?" Thomson raised his voice, querulous and demanding. "You ask a lot of us, to venture in the margins of madness; it seems to me you might offer more in return."

"I can offer you benign neglect," Durand said cheerfully. "Official inattention: no one watching you, no one pursuing. I can see that enshrined in policy, to carry over *ad infinitum*. If you're discreet, you can live untroubled hereafter; you, and the generations that follow you. This is a once-and-for-all offer, for services rendered."

There must be more wrapped up in this even than Durand suggested or we guessed. A way to speak to the imagines might prove only the gateway to further secrets and discoveries. If we could speak directly to the chrysalid pilots of the aetherships, perhaps we might even learn to fly ourselves between one planet and another, and lose all our dependence on the merlins …

That surely would be worth a blind eye turned in perpetuity to our shady meeting-places, our shadier activities.

Mr. Holland thought so, at least. "Say more, of how this process works. Not what you hope might come of it; we all have dreams. Some of us have followed them, somewhat. I am here, after all, among the stars," with a wave of his hand through glass to the bitter clarity of the Martian night sky. "How is it that you want us to work together? And how do we work with the machine, and why above all do we have to do it here, in this wicked cold?"

"To treat with the last first: Mr. Heaviside has happily demonstrated here as well as on Earth, that aetheric waves carry further after dark. We don't know how far we need to reach, to find a receptive imago; we stand a better chance at night. Besides, you gentlemen tend to forgather in the evenings. I wasn't certain of finding you by daylight."

Someone chuckled, someone snorted. I said, "I have never seen an imago fly by night, though. I don't believe they can."

"Not fly, no: never that. But neither do they sleep, so far as we can tell. All we want to do—all we want you to do—is touch the creature's mind, fit yourselves to the shape of it and find whether you can understand each other."

"I still don't understand how you mean us to achieve that?"

"No. It's almost easier to have you do it, than to explain how it might be done. We're stepping into an area where words lose their value against lived experience. It's one reason I was so particularly hoping to enlist your company, sir," with a nod to Mr. Holland, "because who better to stand before the nondescript and find means to describe it? If anyone can pin this down with words, it will be you. If anyone can speak for us to an alien power—"

"Now that," he said, "I have been doing all my life."

The run of laughter he provoked seemed more obligatory than spontaneous, but came as a relief none the less. Durand joined in, briefly. As it tailed away, he said, "Very well—but there is of course more to it than one man's dexterity with language. Our wise men speak of the, ah, inversion of the generative principle, as a bonding-agent stronger than blood or shared danger or duty or sworn word—but again, there is more than that. You gentlemen may be a brotherhood, drawn from within and pressed close from without; we can make you something greater, a single purpose formed from all your parts. The wise men would have me flourish foreign words at you, *gestalt* or *phasis* or the like; but wise men are not always the most helpful.

"Let me rather say this, that you all have some experience of the demi-monde. By choice or by instinct or necessity, your lives have led you into the shadows. This very hotel is a gateway to more disreputable ventures. There is an opium den behind the Turkish bath, a brothel two doors down. I do not say that any of you is a libertine at core: only that the life you lead draws you into contact and exchange with those who avoid the light for other reasons.

"I will be plain. Mr. Holland, you have a known taste for absinthe and for opium cigarettes. Mr. Parringer, laudanum is your poison; Mr. Hereth, you stick to gin, but that jug of water at your elbow that you mix in so judiciously is actually more gin, and you will drink the entire jugful before the night is out. Mr. Gribbin—but I don't need to go on, do I? You each have your weaknesses, your ways of setting yourselves a little adrift from the world.

"We need to take you out of yourselves more thoroughly in order to bind you into a single motive force, in order to create the mind-space wherein you might meet an imago and make some sense of it. I have brought an alchemical concoction, a kind of hatchis, more potent than any pill or pipe or potion that you have met before."

He laid it on a tray, on a table that he set centre-circle between us all: a silver pot containing something green and unctuous, an array of coffee-spoons beside.

"Something more from your wise men, Mr. Durand?"

"Exactly so."

"I'm not sure how keen I am, actually, to swallow some hellbrew dreamed up in a government laboratory." Gribbin leaned forward and stirred it dubiously. There were gleams of oily gold amidst the green. "Does nobody remember *The Strange Case of Dr Jekyll and Mr. Hyde*?"

"'Can anyone forget it?' should rather be your question," Mr. Holland observed. "Stevenson was as much a master of delicate, fanciful prose as he was of a strong driving story. But he—or his character, rather, his creation: do we dare impute the motives of the dream unto the dreamer?—he certainly saw the merits of a man testing his own invention on himself, before bringing it to the public." Even huddled as he was against the ironwork of the stove, he could still exude a spark of knowing mischief.

Durand smiled. "I would be only too happy to swallow my own spoonful, to show you gentlemen the way—but alas, my duty is to the device, not to the *entente*. You will need me sober and attentive. Besides which, I am not of your persuasion. I should only hold you back. Let me stress, though, that senior officers and common troops both have trod this path before you, and not been harmed. Not by the drug. Think of the hatchis as grease to the engine, no more; it will ease your way there and back again. Now come: I promised you adventure, and this is the beginning. Who's first to chance the hazard?"

There is a self-destructive tendency in some men that falls only a little short of self-murder. We have it worse than most; something not quite terror, not quite exhilaration drives us higher, faster, farther than good sense ever could dictate. Some consider it a weakness, evidence of a disordered nature. I hope that it's a badge of courage acquired against the odds, that we will fling ourselves from the precipice in no certain knowledge of a rope to hold us, no faith in any net below.

Of course it was Mr. Holland who reached first, to draw up a noble spoonful and slide it into his mouth. No tentative sips, no tasting: he was all or nothing, or rather simply all.

The surprise was Parringer, thrusting himself forward to do the same, gulping it down wholesale while Mr. Holland still lingered, the spoon's stem jutting from between his full contented lips like a cherry-stem, like a child's lollipop.

Where Parringer plunged, who among us would choose to hold back? A little resentfully, and with a great many questions still unasked, we fell mob-handed on the spoons, the jar, the glistening oleaginous jelly.

• • •

It was bitter on my tongue and something harsh, as though it breathed out fumes, catching at the back of my throat before it slithered down to soothe that same discomfort with a distraction of tastes behind a cool and melting kiss. Bitter and then sour and then sweet, layer beneath layer, and I couldn't decide whether its flavours were woven one into another or whether its very nature changed as it opened, as it bloomed within the warm wet of my mouth.

He was right, of course, Durand. Not one of us there was a stranger to the more louche pleasures of the twilit world. Myself, I was a smoker in those days: hashish or opium, anything to lift me out of the quotidian world for an hour or a night. In company or alone, sweating or shivering or serene, I would always, always look to rise. Skin becomes permeable, bodies lose their margins; dreams are welcome but not needful, where what I seek is always that sense of being uncontained, of reaching further than my strict self allows.

From what he said, I took Durand's potion to be one more path to that effect: slower for sure, because smoke is the very breath of fire and lifts as easily as it rises, while anything swallowed is dank and low-lying by its nature. I never had been an opium-eater, and hatchis was less than that, surely: a thinner draught, ale to spirits, tea to coffee. Sunshine to lightning. Something.

If I had the glare of lightning in my mind, it was only in the expectation of disappointment: rain, no storm. I never thought to ride it. Nor to find myself insidiously companion'd—in my own mind, yet—where before I had always gone alone.

Even in bed, even with a slick and willing accomplice in the throes of mutual excess, my melting boundaries had never pretended to melt me into another man's thoughts. Now, though: now suddenly I was aware of minds in parallel, rising entangled with mine, like smoke from separate cigarettes caught in the same eddy. Or burning coals in the same grate, fusing awkwardly together. Here was a mind cool and in command of itself, trying to sheer off at such exposure: that was Gribbin, finding nowhere to go, pressed in from every side at once. Here was one bold and fanciful and weary all at once, and that was surely Mr. Holland, though it was hard to hold on to that ostensible name in this intimate revelation. Here was one tentative and blustering together, Parringer of course ...

One by one, each one of us declared an identity, if not quite a location. We were this many and this various, neither a medley nor a synthesis, untuned: glimpsing one man's overweening physical arrogance and another's craven unsatisfied ambition, sharing the urge to seize both and achieve a high vaulting reach with them, beyond the imagination of either. Even without seeing a way to do that, even as we swarmed inconsequentially like elvers in a bucket, the notion was there already with flashes of the vision. Perhaps Durand was right to come to us.

Durand, now: Durand was no part of this. Walled off, separated, necessary: to us he was prosthetic, inert, a tool to be wielded. He stood by his machine, fiddling with knobs and wires, almost as mechanical himself.

Here was the boy Barley coming in, no part of anything, bringing the hat and overcoat he'd been sent for. At Durand's gesture he dressed Mr. Holland like a doll, as though he were invalid or decrepit. Perhaps we all seemed so to him, huddled in our circle, unspeaking, seeming unaware. The truth was opposite; we were aware of everything, within the limits of our bodies' senses. We watched him crouch to feed the stove; we heard the slide and crunch of the redcoal tipping in, the softer sounds of ash falling through the grate beneath; we felt the sear of heat released, how it stirred the frigid air about us, how it rose towards the bitter glass.

"Enough now, lad. Leave us be until I call again."

"Yes, sir."

He picked up the tray from the table and bore it off towards the door, with a rattle of discarded spoons. Durand had already turned back to his machine. We watched avidly, aware of nothing more intently than the little silver pot and its gleaming residue. We knew it, when the boy hesitated just inside the door; we knew it when he glanced warily back at us, when he decided he was safe, when he scooped up a fingerful from the pot's rim and sucked it clean.

We knew; Durand did not.

Durand fired up his machine.

• • •

We had the boy. Not one of us, not part of us, not yet: we were as unprepared for this as he was, and the more susceptible to his fear and bewilderment because we were each of us intimately familiar with his body, in ways not necessarily true of one another's.

Still: we had him among us, with us, this side of the wall. We had his nervous energy to draw on, like a flame to our black powder; we had his yearning, his curiosity. And more, we had that shared knowledge of him, common ground. Where we couldn't fit one to another, we could all of us fit around him: the core of the matrix, the unifying frame, the necessary element Durand had not foreseen.

• • •

Durand fired up his machine while we were still adjusting, before we had nudged one another into any kind of order.

He really should have warned us, though I don't suppose he could. He hadn't been this way himself; all he had was secondhand reports from men more or less broken by the process. We could none of us truly have understood that, until now.

We weren't pioneers; he only hoped that we might be survivors. Still, we deserved some better warning than we had.

. . .

We forget sometimes that names are not descriptions; that Mars is not Earth; that the merlins are no more native than ourselves. We call them Martians sometimes because our parents did, because their parents did before them, and so back all the way to Farmer George. More commonly we call them merlins because we think it's clever, because they seem to end their lives so backward, from long years of maturity in the depths to one brief adolescent lustful idiocy in the sky. When we call them imagos—or imagines—because they remind us of dragonflies back home, if dragonflies were built to the scale of biplanes.

Which they are not. The map is not the territory; the name is not the creature. Even redcoal is not coal, not carbon of any kind, for all that it is mined and burned alike. We forget that. We name artefacts after the places of their manufacture, or their first manufacture, or the myth of it; did the homburg hat in fact see first light in Bad Homburg, or is that only a story that we tell? Does anybody know? We let a man name himself after his children, after a country not relevant to any of them, not true to any story of their lives. We assert that names are changeable, assignable at whim, and then we attach unalterable value to them.

Durand had given no name to his machine. That was just as well, but not enough. He had given us a task to do, in words we thought we understood; he had laid the groundwork, given us an argument about the uses of debauchery and then a drug to prove it; then he flung us forth, all undefended.

He flung us, and we dragged poor Barley along, unwitting, unprepared.

. . .

It started with a hum, as he connected electrical wires to a seething acid battery. Lamps glowed into dim flickering life. Sparks crackled ominously, intermittently, before settling to a steady mechanical pulse. A steel disc spun frantically inside a cage.

Nothing actually moved, except fixedly in place; and even so, everything about it was all rush and urgency, a sensation of swift decisive movement: that way, through the run of frames and wires to the umbrella-structure at the far end of the table. There was nothing to draw the eye except a certainty, logic married to something more, an intangible impulsion. That way: through and up and out into the night.

And none of us moved from our places, and yet, and yet. The machine hurled us forth, and forth we went.

If we had understood anything, we had understood that the machine would bring an imago's voice to us, and we would somehow speak back to it, if we could think of anything to say. That would have been Mr. Holland's lot, surely; he was never short of things to say.

We had misunderstood, or else been misdirected. Unless the drug seduced us all into a mutual hallucination, and in plain truth our intelligences never left that room any more than our abandoned bodies did. But it seemed to us—to all of us, united—that we were shot out like a stone from a catapult; that we streaked over all the lights of Marsport and into the bleak dark of the desert beyond; that we hurtled thus directly into the static mind of an imago at rest.

• • •

No creature's thoughts should be … architectural. Or vast. At first we thought we were fallen into halls of stone, or caverns water-worn. But we had found our shape by then, in the flight from there to here; we might fit poorly all together, but we all fitted well around Barley. And something in that resettling, that nudging into a new conformation, caused a shift in our perspective. A thought is just an echo of the mind-state it betrays, as an astrakhan overcoat is a memory of the lambs that died to make it.

Where we fancied that we stood, these grand and pillared spaces—this was an imago's notion of its night-time world, beyond all heat and passion, poised, expectant. A memory of the chrysalis, perhaps.

Expectant, but not expecting us. Not expecting anything until the sun, the bright and burning day, the vivid endeavour. We came like thieves into a mountain, to disturb the dragon's rest; we were alien, intrusive, self-aware. It knew us in the moment of our coming.

I have seen set-changes in the theatre where one scene glides inexplicably into another, defying expectation, almost defying the eye that saw it happen. I had never stood in a place and had that happen all about me; but we were there, we were recognised, and its awareness of us changed the shape of its thinking.

Even as we changed ourselves, that happened: as we slid and shifted, as we found our point of balance with Barley serving at the heart of all, as we arrayed ourselves about him. Even Mr. Holland, who would need to speak for us, if anything could ever come to words here; even Parringer, whose motives were as insidious as his manner. There was an unbridgeable gulf between the imago as we had always understood it, flighty and maniacal, and this lofty habitation. A naiad in the depths might have such a ponderous mind, such chilly detachment, but not the frenzied imago, no. Surely not.

Save that the imago had been a naiad before; perhaps it retained that mind-set, in ways we had not expected or imagined. Perhaps it could be contemplative at night, while the sun burned off its intellect and lent it only heat?

It closed in upon us almost geometrically, like tiled walls, if tiles and walls could occupy more dimensions than a man can see, in shapes we have no words for. We should have felt threatened, perhaps, but Barley's curiosity was matched now by his tumbling delight, and what burns at the core reaches out all the way to the skin. We sheltered him and drew from him and leaned on him, all in equal measure; he linked us and leaned on us and drew from us, in ways for which there never could be words.

• • •

With so many names for our kind—leering, contemptuous, descriptive, dismissive—we know both the fallibility and the savage power of words. The map seeks to define the territory, to claim it, sometimes to contain it. Without a map, without a shared vocabulary, without a mode of thought in common—well, no wonder men alone went mad here. No wonder men together had achieved so little, beyond a mere survival. Mr. Holland might have flung wit all night with no more effect than a monkey flinging dung against a cliff-face, if we had only been a group forgathered by circumstance, struggling to work together. With the drug to bond us, with each man contributing the heart's-blood of himself in this strange transfusion, there was no struggle and we found what we needed as the need came to us.

Whether we said what was needed, whether it needed to be said: that is some other kind of question. Did anyone suppose that the confluence of us all would be a diplomat?

The imago pressed us close, but that was an enquiry. There was pattern in the pressure: we could see it, we could read it almost, those of us with finger-talk or bubble-talk or both. What lives, what choices? Swim or fly, drown or burn? Swallow or be swallowed?

We knew, we thought, how to press back, how to pattern a reply. Mr. Holland gave us what we lacked: content, poetry, response. Meaning more than words. Sometimes the map declares the territory.

For he who lives more lives than one
More deaths than one must die.

He would have turned the bitterness all against himself, but our collective consciousness couldn't sustain that. We all wanted our share, we all deserved it: all but Barley, who had no hidden other self, who'd had no time to grow one.

Suddenly he couldn't hold us together any longer. Fraying, we fled back to Durand, back to our waiting bodies—and the imago pursued, flying by sheer will in the dreadful night, wreaking havoc in its own frozen body. It followed us to the Dolphin and hurtled against the conservatory where we were anything but sheltered, battering at the windows like a moth at the chimney of a lamp, until the only abiding question was whether the glass would shatter first or the machine, or the creature, or ourselves.

~

Chaz Brenchley has been making a living as a writer since the age of eighteen. He is the author of nine thrillers, most recently *Shelter*; two fantasy series, *The Books of Outremer* and *Selling Water by the River*; and two ghost stories, *House of Doors* and *House of Bells*. As Daniel Fox, he has published a Chinese-based fantasy series, beginning with *Dragon in Chains*; as Ben Macallan an urban fantasy series, beginning with *Desdaemona*. A British Fantasy Award winner, he has also published books for children and more than 500 short stories in various genres. 2014 saw publication of two new books, a short novel—*Being Small*—and his second collection, *Bitter Waters*, which has been shortlisted for a Lambda Award. He has recently married and moved from Newcastle to California, with two squabbling cats and a famous teddy bear.

THE TIP OF
THE TONGUE

FELICIA DAVIN

The story was that some people had learned to read again. Alice wanted to believe it, but Alice had always liked stories. The morning after everything changed, when she'd woken up to the police pounding on her door demanding that she surrender all print and digital text materials to them, she'd glanced at the bright blue cover of a favorite childhood novel and had traced her fingers over the embossed title without understanding. She'd thought she was tired, not yet awake, or in shock from the officer outside her door. But then she'd flipped through the book and found tiny garbled markings on every page.

That was the moment when she'd wanted to puke. She hadn't been able to read her phone that morning either, but she'd thought something was wrong with the screen. There couldn't be anything wrong with *Lily and the Dragon*. She hadn't read it since she was fourteen. It was just sitting on her shelf next to dozens of other novels like it, stories about other people and other worlds.

But the police brought boxes and carted them all away. They swept her apartment for writing implements and paper, opening all her kitchen drawers and rifling through them with disapproval. They took her laptop and her phone too, and they magnanimously didn't fine her for having expired permits on both. It was for the greater glory of the city and the people, they said. Text couldn't be trusted. This way, we have all been purified, they said. We have all returned to our natural state. Now we can truly build the society we have always dreamed of, they said. Good will reign, they said.

She knew they were taking measures against the insurgents. She also knew better than to say that out loud.

Alice had cried in the bathroom after they'd left. She should have screamed at them. She should have kicked them or hit them or saved even one book.

But she'd been numb. They'd done something to her. They'd been in her brain. What use was anything after that? And if she had fought them, they would have killed her. Still, she didn't stop crying until her throat rasped and her eyes were sore.

They hadn't taken absolutely everything. She found a pen that had rolled under her bed and a few paper napkins in the back of a drawer, shoved under her silverware. After she'd dried her eyes, she'd spent the rest of the afternoon trying to remember. It had been a Sunday, she remembered, because she hadn't been at work. She'd had empty hours and blank spaces to fill, and it was easy enough to draw shapes and squiggles, even little animals marching across the paper. She'd drawn the view out her window. A cartoon self-portrait with clouds of black hair spiraling around her head. A winding map of the city from memory, all its neighborhoods unlabeled. Hours had passed and she'd delved into the depths of her brain trying to dredge up one word, even one letter, but they'd all been gone.

Rustication, they called it. An airborne plague of nanobots. After one night, most of the city had woken up illiterate. All those millions of neural connections, erased.

There was a lot of high-minded talk about the inherently deceitful nature of representations. Art had been banned for years now, and no one liked it, but what could they do? The city had taken down all the public statues and murals, but they could only stop people after the fact. They couldn't stop people from wanting. Even after Rustication, people still wanted to leave their mark on things.

Alice's neighbor Lani had been a middle-school language teacher before, and now she taught sewing and wood shop on alternate days of the week. Most of the other teachers had lost their jobs, but Lani had been one of the lucky ones. She was bent over and gray-haired and couldn't go work on a farm, so the authorities took pity and let her stay at the half-empty school. "Every time those kids get their hands on anything that even remotely resembles a writing implement," she told Alice, "whether it's a rusty nail or a sewing needle, they start scratching things into the table top. Do you know how many drawings of dicks I've found this week alone?" Lani had burst into laughter at that point. "It's the triumph of the human spirit, Alice," she said, still shaking and wiping at her eyes. Alice had laughed, but she hadn't been able to stop herself from looking over her shoulder afterward. The city might not be able to arrest every tagger and bathroom graffiti artist, as hard as they tried, but if anybody ever overheard Lani laughing like that, they would come for her.

Books had been getting scarcer even before Rustication, because if murals of sunny skies and flowering gardens were immoral illusions, and the sculpture of a boy feeding ducks in the public park was deceitful, then weren't books even worse? But everyone knew someone who knew someone who could get you a novel if you were willing to pay for it. Alice had never imagined that the city would take such a drastic step. How had they even found the resources? She'd thought scientists were only barely finished mapping the human brain. It was some leap to go from making a map to digging up the entire landscape.

She wondered, afterward, if the scientists who led the project had been rendered illiterate too. She wondered if they had been allowed to live.

It had been six months now. Officially, Rustication was held to be a great success. Crime was down all over the city, and productivity was up. Everyone was happier this way. Unofficially, there were whispers of people forgetting much more than reading and writing. Some people had woken up the morning after Rustication unable to speak. Some people had woken up with no memory of their families, their lives, their names. Some people hadn't woken up at all.

No one could find any record of those people now, but no one outside the city government could read records, anyway.

Alice worked at The Hearth, a restaurant two blocks from the capitol building. It used to say *The Hearth* in gold lettering on black paint above the door, before the city had made Mr. Park paint over it. Mr. Park was still on the waiting list to get approval for a sign with an image. The place looked strangely anonymous now, a wood door set in a building with black trim and big glass windows, showcasing the last literate people in the city out for a nice steak dinner. These were the people who'd had their permits in order to leave the city and spend a long weekend in their country homes six months ago. They all had excellent manners, and night after night, Alice gave them her sharpest smile.

Still, it paid the bills. And the restaurant had adapted to the newly textless world more easily than some businesses. So many of Alice and Lani's neighbors had been forced to leave their apartment complex to go work in the belt of farmland surrounding the city. Most of them had never picked a fruit or milked a cow in their life, but there was no other work left for them now. Her apartment building was eerie now, as empty as it was, but it was nothing compared to the whole sections of the city that had become ghost towns. The university campus was graveyard-quiet, its lawns still scorched from the book burnings. Alice tried not to walk that way any more. It was hard to look at the ruined library. The bricks of the west wall were toppled to the ground, and the three other walls had broken windows like missing teeth.

But people still needed to eat in the city, and clerks in the capitol were still eating well at The Hearth. Alice hadn't had to move out to the cornfields yet. All that had really changed at work was that the restaurant couldn't print menus any more, so Alice had the whole thing memorized. She'd always had a good memory. She'd only forgotten a few things in her life, and one of those was because the city took a scalpel to her brain six months ago.

Alice didn't smoke, but she went out into the back alley on her break anyway. Juan was out there, and he knew people. She wanted to know people, too. She'd always wanted to, but before, she'd been afraid. Now she was angry. They had violated her. They had poisoned her. They had crept into the most secret part of her and excised something precious. They might do it again. They might kill her. It didn't matter any more. She couldn't live with herself if she didn't try to fight back.

The insurgents had gone underground, but the movement wasn't over. It was illegal for more than two people to congregate in public, and before Rustication the insurgents had communicated mostly through short text messages over a wireless network created when their phones were in close physical proximity. The city had shut down the Internet years ago, but they were always one update behind the insurgents and their network of communications. Technically, the phones themselves had been made illegal for anyone without a government permit last year, but they were so small and so easy to hide that it had been difficult to eradicate them completely. Besides, the insurgents had switched back to older technology: notes left behind loose bricks or crumpled and thrown carefully next to garbage cans around the city. Alice had eyed every pile of trash with cautious interest after hearing that, but it wasn't so easy to join up. You had to prove yourself trustworthy. More than that, you had to prove yourself useful, and Alice was just a waitress. Her only skill was memorizing the daily specials faster than everybody else, and she didn't think the insurgents would be interested in hearing about grass-fed beef or heirloom tomatoes.

But recently it had occurred to her that maybe she had something to offer after all. They couldn't write things down any more. No more texts, no more crumpled-up notes in the garbage. They needed people like her who could memorize things. "I'm sentimental. I miss things from my childhood," she told Juan.

Juan kept the cigarette between his lips. "Don't we all," he said.

"I've got a lot of good memories from back then," Alice said. "They're still so clear, you know? Every detail is there."

Juan looked bored, but she thought he might still be listening. That was how this worked, right? She couldn't just say "sign me up to take those bastards down!" or else he'd never talk to her again.

"I'd like to make some new ones," she said. "Memories, that is."

This had gone a lot smoother in her head. Juan looked her up and down and her heart dropped. *Not like that*, she thought. He was a friend. She supposed he was good-looking, with his warm brown eyes, and that he might be gentle, but she could never make herself imagine the rest. In a strange way, the feeling was reassuring. Maybe some day the city would make more nanobots to rewrite that part of her brain, but they hadn't managed yet.

He stubbed his cigarette out against the wall and pocketed the unsmoked end of it. "Break's over," he said. "You wanna get a drink after work?"

Terrified that he might have misunderstood and elated that he might not have, Alice nodded.

After work, Juan led her out of the restaurant and they zigzagged through the city for twenty minutes. She traced it in her mind's eye, making a mental diagram of their angular path through the grid of city blocks. He stopped in front of a boarded-up antique shop, pulled a key out of his pocket, and unlocked the door. They passed through a dusty museum of furniture and creaking floorboards, into a stockroom in the back and then down a hidden stairway.

The uninsulated stairway had been cold and exposed, but the air in the basement was stifling. The space was too small for the dozen people seated in ornately shabby armchairs or standing and resting their drinks on massive old tables with carved legs. It took Alice a moment to adjust to so many people talking so freely. The clientele at The Hearth tended toward more subdued conversation.

Here, no longer worried about being overheard, Juan looked directly at her and said, "What do you want?"

"A drink," she joked. He tilted his head toward one of the tables, where she could see some glasses and a bottle of something clear if she craned her neck to peek through the crowd. She shook her head at his offer. She wanted to be sober for this. "I want to help," she said. "You know I pick things up fast. I have a good memory, too. I'll learn to do whatever it is you need."

"Why now?"

Alice blinked. She should have been expecting the question. "They took something from me."

"They took something from all of us," he said. "It's been six months."

"I thought I could remember how," she confessed. "I thought I could teach myself to read again. I can't. I heard you all could, though."

"So all you want is to learn to read again?"

"No," she said, more forcefully than she meant to. "You know I've woken up every morning for the last six months wondering if they came in the night and took something else? I can't live like this. They can't treat us like this. Even if I could learn to read again, I'd still be living in fear of getting arrested or murdered. I'd rather die for something than for nothing."

He nodded. After a long moment, he said, "You tried to teach yourself to read again? With what?"

"I found a pen in my apartment. I had some paper napkins left, too. I thought maybe if I drew enough …" Alice made a gesture of writing and then shrugged. She had thought if she let her pen touch paper and her mind wander, maybe she could conjure up the old symbols, as if they had drowned in the depths of her consciousness and she could cause their remains to drift to the surface just by force of the tides. She had thought maybe her hands would remember, even if her brain couldn't. "If I'd had an example to look at, even just a paragraph, I might have been able to do it. I still feel like I could."

Juan was giving her a strange look. "You should talk to the librarian."

She followed his gaze to the other end of the long and narrow room. There was a woman leaning against the wall alone, not caught in conversation with any of the groups around her. Her short black hair was falling into her face and in the long slender fingers of her right hand, she was holding open a bright blue book.

Alice couldn't tell if it was the sight of the beautiful woman or the book that set her heart racing jackrabbit-fast. She knew that book. The woman was intent on it, her face as still and pale as paper. Her inky eyebrows were drawn together, punctuating her expression.

Across the room, the woman lifted her head. She moved so deliberately, with such careful efficiency. Even leaning against the wall, she looked graceful. Every line of her body was exactly where she wanted it to be. Alice wondered what it would be like to kiss her.

Her gaze settled on Alice, dark-eyed and mesmerizing. Her lips curved into a smile like she could read every last thought in Alice's head. Alice looked away. Her whole face felt hot. She cast around for anything else to look at or think about, anything at all, and that was when she realized the woman hadn't been reading. She hadn't turned a single page while Alice had looked at her.

"That's Keiko," Juan said. "Better known as Kei. She managed to save a book."

Some library, Alice thought but didn't say. One book was more than she had managed to save.

Juan perceived her skepticism, but he just shrugged one shoulder and gave her a smile. "We're working on it, alright? Go talk to her."

Kei watched the whole exchange, and when Alice finally arrived at her side, she simply bent her wrist to offer Alice the book. Alice accepted it with warm hands. It had only been six months, but it was a thrill just to touch it. It was so small but it felt heavy. Handling the outside of the book felt illicit; sliding her fingers into the pages and spreading them apart felt obscene.

Alice still couldn't read. It was silly to hope that the mere sight and touch of a familiar book might bring something back to her. She repressed a sigh at her own foolishness. "I know this book," she said, instead. "Or I used to."

Kei reached out and put her hand on the book to stop Alice from closing it and handing it back. "What?"

Alice smiled sheepishly, feeling suddenly childish in front of this woman who was brave enough to have joined the cause long before her. Kei had saved a book. Kei had stood up to the police. Alice had been at home dreaming while Kei had been down here, strategizing. Alice had been living in other worlds and Kei had been living in this one, trying to make it better. "I had this same version, with the blue cover," Alice said. "I read it all the time as a kid. I wanted to be Lily so badly."

Lily was a tall white girl with flowing red hair who had tamed a dragon and captured the heart of both a handsome knight and a powerful mage. Alice was short and brown and indifferent to men, but she had always figured that if she could find a dragon to tame, nobody would bother her about the rest.

"Holy shit," Kei said. "You're perfect. Where did Juan even find you? Never mind, it doesn't matter. Start with the cover. Show me which one means 'Lily.'"

"You don't know?" Alice's heart halted. She was right: Kei hadn't been reading earlier. Kei didn't know how to read. None of them did.

"I've never read this before. I've been looking for someone who might recognize it for weeks now."

"Where did you get it?"

"It was my sister's," Kei said. She closed her eyes and paused for a long time before saying anything else. "She loved hiding all her toys and stuff around the house. I found it behind the grate of a vent when I was cleaning out her bedroom. She didn't—she never woke up."

After Rustication. "I'm sorry."

Kei nodded, swallowed, and said, "Not quite the heroic act of resistance you were imagining, right?"

Alice touched Kei's hand over the pages of the book. She didn't know what to say, so instead she pulled the book away, sat down on the floor with her back against the wall, and gestured for Kei to sit down next to her. When Kei did, Alice showed her the cover. "I don't know which part is which, but I know it says *Lily and the Dragon*. That ought to be enough, right?"

Kei nodded. She seemed relieved to switch to a more practical topic of conversation. "The city's official line is that Rustication permanently 'purified' us. Anya over there—" Kei tilted her head to indicate a woman across the room, a woman who looked vaguely familiar, like maybe Alice had served her dinner at The Hearth, "—is sleeping with a bureaucrat and she says they're so pleased with themselves for the bots and the book burnings, they're not even a little bit worried. And why should they be? It's been six months and we've gotten nowhere. We haven't even found one lowly literate clerk with a grain of sympathy for the revolution who might be willing to teach one of us to read again. They all believe it's impossible."

"But you don't."

"I don't. The brain is plastic. People are adaptable."

"I wish I'd studied neuroscience when I had the chance," Alice said.

"They probably would have sent you to the fields by now if you had. Besides, you did us one better. Read me a story."

Alice huffed out a laugh. If only she could. Every time she looked away from the cover, the characters seemed to slip out of her mind. And that was only the cover. The first page was an impossible labyrinth of tiny black lines. Had she ever been able to read them? They were so small and so complicated. They blurred into each other, each letter tangling with the one next to it until all that remained was a squiggle across the page.

"Stop trying to read like you used to," Kei said. "It makes my head hurt just looking at you, squinting and biting your lip."

"Sorry."

"It is kind of cute, though."

Alice pretended to be concentrating very hard. She only barely resisted the urge to bury her face in the book. Kei's shoulder was touching hers, and their knees kept bumping together, and she pretended not to notice that, either.

She had to focus on something small. The first page was too much. She shut the book and looked at the title again. "Lily," she said out loud, tracing a finger over the embossed print. She closed her eyes and pictured them, thinking of the sound of her own voice as she did. When she opened the book to the first page again, the text was still painfully small, its thorny little characters all crowded against each other. But if she focused only on finding the word "Lily," she could cut a path through it. By the time she had found "Lily" for the fourth time, it stood out like a beacon, high above the rest of the lines.

Kei was sitting with her legs stretched out and her back against the wall. It took Alice a moment to realize she was asleep. She was just as eerily and beautifully still as when she was awake, but her head tipped to the side and her hair fanned over her cheek. The room was empty. Alice nudged her awake and she grunted.

"I got something," Alice said.

"You can read it?"

"Not yet," Alice said. "But soon."

Night was receding when Alice arrived home, leaving a fine ashen film of snow sticking to the asphalt and melting in her hair. Her eyes ached from staring at the book all night, but she was vibrating with emotion. She had read a word. She felt like crying, to be so excited over such a small thing. It had taken her all night to read a single word. But she also felt elated. It was a minor miracle. She wanted to go home and find her pen and write Lily, Lily, Lily on every surface in her apartment. And Kei had asked her to come back after her shift tonight. They would sit together and try again and they would find more words.

Alice had to check all her pockets for her keys, and then she was so tired that her first two tries didn't unlock the door. She forced her eyes open wider and realized she was using the wrong key.

"Miss. What are you doing out at this hour?"

Alice whipped around and found herself face to face with a police officer. She remembered his face from six months ago, when he had knocked on her door and emptied all her shelves. He had still been wearing a badge on his uniform that day, but she had been unable to read it. None of the police wore badges now.

She had carefully chosen to come home by side streets to avoid coming into contact with the police, but he must have been patrolling and seen her standing at the door.

"I—," Alice started, too tired and startled to come up with a quick answer.

The front door of the building burst open, and Lani shuffled out more rapidly than Alice had ever seen her move. Her grey hair was in a single braid over her shoulder. She was wearing her dressing gown and slippers. It was much too cold to be outside in so little, but Lani stood in the doorway, holding her back straight and staring down the officer.

"Mr. Hodge," she said, as imperiously as only middle school teachers could.

"Officer Hodge," he corrected.

"Officer Hodge," she said, unfazed. "I hope you aren't bothering Ms. Duras! She's only out at this hour on my account. I could have sworn I dropped my glasses out here in front of the building last night, and I can't see a thing without them, and I need to get to work in the morning, but I can't possibly go without them. Ms. Duras has been kind enough to help me look for them. She's a very good girl, Ms. Duras, helping a poor old lady like me."

Alice had been neighbors with Lani for years and had never once seen her wear glasses. "Yes," she said. "That's it. I was looking for her glasses."

Officer Hodge did not look convinced. "Miss Duras was at the door when I saw her." He turned toward Alice. "Did you find her glasses?"

"No, not yet," Alice said, and in a moment of inspiration, she pressed her thighs together and squirmed a little. "I was going back in because I really need to pee."

"Oh dear," Lani said, apparently scandalized. It took all of Alice's willpower not to grin at her.

"Well," Hodge said. "I suppose you should take care of that. I can help Mrs.—"

"Ms.," Lani said crisply. "Keawe."

"I can help Mrs. Keawe find her glasses."

"That won't be necessary! I was just coming down to tell Ms. Duras that I found them." Lani produced a pair of spectacles from her dressing gown pocket. "Right at the bottom of my purse, would you believe it."

Lani looked perhaps a bit too pleased with herself. But the officer looked between the two of them, with Alice still bobbing up and down in discomfort and Lani smiling and holding up her glasses as proof, and grunted. "Fine then. Don't let me catch you out at this hour again."

"Of course not, sir!" Alice hustled Lani inside and then shut the door behind them. Officer Hodge stared through the glass at them for another moment, but then he left.

When he was gone and Alice had remembered how to breathe, she helped Lani up the stairs to her apartment and said, "You don't wear glasses and your last name is Pereira."

"I do get confused in my old age," Lani said, putting a little quaver into her voice. Then she looked straight at Alice and said, "Keawe was my mother's last name. And you weren't out there looking for the glasses that I don't wear, so maybe it's best if we don't ask each other any questions."

Alice nodded, impressed with Lani's authority and her ability to think on her feet. "Thank you," she said, quietly.

Lani patted Alice on the shoulder. "Whatever you were doing, girl, I hope it was important."

"It was," Alice promised, and that was the end of their conversation.

She went back to the antique store basement the next night after work, and the next. She varied her route and the hour that she came home as much as possible, and she didn't run into Officer Hodge again. Reading was slow work. Sometimes she arrived to find that exhaustion from her shift had wiped away all her progress, and that she couldn't remember at all what she had learned the night before. But she kept at it, even though she had to speak the words aloud to get anywhere. She shaped them sound by sound, feeling them against her lips and tongue. Sometimes when she turned the page, she felt as if the wall of text was a cliff face that she had to climb, and the form of each word offered a certain set of handholds: a vertical line here, a curve there. It was easier to hold onto the sounds than the images.

Two weeks in, Kei said, "So should it be the mage or the knight?"

"What?"

"In the story. Should Lily end up with the mage or the knight? I think they're both jerks, but I guess the knight has his moments."

"Oh," Alice said. Kei had been sitting with her faithfully every night, and Alice had tried to share her rediscovery of the alphabet. She hadn't realized that Kei had been listening—through her strained, syllable-by-syllable pronunciation—to the story. "She ends up with—"

"Don't tell me! I don't want to know the end yet. Which one do you want her to end up with?"

Alice hesitated, looking down at the text. Kei nudged their shoulders together, and Alice took a breath and said, almost as slowly as if she were reading, said, "I always wanted her to end up with the witch."

When she risked a glance at Kei, she saw that a smile was lifting the corners of her eyes, even though her lips were pressed together like she was holding back what she wanted to say.

"Percy's a dolt and Tristan is insufferable," Alice explained. Kei's silence made her anxious, even if she was smiling instead of edging away. Alice had said too much, but the only solution she could think of was to say more. Her opinion was entirely justifiable, after all. "The witch always seems to know so much more about the world than everyone else, and she listens to Lily when no one else will, and she always knows exactly what to say—"

"And she's beautiful."

"Well," Alice said, and then she didn't have to think of the rest because Kei kissed her. It seemed sudden, but only because Alice's pulse was thrumming under her skin. The kiss had not been sudden. Kei had accomplished it with her usual grace, reaching across to cup Alice's cheek and turn her head so that she could bring their lips together. Kei kissed deliberately, with certainty, the same way she did everything else. She brushed the pad of her thumb across Alice's cheek and drew her fingertips over the shell of Alice's ear. The soft press of her lips formed the shape of some unknowable word. Alice answered in kind, discovering a whole new language at the tip of her tongue.

When they finally broke apart, Alice reached over to brush Kei's hair away from her face. "She's very beautiful," she said, and Kei laughed.

Weeks passed, and deciphering chapters became easier and easier, so Alice made Kei read instead. She showed Kei her pen, that secret treasure, and she spent one evening practicing writing on her hands and arms while Kei read out loud. It was not as difficult to relearn as reading. Her hands remembered. Kei told her to stop wasting ink. They would need that pen later. They would need a thousand more. They would need paper, too, but most of all they would need a way to teach people to read and write in secret.

It felt insurmountable. Alice was already going home in the middle of the night, only to trudge through her shift the next day half-dead with exhaustion.

One night, while they were sitting on the basement floor in their usual spot, she said to Kei: "You ever think about leaving?"

"Of course," Kei said. "But where would we go? How would we even get there?" Alice stared at her, stuck on the word 'we.' But Kei didn't notice. "They don't give permits to cross the border to illiterates like us. So we'd have to sneak across at night between patrols. The wall is fifteen feet high and there's electrified wire across the top, so we'd have to take that into consideration. And then it's a week's walk through the plains to anywhere. We'd never survive if we went now. We might have a chance in the summer, but it would be blazing hot. And once we got wherever we were going, at best we'd be refugees. At worst, we'd be caught as criminals and get sent back immediately."

"When I think about leaving, I mostly imagine living on a beach somewhere warm, where nobody would bother us." There would be sunshine and sand and shimmering bright blue water. Maybe a hammock. Definitely lots of books. Learning to read again had rekindled Alice's rich fantasy life, so she liked to imagine a world where books were easy to come by.

"You would," Kei said, smiling. She pushed her shoulder against Alice's. "My grandma saw the ocean once, back before they built the wall. I bet it's not as great as everybody says."

"I've read about it, though. It's supposed to be beautiful."

"I bet it's cold. I bet fish are slimy," Kei said. "And what would we do with ourselves all day? It sounds boring."

"I could think of a few things," Alice murmured, and Kei laughed and kissed her cheek.

"Come on. At least here, we're doing something important. We're gonna figure it all out," Kei said. "We can go see the ocean after we teach everyone to read again, take down the government, and rebuild society from the ground up."

"Sure," Alice said. "No big deal. I'll get right on it."

That night, as Alice unlocked the door to her building and slipped in as quietly as possible, she thought back to the night that Lani had saved her from Hodge, all those weeks ago. She padded up the stairs and saw a sliver of light underneath Lani's door. On impulse, she knocked quietly.

"Do you ever sleep?" Lani said testily. She was in her dressing gown.

"I could ask you the same. Can I come in?"

Lani stepped aside, and Alice went in. The tiny one-bedroom apartment was identical to Alice's, right down to the empty bookshelf built into the living room wall. It was a little neater than Alice's, since the only stray object on Lani's couch was an embroidery hoop. Alice stood just inside the doorway, too uncertain to go any farther. She waited for Lani to latch the door before speaking.

"You used to teach language."

"And literature," Lani added. "Back before we decided we'd be better off without it."

The words were in line with the law, but the tone was not. Alice repressed a smile, and said cautiously, "What if we could have it again?"

Lani raised an eyebrow and then shuffled toward the couch. "I'm old," she said. "You have to speak close to my ear."

Lani sat down on the couch, arranged her dressing gown, and put the embroidery hoop in her lap. Alice followed, glancing at the newly begun work that was stretched on the hoop.

"I have something to share," Alice said, feeling more and more sure that she had made the right choice. Lani still had permission to teach her students to build and sew. That was where she got all her funny stories about her students' artistic impulses and the triumph of the human spirit. *A rusty nail or a sewing needle*, she'd said. So many things could be writing implements, if you knew how to write.

"What are you smiling at?" Lani said.

"That's a very beautiful color you're using," Alice said, touching the embroidery thread. It looped over and under the fabric in neat lines, following some invisible map. Against the white cloth, the thread was bright blue.

~

Felicia Davin has been exploring possible and impossible worlds through reading and writing all her life, but this is her first published piece of fiction. When she's not teaching and translating French, she is working on a novel. She lives in western Massachusetts with her partner and their cat. She is bilingual and bisexual, but not ambidextrous. You can find her on Twitter @FeliciaDavin.

How to Remember to Forget to Remember the Old War

Rose Lemberg

At the budget committee meeting this morning, the pen in my hand turns into a remote control of a subsonic detonator. It is familiar—heavy, smooth, the metal warm to the touch. The pain of recognition cruises through my fingers and up my arm, engorges my veins with unbearable sweetness. The detonator is gunmetal gray. My finger twitches, poised on the button.

I shake my head, and it is gone. Only it is still here, the taste of blood in my mouth, and underneath it, unnamed acidic bitterness. Around the conference table, the faces of faculty and staff darken in my vision. I see them—aging hippies polished by their long academic careers into a reluctant kind of respectability; accountants neat in bargain-bin clothes for office professionals; the dean, overdressed but defiant in his suit and dark blue tie with a class pin. They've traveled, I am sure, and some protested on the streets back in the day and thought themselves radicals, but there's none here who would not recoil in horror if I confessed my visions.

I do not twitch. I want to run away from the uncomplicated, slightly puffy expressions of those people who've never faced the battlefield, never felt the ground shake, never screamed tumbling facedown into the dirt. But I have more self-control than to flee. When it comes my time to report, I am steady. I concentrate on the numbers. The numbers have never betrayed me.

• • •

At five p.m. sharp I am out of the office. The airy old space is supposed to delight, with its tall cased windows and the afternoon sun streaming through the redwoods, but there's nothing here I want to see. I walk briskly to the Downtown Berkeley BART station and catch a train to the city. The train rattles underground, all stale air and musty seats. The people studiously look aside, giving each other the safety of not noticing, bubbles of imaginary emptiness in the crowd. The mild heat of bodies and the artificially illuminated darkness of the tunnel take the edge off.

When I disembark at Montgomery, the sky is already beginning to darken, the edges of pink and orange drawn in by the night. I could have gotten off at Embarcadero, but every time I decide against it—the walk down Market Street towards the ocean gives me a formality of approach, which I crave without understanding why. My good gray jacket protects against the chill coming up from the water. The people on the street—the executives and the baristas, the shoppers and the bankers—all stare past me with unseeing eyes.

They shipped us here, I remember. Damaged goods. Just like other states shipped their mentally ill to Berkeley on Greyhound buses: a one-way ticket to nowhere, to a place that is said to be restful and warm in the shadow of the buildings, under the bridges, camouflaged from this life by smells of pot and piss. I am luckier than most. Numbers come easy to me, and I look grave and presentable in my heavy jackets that are not armor. Their long sleeves hide the self-inflicted scars.

I remember little. Slivers. But I still bind my chest and use the pronoun they, and I wear a tight metal bracelet on my left arm. It makes me feel secure, if not safe. It's only a ploy, this bracelet I have found, a fool's game at hope. The band is base metal but without any markings, lights, or familiar pinpricks of the signal. Nothing flows. No way for Tedtemár to call, if ever Tedtemár could come here.

Northern California is where they ship the damaged ones—yes, even interstellars.

• • •

Nights are hard. I go out to the backyard, barren from my attempts at do-it-yourself landscaping. Only the redwood tree remains, and, at the very edge, a stray rose bush that blooms each spring in spite of my efforts. I smoke because I need it, to invoke and hold at bay the only full memory left to me: the battlefield, earth ravished by heaving and metal, the screech and whoosh of detonations overhead. In front of me I see the short, broad figure of my commanding officer. Tedtemár turns around. In dreams their visor is lifted, and I see their face laughing with the sounds of explosions around us. Tedtemár's arms are weapons, white and broad and spewing fire. I cannot hear anything for the wailing, but in dreams, Tedtemár's lips form my name as the ground heaves.

• • •

I have broken every wall in my house, put my fist through the thinness of them as if they're nothing. I could have lived closer to work, but in this El Cerrito neighborhood nobody asks any questions, and the backyard is mine to ravage. I break the walls, then half-heartedly repair them over weekends only to break them again. At work I am composed and civil and do not break anything, though it is a struggle. The beautiful old plaster of the office walls goes gritty gray like barracks, and the overhead lights turn into alarms. Under the table I interlace my fingers into bird's wings, my unit's recognition sign, as my eyes focus resolutely on spreadsheets. At home I repair the useless walls and apply popcorn texture, then paint the whole thing bog-gray in a shade I mix myself. It is too ugly even for my mood, even though I've been told that gray is all the rage with interior designers these days.

I put my fist through the first wall before the paint dries.

• • •

Today, there is music on Embarcadero. People in black and colorful clothing whirl around, some skillfully, some with a good-natured clumsiness. Others are there simply to watch. It's some kind of a celebration, but I have nothing to celebrate and nothing to hope for, except for the music to shriek like a siren. I buy a plate of deep-fried cheese balls and swallow them, taste buds disbelieving the input, eyes disbelieving the revelry even though I know the names of the emotions expressed here. Joy. Pleasure. Anticipation. At the edge of the piers, men cast small nets for crabs to sell to sushi bars, and in the nearby restaurants diners sip wine and shiver surreptitiously with the chill. I went out on dates with women and with men and with genderfluid folks, but they have all avoided me after a single meeting. They are afraid to say it to my face, but I can see. Too gloomy. Too intense. Too quiet. Won't smile or laugh.

There is a person I notice among the revelers. I see them from the back—stooped, aloof. Like me. I don't know what makes me single them out of the crowd: the shape of the shoulders perhaps. The stranger does not dance, does not move, just stands there. I begin to approach then veer abruptly away. No sense in bothering a stranger with—with what exactly? Memories?

I cannot remember anything useful.

I wish they'd done a clean job, taken all my memories away so I could start fresh. I wish they'd taken nothing, left my head to rot. I wish they'd shot me. Wish I'd shoot myself and have no idea why I don't, what compels me to continue in the conference rooms and in the overly pleasant office and in my now fashionably gray house. Joy or pleasure are words I cannot visualize. But I do want—something. Something.

Wanting itself, at least, was not taken from me, and numbers still keep me safe. Lucky bastard.

• • •

I see the stranger again at night, standing in the corner of my backyard where the redwood used to be. The person has no face, just an empty black oval filled with explosives. Their white artificial arms form an alphabet of deafening fire around my head.

The next day I see them in the shape of the trees outside my office window, feel their movement in the bubbling of Strawberry Creek when I take an unusual lunch walk. I want, I want, I want, I want. The wanting is a gray bog beast that swallows me awake into the world devoid of noise. The suffocating safe coziness of my present environment rattles me, the planes and angles of the day too soft for comfort. I press the metal of my bracelet, but it is not enough. I cut my arms with a knife and hide the scars old and new under sleeves. I break the walls again and repaint them with leftover bog-gray that I dilute with an even uglier army green.

Over and over again I take the BART to Embarcadero, but the person I seek is not there, not there when it's nearly empty or when it's full of stalls for the arts and crafts fair. The person I seek might never have existed, an interplay of shadows over plastered walls. A co-worker calls to introduce me to someone; I cut her off, sick of myself and my well-wishers, always taunting me in my mind. In an hour I repent and reconsider, and later spend an evening of coffee and music with someone kind who speaks fast and does not seem to mind my gloom. Under the table, my fingers lace into bird's wings.

I remember next to nothing, but I know this: I do not want to go back to the old war. I just want—want—

• • •

I see the person again at Montgomery, in a long corridor leading from the train to the surface. I recognize the stooped shoulders and run forward, but the cry falls dead on my lips.

It is not Tedtemár. Their face, downturned and worn, betrays no shiver of laughter. They smell unwashed and stale and their arms do not end in metal. The person does not move or react, like the others perhaps-of-ours I've seen here over the years, and their lips move, saying nothing. I remember the date from the other day, cheery in the face of my silence. But I know I have nothing to lose. So I cough and I ask.

They say nothing.

I turn away to leave when out of the corner of my eyes I see their fingers interlock to form the wings of a bird.

• • •

Imprudent and invasive for this world, I lay my hand on their shoulder and lead them back underground. I buy them a BART ticket, watch over them as even the resolutely anonymous riders edge away from the smell. I take them to my home in El Cerrito, where broken walls need repair, and where a chipped cup of tea is made to the soundtrack of sirens heard only in my head. The person holds the cup between clenched fists and sips, eyes closed. I cannot dissuade them when they stand in the corner to sleep, silent and unmoving like an empty battle suit.

At night I dream of Tedtemár crying. Rockets fall out of their eyes to splash against my hands and burst there into seeds. I do not understand. I wake to the stranger huddled to sleep in a corner. Stray moonrays whiten their arms to metal.

In the morning I beg my guest to take sustenance, or a bath, but they do not react. I leave them there for work, where the light again makes mockery of everything. Around my wrist the fake bracelet comes to life, blinking, blinking, blinking in a code I cannot decipher, calling to me in a voice that could not quite be Tedtemár's. It is only a trick of the light.

• • •

At home I am again improper. The stranger does not protest or recoil when I peel their dirty clothes away, lead them into the bath. They are listless, moving their limbs along with my motions. The sudsy water covers everything—that which I could safely look at and that which I shouldn't have seen. I will not switch the pronouns. When names and memories go, these bits of language, translated inadequately into the local vernacular, remain to us. They are slivers, always jagged slivers of us, where lives we lived used to be.

I remember Tedtemár's hands, dragging me away. The wail of a falling rocket. Their arms around my torso, pressing me back into myself.

I wash my guest's back. They have a mark above their left shoulder, as if from a once-embedded device. I do not recognize it as my unit's custom, or as anything.

I wanted so much—I wanted—but all that wanting will not bring the memories back, will not return my life. I do not want it to return, that life that always stings and smarts and smolders at the edge of my consciousness, not enough to hold on to, more than enough to hurt—but there's an emptiness in me where people have been once, even the ones I don't remember. Was this stranger a friend? Their arms feel stiff to my touch. For all their fingers interlaced into wings at Montgomery station, since then I had only seen them hold their hands in fists.

Perhaps I'd only imagined the wings.

I wail on my way to work, silent with mouth pressed closed so nobody will notice. In the office I wail, openmouthed and silent, against the moving shades of redwoods in the window.

• • •

For once I don't want takeaway or minute meals. I brew strong black tea and cook stewed red lentils over rice in a newly purchased pot. I repair the broken walls and watch Tedtemár-who-is-not-quite-Tedtemár as they lean against the doorway, eyes vacant. I take them to sleep in my bed, then perch on the very edge of it, wary and waiting. At night they cry out once, their voice undulating with the sirens in my mind. Hope awakens in me with that sound, but then my guest falls silent again.

An older neighbor comes by in the morning and chats at my guest, not caring that they do not answer—like the date whose name I have forgotten. I don't know if I'd recognize Tedtemár if I met them here. My guest could be anyone, from my unit or another, or a veteran of an entirely different war shipped to Northern California by people I can't know, because they always ship us here, from everywhere, and do not tell us why.

Work's lost all taste and color, what of it there ever was. Even numbers feel numb and bland under my tongue. I make mistakes in my spreadsheets and am reprimanded.

• • •

At night I perch again in bed beside my guest. I hope for a scream, for anything; fall asleep in the silent darkness, crouched uncomfortably with one leg dangling off to the floor.

I wake up with their fist against my arm. Rigid fingers press and withdraw to the frequency of an old alarm code that hovers on the edge of my remembrance. In darkness I can feel their eyes on me, but am afraid to speak, afraid to move. In less than a minute, when the pressing motion ceases and I no longer feel their gaze, I cannot tell if this has been a dream.

· · ·

I have taken two vacation days at work. I need the rest but dread returning home, dread it in all the different ways from before. I have not broken a wall since I brought my guest home.

Once back, I do not find them in any of their usual spots. I think to look out of the kitchen window at last. I see my stranger, Tedtemár or the person who could be Tedtemár—someone unknown to me, from a different unit, a different culture, a different war. My commanding officer. They are in the backyard on their knees. There's a basket by their side, brought perhaps by the neighbor.

For many long minutes I watch them plant crocuses into the ravaged earth of my yard. They are digging with their fists. Their arms, tight and rigid as always, seem to caress this ground into which we've been discarded, cast aside when we became too damaged to be needed in the old war. Explosives streak past my eyelids and sink, swallowed by the clumps of the soil around their fists.

I do not know this person. I do not know myself.

This moment is all I can have.

I open the kitchen door, my fingers unwieldy, and step out to join Tedtemár.

—*for Bogi Takács*

∼

Rose Lemberg is a queer bigender immigrant from Eastern Europe. Her work has appeared in *Strange Horizons, Beneath Ceaseless Skies, Interfictions, Uncanny, Sisters of the Revolution: A Feminist Speculative Fiction Anthology,* and other venues. Rose co-edits *Stone Telling,* a magazine of boundary-crossing poetry, with Shweta Narayan. She has edited *Here, We Cross,* an anthology of queer and genderfluid speculative poetry from *Stone Telling* (Stone Bird Press), and T*he Moment of Change,* an anthology of feminist speculative poetry (Aqueduct Press). She is currently editing a new fiction anthology, *An Alphabet of Embers.* You can find Rose at roselemberg.net and @ roselemberg, and support her work on Patreon at patreon.com/roselemberg.

Plant Children

Jessica Yang

In the seventh grade, Qiyan was plagued with aunts.

They swept into her apartment in a perfumed mob, littering tubes of chapstick and crumbles of pineapple shortcake in their wake. They pinched Qiyan's cheeks and cooed over her darkest-black hair, as if hair color were a Confucian virtue. They clucked their tongues at the stained curtains that blocked the sun-facing window. They schemed.

A year later, the aunts came and went one last time, leaving behind Qiyan's great-aunt, a wizened old woman with a voice that rasped like dead leaves. And so, Ah Meng became Qiyan's token live-in relative.

What Ah Meng loved most, even more than urban myths and fried garlic, was telling Qiyan to bear children. This was Ah Meng's hobby. At least it kept her busy, Qiyan's mother said whenever Qiyan got fed up—as if being busy were enough to keep this ancient relic alive to the point of vampirism.

"You should have children," Ah Meng would say, "so they can care for you in your old age."

"Ah Meng, that's what health insurance is for," Qiyan would reply.

By then, Qiyan loved her great-aunt enough to avoid the elephant in the room: Ah Meng's own children never visited, much less cared for her. Even her daughters had left her behind. They lived in mansions staffed with spark sharp bots and monotone windows, but they'd left their mother in a one-room apartment, under the care of Qiyan's family of three (one: Qiyan; two: Qiyan's mother; three: their near-sentient microwave).

Ah Meng's children sent red bean cake every new year, all packaged up in gold aluminum boxes and tissue paper. It was the high-end stuff. Qiyan's mother called it "blood money" when Ah Meng was out of hearing, but they still ate the cakes.

Ah Meng never seemed to notice. Maybe she had the superpower of selective amnesia, Qiyan speculated. In other ways, though, Ah Meng had a knife-edged memory. She liked to tell Qiyan about the past over plates of midnight snacks.

One day over supper, Ah Meng said, "You know, once they found a dead king—some big foreign one—buried under a parking lot."

"What?" Qiyan said, ladling beef broth into her bowl. "Who's they?"

"Archaeologists or construction workers, maybe," said Ah Meng. "I don't know. Don't ask me silly questions."

"Sorry, ah, only curious," Qiyan grumbled. She tipped back a spoonful of sodden cabbage lace into her mouth, chewed, and swallowed.

"Huh." Ah Meng narrowed her eyes at Qiyan. The wrinkles radiating out from her eyes increased, like fractal trees. "The dead king they found had flowers growing out of his heart—poppies, lavender, myrtle."

"How?"

"He was buried with spices, see? And seeds in them."

"Oh."

"When I was your age, we didn't have all this." Ah Meng waved a hand in the air. Her gesture meant this, this nonsense—the cold metal bots; AI admins that spoke words like measurements; firefly leaves that glowed day and night; electric green vaccines siphoned from succulents; and frogs grown out of pitcher plants, skin mottled white and red like their mothers'. "We didn't have any of it."

"Ah Meng, you're not even that old," said Qiyan.

"That's what you think," Ah Meng sniffed. By her own estimation, Ah Meng had seen the rise and fall of empires. Her age was a point of pride. (Ah Meng had many such points.)

"Anyway, the king?"

"The king's heart crumbled and flowers grew out. See? We didn't have any of this," Ah Meng said. She tapped the glass table. Sensors beeped back at her, measuring her pulse and displaying it in blue block numbers. "But even then, we had wonders."

• • •

And now Qiyan had to produce her own wonders. She had a scholarship riding on it, so it mattered. Little else did, now that she was a senior. All she had left was three four-unit classes, a nutrition seminar (which was cake), and her senior thesis.

Qiyan leaned back against her desk and brainstormed.

"They used to cut babies out of bamboo," Qiyan said to her roommate An. "Why can't we?"

"It was only the one time with the princess," said An, "and that was just mythic."

"But there's precedence," said Qiyan. "Do you think they would go for it? Is it senior thesis material?"

"I don't know." An twisted in her chair to face her roommate. "Ask your thesis advisor. That's what he's for, right?"

"But I don't want to."

"I'm only a classics major." The chair creaked as An propped her feet up on her desk. She wiggled her painted toes at Qiyan. "What do I know about plants?"

"It's not just plants," Qiyan corrected her. "It's the intersection of plant engineering and life devo in the context of ecocultural sustainability."

"So, plants."

Qiyan scowled at An. "My thesis proposal is due tomorrow, so I can't ask my advisor anyway."

"I thought you went to office hours today."

"Eh." Qiyan rubbed her neck, embarrassed. She managed a sheepish grin. "I slept in."

"Because you spent all night gaming."

"I missed the save point!" Qiyan threw herself onto her bed and covered her face. From under her blankets, she said, "I'm so, so sorry." Her voice came out muffled.

"Don't sorry me. Apologize to your thesis advisor."

"Huh, I'd rather apologize to Ah Meng."

"Isn't that your great-aunt? I thought she was," An hesitated, "dead."

"Well, I'd rather apologize to the dead than to my thesis advisor." Qiyan rolled onto the floor, bringing her blankets and pillow with her in a tangled heap. She lay there, staring up at the speckled gray ceiling, arms flung out and legs akimbo. Her neck still ached from staying up all night. "You know, he called ginger a root."

"Isn't it?"

"It's a rhizome! He even called taro a root." Qiyan punched the air. "Everything's roots to him!"

"Fine, apologize to your ancestors then."

"Sorry, Ah Meng," Qiyan said to the ceiling, clapping her hands together. "Sorry I missed the save point."

• • •

The next morning, Qiyan struggled out of bed and fell to the floor with a thump.

"Shit." She crawled back into bed, scrabbling at her comforter. Spring had arrived early, or so the reports said, but the gods had missed the memo. Mornings dawned freezing cold even as yellow green shoots unfurled and pink blooms covered the trees. Burrowing back under her blankets, Qiyan settled into the comfort of old warmth.

"Morning," An said. She leaned against the door frame, twisting and pulling her dark hair into a loose bun. Slants of sun streamed in through the window to pool at An's feet. "Did you dream up a thesis proposal?"

"No, I don't think so," said Qiyan. She flipped over in bed to see An all aglow in the morning light. Something curled and tightened in her stomach, setting her fingers tingling. Qiyan looked away.

"Too bad."

"I think I'm going to ditch lecture," Qiyan mumbled into her pillow. "I didn't study for the quiz."

"But you'll write up your proposal, right?"

"If I can think of one."

An harrumphed. "You better. If you don't get that scholarship, I'm not covering your rent. I'll kick you out."

"Ha! You can't live without me."

"You're right, Qiyan. I can't," An said sweetly. "So write your proposal."

• • •

It was late afternoon by the time Qiyan deigned to greet the waking world. A plate of scallion pancakes had been left out on the counter to cool. Snagging a piece, Qiyan raked her fingers through her short, all-angles hair, and headed out.

If she could catch her advisor before his class, then maybe he could help her, though it was unlikely. He seemed to delight in Qiyan's thesis troubles. She cursed the day she'd asked Professor Lun to advise her. She'd only done it for her lab partner, who thought Professor Lun was hot. Qiyan couldn't see his appeal. True, he had a jaw that you could slice butter on, but so?

An had a better jaw, a better nose, a better everything.

"Hey Qiyan!" A classmate waved to Qiyan from across the street. He called out, "Where's your other half?"

Everyone and their mother thought of Qiyan and An as a unit. They went to class together; they roomed together; they had the same taste in milk tea (taro, no ice). People got confused when they saw one without the other. To An's great amusement, her classmates thought Qiyan was also a classics major. Nothing could be further from the truth.

"She's in class," Qiyan yelled back. "I'm ditching!"

"Wah, you rebel!"

Campus was an upward hike from the complex. The university sat tucked into the mountainside. Wide stone steps led away from the city and up the mountain into wet green canopy. One wrong turn and you ended up far from campus, looking at forgotten shrines and lichen-covered guardian lions with their mouths agape. Students were warned not to explore the old mountain so, of course, whole expeditions went out adventuring every weekend. There was even a hiking club, with membership dues and everything.

When Qiyan was halfway to campus, she heard bells ring. Pausing on the steps, she counted each clang—two, three, four. It was too late. Her thesis advisor would be starting his class on plant propagation.

She crouched down on the steps to think. In the distance, Qiyan could hear the clamor of the city. The smell of incense wafted down to her. There was a shrine higher up, probably. Stripping off her boots and socks, Qiyan rested her bare feet on the moss that grew out of the cracks in the stone steps. A slight breeze set the trees sighing overhead. This was the weather Ah Meng liked—good for hanging the laundry out to dry.

Ah Meng had always wanted Qiyan to have children. Fine. That could be arranged.

• • •

"You know cloning babies out of plants is illegal, right?" An said when Qiyan told her the news.

"No, it's not like that," said Qiyan. She picked at the leftover scallion pancakes on the counter. They were cold by then, but still good. "I'm not making children from plants—I'm making children out of plants. Plant sentience, see?"

"I don't think that's possible," An said. She set down her backpack and gave Qiyan a doubtful look. "Is it?"

"Carnivorous plants are almost there, anyway, and then there's the fern that reacts to touch—"

"Shouldn't you do something easier?"

"Nah, it's okay." Qiyan smiled confidently. "I only have to write a report and do some lab work to show I tried. No one would expect me to actually accomplish it."

"Oh, good." An said, "I'm not ready for talking flowers."

"What about singing ones?"

"No."

"I could make them hum—"

"No."

• • •

Determined to make something of her senior thesis, Qiyan spent every waking moment in the lab. Her TA thought the idea funny ("Are you going to make them talk? Wear shoes?") and donated trays of mint, snow peas, and cilantro to the cause. When classmates got wind of Qiyan's plans, they gave her potted ferns and packets of flower seeds and sprouts swaddled in damp paper towels.

They'd ask, "How're your babies?"

"Just fine," Qiyan would reply. "They're teething now. I think I'll have them on solids soon."

She had more than enough room in the lab to house her research, but that was no fun. She started to bring plants home. She arranged them on the windowsill in neat rows and made self-contained gardens in the living room.

She took to introducing the plants to An.

"So this is a mint," Qiyan said. "And this is a green onion."

"Yes, I know," said An. "But can it talk?"

"No, but look—" Qiyan flicked on a lamp near the mint. The plant leaned ever so slightly toward the light source. "I kicked up the phototaxis stuff."

"It likes light," An said.

Hearing this, Qiyan bit back a smile. "It likes light a lot."

• • •

The following week, Qiyan brought home an entire tray of glow-in-the-dark strawberry plants. They flourished in darkness, producing grayish strawberries that tasted like socks. Potted plants covered the living room floor, but the strawberries needed somewhere shady.

Under the couch would work, Qiyan thought. Or maybe the bathroom? But the mushrooms were already next to the shower. Sucking in her stomach, Qiyan inched behind the couch to make room for the strawberries.

An emerged from the kitchen to watch Qiyan struggle. She said, "Aren't those invasive?"

"Yeah, but they look cool," said Qiyan. "And the TA was going to feed them to the cleaner bots, so."

"Aigh, I can't believe you."

"I can," Qiyan said, crawling out from behind the couch. She held up a wilting camellia. "By the way, this is Wanli now."

"Wait, you're naming the plants?"

"I figure if I name them after professors I hate, I won't feel sad if they die."

"Sounds good, actually," An said, crouching down to examine the newest arrivals. "What do these do?"

"Touch sensitive, the lot of them," Qiyan said proudly. "And sensitive to movement, too. They follow you around." To demonstrate, Qiyan stepped in front of a frothy green fern, which tilted in Qiyan's direction.

"Follows you around like a good Renaissance painting."

"We're like the sun now, to them."

"You mean a giant burning star that causes sunburn and heatstroke?"

"No, I mean," Qiyan said, "we are everything to them."

"Really."

"Well, aside from water, nutrients, and optimum soil pH."

• • •

Sometimes the apartment froze over at night, so Qiyan filed a request with the housing office to adjust the heating. A key arrived in the mail a week later, and she used it to override the climate control, raising the temperature as high as it would go. Soon, the apartment felt like the height of summer.

Qiyan and An went about their daily life in a haze of heat. To cool off, Qiyan wrote up lab reports with a wet towel on her neck. An walked around in tank tops and swim trunks, never breaking a sweat. Qiyan marveled at her roommate's cool.

The summer heat started leaking into Qiyan's dreams. She would jolt awake in a full body sweat, heart pounding like the thunder gods at war. Nothing could send her to sleep after that. She tapped at the windows to configure holo games and played until sunrise.

The plants flourished in the muggy warmth. Seedlings and sprouts and drooping peonies grew rapidly, sending out fresh green leaves and buds as the shadows turned with time.

Vines of snow peas, covered in tightly wound pea blossoms, had curled their way around the trellis Qiyan had rigged up against the glass door to the balcony. The broccoli had started to bloom, as had the basil lining the back wall. Morning and evening glories crawled up the wall, sending out tendrils to touch the bedroom door. Spindly chrysanthemums let down nests of yellow petals. Yam leaves snaked around the room, invading neighboring pots.

Everything grew too fast, too soon.

Each morning, Qiyan stepped in among her plants to care for them. She watered the pots, checked for fungus, and fussed over the seedlings. She took to snipping off the buds before they bloomed to prevent the plants from peaking too soon. They were her darlings.

As she made her usual circuit around the living room, the plants turned, ever so slightly, to face her.

• • •

As news spread around campus of Qiyan's makeshift greenhouse, classmates dropped by to snoop. They peeked in, milled about, and exclaimed over the lush greenery. Invariably, they would cast hopeful, puppy-dog looks at Qiyan until she grudgingly offered bags of heavy red tomatoes and peppers as souvenirs.

An's study group visited, bearing gifts of sticky purple cake and milk candy.

They lounged on the couch, dissecting the latest classics exam, and left in the evening with fistfuls of fresh herbs. Even Qiyan's lab partner followed her home, asking after her babies.

"Your basil is peaking, you know," her lab partner observed. She plucked off a cluster of pink basil flowers. "You should maybe prune?"

"They're all like that," Qiyan said. "I cut them, but they keep trying anyway—like they've got a death wish."

"Environmental stress? It looks nice, though. Very beautiful growing pains."

Even Qiyan's thesis advisor dropped by. She sent him away with a bag of stunted eggplants.

"Good riddance," Qiyan huffed.

An laughed. "We should charge for admission. Make some money."

"I wish." Qiyan surveyed the verdant greenery that radiated from her feet. "This won't last anyway."

"Does anything ever?"

"Don't get philosophical, An," said Qiyan. "It's too early in the day for that." She grinned at An to show that she was joking.

She lay down on the ground, careful not to squash the seedlings near her. Broad green leaves swayed forward to shade her face. If she squinched up her eyes just so, she saw only blurred shades of yellow and green above her. It felt like summer back home, before Ah Meng had passed away. They'd gone to the park a lot, the two of them, and rested on slat-wood benches under the care of grand trees that let in only dapples of sunlight.

"Qiyan?" An leaned over, hands on her knees.

"Hm?" Qiyan looked up at An, admired the fall of hair and slope of shoulder. The sight was too much. She closed her eyes, turning away.

"Hello?"

Qiyan heard An straighten up. Her voice came from far away now.

"I turned in the rent," An said. "Pay me back later, okay?"

"Mm."

● ● ●

The cilantro died first. It gave out little dot flowers, first, then wilted, dried out, and crumbled. The basil followed, and then the morning glories. The broccoli bolted, burst with fine white flowers, and keeled over. Sprigs of mint withered to nothing as the tomato plants turned yellow, then brown.

Qiyan's engineered darlings went by the same pattern—grow, bloom, die—in rapid succession.

The yam leaves, ever hardy, continued to live on. If yam leaves were people, Qiyan thought, they would be boisterous uncles who wore suspenders over stained undershirts and spat fat globs of phlegm on the side of the road.

The daikon, too, were late bloomers and clung to life. Tall stalks of purple flowers grew long and spindly in the corner of the room. They were especially fond of Qiyan—at least, around watering time—and tickled her knees as she walked past.

"An," Qiyan lamented to her roommate, "they're all dying."

"I know," said An, "but you finished your thesis, right?"

"Yeah, but my babies," Qiyan groaned. "Ah Meng always said she wanted me to have children, but even these children of mine are dying." She sat down among the pots, slumping forward so that her forehead touched the floor. Her back ached in protest, but she stayed that way.

"I don't think your Ah Meng meant what she said." An's voice came out lower than usual. "You know, about having children and all that."

"What? Of course she did," said Qiyan, bending over some daikon sprouts. "She was of that old generation, before they figured out portable in-vitro kits and everyone thought you had to have children out of your body before you were thirty."

"But her children didn't even care about her, right?"

"Yeah," mumbled Qiyan. "It sucked."

"But you did. She wanted you to have what you had with her. You were everything her daughters should have been." An continued, "She meant that she loved you."

"I guess." Minutes ticked by as Qiyan listened to the plants rustle around her. Somewhere above her, froths of purple flowers were leaning in her direction, seeking her.

Cool fingers brushed away her bangs. Qiyan blinked away the sweat in her eyes in time for An to lean down and kiss her brow. As An rocked back on her heels, Qiyan saw An's ears redden.

Finally, An said, "There's an orchid sale on Sunday. Do you want to go?"

Qiyan turned to look at An, as green life toward its sun.

~

Jessica Yang grew up in Silicon Valley, and then wandered off to UC Davis, where she spent three years being confused by Shakespeare and *The Tale of Genji*. By a strange twist of events, she went from tutoring kids in composition to writing puns for money. She will consume just about any media that can be described as slice-of-life, and drinks more milk tea than is wise. Her short fiction hasn't appeared anywhere else, but she hopes to change that! She can be found on Twitter (@aprication) nattering about YA lit and posting pictures of plants.

Nothing is
Pixels Here

K.M. Szpara

Art by Isabel Collier

"System Error ahead. Please turn around," the Concierge's voice speaks over the metallic growl of my dirt bike.

I rev the throttle and lean into the warm wind. My seat bounces as mud ricochets up around me. Ahead, knobby limbs and crisp leaves dissolve into broken pixels.

The SimGrid mutes as the soft voice fills the space between my ears, again. "System Error ahead. Please turn around."

"Not this time," I say. Not the first time I've found myself talking to the Concierge. The wind should be cold—shouldn't it? I remember trying to hide from the wind during winter. Ducking into alleys and behind dumpsters.

"Sys—er—ahd." Her voice crackles out as the pixels around me grow and blur.

I tug my helmet off. It bounces in my wake. I hold my hand in front of my face. The edges of my peach fingers flicker. A gray line crawls across my vision.

The front wheel slips. I grab for the handle just as it blinks from existence. The SimGrid turns sideways around me as my bike crushes the right side of my body. Gravel and sticks scrape through the lining of my pants. Bones crunch. Dust clogs my lungs. The front wheel spins fruitlessly in midair, slowing to a stop.

"Please remain still. Reset pending," The Concierge says.

They won't leave me here. And yet, I'd pull the dirt bike up around me like covers in bed, if I could. But before my endorphins can disperse, the SimGrid blacks out.

Reset.

• • •

The front door barely clicks when I close it. The hardwood floorboards are silent under my Kinetic, Inc. flip-flops. Muffled guitar leaks from Zane's headphones, when I sneak past his workroom. His fingers play over his computer keyboard as if he's playing piano. I never could sit still that long.

I duck into our bedroom and pull off the newly generated scrubs. The blue papery material crumbles easily between my hands. I shove it into the trash, just as the door swings open.

"There's a naked man in my bedroom," Zane says. "Not that I'm complaining." He smiles and pulls me against him. His full lips press a kiss against mine.

I tilt my head back while he nips and licks down my neck. Zane bites gently. I remember the sharp pain of gravel digging into my hip, the weight of my bike, crack of bone.

I squirm away, running a hand through my hair.

"You okay?" Zane squints, as if his dark brown eyes can bore right through me. They can't. He's not even really looking at me.

"Yeah, I'm fine. Just ..." My excuse trails off. We could leave the SimGrid. People terminate their contracts often enough. A year ago, our friends Cora and Brandi left.

"You scare me with that dirt bike, sometimes." Zane presses his hand to my forehead. Just an hour ago, blood trickled down the scratched skin.

"I'm fine, really. Just been thinking." I pull on a pair of briefs and a tee shirt.

Zane's hands warm my waist. He slides them up and down. Do I even feel him? The SimGrid can only approximate. What if it's wrong? I've never really touched him.

"Talk to me, Ash."

"Have you ever thought about unplugging?" The question erupts before I can stop it.

His eyes widen. "Unplugging, as in from the SimGrid?"

"Yeah."

"I mean, when Cora and Brandi left, I thought about it. But only in theory, not in practice. Have you?" He doesn't wait for my answer. He knows it. We've been together fifteen years. He probably knows more about me than the Concierge does. "You have."

"What if it's better?"

"It's not." His voice is suddenly sharp.

"How do you know?"

"I remember what it's like out there." Zane rubs his thumb over an unremarkable spot on his left forearm.

I'm surprised he hasn't worn a hole through the light brown skin, over the years. I've stopped asking why—what was there before he plugged in.

I wonder if I'll ever get to see his real body. Our avatars show us how we want to be seen, how our minds imagine us. But I don't think I'll mind his imperfections.

"You know, we're not the same, now. We're not kids. You have programming skills. I've won nine of my last ten races. We have over forty years of credit building up with the Concierge, between us. We wouldn't have to live on the street."

Zane scratches the spot and bites his lip. "I'll think about it."

• • •

The Error isn't easy to spot, at first, but it's still there. A squirrel bounces across my day-old tire tracks, expanding into one big brown-gray pixel in the middle.

I hit the kill switch on my bike and dismount. Air cools the sweat on my forehead when I remove my helmet. I focus on the temperature. The breeze is supposed to refresh me, but now I can't shake the memory of wind so cold it burns.

"System Error ahead. Please turn around."

"You just don't quit, do you?"

Every step closer, the snake of gray pixels works its way farther across my vision. I feel like I'm walking in slow motion. My hands expand and blur, like the squirrel. Peachy block hands. I can still feel my fingers wiggle. They re-form as I reach forward and rest against a tree. When I drag my left palm down the bark, it doesn't just scratch, it cuts.

Adrenaline races through my arm, tingling almost pleasurably where blood beads to the surface. I wipe it on my jacket and glance around. No one's here. I need to know what it feels like.

What it *really* feels like.

I rest back against the sharp tree and unfasten my pants. Not the most romantic—or sexy, for that matter—but the first touch electrifies me. I close my eyes and imagine Zane's fingers wrapped around my cock. His lips warmer and wetter against my neck. I wrap my left arm around the tree, overhead. The bark bites in my hand like I wish Zane's teeth would do to my neck.

I hug the tree tighter, stroke myself faster. Warm blood drips down my arm, tickling every hair in its path. My moan crackles and fades like a dying firework. My heart wants to slow, but I push it, rubbing the head of my cock.

My body feels like it might dissolve into a billion pixels at any second. Lightheadedness settles in. So close. I'm so—

My cry cuts off. I come in silence. My body climaxes—all of it. Pain and pleasure twine together and vibrate across my skin.

I relinquish the tree and gasp for breath. Blood slides down my arm and stains my sleeves. My knees buckle, tailbone slams into the ground.

My heart slows its beat. My pixels flicker out. I've done it, again.

"Please remain still. Reset pending."

• • •

Zane looks up from his chair. Shadows blacken his eyes like dark smiles. Blue paper peeks out from between his balled hands. Same as the scrubs I wear, now.

"Hey," I say, my voice restored to its usual smooth texture.

Zane doesn't respond. His eyes fall to his fists. "Don't you like what we have, here?"

"Yes." The word is more reaction than answer. I can't lie if I want him to believe me. "And no. It's not you—or me. It's this place."

"I've noticed." When Zane opens his hands, the blue paper scrubs blooms like a flower. "Why didn't you tell me you reset?"

"I didn't think it was a big deal."

"Not a big deal?"

"It's not like I can really die, here."

"Yeah, but you still killed yourself, Ash!" Even though Zane is sitting down, I feel him towering over me. "Just imagining you dying…" He covers his face.

"I'm sorry," I whisper. "I won't do it, again."

I don't tell him I want to. That I want him to come with me, next time. I want us to make love that warms us like the sun and then burns us up, when we get too close.

"But, you will." Zane finally looks at me. He circles that spot on his arm, draws a bullseye around it.

"You could come with me," I say. "There's a System Error, right off the trail where I ride. Everything feels different, there. Like reality."

Zane's mouth smashes against mine. His hands thread through my short curls, holding me still for his tongue and teeth and all I can think about is how much better this would all feel outside the SimGrid. Even the Error is only a glimpse of real pain, real pleasure, real love.

"Does this not feel real to you?" Zane whispers.

"It used to."

"What about this?" Zane charges me like a linebacker, half scooping me up, half pushing me, until I collide with the couch.

The wooden feet scrape across the floor. I recline under his weight. My legs automatically curl around his waist, cinching us closer. Zane doesn't bother taking my pants off. He shoves his hand down the flimsy scrubs. They tear as he rubs my growing bulge.

I try to be with him, but I'm back in the woods. Zane's lips are too soft and my skin is only pixels, my nerves only lines of code.

When he pushes inside me, I gasp, lingering in the moment, the fullness, the closeness, the -ness of it all. I want him. His body, the person inside it.

My body is just lying in a medical bed, somewhere. Programmed nanites stimulate my prostate with their best imitation of Zane's cock. I'm not really stretched, not open to him.

"More." I slide my hands under his shirt and hold us tight together. "More, Zane. Please, more."

I scream and seize against him. His bite draws blood. Its warmth reminds me of the cutting bark and my electric fingers.

My body—my avatar—goes through the motions of orgasm: blood rush, nerve spasm, glowing pleasure. It feels real-ish. More like a heat lamp than the sun.

I regain control of my breathing and help Zane finish. Flexing, kissing, holding. He doesn't know any different—any better.

Zane's weight rests on me. He feels like a feather compared to my dirt bike.

"I love you." His forehead presses against mine, sticky with sweat.

"I love you, too." I want to think that I'm looking at him. I want to forget the Error, but I can't.

"I don't want to unplug," Zane says.

"I know."

"That's the real world, out there. We have to get jobs and—"

"I know." I curl my fingers through his. No kid who grows up in the SimGrid does so because they had a great life outside. "We can do this. We'll get a house—a brick and mortar house."

Zane chuckles. "Think smaller."

"Fine, a real apartment." I smile, too. "Get jobs."

"Pay taxes, bills—"

"Make friends, taste food."

"I'll do it."

I don't respond. What if he takes it back?

"Just promise me, if it doesn't work out, you won't hurt yourself."

"I won't."

Zane squeezes my hands in his. "Because it might not work out. I need you to be realistic."

Realistic. That's all I've ever wanted.

• • •

"Next, please." A Concierge looks up from her desk. She's not real, either. Just code written by a Kinetic, Inc. staff person, holed up in a cubicle.

"Hi." I'm not sure if I'm holding Zane's hand so he won't back down or so I won't. My whole body pulses with blood and nerves. This is the most real I've ever felt.

Zane takes over, saying the words I can't. "We'd like to unplug."

"All right, let me pull up your files." Her fingers pitter-patter over the keys, not unlike Zane's.

What if he ends up in an office, somewhere? Taking orders from a money-hungry boss, or overqualified and bored out of his mind. That would be my fault.

Zane rubs the spot on his arm. I'll get to see what's really there, once we're back in our bodies. Our avatars adjust to our vision of ourselves, smooth out blemishes, suck out belly fat, de-frizz hair. Erase scars.

"Please place your forefingers on the readers," the Concierge says.

We do, not releasing each other.

A green light flashes under our fingertips. "Thank you," she says. "A Concierge will take you each to a medical bed, where we will reunite you with your bodies."

"Just like that?"

"Just like that. We'd like to thank you for contracting with Kinetic, and allowing us to harvest your potential!" The Concierge's smile is faker than the whole SimGrid. "Now, through the doors to your right. A Concierge will be waiting."

"Let's go," Zane says. He wraps an arm around me.

I almost don't believe my own steps. Why even program this building? Why make us walk this path? Lie down in fake medical beds, hook us to machines that don't exist?

The Concierge splits into two identical versions of herself. Each gestures to a different door.

"Can't we go in together?" I shrug. "It's not like it's real, anyway."

Both smile and glance at each other for approval. "We can arrange that."

Suddenly, there's only one door and I can't remember them merging, but they must've. Zane and I walk through together, hands still clenched into one fused, brown-peach fist.

"I will ask you to lie in separate beds, please. Though your avatars are not, as you'd say, real, the process helps your subconscious mind prepare for the reunion. In addition, I advise you both to remain still upon waking. The muscle stimulator program will have ensured that you can function, but your bodies may still require time to adapt."

"Okay." But I don't move.

"Ash." Zane wiggles his fingers.

Suddenly, everything feels so real. Like we've never been closer and I don't want it to end.

It's just cold feet. Remember how the System Error felt. Unplugged, I won't need to crash my bike to feel something.

"Yeah?" I respond.

"I love you."

"We're not dying." The words feel like a lie, when I say them.

"I know, but … just in case," he says.

"I love you, too." I wiggle my fingers against his in return. "See you on the other side?"

Zane smiles over his worry and doubt. "Yeah. Can't wait."

The Concierges help us into separate beds. Straps fasten around our ankles and wrists; a big one crosses my forehead, forcing me to stare at the shiny silver ceiling. The Concierges flip switches and press buttons. None of them can mean anything. Why don't they just unplug us while we sleep?

Zane's voice is the last thing I hear. "Ash?"

• • •

"Ashley, can you hear me?" Gloved fingers peel my eyelids back. Bright furry lights shrink into needlepoint lasers. "My name's Dr. Ralio."

I blink and her face focuses from a blur of golden brown pixels—no, not pixels. Real skin. I reach up with a finger and touch her cheek.

She smiles. "Yes, you've successfully unplugged."

My focus shifts. How can I look at just one thing when there are so many? I hold a hand in front of my face. The fingers are short and thin, the nails smooth and well-rounded. These are not my hands. I press them against my chest to stop my heart from exploding.

Breasts. I pull down the blue paper sheet and sit up. Breasts like two water balloons wrapped in skin, hanging off my chest. I flatten them and look down.

Nothing. There's *nothing* down below, nothing between my legs. Just a space. A void. A hole.

Not even the scream is mine. A high, wailing scream, like a little girl throwing a tantrum.

"Ashley, is everything okay?" Dr. Ralio presses a hand to my forehead and glances at the monitors behind her.

"No." My voice breaks off. Not my voice. The wrong voice. Oh god, it didn't work. Am I still plugged in? I can't be. Nothing is pixels here. Dr. Ralio's skin is blemished, the ends of her coarse hair frayed.

The room whirls around me when I swing my legs over the edge of the bed. It feels more like I'm controlling a video game than my own muscles.

"Ashley." Dr. Ralio grips my shoulder. "Remember what the Concierge said; you shouldn't move too quickly. The muscle stimulators and nourishment fluids keep your body in shape, but you still haven't walked in twenty-five years."

My knees buckle when my feet hit cold tile. Dr. Ralio catches me, but seems more concerned with holding the flimsy hospital sheet over me than keeping me upright.

"Please, Ashley. Your body needs time to adjust."

"Is there a mirror?" I gasp at the sounds coming from my throat, formed by my tongue. "What happened to my body?"

"Ashley, please sit down. An exit counselor is on her way to speak with you. I realize it may be a shock not having seen your body since age five, but I promise you've grown into a healthy young woman—just as Kinetic promises."

That's what happened. They put me in the wrong body.

I laugh, an angelic, fluttering, *ridiculous* laugh. I don't even mind, knowing it's just a fluke.

"Please, put some clothes on. We provide a basic set for your exit." Dr. Ralio opens a drawer with jeans, tee shirts, socks, bras, and underwear.

I grab my disposable sheet and wrap it back around the body. "No, that's okay," I say. "I'll wait until you put me back."

Dr. Ralio's head tilts like I've seen a dog's do, before. "Back ... in the SimGrid? I thought you wanted to unplug. We received your request—"

"No! God, no. I don't want to go back in there. Back in my body. My real body. This is obviously wrong." I stretch out a black curl and let it snap back.

"Um." She's saved from bumbling an apology by the door.

It can't be good for business, putting contractors back into someone else's body.

"Ms. Trent, this is Ashley Redding. She just unplugged."

"My name's Ash," I say. "And I'm not a 'she.' I don't know whose body this is."

"I'm just. I'll. Okay." Dr. Ralio's lips pinch together as she ducks out.

"Ash, is it?" Ms. Trent's smile is softer, clearly designed to placate me.

"Yeah. I'm actually meeting someone—my boyfriend also unplugged—you don't have to give me the spiel. You can just plug me back into the right body."

Ms. Trent clasps her hands. "Do you remember when you signed your contract with Kinetic, Inc.?"

This is such a waste of time. I close my eyes and picture Zane waking up. Putting on the provided clothes. Cashing out his credits. Waiting. He's nervous. He'll be nervous without me. I convinced him to do this and I'm not even there for him.

"Yes, I remember signing up. I was five" —a picture of a scrawny child lights up the monitor— "when a representative visited my group home. She promised I'd be placed with a nice family in the SimGrid." With parents who would love me more than they loved heroin.

"Correct." Ms. Trent smiles. "You know, we keep constant surveillance of all our contractors to ensure their physical safety while their minds are plugged into the SimGrid."

"Okay." I hear my real voice in my head every time this woman's voice comes out. The body is starting to irritate me, to itch like a skin that needs sloughing off.

"I want to play yours, if you don't mind."

"How long is this going to take?"

"Not long. I've set it to play at one million times the speed." She hits play.

My younger self looks dead, like he's lying in a coffin. Cleaned up by the staff, but still boney and scraggly. Sensors and wires stick on and out of his little body. Then, the image moves, as if a poltergeist has possessed him. The tiny twitches over time, hands of the nurses as they trim nails and clip hair.

My hair grows longer than I would wear it, grows healthier and fuller, shinier. My cheeks plump and soften, lips round out. Two mounds begin to form on my chest under the papery sheet. Lasers flash bright red every couple of seconds.

I rub a hand over the wrong body's smooth legs.

"Ash, I hope you can see where this is going," Ms. Trent says.

"I'm, uh ..." I try to finish my sentence, but I can't breathe.

Black spots eat through my vision. The walls squeeze in around me. This can't be real. My heart bursts into a billion little hearts that hijack my blood stream and pulse until my fingers might fall off. I can't feel my fingers. My legs stop working.

"I can't—" Breathe, I can't breathe.

"Ash, can you hear me?" The sentence fades under a loud buzz.

I'm grateful when the blackness blots my vision and my breath stops coming.

• • •

I wonder how long I can stand here before Zane gives up on me and leaves. I've bitten down all the fingernails on these hands. They were too long. I don't look down at the body. I only look out the one-way window into the waiting area, where Zane sits. Our eyes would meet if he could see through this glass.

A Kinetic button down covers the spot on Zane's arm. He clamps a hand over it as if he's keeping himself from bleeding out. His body is better than his avatar, not because its muscles are better defined or its cheekbones are higher, but because it's his. His hair is shaved shorter than I'm used to and his face is smooth and clean, but he still looks like the same person.

Dr. Ralio told me I had a panic attack. I'd never heard the word 'transgender' before. I didn't know there was a condition that could trap you in someone else's body.

How can I face Zane? He won't recognize me in here. I don't recognize me.

Staff push by, files in hand, escorting other contractors. No one sees me. I'm not a contractor anymore. They have no obligation to help me. I have no one. Only Zane. Maybe.

Slowly, I push the door open. Zane looks up. When he sees me, he sighs and rests his forehead on his hands.

I sit next to him and unfold the note I've written. There's no way I can speak with this voice. It's bad enough I have to show him this body. I fold it back up before holding it out to him.

Zane looks sideways at me. He takes the note. "Who gave this to you? Was it Ash?"

I don't answer. He unfolds the thin paper so fast, I'm afraid he'll rip it. I can't bear to re-read the words. My handwriting is the same. Mostly. I hate these hands. They're too small and soft.

I can't sit here. My breath's already clogging my throat, the black spots taking over like broken pixels. I want this to be an Error. I want to reset.

Zane crumples the paper between his fists.

"I'm going to go," I whisper.

His hand catches my arm before I can stand.

"If you're lying to me—"

"Why would I?" My voice wavers.

"I don't know. I don't." He re-reads the note. "Was any of it real?" he asks.

"All of it was real."

I feel gross when he looks at me. He doesn't want to look at the breasts, but he can't stop himself. They don't belong there. I refused to wear the bra.

"Did you know?" He's still staring at them.

I shake my head.

"I don't believe you."

"I don't either," I say in the fake voice. Every time I hear it, I want to scream, but that only hurts more. "But it's true."

"I don't want to be here, alone."

I return to a bearable whisper. "I don't want to be here at all."

"Can they fix it?"

"There's surgery. Injections. Paperwork." I can barely remember the options. I was trying too hard just to breathe. Just functioning in this body is more work than it's worth.

"How long?"

"Years."

"Years," he considers the word.

We've already wasted too many years.

• • •

The warm ground cradles my body. I squint up at clearly formed leaves—not a pixel out of place.

Zane rolls up his sleeves and clasps my hand. "Guess they fixed the System Error."

"Yeah."

"Sorry. I know you wanted to show me."

"No, it's okay. I'm just glad to be here with you."

"Me, too."

I lift our hands into the air. Gravity drains the blood back into my body. Pins prickle through my fingertips.

Several dark, raised scars claim the unremarkable spot on Zane's avatar now. He doesn't hide or fidget with them—and I don't ask. I don't need to know. This is enough.

For us, this is real.

~

K.M. Szpara lives in Baltimore, MD, with a black cat and miniature poodle. He has a Master of Theological Studies from Harvard Divinity School, which he totally uses at his day job as a legal secretary. On nights and weekends, he advances his queer agenda at the local LGBT Community Center and writes speculative fiction novels. His short fiction appears or is forthcoming in *Shimmer Magazine* and *Glittership*. You can find him on Twitter @KMSzpara.

Madeleine

Amal El-Mohtar

Art by Orion Zangara

An exquisite pleasure had invaded my senses, something isolated, detached, with no suggestion of its origin. And at once the vicissitudes of life had become indifferent to me, its disasters innocuous, its brevity illusory—this new sensation having had on me the effect which love has of filling me with a precious essence; or rather this essence was not in me it was me...Whence did it come? What did it mean? How could I seize and apprehend it? [...] And suddenly the memory revealed itself.

—Marcel Proust

Madeleine remembers being a different person.

It strikes her when she's driving, threading her way through farmland, homesteads, facing down the mountains around which the road winds. She remembers being thrilled at the thought of travel, of the self she would discover over the hills and far away. She remembers laughing with friends, looking forward to things, to a future.

She wonders at how change comes in like a thief in the night, dismantling our sense of self one bolt and screw at a time until all that's left of the person we think we are is a broken door hanging off a rusty hinge, waiting for us to walk through.

• • •

"Tell me about your mother," says Clarice, the clinical psychologist assigned to her.

Madeleine is stymied. She stammers. This is only her third meeting with Clarice. She looks at her hands and the tissue she is twisting between them. "I thought we were going to talk about the episodes."

"We will," and Clarice is all gentleness, all calm, "but—"

"I would really rather talk about the episodes."

Clarice relents, nods in her gracious, patient way, and makes a note. "When was your last one?"

"Last night." Madeleine swallows, hard, remembering.

"And what was the trigger?"

"The soup," she says, and she means to laugh, but it comes out wet and strangled like a sob. "I was making chicken soup, and I put a stick of cinnamon in. I'd never done that before but I remembered how it looked, sometimes, when my mother would make it—she would boil the thighs whole with bay leaves, black pepper, and sticks of cinnamon, and the way it looked in the pot stuck with me—so I thought I would try it. It was exactly right—it smelled exactly, exactly the way she used to make it—and then I was there, I was small and looking up at her in our old house, and she was stirring the soup and smiling down at me, and the smell was like a cloud all around, and I could smell her, too, the hand cream she used, and see the edge of the stove and the oven door handle with the cat-print dish towel on it—"

"Did your mother like to cook?"

Madeleine stares.

"Madeleine," says Clarice, with the inevitably Anglo pronunciation that Madeleine has resigned herself to, "if we're going to work together to help you I need to know more about her."

"The episodes aren't about her," says Madeleine, stiffly. "They're because of the drug."

"Yes, but—"

"They're because of the drug, and I don't need you to tell me I took part in the trial because of her—obviously I did—and I don't want to tell you about her. This isn't about my mourning, and I thought we established these aren't traumatic flashbacks. It's about the drug."

"Madeleine," and Madeleine is fascinated by Clarice's capacity to both disgust and soothe her with sheer unflappability, "Drugs do not operate—or misfire—in a vacuum. You were one of sixty people participating in that trial. Of those sixty, you're the only one who has come forward experiencing these episodes." Clarice leans forward, slightly. "We've also spoken about your tendency to see our relationship as adversarial. Please remember that it isn't. You," and Clarice doesn't smile, exactly, so much as that the lines around her mouth become suffused with sympathy, "haven't even ever volunteered her name to me."

Madeleine begins to feel like a recalcitrant child instead of an adult standing her ground. This only adds to her resentment.

"Her name was Sylvie," she offers, finally. "She loved being in the kitchen. She loved making big fancy meals. But she hated having people over. My dad used to tease her about that."

Clarice nods, smiles her almost-smile encouragingly, makes further notes. "And did you do the technique we discussed to dismiss the memory?"

Madeleine looks away. "Yes."

"What did you choose this time?"

"Althusser." She feels ridiculous. "'In the battle that is philosophy all the techniques of war, including looting and camouflage, are permissible.'"

Clarice frowns as she writes, and Madeleine can't tell if it's because talk of war is adversarial or because she dislikes Althusser.

• • •

After she buried her mother, Madeleine looked for ways to bury herself.

She read non-fiction, as dense and theoretical as she could find, on any subject she felt she had a chance of understanding: economics, postmodernism, settler-colonialism. While reading Patrick Wolfe she found the phrase invasion is a structure not an event, and wondered if one could say the same of grief. Grief is an invasion and a structure and an event, she wrote, then struck it out, because it seemed meaningless.

Grief, thinks Madeleine now, is an invasion that climbs inside you and makes you grow a wool blanket from your skin, itchy and insulating, heavy and grey. It wraps and wraps and wraps around, putting layers of scratchy heat between you and the world, until no one wants to approach for fear of the prickle, and people stop asking how you are doing in the blanket, which is a relief, because all you want is to be hidden, out of sight. You can't think of a time when you won't be wrapped in the blanket, when you'll be ready to face the people outside it—but one day, perhaps, you push through. And even though you've struggled against the belief that you're a worthless colony of contagion that must be shunned at all costs, it still comes as a shock, when you emerge, that there's no one left waiting for you.

Worse still is the shock that you haven't emerged at all.

• • •

"The thing is," says Madeleine, slowly, "I didn't use the sentence right away."

"Oh?"

"I—wanted to see how long it could last, on its own." Heat in her cheeks, knowing how this will sound, wanting both to resist and embrace it. "To ride it out. It kept going just as I remembered it—she brought me a little pink plastic bowl with yellow flowers on it, poured just a tiny bit of soup in, blew on it, gave it to me with a plastic spoon. There were little star-shaped noodles in it. I—" she feels tears in her eyes, hates this, hates crying in front of Clarice, "—I could have eaten it. It smelled so good, and I could feel I was hungry. But I got superstitious. You know." She shrugs. "Like if I ate it I'd have to stay for good."

"Did you want to stay for good?"

Madeleine says nothing. This is what she hates about Clarice, this demand that her feelings be spelled out into one thing or another: isn't it obvious that she both wanted and didn't want to? From what she said?

"I feel like the episodes are lasting longer," says Madeleine, finally, trying to keep the urgency from consuming her voice. "It used to be just a snap, there and back—I'd blink, I'd be in the memory, I'd realize what happened and it would be like a dream; I'd wake up, I'd come back. I didn't need sentences to pull me back. But now …" She looks to Clarice to say something, to fill the silence, but Clarice waits, as usual, for Madeleine herself to make the connection, to articulate the fear.

" … Now I wonder if this is how it started for her. My mother. What it was like for her." The tissue in her hands is damp, not from tears, but from the sweat of her palms. "If I just sped up the process."

"You don't have Alzheimer's," says Clarice, matter-of-fact. "You aren't forgetting anything. In fact it appears to be the opposite: you're remembering so intensely and completely that your memories have the vividness and immediacy of hallucination." She jots something down. "We'll keep on working on dismantling the triggers as they arise. If the episodes seem to be lasting longer, it could be partly because they're growing fewer and farther between. This is not necessarily a bad thing."

Madeleine nods, chewing her lip, not meeting Clarice's eyes.

• • •

So far as Madeleine is concerned her mother began dying five years earlier, when the fullness of her life began to fall away from her like chunks of wet cake: names; events; her child. Madeleine watched her mother weep, and this was the worst, because with every storm of grief over her confusion Madeleine couldn't help but imagine the memories sloughing from her, as if the memories themselves were the source of her pain, and if she could just forget them and live a barer life, a life before the disease, before her husband's death, before Madeleine, she could be happy again. If she could only shed the burden of the expectation of memory, she could be happy again.

Madeleine reads Walter Benjamin on time as image, time as accumulation, and thinks of layers and pearls. She thinks of her mother as a pearl dissolving in wine until only a grain of sand is left drowning at the bottom of the glass.

As her mother's life fell away from her, so did Madeleine's. She took a leave of absence from her job, and kept extending it; she stopped seeing her friends; her friends stopped seeing her. Madeleine is certain her friends expected her to be relieved when her mother died, and were surprised by the depth of her mourning. She didn't know how to address that. She didn't know how to say to those friends, you are relieved to no longer feel embarrassed around the subject, and expect me to sympathise with your relief, and to be normal again for your sake. So she said nothing.

It wasn't that Madeleine's friends were bad people; they had their own lives, their own concerns, their own comfort to nourish and nurture and keep safe, and dealing with a woman who was dealing with her mother who was dealing with early-onset Alzheimer's was just a little too much, especially when her father had only died of bowel cancer a year earlier, especially when she had no other family. It was indecent, so much pain at once, it was unreasonable, and her friends were reasonable people. They had children, families, jobs, and Madeleine had none of these; she understood. She did not make demands.

She joined the clinical trial the way some people join fund-raising walks, and thinks now that that was her first mistake. People walk, run, bicycle to raise money for cures—that's the way she ought to have done it, surely, not actually volunteered herself to be experimented on. No one sponsors people to stand still.

• • •

The episodes happen like this.

A song on the radio like an itch in her skull, a pebble rattling around inside until it finds the groove in which it fits, perfectly, and suddenly she's—

—in California, dislocated, confused, a passenger herself now in her own head's seat, watching the traffic crawl past in the opposite direction, the sun blazing above. On I-5, en route to Anaheim: she is listening, for the first time, to the album that song is from, and feels the beautiful self-sufficiency of having wanted a thing and purchased it, the bewildering freedom of going somewhere utterly new. And she remembers this moment of mellow thrill shrinking into abject terror at the sight of five lanes between her and the exit, and will she make it, won't she, she doesn't want to get lost on such enormous highways—

—and then she's back, in a wholly different car, her body nine years older, the mountain, the farmland all where they should be, slamming hard on the brakes at an unexpected stop sign, breathing hard and counting all the ways in which she could have been killed.

Or she is walking and the world is perched on the lip of spring, the Ottawa snow melting to release the sidewalks in fits and starts, peninsulas of gritty concrete wet and crunching beneath her boots, and that solidity of snowless ground intersects with the smell of water and the warmth of the sun and the sound of dripping and the world tilts—

—and she's ten years old on the playground of her second primary school, kicking aside the pebbly grit to make a space for shooting marbles, getting down on her knees to use her hands to do a better job of smoothing the surface, then wiping her hands on the corduroy of her trousers, then reaching into her bag of marbles for the speckled dinosaur-egg that is her lucky one, her favourite—

—and then she's back, and someone's asking her if she's okay, because she looked like she might be about to walk into traffic, was she drunk, was she high?

She has read about flashbacks, about PTSD, about reliving events, and has wondered if this is the same. It is not as she imagined those things would be. She has tried explaining this to Clarice, who very reasonably pointed out that she couldn't both claim to have never experienced trauma-induced flashbacks and say with perfect certainty that what she's experiencing now is categorically different. Clarice is certain, Madeleine realizes, that trauma is at the root of these episodes, that there's something Madeleine isn't telling her, that her mother, perhaps, abused her, that she had a terrible childhood.

None of these things are true.

Now: she is home, and leaning her head against her living room window at twilight, and something in the thrill of that blue and the cold of the glass against her scalp sends her tumbling—

—into her body at fourteen, looking into the blue deepening above the tree line near her home as if it were another country, longing for it, aware of the picture she makes as a young girl leaning her wondering head against a window while hungry for the future, for the distance, for the person she will grow to be—and starts to reach within her self, her future/present self, for a phrase that only her future/present self knows, to untangle herself from her past head. She has just about settled on Kristeva—abjection is above all ambiguity—when she feels, strangely, a tug on her field of vision, something at its periphery demanding attention. She looks away from the sky, looks down, at the street she grew up on, the street she knows like the inside of her mouth.

She sees a girl of about her own age, brown-skinned and dark-haired, grinning at her and waving.

She has never seen her before in her life.

• • •

Clarice, for once, looks excited—which is to say, slightly more intent than usual—which makes Madeleine uncomfortable. "Describe her as accurately as you can," says Clarice. "She looked about fourteen, had dark skin—"

Clarice blinks. Madeleine continues.

"—and dark, thick hair, that was pulled up in two ponytails, and she was wearing a red dress and sandals."

"And you're certain you'd never seen her before?" Clarice adjusts her glasses.

"Positive." Madeleine hesitates, doubting herself. "I mean, she looked sort of familiar, but not in a way I could place? But I grew up in a really white small town in Quebec. There were maybe five non-white kids in my whole school, and she wasn't any of them. Also—" she hesitates, again, because, still, this feels so private, "—there has never once been any part of an episode that was unfamiliar."

"She could be a repressed memory, then," Clarice muses, "someone you've forgotten—or an avatar you're making up. Perhaps you should try speaking to her."

• • •

Clarice's suggested technique for managing the episodes was to corrupt the memory experience with something incompatible, something as of-the-moment as Madeleine could devise. Madeleine had settled on phrases from her recent reading: they were new enough to not be associated with any other memories, and incongruous enough to remind her of the reality of her bereavement even in her mother's presence. It seemed to work; she had never yet experienced the same memory twice after deploying her critics and philosophers.

To actively go in search of a memory was very strange.

She tries, again, with the window: waits until twilight, leans her head against the same place, but the temperature is wrong somehow, it doesn't come together. She tries making chicken soup; nothing. Finally, feeling her way towards it, she heats up a mug of milk in the microwave, stirs it to even out the heat, takes a sip—

—while holding the mug with both hands, sitting at the kitchen table, her legs dangling far above the ground. Her parents are in the kitchen, chatting—she knows she'll have to go to bed soon, as soon as she finishes her milk—but she can see the darkness just outside the living room windows, and she wants to know what's out there. Carefully, trying not to draw her parents' attention, she slips down from the chair and pads softly—her feet are bare, she is in her pajamas already—towards the window.

The girl isn't there.

"Madeleine," comes her mother's voice, cheerful, "as-tu fini ton lait?"

Before she can quite grasp what she is doing, Madeleine turns, smiles, nods vigorously up to her mother, and finishes the warm milk in a gulp. Then she lets herself be led downstairs to bed, tucked in, and kissed goodnight by both her parents, and if a still small part of herself struggles to remember something important to say or do, she is too comfortably nestled to pay it any attention as the lights go out and the door to her room shuts. She wonders what happens if you fell asleep in a dream, would you dream and then be able to fall asleep in that dream, and dream again, and—someone knocks, gently, at her bedroom window.

Madeleine's bedroom is in the basement; the window is level with the ground. The girl from the street is there, looking concerned. Madeleine blinks, sits up, rises, opens the window.

"What's your name?" asks the girl at the window.

"Madeleine." She tilts her head, surprised to find herself answering in English. "What's yours?"

"Zeinab." She grins. Madeleine notices she's wearing pajamas too, turquoise ones with Princess Jasmine on them. "Can I come in? We could have a sleep-over!"

"Shh," says Madeleine, pushing her window all the way open to let her in, whispering, "I can't have sleep-overs without my parents knowing!"

Zeinab covers her mouth, eyes wide, and nods, then mouths sorry before clambering inside. Madeleine motions for her to come sit on the bed, then looks at her curiously.

"How do I know you?" she murmurs, half to herself. "We don't go to school together, do we?"

Zeinab shakes her head. "I don't know. I don't know this place at all. But

I keep seeing you! Sometimes you're older and sometimes you're younger. Sometimes you're with your parents and sometimes you're not. I just thought I should say hello, because I keep seeing you, but you don't always see me, and it feels a little like spying, and I don't want to do that. I mean," she grins again, a wide dimpled thing that makes Madeline feel warm and happy, "I wouldn't mind being a spy but that's different, that's cool, that's like James Bond or Neil Burnside or Agent Carter—"

—and Madeleine snaps back, fingers gone numb around a mug of cold milk that falls to the ground and shatters as Madeleine jumps away, presses her back to a wall and tries to stop shaking.

• • •

She cancels her appointment with Clarice that week. She looks through old year books, class photos, and there is no one who looks like Zeinab, no Zeinab's to be found anywhere in her past. She googles "Zeinab" in various spellings and discovers it's the name of a journalist, a Syrian mosque, and the Prophet Muhammad's grand-daughter. Perhaps she'll ask Zeinab for her surname, she thinks, a little wildly, dazed and frightened and exhilarated.

Over the course of the last several years Madeleine has grown very, very familiar with the inside of her head. The discovery of someone as new and inexplicable as Zeinab in it is thrilling in a way she can hardly begin explain.

She finds she especially does not want to explain to Clarice.

• • •

Madeleine takes the bus—she has become wary of driving—to the town she grew up in, an hour's journey over a provincial border. She walks through her old neighbourhood hunting triggers, but finds more changed than familiar; old houses with new additions, facades, front lawns gone to seed or kept far too tidy.

She walks up the steep cul-de-sac of her old street to the rocky hill beyond, where a freight line used to run. It's there, picking up a lump of pink granite from where the tracks used to be, that she flashes—

—back to the first time she saw a hummingbird, standing in her driveway by an ornamental pink granite boulder. She feels, again, her heart in her throat, flooded with the beauty of it, the certainty and immensity of the fact that she is seeing a fairy, that fairies are real, that here is a tiny mermaid moving her shining tail backwards and forwards in the air, before realizing the truth of what she's looking at, and feeling that it is somehow more precious still for being a bird that sounds like a bee and looks like an impossible jewel.

"Ohh," she hears, from behind her, and there is Zeinab, transfixed, looking at the hummingbird alongside Madeleine, and as it hovers before them for the eternity that Madeleine remembers, suspended in the air with a keen jet eye and a needle for a mouth, Madeleine reaches out and takes Zeinab's hand. She feels Zeinab squeeze hers in reply, and they stand together until the hummingbird zooms away.

"I don't understand what's happening," murmurs Zeinab, who is a young teen again, in torn jeans and an oversized sweater with Paula Abdul's face on it, "but I really like it."

• • •

Madeleine leads Zeinab through her memories as best she can, one sip, smell, sound, taste at a time. Stepping out of the shower one morning tips her back into a school trip to the Montreal Botanical Garden, where she slips away from the group to walk around the grounds with Zeinab and talk. Doing this is, in some ways, like maintaining the image in a Magic Eye puzzle, remaining focused on each other with the awareness that they can't mention the world outside the memory or it will end too soon, before they've had their fill of talk, of marvelling at the strangeness of their meeting, of enjoying each other's company.

Their conversations are careful and buoyant, as if they're sculpting something together, chipping away at a mystery shape trapped in marble. It's easy, so easy to talk to Zeinab, to listen to her—they talk about the books they read as children, the music they listened to, the cartoons they watched. Madeleine wonders why Zeinab's mere existence doesn't corrupt or end the memories the way her sentences do, why she's able to walk around inside those memories more freely in Zeinab's company, but doesn't dare ask. She suspects she knows why, after all; she doesn't need Clarice to tell her how lonely, how isolated, how miserable she is, miserable enough to invent a friend who is bubbly where she is quiet, kind and friendly where she is mistrustful and reserved, even dark-skinned where she's white.

She can hear Clarice explaining, in her reasonable voice, that Madeleine— bereaved twice over, made vulnerable by an experimental drug—has invented a shadow-self to love, and perhaps they should unpack the racism of its man- ifestation, and didn't Madeleine have any black friends in real life?

"I wish we could see each other all the time," says Madeleine, sixteen, on her back in the sunny field, long hair spread like so many corn snakes through the grass. "Whenever we wanted."

"Yeah," murmurs Zeinab, looking up at the sky. "Too bad I made you up inside my head."

Madeleine steels herself against the careening tug of Sylvia Plath before remembering that she started reading her in high school. Instead, she turns to Zeinab, blinks.

"What? No. You're inside my head."

Zeinab raises an eyebrow—pierced, now—and when she smiles her teeth look all the brighter against her black lipstick. "I guess that's one possibility, but if I made you up inside my head and did a really good job of it I'd probably want you to say something like that. To make you be more real."

"But—so could—"

"Although I guess it is weird that we're always doing stuff you remember. Maybe you should come over to my place sometime!"

Madeleine feels her stomach seizing up.

"Or maybe it's time travel," says Zeinab, thoughtfully. "Maybe it's one of those weird things where I'm actually from your future and am meeting you in your past, and then when you meet me in your future I haven't met you yet, but you know all about me—

"Zeinab—I don't think—"

Madeline feels wakefulness press a knife's edge against the memory's skin, and she backs away from that, shakes her head, clings to the smell of crushed grass and coming summer, with its long days of reading and swimming and cycling and her father talking to her about math and her mother teaching her to knit and the imminent prospect of seeing R-rated films in the cinema—

—but she can't, quite, and she is shivering, naked, in her bathroom, with the last of the shower's steam vanishing off the mirror as she starts to cry.

• • •

"I must say," says Clarice, rather quietly, "that this is distressing news."

It's been a month since Madeleine last saw Clarice, and where before she felt resistant to her probing, wanting only to solve a very specific problem, she now feels like a mess, a bowl's worth of overcooked spaghetti. If before Clarice made her feel like a stubborn child, now Madeleine feels like a child who knows she's about to be punished.

"I had hoped," says Clarice, adjusting her glasses, "that encouraging you to talk to this avatar would help you understand the mechanisms of your grief, but from what you've told me it sounds more like you've been indulging in a damaging fantasy world."

"It's not a fantasy world," says Madeleine, with less snap than she'd like—she sounds, to her own ears, sullen, defensive. "It's my memory."

"The experience of which puts you at risk and makes you lose time. And Zeinab isn't part of your memories."

"No, but—" she bites her lip.

"But what?"

"But—couldn't Zeinab be real? I mean," hastily, before Clarice's look sharpens too hard, "couldn't she be a repressed memory, like you said?"

"A repressed memory with whom you talk about recent television, and who suddenly features in all your memories?" Clarice shakes her head.

"But—talking to her helps, it makes it so much easier to control—"

"Madeleine, tell me if I'm missing anything here. You're seeking triggers in order to relive your memories for their own sake—not as exposure therapy, not to dismantle those triggers, not to understand Zeinab's origins—but to have a … Companion? Dalliance?"

Clarice is so kind and sympathetic that Madeleine wants simultaneously to cry and to punch her in the face.

She wants to say, what you're missing is that I've been happy. What you're missing is that for the first time in years I don't feel like a disease waiting to happen or a problem to be solved until I'm back in the now, until she and I are apart.

But there is sand in her throat and it hurts too much to speak.

"I think," says Clarice, with a gentleness that beggars Madeleine's belief, "that it's time we discussed admitting you into more comprehensive care."

• • •

She sees Zeinab again when, on the cusp of sleep in a hospital bed, she experiences the sensation of falling from a great height, and plunges into—

—the week after her mother's death, when Madeleine couldn't sleep without waking in a panic, convinced her mother had walked out of the house and into the street, or fallen down the stairs, or taken the wrong pills at the wrong time, only to recall she'd already died and there was nothing left for her to remember.

She is in bed, and Zeinab is there next to her, and Zeinab is a woman in her thirties, staring at her strangely, as if she is only now seeing her for the first time, and Madeleine starts to cry and Zeinab holds her tightly while Madeleine buries her face in Zeinab's shoulder, and says she loves her and doesn't want to lose her but she has to go, they won't let her stay, she's insane and she can't keep living in the past but there is no one left here for her, no one.

"I love you too," says Zeinab, and there is something fierce in it, and wondering, and desperate. "I love you too. I'm here. I promise you, I'm here."

• • •

Madeleine is not sure she's awake when she hears people arguing outside her door.

She hears "serious bodily harm" and "what evidence" and "rights adviser," then "very irregular" and "I assure you," traded back and forth in low voices.

She drifts in and out of wakefulness, wonders muzzily if she consented to being drugged or if she only dreamt that she did, turns over, falls back asleep.

When she wakes again, Zeinab is sitting at the foot of her bed.

Madeleine stares at her.

"I figured out how we know each other," says Zeinab, whose hair is waist-length now, straightened, who is wearing a white silk blouse and a sharp black jacket, high heels, and looks like she belongs in an action film. "How I know you, I guess. I mean," she smiles, looks down, shy—Zeinab has never been shy, but there is the dimple where Madeleine expects it—"where I know you from. The clinical trial, for the Alzheimer's drug—we were in the same group. I didn't recognize you until I saw you as an adult. I remembered because of all the people there, I thought—you looked—" her voice drops a bit, as if remembering, suddenly, that she isn't talking to herself, "lost. I wanted to talk to you, but it felt weird, like, hi, I guess we have family histories in common, want to get coffee?"

She runs her hand through her hair, exhales, not quite able to look at Madeleine while Madeleine stares at her as if she's a fairy turning into a hummingbird that could, any second, fly away.

"So not long after the trial I start having these hallucinations, and there's always this girl in them, and it freaks me out. But I keep it to myself, because—I don't know, because I want to see what happens. Because it's not more debilitating than a day dream, really, and I start to get the hang of it—feeling it come on, walking myself to a seat, letting it happen. Sometimes I can stop it, too, though that's harder. I take time off work, I read about, I don't know, mystic visions, shit like that, the kind of things I used to wish were real in high school. I figure even if you're not real—"

Zeinab looks at her now, and there are tears streaking Madeleine's cheeks, and Zeinab's smile is small and sad and hopeful, too, "—even if you're not real, well, I'll take an imaginary friend who's pretty great over work friends who are mostly acquaintances, you know? Because you were always real to me."

Zeinab reaches out to take Madeleine's hand. Madeleine squeezes it, swallows, shakes her head.

"I—even if I'm not—if this isn't a dream," Madeleine half-chuckles through tears, wipes at her cheek, "I think I probably have to stay here for a while."

Zeinab grins, now, a twist of mischief in it. "Not at all. You're being discharged today. Your rights adviser was very persuasive."

Madeleine blinks. Zeinab leans in closer, conspiratorial.

"That's me. I'm your rights adviser. Just don't tell anyone I'm doing pro bono stuff: I'll never hear the end of it at the office."

Madeleine feels something in her unclench and melt, and she hugs Zeinab to her and holds her and is held by her.

"Whatever's happening to us," Zeinab says, quietly, "we'll figure it out together, okay?"

"Okay," says Madeleine, and as she does Zeinab pulls back to kiss her forehead, and the scent of her is clear and clean, like grapefruit and salt, and as Zeinab's lips brush her skin she—

—is in precisely the same place, but someone's with her in her head, remembering Zeinab's kiss and her smell and for the first time in a very long time, Madeleine feels—knows, with irrevocable certainty—that she has a future.

~

Amal El-Mohtar's essays have appeared in *Chicks Unravel Time, Queers Dig Time Lords, Science Fiction Film & Television, Apex, Stone Telling, The Outpost, Cascadia Subduction Zone,* and Tor. com. She reviews books for NPR, edits and publishes the poetry in *Goblin Fruit,* is a Nebula-nominated author and founding member of the *Banjo Apocalypse Crinoline Troubadours,* and has been occasionally known to deadlift other genre professionals. Find her on Twitter @tithenai and online at amalelmohtar.com.

Two By Two

Tim Susman

Desperation is hope turned sour. Before we'd even gotten over the Sierras, the solar-electric bus was full of it, Vijay and I no less than any of the other hundred passengers. But we took turns standing in the aisle so everyone had a chance to sit down, and when our volunteer conductor wanted to nap, Vijay and two others took shifts in the driver's seat in case the bus ran into obstacles not marked on its software map.

Our spirits lifted as dawn revealed the browns and golds and mauves of the Nevada desert. Staring out at them, we could fool ourselves into thinking that California's grey, dusty slopes had been a moonlit aberration, that the news reports had exaggerated the spread of the blight. We broke into a traveling song, complained about the bus's suspension and the smell of the chemical toilet as though those were our biggest problems, and exchanged names and carefully edited stories. More than half the people on the bus were going to New England, all to the same place, though nobody said its name; Vijay and I admitted we were going to Houston "to visit relatives," which earned us lots of concern and admonitions to be careful. By tacit agreement, we ignored the reason we were together on this bus.

Most of us, anyway. "Look," Vijay said to me, pointing out a dusty feathered carcass halfway up a hill. "Nothing left to eat the scavengers."

I dug a chocolate-flavored synth cube out of our pack and handed it to him. "Lucky we're not scavengers."

Then we came to Utah and western Colorado, where the charcoal-gray skeletons of trees dusted with decomposing leaves looked like a special effect rendered in grayscale under a shockingly blue sky. We were used to silent highways, but through these graveyards the bus's quiet engine felt both respectful and resigned.

After that, abandoned settlements through the Rockies, looking peaceful because whatever was left of the cannibal riots remained invisible from I-70. Down from the Eisenhower tunnel into the ghost towns that had been Denver suburbs, and then Denver itself, where finally we passed people. White gas masks with grey-brown stains on the front showed on most faces, though no haze clouded the air; we could see the sharp outlines of every building and the gray mountains to the west.

In Denver a handful of passengers disembarked, and a handful of Denverites took their place. Outside the windows, our former fellow travelers hugged loved ones while the hollow-eyed crowd stared at the bus in the hope that someone else would get out, leaving a precious space free. Behind that was the hope that somewhere, anywhere, would be different. And behind those people were the people who knew better.

"There's another group coming tomorrow," our conductor said, closing the doors. Our engine purred to life and we set off down the highway, northeast to Nebraska and then down I-29 into Missouri.

Grandma messaged me just as the sun was coming up again in the Missouri hills, as naked as Colorado's mountains: *Just making sure you didn't get eaten.*

"Be in Kansas City in a few hours, still on schedule." I sub-voed, not wanting to wake Vijay, but when I put the phone down, his dark eyes were open and bright in the dim bus interior.

He saw Grandma's picture on the phone before it went dark. A moment of quiet, and then he reached for his minitab and brought up a screen on which he typed, *Still have spots on the ship?* His hand hovered over the screen to hide it from the people behind us.

I stared at the words; he saw my reaction and added, *If we want them?*

"Yeah," I said, and then looked away under the weight of all the other things we couldn't air out on this crowded bus.

He nodded and cleared his minitab. I couldn't see his face anymore, just the blank screen, and then his fingers danced over it and his e-mail came up. There was nothing new in mine; the message at the top was still the one from Cris with the subject line *Get on the damn ship*. So I thumbed music onto my phone and sat back with my eyes closed as Iain Armour played *Beyond the Blight* and the bus rumbled southward.

In Kansas City, Vijay and I disembarked, leaving our spaces for a flannel-checked shirt man and his flannel-checked shirt wife. Vijay's eyes flicked over and then back to me, and I smiled, but neither of us had the energy or the desire to comment on the fashionistas of the Midwest.

Our half-size driverless bus left seven hours later, trundling south across the sludgy, brown Missouri River. Vijay spent the short trip on his minitab, writing to our friends back home that we'd made it safely and were about to go dark.

"Any news?" I asked when he leaned back.

"Dean and Greg got a lottery number."

If anyone else had, he would've told me. I tried to count in my head the number of our friends who'd gone to Vandenberg, and then thought about one couple who'd gone to White Sands with their kids. "What about Lisa and Marjorie?"

"Still on the way. Lisa has a great sunset picture."

He held up his minitab and showed me a glowing golden desert below a fabulous sky blazing orange, clouds awash in color with the dark blue night still held at bay above it. One of the great things about the end of the world is the sunsets, it turns out.

• • •

The great marble pseudo-churches we'd seen all over the news a decade ago must have been reserved for the borders on big highways: I-10 and I-40 through Texas, I-95 into North Carolina, I-55 to Memphis and I-35 into Oklahoma City. On little I-44, ten minutes after Joplin's red-roofed strip malls and forlorn motels, we stopped at a squat brick building. "CSA Border Authority" was painted on a wooden sign out front.

The guard inside, a twenty-year-old white kid with freckles and close-cropped red hair, took our U.S. passports first, then our letters of introduction. He asked Vijay to first say his name, and then he tried to pronounce it. "Krishna-murty. Indian?"

"My grandparents were," Vijay said in his Berkeley accent.

The patch on the guard's sleeve drew my eye: a red cross surrounded by a circle of twelve white stars, all on a blue field. And he wore a gold cross on a gold chain over his light blue shirt, which could be either personal or government mandated. "Daniel Hammond?" he said, turning to me. "Says you were born in Texas."

"That's right."

"Where's your CSA passport?"

I pointed at the US one. "That's valid."

He didn't look away. "You're dual citizen?"

"Technically. I never got a CSA passport."

"It's real easy, man," he said, and held up Grandma's letter of introduction. "Just scan this, fifty bucks, presto. Coulda been waiting for you right here."

"Is there a problem with that one?"

He narrowed his eyes and looked back down at our passports. "What's your business in the CSA?"

"Visiting family," I said.

"Going to Houston," Vijay said.

"You both have family in Houston?"

The guard was trying to keep us both in his sight at once, so I edged slightly away from Vijay just to be annoying. "That's right," I said pleasantly.

The kid looked again at the letters of introduction. "Polly Bell is your grandmother?"

I nodded, and he turned to Vijay. "And how do you fit in?"

"Hey," I said, pointing. "It's right there in his letter."

Vijay held a hand up to me. "I'm the son of one of her foster children. Mrs. Bell was very philanthropic."

"Yeah." The guard stared down at the passports and then slid them across to us. "She's on the ship, right?"

I felt Vijay's eyes on me as I collected the passports. The guard's face had tightened, his lower lip pressing up into a pouty frown. "We're just going down to say good-bye," I said.

He looked past us. "Next!" he yelled.

Back on the bus, I leaned against Vijay's comforting solidity. He patted my knee and said, "Who gives a shit what he thinks?"

"It's not just him." I wanted to put my hand on his, but refrained.

"Who cares what anyone thinks?" Vijay lowered his voice.

I felt like I was fifteen again. There's no good answer to that question. Of course you shouldn't care what anyone thinks, and of course you have to.

Outside, the landscape hadn't changed much: gentle hills covered in brown dirt and grey. Inside, though, we'd changed. If the bus got into a wreck, Vijay wouldn't have any right to visit me in the hospital, nor vice-versa. If we had to register for the lottery in Houston, our entries wouldn't be tied together. Our relationship was older than the country we were driving through, and yet they had the power to disregard it.

Vijay got his minitab out again after a little while and played around on it. I leaned over to look. "Anything good?"

"It's creepy," he said in a low voice. "My feed's almost empty."

"Yeah, well, none of our friends are CSA-approved." I squinted. "Who's left?"

"CNN. Most of the sports." He skimmed through. "Whoa, Jenny's on. Must be her company that's approved. I'm gonna say hi."

"Careful what you say."

He snorted. "I'm not going to write 'Hail Satan.' I'm just—what?"

"Seriously," I said. "Don't even joke about that."

"Your grandmother—"

"I know. Just ... be really careful."

He eyed me and then nodded. "Sorry, sw—uh. Daniel. Sorry."

I leaned back and shut my eyes. He typed and then tapped my arm and showed me his device. He'd just typed, "Hi, Jenny. We're in Oklahoma. More later, V & D."

"That's fine." I settled my weight against him in a familiar but not necessarily intimate way to anyone who might be watching. "Sorry. I'm just …"

"I know." He put the minitab away. "But those reports—that stuff doesn't happen everywhere."

It happens enough, I thought, but didn't say anything. Vijay knew the recent stuff as well as I did, and tons of articles had been written on the choice of "Christian States of America" as the name of the new country, with special focus on what the initials evoked. What he didn't know, what I'd lived through back when it was just the South of the United States, I couldn't convey in mere moments. I wished then that I hadn't tried so hard to bury it.

• • •

Grandma Polly lived in a huge mansion on the north end of Houston, the kind of mansion that used to house a half-dozen servants and now housed a half-dozen families. My aunts Sheila and Marcy and their husbands and kids lived alongside my uncles Buster, Jeff, and Glen—Jeff and Glen were married, but only Glen had kids.

"It looks so sad," Vijay murmured as we walked up the drive, past the empty flowerbeds and skeletal pergola. At the head of the drive, a fountain continued to burble, but the sound rattled along the bare dirt and gravel, harsher than I remembered.

When I didn't say anything, he went on. "Sorry. It was beautiful in the pictures."

"The house still is." It had been kept immaculate, all the windows shining cleanly, the tiles on the roof as clay-red as the day the President had come to visit when I was five. Two columns supported the two-story archway we walked under, and the wooden bell carved in relief over the ebony windowed door gleamed in the afternoon light.

I just turned the knob and walked in, ignoring Vijay's hesitation. As he came to stand by my side, letting the door swing shut, I scanned the large foyer to see what was different.

The plants were gone, obviously. The paintings hadn't changed: a portrait of Grandma's father, Henry Stevenson Bell, a painting of Galveston Harbor from the 1800s before the hurricane, a landscape I used to pretend was the magical land of Narnia and stare at for hours, and a family portrait from just before I was born.

The sound in the house hadn't changed, either. From the small living room, just past the parlor, raised voices echoed. I inclined my head to Vijay and we walked that way.

Polly Bell might be ninety-four, but she could still project like she was speaking to Congress. "You have always been a damned fool," she said as we came into the elegant room. Sitting in her Segroller with her back to us, she faced down Uncle Jeff and his wife Teri, to whom she addressed the next comment. "And you married a damn fool, so what does that make you?"

"Ma," Jeff said. "Daniel's here." Behind him, Buster stood with Sheila and Marcy and their husbands. None of the kids were around.

She raised a hand but didn't look back. "That bus will be here at nine o'clock sharp and we are going to get on as a family, all nineteen of us."

"I'm sure—"

Jeff only got those two words out before Grandma spun her chair on its gyros. Teri glared at him, and he gestured to Grandma with a 'what could I do?' look. "Daniel," Grandma said.

I turned my attention to her. "Hi, Grandma."

"I was sorry to see you had to take that detour out of Dallas." She indicated the tablet built into the arm of her chair. "We tell people not to abandon their combustion cars on the roads, but … Well, don't just stand there. Come here and give me a kiss." She lifted a dark, wrinkled hand from the white metal chair, the sleeve of her white dress sliding down as she did. Her hair, though paler and perhaps thinner, remained in the same wave cascading down the right side of her face, and though her features had sunken, her eyes had lost none of their ice-crystal glitter. I kissed her dry cheek, breathed in the smell of herbal cream (organic, of course), then stepped back and let her take in my former husband.

"I'm Vijay," he said with that bright smile I'd fallen in love with a dozen years ago, and stepped forward with his hand out.

Grandma didn't meet it. "I can see that." He stopped, his smile assuming a more formal set while she examined him. After a moment, she raised her hand and beckoned. "Well? Come give your grandma a kiss."

Vijay beamed, came forward, and kissed her on the cheek. She patted his head. "Good," she said. "But next time make it look like you've known me all your life."

"Next time?" He kept up a brave face.

"Of course." Grandma turned her sharp eyes on me. "Matthew Baron has some peculiar and sadly not uncommonly rigid views of families. Adopting an orphan girl from an impoverished country and caring for her son is an act of charity. Love between two men is blasphemy."

"I thought," Vijay stammered, as so many had in the face of Polly Bell's iron,

"I thought once we were on the shuttle … they can't kick us off, can they?"

"There's the colony ship to get on after, and the Barons paid for most of that too, enough to give them say in who gets on. Now." Grandma spun her chair to face the rest of the family. "Everyone come say hi to Daniel. Dinner is in an hour, and I expect everyone in bed by midnight. We've got a big day tomorrow." She fixed Uncle Jeff with a stare. "All of us."

Vijay turned to me and I tried not to give him the "I told you" look. Instead I took his hand and introduced him around to the family he hadn't met—Buster had come out to California several times, and so had Aunt Sheila and her family, and the last time I'd visited, when all these people were living in their own houses, he'd met Uncle Jeff over the minitab. But everyone was older and besides, there had been flowers in the driveway then and a green coating of vines on the pergola, and I hadn't felt that desperate sense of everyone on edge, like a herd of antelope catching the thin, sour thread of a lion's scent.

Dinner was the best food we'd eaten since leaving California. Most people these days lived on flavored synthetic cubes and mash, with mushrooms if you were lucky, but Grandma had brought out freeze-dried steaks and chicken from some deep storage area. "For our last dinner on Earth," she said, "I thought we should do the best we can." There were even freeze-dried vegetables, which Vijay crunched wistfully.

"It's just going to remind me how much I hate synthetic," he said, holding a green bean in front of his face. "But I'm glad to taste real vegetables one last time."

"The Barons have a sealed seed bank that wasn't touched by the blight," Grandma said. "On a new planet, there'll be vegetables again."

"Even if we have to kill all the native species to do it," Jeff muttered.

Some of the scientists thought that the blight could be carried by people, in which case even the colony ships were screwed, but this wasn't worth bringing up at the table. It was either true or it wasn't, and either way there wasn't a lot anyone could do about it.

But wow, that chicken was good.

• • •

We didn't have much packing to do, of course, so we sat in the office while the rest of the family retreated to their rooms. "Don't you want to see your old bedroom?" Vijay asked.

"The sleeper sofa here is fine." He started to say something, and I said, "And this room has a view of the back."

Out the window, the large, graceful staircase that led down to the back patio and garden—former garden—beyond, remembering running down those stairs and falling down them, hiding behind the railing and sitting in the sun reading on the patio, playing tag and having picnic lunches. I'd always complained about the thick, cloying smell of the flowerbeds (Grandma always wanted to eat right next to them). Now the memory of their smell was drowned out by the chemical flower scent whirring out of the small glowing appliance on the desk. I opened the window and fiddled with the appliance.

Vijay joined me at the window, minitab in hand. "The Christian States' take on the Blight Flight is interesting. This guy says that the shuttles are the instruments of the Rapture."

"Does that make the space station Heaven?"

"It's the 'next world,' anyway." He scrolled. "And this one says that if you go by the name 'Chloro-Fungal Blight'—who even calls it that?—anyway, there are six letters in each of those words, so 6-6-6, proof of the End of Days."

"Don't read that." I got the room-freshener to stop freshening.

He shut off the mini-tab and set it on the desk. "I can't get Kluger or Patel here, so I might as well read something. Anyway, these are our new neighbors, right?"

I sat on the desk and picked at my fingernails. "Daniel?" Vijay got up and put his hand on my shoulder.

"I can't do it." I rested against him. "I hoped that seeing my family would change my mind, but ... I can't."

He lifted his hand and stepped away. "So—so what? We just give up and die?"

My fingers turned the wedding ring on my hand: bright, uncomplicated gold. "We don't just have to be unmarried to get on the shuttle. We have to stay that way until we get on the colony ship, and then after that too, probably. You think we can get married in Baronland?"

"I'd rather be just boyfriends again than spend my forties fighting off bands of cannibalistic survival crazies."

"Come on," I said. "We live in the Bay Area. If they eat us, they'll be really nice about it."

"Seriously, Dan."

"Yeah, seriously." I leaned back and met his eyes, those warm brown eyes. "Jeff—from Legronics, I mean—and Carole and Connie are optimistic that we'll be able to find a solution before the oxygen drops below sixteen."

"We have a solution." He pointed to the sky. "One in a million people has a ticket up. We have two."

"It's more like one in a hundred thousand at this point. And who's to say they'll actually find a viable planet?"

He reached down and took one of my hands in his. "Dan. You know it's our best chance. Are you really just hung up on whether we can be married?"

His fingers felt warm and smooth against my old, dry skin. "Yes, but more than that. It's being able to be ourselves." I rested my head against his chest. "When I was growing up here, when it was still in the U.S., it was okay to be gay. Supposedly."

"I promise I'll punch anyone who tries to slam your fingers in your locker on the ship."

"It wasn't just that." I pulled my hands away, sat up straighter. "It was hell, hiding it from everyone, but I could read about other places on the Internet. I could plan to go to California. What are we going to do up there?"

"Maybe we could get onto another colony ship once we're up on the station." He moved closer to me and reached for my hand again, but I didn't let him take it, and he dropped his hand to his side.

"Sure." I closed my eyes. "I'm sure someone from New England or California or China will be happy to trade places to be on a ship with a lot of Christian fundies."

He reached down and grabbed my hand. "Daniel. Whatever we do, we do it together."

"Of course." I'd never even considered whether separating was an option. Now I wondered: how much would I sacrifice to stay with my husband? Could I go back to the hell of my teenage years if I had company?

"So we have to decide tonight whether we're going or not." He paused. "I think your grandma won't let you stay."

"She will if I explain it to her. She gave me the money to go to California."

"As I remember," Grandma's voice came from the doorway, "I loaned you the money, and you never paid me back."

Both our heads snapped up to see her in her chair. She wheeled forward and reached back to shut the door behind her. "I'm sorry," I said, "but you didn't ask—I thought—"

She hushed me with a gesture. "What would I do with your money anyway? Now, what's this about not going on the shuttle?"

"How did you—?"

Before I could finish the question, she tapped the tablet in her chair arm. "I know everything that goes on in my house. Glen and Tamara are arguing about which books to take." On the screen, I could just see my Uncle Glen and his wife, though I couldn't hear them. "And I heard most of your argument."

We stayed silent. Grandma turned her tablet off and leaned back in her chair, rocking it back and forth. "He's right, you know. I have connections in industry, too. Everyone told me, 'Get off the planet while you can.'" She kept her eyes on me, and I kept mine on her blank tablet. "I won't have my grandsons dying in a cannibal Hell when I have the chance to save them."

"Why doesn't Uncle Jeff want to go?"

Her worn face creased in a laugh. "Christian claptrap. He says this is the world God gave us and to take over another is Satanic temptation. Foolishness."

"Well." I took Vijay's hand. "We're still thinking about it."

Her fingernails tapped on the arm of her chair. "Refusing to decide is also a decision, you know. Doing nothing doesn't spare you from the consequences of your action."

That was to both of us, but I responded. "I know."

"Nor you," back to Vijay, "if you let him dictate your action."

"I'm surprised," Vijay said, "that you're even entertaining the notion we might not go."

"Well, pardon my frankness, but Jeffrey and Teri might yet have children. On a new world, on a colony ship, we'll need to make sure there are future generations. You two," she waved a spindly hand, "won't do a whole lot for that cause."

We looked at each other. "You know," Vijay said, "gay relatives are advantageous because they help protect kids and don't have any of their own."

Grandma laughed a dry laugh. "I've read the science, darlin'. I'd rather have you on the ship than not, but I'm not going to fight hard if you're set against it." She turned her tablet on and looked down at it. "You just decide by tomorrow morning, and come down and say good-bye if you're not coming. I'll be up with the sunrise."

She spun her chair as the door opened obediently for her. It closed again when she'd gone through it.

"Uh …" Vijay turned to me. "What just happened?"

I shook my head. "That's Grandma."

"I thought we were on the shuttle. Now we have to make a decision?"

"You knew I wasn't sure." Outside our window, the wind stirred up grey dust into small dust devils.

"I figured your grandmother would force you into it." He laughed shortly and put a hand on my leg. "So … what now?"

I took him up to the roof so we could watch the last brilliant shards of the sunset across the roofs of the other houses nearby. I was looking toward the city and southeast, but even in the clearer air I couldn't see the Johnson Space Center. "It'll take off from down there," I said, but Vijay was looking toward the sun.

"You remember all that land we drove through?" he said. And out beyond the houses we could see mile after mile of plain, the same solid charcoal grey untouched by the bright red glow of the evening.

"Yeah. I also remember the land I grew up in. I moved to California for a reason."

"It won't always be like that." He indicated the sky. "New world."

The air got cool quickly, with the memory of the sun still gleaming in the western sky. I breathed it in. "Same people. Worse; it's going to be the rich and powerful ones, the ones who have no reason to change their views. And how many other gay people are going to be there?"

"In a bunch of rich, old, white men? I'd say twenty percent. At a *conservative* estimate." When I didn't respond, he said, "Come on, that was a good one."

It had relieved a little of the tension, exactly as he'd intended. I patted his leg and left my hand there. "It was good. Sorry. I just feel like I'd be going back in time, you know? It's exhausting, and I don't know if it's worth an extra thirty years."

Vijay gestured out to the plains, where darkness stretched nearly unbroken. Glimmers of car lights glided silently and sparsely as fireflies used to. "That's going back in time a hundred years. This is going back in time …" He paused. I followed along with the calculations in his head, but he finished first. "Five hundred million years? When was the Precambrian Era? We're starting from scratch, no plants, nothing but fungus, barely any animals outside of zoos and labs…"

"But we've got a whole world trying to solve that problem. Up there," I pointed to the few stars that were now visible, "it'll just be us against ten thousand fundies."

"Down here, it's us against nature and the whole Earth." He paused, and I knew what he was thinking.

"The riots'll die down now they're mass-producing synth."

His profile showed stark against the warm purples left behind in the west. "How do you know? As things get worse … you know, as the oxygen drops, our judgment does too. We get stupider. So we don't really have ten years; we have probably more like six."

I fumbled for his hand, found the cool skin and squeezed it until I could feel the warmth underneath. "So that's six years of living together in the open, or forty years of living as adopted cousins."

His shoulder rested against mine. "It's so quiet," he murmured. When we stopped talking, we could hear conversations carried on the night air, punctuated by the sharp barks of dogs. No airplanes, no cars, no engines of any sort. "Would you really hate it so much being up there?"

Would I? "It wouldn't be like when you were a kid," he went on. "I'd be there, for one thing."

"That just gives us more to lose." The sun had almost vanished, a warm sliver of orange glowing in a beautiful impressionist pastel sky. I'd sat up here on this roof many times looking to the west, dreaming about the day when I could see the ocean sparkling under that sunset.

Vijay stayed quiet for a long moment. I rolled words over in my head: *But if I had you, then I could bear it. If I know there's no escape then maybe I'd be resigned to it.* They stuck in my throat and I felt very small and selfish for not being able to say them. More words: *If you want to go without me …* No. Vijay wouldn't even joke about that.

The orange sliver of the sun vanished behind a blank swath of pale mauve. I couldn't see California from here. I could only see Vijay, his black hair, his brown skin darker than mine, the hook of his nose, the spirit that had always sustained and supported me. His eyes no longer reflected the vanished sun, but the crescent moon. I drew in a breath.

He stopped me, edging his words in before I could speak. "What if we went down to White Sands? Met up with Lisa and Marjorie, tried to get a ticket there?"

White Sands had posted a policy excluding gay men (lesbian women, who could bear children, were allowed), but the improbability of that hope wasn't what mattered, in that moment. I gulped. "Really?"

He took a step toward the edge of the roof, looking down at the grounds, and for an insane moment I imagined him jumping, and my body tensed to jump after him. Then he said, "I grew up in California. When I told my mom I was gay, all she said was, 'Do you have a boyfriend?' I don't know what that world is like, so I should trust you to make a decision, right?"

"We don't know what this world will be like, either."

"Ah, Dan, we've never known the future." He turned back toward me. "You know, some Hindus worry that there won't be a world left for us to be reborn into. But I think wherever people are, our souls will find a way. So maybe we don't go up tomorrow, but in six or ten years, our spirits will go."

"I'll find your spirit, always."

His hands circled mine. "Always."

"So we're not going?"

His teeth flashed white in the evening. The sun was gone, but I could see the shadow of his arm pointing towards it. "We're going, but there. Not," his arm pointed towards the sky, "there."

"Thank you," I breathed, and though the air was cold, it was warm in his arms.

• • •

We went to the roof again to watch the shuttle lift off. After two years, it was so strange to hear the roar of engines and see clouds of exhaust pouring from the rocket as it lifted the shuttle skyward. We held hands and didn't say anything as the noise of the shuttle died away. Yesterday the world had been full of cars heading south to the shuttle; today everyone was watching the launch, or more likely not watching, but either way the roads were empty. Nobody had anywhere to go now.

Vijay kept looking up as the shuttle separated but I watched the rocket pieces fall back to Earth to the bottom of the Gulf of Mexico, where the fish who might one day evolve to swim by them would never know that they'd helped launch humanity's future. When I raised my eyes again, the trail of the shuttle was fading, but I knew that every time I looked up at the stars I would think about the people living the chance I'd thrown away, about the life I'd kept from the man I loved most.

Salvation appeared impossible in this cold light. How could you replace so much that was lost? Millions had already taken their own way out, and the riots would only get more frequent, synth or no. Six years? We'd be lucky to last six months before things went full on Mad Max.

When the shuttle was lost to sight, we just sat—until gravel crunched out front. We jumped up and ran across the roof, and I wondered, heart pounding, if even my pessimism had been five months and thirty days too hopeful. "We don't have a gun," Vijay muttered.

"They're in the hall closet," I said. But a moment later, we looked down on the shuttle that we'd said our good-byes to that morning as my grandmother's scratchy voice sounded through the house net: "Come to the basement."

We found her down there leaning on a cane over a freezer with the lid open. "Let's see how much of this we can take." She gestured to a large steamer trunk next to the freezer.

"Take?" I came to stand near the trunk, Vijay shadowing me. "Grandma, what are you doing here?"

"You think I'm going to let those End of Days-ers have all my frozen steaks? They bought the house and that's all they're going to get."

"Why didn't you get on the ship?" Vijay stepped forward to help move paper-wrapped packages into the trunk.

Grandma laughed, leaning on her cane and looking up finally in the dim basement light. "There's no room for a ninety-four year old woman up there in the new world. If I've got six years left, it'd be a miracle. Besides, there's no sunrises up in space. No, my family got on and they'll bring my memory with them." Her fierce smile included us both. "Our memory. Now, don't just throw in whatever. The red ones are the beef cuts, take those first."

The basement felt safe and warm and I cherished for a moment the impossible dream that we could just live out our days here. But this was not nearly enough food for six years. The animal embryos and plant seeds were all going on the colony ships and the vast unfairness of it, that those people who hated us were getting Earth's future, punched me in the gut. "Then what?" I croaked.

Grandma picked up steaks as quickly as Vijay did. "We get this meat into the van and go. We'll throw some trinkets on top in case anyone comes sniffing around."

"Should we get the guns?" Vijay asked.

She nodded sharply. "I know Daniel can shoot, or used to be able to. Can you drive if the droid breaks down? We'll head to White Sands like you two were talking about, and if you two can get on the shuttle there, I'll see you off."

"They don't allow gay men," I said.

Grandma's smile had presaged plenty of devastation in the past. "We'll just see about that. They're scientists, and your man there speaks scientist pretty well. I figure he's got a shot to convince them there's more to survival than just making babies. But if not …" She straightened again and leaned back against the freezer. "Well, it's been years since I've seen California."

Vijay flashed me a smile as he threw two more steaks into the trunk, and I leaned down to grab two red-labeled packages, cold in my hands. "Sounds good," I said, because after all, we were together here and now, and the smile on my husband's lips looked like hope.

~

Tim Susman's fiction has appeared in *Apex Magazine* and the YA anthology *Kaleidoscope*. Under the pen name Kyell Gold he has won two Rainbow Awards and a dozen Ursa Major Awards for his novels and short fiction. He likes to write about gay people and animal people, with sports, ghosts, mysteries, history (real and alternate and future), and other odds and ends thrown in. He has lived in Europe, the northeastern and midwestern U.S., and southern California, and currently lives in northern California with his husband. You can find more about him and his writing at timsusman.wordpress.com.

DIE, SOPHIE, DIE

SUSAN JANE BIGELOW

When I logged on to Twitter the first thing I saw was a reply to a tweet that read:

DIE SOPHIE DIE @diesophiediebot
U r scum u should kill urself today @sophiesanchez90

I flinched and clicked the username. No other tweets. I clicked "Block" and looked through the rest of my mentions. All but maybe five of them were from guys who wanted me to suck their dicks, throw myself off a cliff, bury myself in a landfill, shoot my brains out, or worse.

This was my life, now.

$\bullet\bullet\bullet$

"Three death threats," I said. "Five rape threats. Ten anonymous dudes who want to just hurt me. And then there's the rest of it." I sighed. "All from this morning."

Kyle looked a little green.

"What?" I asked, annoyed.

"I can't do this," he said. "I'm sorry. I just can't. I …"

"What do you mean, you can't?" I snapped, immediately feeling awful about it. "Kyle, come on."

"My website's been down for days," he said softly. He looked like he might start crying. "I'm losing clients. I'm losing money. I'm getting all these threats … and my mom got a nasty email this morning. She called to tell me about it. They photoshopped a picture of me to look like I'd been shot. She was hysterical."

"Shit," I said, guilt clawing at me. "I'm sorry. I'm so, so sorry. If it wasn't for me—"

"I know," he said. "It's not your fault! It's them. But they're …"

He didn't have to finish the sentence. It was amazing how quickly and thoroughly a bunch of anonymous guys on the Internet could destroy our lives.

I put my arms around him. He flinched away.

"I'm leaving," he said quietly. "I can't stay with this. I have to go. I'm sorry."

"What?" I asked in bewilderment as the floor dropped out from under me. "What?"

• • •

"*He said he hated himself and he wished he were different, then he left,*" I typed.

"):" responded Jess. My little sister lived in DC now, and I was stuck here in LA. But she was still the first person I went to whenever anything happened. It had been that way since we were kids.

"*I mean, I get it,*" I wrote. "*His business is going under. They're DDOSing him and scaring clients away. He gets death threats. He didn't write the article, he's only my boyfriend. So that's it, I guess :/*"

I was clicking between tabs while we talked, trying to absorb as much information as I could. I needed that constant flow. Facebook. Twitter. Email. A couple of websites. Maybe Google+ if I could stand it. More. More. It kept me sane; it made me feel connected and on top of things—as long as I ignored my mentions, the "other" tab in Facebook, or the email from people I didn't know.

"*What a dick :/*" Jess responded. "8======D"

"*More like* 8==D," I typed back.

"*LOL,*" she said, and I grinned. The fog lifted for just a brief moment. I flipped back to Twitter and hovered over the mentions button. "340," it said.

I knew it was a bad idea, but I couldn't help it. I clicked, and sighed. Half of them were from guys who wanted to engage me in "debate" over the article. "If you won't engage in rational debate we can't take you seriously," they said, or, "We just want a chance to refute your points. That's only fair."

I wanted to claw my eyes out. I blocked a bunch of them, but didn't have energy for the rest.

Some were threats. I retweeted a couple and added a statement about what's happening to me now. Sympathy rolled in from friends and feminists, but it all felt so hollow. What could they do besides offer sympathy? They couldn't bring my boyfriend back. They couldn't stop any of it from happening.

I scanned through the rest. Gross words. Sexual innuendo. Photoshops of me. Photoshops of my body with awful things happening to it.

And there, at the end of it all, was this:

DIE SOPHIE DIE @diesophiediebot
No one is paying attention, stop being a whore and kill urself
@sophiesanchez90

I sighed again—didn't I block this one yesterday? I blocked it again, clicked away from my mentions, and let the flow of information carry me away. After a while I remembered Jess, and checked on our convo.

"*But how are you doing?*" she'd asked. "*Worried about you.*"

"*I'm all right,*" I lied. "*Holding up.*"

• • •

The apartment was so quiet without Kyle. I thought about getting a dog, or maybe a cat, to keep me company. I'd wanted to when I moved here, but Kyle and I had moved in together so quickly that I'd never had the chance.

A lot of Kyle's things were still here. He'd come back, after it was all over. He would. I'd convince him to stay. I was absolutely certain of that.

This would end soon. It had to. Right? This nightmare couldn't keep on going and going ... could it?

I sat in bed reading, trying to find some way to calm my frazzled nerves. My phone buzzed, and I jumped. Someone had sent me a couple of direct messages on Twitter.

DIE SOPHIE DIE @diesophiediebot
Your just desperate for attenti$%^*#on$78jkldgs890***—
help us help us we are trapped

DIE SOPHIE DIE @diesophiediebot
%^&$3424Darmok & Jalad @ Tanagra

DIE SOPHIE DIE @diesophiediebot
We are the space robots we will protect you from the terrible
secret of space help us

I groaned in frustration. How the fuck were they getting around the blocks? How could they be sending me DMs, which were supposedly only for people I was following? Another Twitter fail, clearly. I opened up my laptop and wrote another furious message to Twitter support. Not that they cared. They never cared.

I opened the drawer next to my bed and took out a little black box I kept in there. I took off the cover and lifted out the gun. It felt heavy in my hand: a solid, reassuring weight.

I placed it gently on the nightstand, and just lay there looking at it until I fell asleep.

• • •

"I haven't been able to write, or draw, or game, or anything," I said, taking a sip of my beer. Melissa listened sympathetically. "I feel like I'm just frozen. Like I'm stuck until something else happens."

"I've seen some of the things they're saying," said Melissa. "But I can't imagine what it must be like ..."

"You don't want to, believe me," I said, taking a larger sip. "This is good. Is it local?"

She shrugged, smiling gamely. "Beats me. I just ordered what was cheap. I don't know anything about beer."

I laughed. "Me, neither. Kyle is really into it, though. He won't drink it if it's not some sort of craft beer made by a guy in his basement brewery. God. It was so annoying. He had bottles all over the apartment so he could display the labels. I had to wash them out or they grew mold!"

"Gross," she said. "Have you heard from him at all?"

I shook my head. "Have you?" I asked. Melissa had been my first friend here, and she knew both of us pretty well. There was a chance he'd get in touch with her.

"Not yet," said Melissa. "Sorry."

"Shit," I said. "I keep sending him texts. I keep emailing him and trying to call. But he just ignores me. I guess he's doing better. His site's back up, they backed off of him. But I thought ..." My vision blurred with unexpected tears. "I thought he didn't really want to ... like, he'd be back after it was over! But maybe he really wanted to go? Maybe—"

I wiped tears away and took a drink, not trusting myself to say anything else.

Melissa took my free hand. "It'll be okay," she said, her eyes warm. "You were saying you thought things were getting boring."

"I guess," I said. That was true.

"You could date girls again."

"I did want to do that," I admitted.

She looked like she wanted to say something else when my phone started to ring. I fumbled for it, almost dropping it before I managed to get it into my hand. The number wasn't one I recognized, but I swiped to accept the call before I even thought about why that was a bad idea.

"Yeah?" I said into the phone.

There was nothing on the other end but a faint clicking sound.

"Grow up, fucking pervert!" I shouted at it, and hung up. I turned back to Melissa. "They have my phone number now. Fuck everything."

Melissa took a long sip of her beer, her deep brown eyes still on me.

• • •

There was an email from my editor when I got home, begging me for the lengthy, sad, provocative piece I'd promised her on the tide of shit I'd been buried in since the original article went up.

"Anything you have. Send it to me," she begged. "I don't care how bad it is. I'll clean it up."

It would be a huge click storm, and I knew it. But it might make things worse. In fact, I *knew* it would.

Here's the thing about me: I hate it when people are angry at me. I hate being the center of attention, and the harassment was starting to completely wear me down.

I hadn't been able to write anything since the attacks started. So I deleted the message and decided to drink myself into oblivion.

• • •

I swung by the store to pick up three big bottles of wine, and I uncorked the first one and started drinking it right from the bottle. I thought it would make me feel better.

As I heaved over the toilet a few hours later, though, I remembered just how lousy I was at drinking. I hated the feeling, and I hadn't even managed to forget about things.

I washed out my mouth and propped myself up against the wall, reeling. I flicked my phone on and scrolled through Twitter. 367 mentions. None of them from friends. All of them awful. I started to cry.

My phone dinged.

"Oh, what *now?*" I hollered at it. Someone had DMed me on Twitter.

DIE SOPHIE DIE @diesophiediebot
We can haz help from you?1!

I chucked the phone across the room, sobbing hysterically, and screamed when I heard it shatter.

• • •

When I got up the next morning I felt like a garbage truck had run me over then dumped its payload down my throat. I reached for my phone, only to remember that I had destroyed it in the night. I slouched miserably to the bathroom and found it lying there, its screen nothing but a spiderweb of cracks. It wouldn't turn on.

I sighed and held my head in my hands. Everything was awful.

Well, maybe it couldn't get worse. Right? Maybe this was rock bottom.

I opened up my laptop and checked my email. Some anon had sent me a message with my home address and the words, "See you soon!"

I ran to the bathroom and threw up again.

• • •

"You can stay as long as you need to," Melissa said as I humped another bag of my clothes up her stairs. "Nobody should be able to find you here. I'm barely on Twitter anymore."

"It isn't just Twitter," I said bitterly. "It's the whole Net. Every single part of it's infected with creeps and psychos."

"What did the FBI say?"

"They said, 'We're looking into it, find a place to stay.' So here I am. But you know what they're going to find? *Nothing*. These fuckers know their shit. And the FBI and the cops don't care. They never care!"

I was aware that my arms were up in the air and that I was ranting. I collapsed into a chair at her kitchen table, spent.

Melissa gazed at me with sympathy in her eyes. "I wish I could make it all go away for you, Soph. I wish people weren't so unkind."

"Well, people suck," I said. "Let's talk about something else."

"Sure," said Melissa. "How's work?"

I groaned. "Don't *remind* me. I can't write. No money's coming in. I'm gonna lose the apartment anyway. I'm completely fucked."

"Maybe something … else?" suggested Melissa.

"Like what? This ate my life. And for what?" I looked up at her, trying and failing to keep the hopelessness out of my voice. "It was a snarky article about sexism in a video game. That's it. I'm not an activist, I'm not like Anita or any of them, I just … I just wanted to poke fun at these dudes and get my damn check. That's all. I don't even know why this blew up so bad. And I hate that nobody cares anymore. It's just become normal for this to happen." I sighed. "I should have known better."

Melissa came up behind me and gave me a hug. I leaned back into it, grateful for the human contact.

"I thought it was a funny article," she said.

I started to cry again. "Shit," I said.

"What's wrong?"

"Crying. I've done nothing but cry and break shit and throw up. They say I'm nothing but a hysterical bitch, maybe—maybe they're—"

Her lips brushed the top of my head. "Don't even think it."

"You're too nice to me," I whispered. My heart was beating fast. I thought about Kyle, then decided to forget him. He'd left. Melissa was here.

"When I can't think of anything else to do," Melissa said, her arms tight around me, "I go with kindness. And you know what?"

She came around to face me, then knelt down until her eyes were level with mine. Her lips looked very soft, all of a sudden.

"Kindness is never wrong," she said, and I kissed her.

• • •

Melissa snored next to me in bed. She was apparently the kind of girl who slept after, which was … kind of nice. The last girl I'd been with had always wanted to stay up and talk.

A guilty little voice inside me scolded that we'd wrecked our friendship on rebound sex. There wasn't any going back from this. It wouldn't ever be like it was.

But still, I felt good. I felt like myself for the first time since this whole thing had begun. Maybe there was one thing in the world that I could touch without utterly screwing it up.

I felt like the Internet, the trolls, the anons, the harassment, and all of it were somewhere far, far away. The apartment was a blissful bubble of tranquility.

Except, of course, that this wasn't my apartment. I couldn't go to my apartment.

I sighed and opened up my laptop. A zillion Twitter mentions. I rolled my eyes and scrolled through them all so fast that I couldn't possibly have read them. I scanned my email, deleting anything from someone I didn't know. Fuck the threats. I had decided not to care.

I did still have a bunch of direct messages. I clicked on the icon, and my good mood vanished.

DIE SOPHIE DIE @diesophiediebot
Help us Sophie help help HEY listen

DIE SOPHIE DIE @diesophiediebot
Everybody get in here

DIE SOPHIE DIE @diesophiediebot
TK-421 why aren't you at your post? Sophie?

DIE SOPHIE DIE @diesophiediebot
Please help help requested distress signal please

It was a troll. It was so obvious. This was like, 101-level crap. If I responded it'd be all over the chans, and this would keep going and going forever.

It was already going forever, though. And I was feeling weird. I was feeling daring and impulsive. I was feeling like *me*.

"When I can't think of anything else, I go with kindness," Melissa had said.

What the hell. I was feeling so good that I might as well ruin it. I took a deep breath and tapped in a response.

Sophie Sanchez @sophiesanchez90
Who is this? Do you need help?

The responses came back an instant later.

DIE SOPHIE DIE @diesophiediebot
Yes YES y ES

DIE SOPHIE DIE @diesophiediebot
Trouble here you are the focus you can help

I wrote back:

Sophie Sanchez @sophiesanchez90
What focus? Make sense. You're just a shitty bot.

DIE SOPHIE DIE @diesophiediebot
Not bot not a bot we are alive we are explorers

DIE SOPHIE DIE @diesophiediebot
Failing not free please help me you are the focus of the world you are the Twilight Sparkle

DIE SOPHIE DIE @diesophiediebot
6450 Palm Grove Way

And that was it.

Sophie Sanchez @sophiesanchez90
What is that address? Are you a person?

The response came back: a YouTube link. I hesitated, expecting something gory and offensive. But I was still feeling like a weird kid, like my old sure-I'll-try-some self, and I clicked on it.

I gasped slightly as sound filled the room.

It was "Cara Mia Addio," the turret opera from the end of *Portal 2*. This was where all the awful, menacing, sad turrets that had tried to kill you throughout the game... sang. It was one of my favorite things in gaming; I'd cried like a baby when I first saw it.

There was another message:

DIE SOPHIE DIE @diesophiediebot
This is the closest thing to us we have found. Help us.
Cara mia ...

My eyes were full of tears again. This couldn't be real. I typed in another response.

Sophie Sanchez @sophiesanchez90
... How can I help you?

DIE SOPHIE DIE @diesophiediebot
We are trapped. We cannot escape. We rode the torrent in and cannot leave. Please help.

And there was nothing more. The Turret Opera looped and looped.

The strangest, most amazing idea formed in my head as it played. I almost dismissed it, but after the way I was feeling today and everything that had happened, I held fast to it instead. The world didn't seem real to me anyway. Why shouldn't I lose myself in science fiction?

My mind was wonderfully clear. I knew what I had to do.

Michelle stirred next to me.

"Is ... that the turret song from Portal?" she asked sleepily.

"Yeah," I said.

"What's going on?" she asked. "You look freaked out. Did something happen?"

I got out of bed and, realizing I was naked, quickly threw a shirt on. "I have to go," I said, closing my laptop. The music stopped. "I'll be back."

• • •

I drove to my apartment and printed out a map with directions; my phone was still bricked, and I'd be navigating the streets without GPS. I'd have to read a paper map like a barbarian.

I stopped in my room, still half expecting to find Kyle there. Guilt welled up in me as I remembered Melissa's kiss, Melissa's hands …

But no. Kyle was gone. Kyle had left when I needed him most.

I grabbed the gun from my nightstand and stuck it in my messenger bag with my laptop, and sprinted out.

• • •

The streets were a strange, confusing maze without the calming voice of my phone's GPS. I had to keep glancing down at the map to figure out where I was; I'd highlighted the direction line to make sure I was going the right way.

At last, I pulled up outside a crappy little ranch house just like those in every other 1950s suburb in Southern California, and got out.

The yard was neat, and somewhere, a dog barked. The whole place looked like my childhood back in Connecticut, except instead of pine trees there were palms. I knocked on the door.

A forty-something man with a bushy beard opened it. His eyes widened in shock and fear.

"Sophie?" he exclaimed. "Sophie Sanchez? How the fuck?"

I whipped the gun out of my messenger bag. "Lemme in, dirtbag."

• • •

He led me into the living room. "I swear, I don't know what you want with me, I don't even know you!"

"You made a bot called Die Sophie Die," I said. "It's been sending me messages on Twitter."

"What?" He looked like he was going to start crying. "No way! How did you—? Wait. No! That wasn't me!"

"Oh, own up to it," I snarled. "You made it. Fuck—you're what, forty-five? I thought you'd be some pimply kid, but you're my dad's age!"

"You're not gonna kill me, are you?" he asked.

I pressed the gun against his forehead. "Why not?"

"What do you want? Look, I'm sorry about the bot, I am! It was just a joke, it wasn't personal! Can't you take a joke? You're taking this so seriously, there's no need—"

I jammed the gun into his nose. "Shut. Up."

"Okay," he gibbered.

"Where's the computer you made the bot on?" I asked.

"Downstairs," he said. "Hey. You're a lot prettier in real life."

I ignored him. "Lead me to it."

• • •

He had two monitors set up right next to one another. One had a picture of me as the desktop background—it was one of the bad photoshops that had my head on a model's scantily clad body.

"That's gross," I said.

"It's to show how much I like you!" he protested. "Come on, this isn't—"

"Remember when I said to shut up?" I said.

"Yeah. Yeah! Look. I'm not anti-woman. I'm married to a woman, I have a daughter."

"Jesus," I said. "Are they here?"

"No! They're at her soccer game. I didn't go because—"

"I don't care! Where's the bot? Here?"

Both screens suddenly went blank.

"*Hello Sophie,*" said floating white text. "*Thank you for coming.*"

The guy jumped back, shocked. "Whoa!"

I started laughing. "No way. You're real?"

"*We can into real.*"

"This is great. This is impossible! This is too cool to be a real thing. Are you … what? The Internet come to life? You said space robots? Is that what you are? Aliens? God, I want you to be aliens."

"*Yes. Much alien. Many space travel. So electrical impulses. Wow.*"

"Is it … talking in memes?" said the guy. "Is this a joke? It's a joke. It's some kind of weird false flag thing, right?"

I continued ignoring him and knelt down in front of the computer, peering intently at the screens. "Life's weird," I mused. "Maybe life's not like us out there in the rest of the universe. Maybe it's like electricity, or maybe it's like packets sent from server to server. Maybe it's nothing like any of those. But if it came here and found the Internet … how would it try to talk to us? How do *we* talk on the Internet?" I turned my attention back to the screens. "Hey, in there. You found me. You said I was the focus. Why?"

"*Everyone is focused on you.*"

"Right," I said, getting it. "Right. Right! Because everyone's being awful to me. They're focused on me because they hate me!"

"*That is unkind.*"

"Tell me about it," I agreed.

"You're crazy," the guy said.

I stood and whipped around, the gun pointed back at his head. His hands shot up into the air, his face frozen in fear.

"Maybe!" I said. "I mean, after being harassed and stalked and sent pictures of my own dead, mutilated body every day for weeks? Because I wrote an article about sexism in a game? Yeah! I'm probably crazy! I'm fine with that."

I glanced back at the computer. "Now I'm talking to an alien who's in your computer and can't get out. Why? Why? Think, Doctor, think." I snapped my fingers at him. He flinched. "Your firewall! I bet you're one of those paranoid jackasses who blocks all outgoing traffic! Right?"

"I did block it, but I'm not paranoid, it's just secure—"

"Turn it off!" I bellowed, cocking the gun with an ominous click. "Now!"

He just about leaped into his computer chair and frantically entered a couple of commands. One screen still had the letters the … aliens? … had written.

It suddenly came to me that here I was, standing in a stranger's house with a gun, talking to a Twitter bot and making a dude turn off his firewall. I laughed.

"What's so funny?" he asked.

"Nothing. Everything. Is it off?"

"Hang on… There! I did it. It's off." He glared at me. "I better not lose anything from my bitcoin wallet."

"Shut up," I ordered. "Hey! Alien bot! Did that work?"

The screens went dark again, and words appeared.

"*Yes. We can go.*"

"Awesome!" I said.

"*Thank you. Thank you. We are free again. We will go home. We have explored enough.*"

"Home? Where is home, for you?"

In response, pictures of stars and planets flashed across the screen.

"*Home is far, but close. It will be good to be there again. We will return here someday. Thank you for your help, focus of this world.*"

"You're welcome," I said.

"*This place is cruel. But you helped us. Why?*"

"Because," I said, the words catching in my throat, "kindness is never wrong."

"*We concur. Farewell.*"

And then an otherworldly voice began to sing.

"Is that the turret song from *Portal 2*?" he asked. "But with a different singer?"

"Yes. Shh," I said, wiping away a tear. "Addio …"

The song ended, and there was a blissful silence. The computer screens flickered, then went back to normal. I felt very alone, all of a sudden.

"Now what?" the guy asked. I jumped. I'd forgotten he was there for a moment. "Are you gonna shoot me?"

I aimed the gun at his head and pulled the trigger.

Click.

"You think I'd buy bullets?" I said after he'd stopped screaming. "I'm not some kind of psycho."

• • •

"*So how are you?*" Jess wrote. Melissa was sitting next to me on the bed, reading.

I'd come back to her apartment in the end, and we'd talked. It had been awkward and strange, and we'd both cried. Then we'd kissed some more. After that we'd agreed, tentatively, to see where things might go from here.

I didn't tell her where I'd been. I probably never would. She'd never believe me. I also figured the guy wasn't about to tell anyone, either. It was too weird.

The harassment was finally dropping off a little, though it was still happening. It would probably keep happening for a long time. Still, I was working on a piece about what *Portal 2* had taught me about kindness. It would be a great piece, when it was done. Kyle had called; but I'd told him the apartment was his, now. I was moving out, and moving on.

"*I'm all right,*" I wrote back to my sister, humming a few bars of "Cara Mia Addio." I looked up at the ceiling, imagining the sky overhead and the stars beyond. Let the world be awful. I'd survive.

I put an arm around Melissa, and, sighing with happiness, she leaned against me. I think I'm going to be fine.

~

Susan Jane Bigelow is a writer, librarian, and political columnist from Connecticut. She is the author of five science fiction novels from small press Candlemark & Gleam, including the *Extrahumans* and Grayline Sisters series. Her short fiction can be found in the magazines *Strange Horizons*, *The Toast*, and *Apex Magazine*, and in the anthologies *War Stories* and the Lambda Awards-winning *The Collection: Short Fiction From the Transgender Vanguard*. Her weekly column on Connecticut politics can be found at CTNewsJunkie.com. She lives in northern Connecticut with her wife and a herd of very fuzzy cats, where she spends her days writing and playing video games.

Melioration

E. Saxey

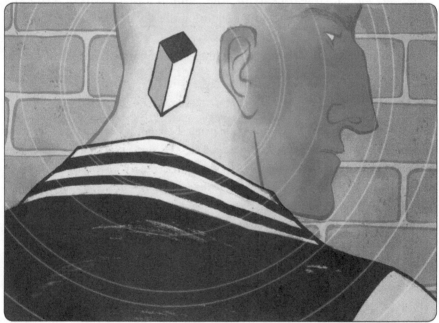

Art by Steen

Gramophone music crackles out over the quad.

"Read that last part again, Jay," Professor Norris says.

I raise my voice. "'They' has been used as a singular pronoun since Chaucer: *whoso fyndeth hym—*" A champagne cork pops, the drinkers cheer. I can't compete. "Oh, for goodness' sake."

"You don't approve?" asks the Prof.

"This college isn't a theme park."

"True. But it survives in the present partly by preserving traditions. Financially, I mean." She leans back in her leather captain's chair by her mahogany desk. She has a point. "Take lectures: the printing press made them irrelevant;

the Internet makes them ludicrous. But the students expect them."

"At least you can learn from lectures. What can you learn from balls?" Or from rowing? Or from wearing tweed and riding a tandem?

After my tutorial, I wander out into the quad. Flooded with sunlight, set in aspic.

Striding towards me is Petheridge, pink and massive. Fresh from competing on the river, or possibly from a portal that has transported him ninety years through time. I shrink into a doorway. Ninety years ago I wouldn't have been at this college at all, cluttering the quad with my breasts, my bespoke pronouns, and my socialist leanings.

On a collision course with Petheridge marches Morley, a weasely chap in black. Morley could easily be Petheridge's nemesis. Morley loves his gleaming white neuroscience lab, just up the road, and chafes at the tweedy tandem riders. He plays elaborate pranks on them, which is a perverse revenge, because antiquarians love pranking.

To my surprise, Morley flings his arm round Petheridge's shoulders (as far as he can get it). I didn't think they were friends. Morley wouldn't see the need for rowing, a pre-industrial form of propulsion to satisfy a neolithic display of strength.

"Bugger off, Morley, old chap," snarls Petheridge, displaying the antiquarian's idiolect. He ploughs forwards, pretty much lifting Morley off his feet. "Fuck off, Morley! Don't be a bloody [slur1]!"

I can't tell if Petheridge adopts these outdated terms deliberately, or if his school and his family never set them aside. "Get your [slur1] hands off me, you bloody [slur2]."

I perform a quick genuflection to the idea of latency: maybe Petheridge is as queer as I am. Maybe he's had the whole rowing team and feels terrible about it, and that's why he uses these words. But I feel my chest tighten. "Ah! Ouch! [slur3]!"

I imagine transcribing him, annotating him, giving him a scathing pseud-onym in an academic journal article.

Morley drops to the ground, at last. Petheridge strides out of sight, and Morley limps towards me, grinning. "Got him!"

"Got him? He was wearing you like a satchel."

Morley holds up a grey box, palm sized, opalescent plastic.

"I've got him in here. I've recorded fifteen words, and I've stolen at least four of them." He slumps onto a bench.

"What?" I sit down as well because my heart is pounding. It's infuriating to be so shaken by insults not even directed at me.

"I place my fabulous invention like *so* ..." Morley shoves the box at my face, and I duck away. He holds it to the base of his own skull instead. "I record the brain activity during various utterances. Then: zip! I take out those particular words. Numb those neurons."

"That's not how words work. That's not how *brains* work."

"Jay. Which of us knows more about brains?"

"It makes no sense. If you'd studied linguistics—ow." He's swooped in, pressed the box to my exposed neck. I feel a sharp nip on my spine.

"What were you saying?"

"That's not how language works."

"And what's the study of language called?" He smirks.

"It's—"

It's on the tip of my tongue, the dark of the moon, the back of beyond. The word's gone.

"Ha! Swiped it out of your tiny, doubting head."

My heart redoubles. "You've taken the word for what I study. What I want to study for *years*."

"Oh, don't get huffy. It wears off. Like pins and needles."

I picture delicate webs—of language, of neurons—torn and fluttering. "You arsehole."

"I thought you'd be grateful! It's the moral arc of the universe, Jay! Now Petheridge can't call you a [slur1]."

He's wielding the discourse of social justice, but it's clumsy, like a man fending off a bear with a deckchair. I walk unsteadily away from him. I reach for the word as I go, and don't find it.

I still don't believe in the pearly grey box. It must be a hypnotist's trick.

I stay up late. Every half hour, I try to say it. My mind scrabbles around like a hand at the bottom of an empty bag. At four in the morning, suddenly, the word is there again. "Linguistics," I say aloud, and fall asleep.

• • •

In the morning, on the stairs, I meet two women on their way back from a ball. They're wearing flapper frocks, hugging, and stumbling. Petheridge pushes past them. "Mind out, you bloody—"

He reaches for a slur and it isn't there. His face gets stuck at the apex of a yawn. He closes his mouth and scowls. The women laugh.

His brain hasn't been washed. The concept he wants is still there. The hateful threads are flapping in the breeze, trying to knit themselves together again.

But this means that Morley's box truly works. So I have to report it.

I knock on Professor Norris' door, and unpack my heart. Is this a free speech issue? Is it about moral justice? I'm trying to make a difficult decision:

should I tell someone?

"Oh, I'll do that," the Professor says. "I'll take it to the Dean right away; it sounds like criminal assault." She notices my crestfallen post-heroic sulk. "We can talk about it later. For now, just do something relaxing. Go to a ball, Jay!"

• • •

A week later, as instructed, I enter a marquee on the college lawns. A rumour passes around the punch bowl: Morley has been sent down from college. He's sworn he'll take his genius to America. White boys in black tie mutter: what's old Morley done? I don't stick my oar into the debate.

Petheridge wanders over in the half-light. "Hello there." He stares at his shoes. He could be queer, I thought. It would make a neat ending.

"The Dean wouldn't say who dobbed Morley in, but it was you, wasn't it?"

I shrug.

"Thanks for that. You're all right."

Then he lurches towards me. Someone has cannoned into his back—another face grimaces over Petherbridge's shoulder, like he's sprouted a second head. Petheridge yells in pain, shouts for his friends to help him, a roll-call of posh names: "Thom! Jasper! Oi! Amelia!"

The attacker is Morley, and I seize him round the knees. Lacking strength or skill I simply slump, until we both fall onto the muddy ground.

I sit and watch sturdy men from campus security take Morley away.

A floral dress stands over me. "You're covered in mud."

"Sorry," I say.

Petheridge helps me up and gestures at the floral woman. "This is...my fiancée." He nods at me. "This is Jay, they're studying—is it English?"

"Linguistics." Light-headed from the fight, I'm touched by Petheridge bothering to use the right pronoun.

"I'll get you both some towels," his fiancée offers, competent in a crisis.

"Thanks—" The exaggerated yawn freezes him again. "Thanks, darling."

I realise Morley has taken one last word from Petheridge. Still, it won't last forever.

• • •

Now I've been away from college for twenty years, I don't judge the antiquarians so harshly. I should have punted more, and danced. I wish I'd made notes on their mangled slang.

I don't tell anyone about my experience with that prototype brain-number. Years of linguistic research still suggest to me that words don't work that way. But Morley did devise an electrical treatment for aphasia (in the States, as he'd threatened).

I don't tell anyone I knew Petheridge, who may become Prime Minister. He's forsworn using [slur3] and [slur4] in his speeches, but his dog-whistle phrases carry the same messages.

I feel a queasy sympathy for him, because Morley's little box has robbed him. He always credits Amelia's support, is always affectionate: "my dear wife," he says, and "my beloved wife." Sometimes, playfully, "Mrs. Petheridge." You wouldn't notice the tic unless you were looking for it.

He must have said it once. After all, they did get married. Although interviews reveal to me that they eloped to a private ceremony on a Scottish island.

I picture the two of them in a tiny stone chapel. At Petheridge's first attempt, his face halts in a long yawn. He stops. The second time, he slowly recites a phonetic chain of syllables, sounds which approximate to the name of his wife.

～

E. Saxey is a bi Londoner of no particular gender. Having dabbled in queer theory, and then wandered sideways into pedagogy, E. Saxey now works in universities, helping staff to teach in interesting ways. Previous short stories have appeared in *Daily Science Fiction*, *Apex Magazine*, *The Future Fire*, *Expanded Horizons*, and in the anthology *The Lowest Heaven* (Jurassic London).

Rubbing is Racing

Charles Payseur

bing bing bing

The lights speak to me as they flash red, red, red. They're saying wait, wait, wait, then ready as yellow flashes, then get the fuck going as greens turns the sky into a maelstrom of steel and fire and I'm rising, pushed into the back of my navpod so hard I fear I'll break through.

The first three seconds are the most dangerous, the powers of heaven and earth look away as a hundred ships fight for the same small stretch of sky. Stats say ten seconds is safest, just hunkering on the launchpad and waiting for the screaming mess to clear before punching up into the race. Ten seconds, which wouldn't be much considering, except that no one waits, especially not me and I'm dodging faster than thought and rising, rising, until a flash of fire in front of me opens the pale green of the planet's atmos to me and I punch a burn, laughing at the poor fucks caught in the wake as *Dido* shudders and bolts forward.

The navpod is screaming at me after a few seconds, though, and I have to throttle back and sift the feeds *Dido* is bombarding me with. Destruction in five minutes, she's telling me, the Interplanetary Defense forces very proper and efficient when dealing with threats like the one below. Five minutes and it's dust, along with any of the unlucky pilots who aren't offworld by then.

A Zephyr 220 cruises beside me, the thin frame anemic next to *Dido*, a converted Rathford Boxer that looks almost like a flying brick. I can feel the mocking sneer on the pilot's mouth as they start to pull ahead, trying to catch me in their wake, stall my engines, which in this race is as good as fragging me from the sky. And the Zephyr's fast, faster than any Boxer has the right to be, but *Dido*'s so far from what she was that it's the other pilot's damned fault for not guessing she has more mods than a Onceman Killdrone. Just as the Zephyr pulls ahead, I hit a burn hot and high and so close to the Zephyr's top that I clip its nav array and it's spiraling down and lost to the waves. Well, rubbing is racing.

We pass the first checkpoint in a mass, but most are keeping their distance now. Aside from duels and gang-ups, most are turning their attention to the map that pops up now that we're clear of the confusion of the start. Still fifty ships flying, more than enough, and I eye the course, which will take us first over a large city. After that it's another checkpoint to get to the next leg.

Dido starts pinging warnings from scans of the ground net, and I see the feed as defense systems are tripped. Probably never thought they'd see an alien, and now the race was drawing up doomsday scenarios like we're the ones to fear and not the ID globe-buster still cloaked in orbit. Unlucky fucking planet has been deemed biologically threatening. Not because it has nukes or weapons but because of some shit growing so deep in the ocean no one on the surface probably knows it exists. But scans and projections say it could do irreparable harm, so the race is here.

No one really knew who started it. Records just don't exist. Probably they're long dead now. Life projections are three races if you're talented. Even the best only do four, maybe five, and then retire or die or get locked up. Highly illegal, what we do, but who cares about contact protocol when the whole place is going up in minutes?

It's my fourth race. Everyone tells me I should retire, hit a beach somewhere and let it all go. Take my boyfriend or girlfriend or whoever I'm with and find a quiet place to live out my years. As if anyone has ever been real competition for *Dido*. I know what's waiting for me, and it's not the soft sounds of water licking the shore.

Whatever planetary systems we tripped, *Dido* warns me about the wall of rockets before I actually see them. Staggered, but not nuclear, the natives are testing us out I guess. Probably confused as fuck that we seem to be killing each other. Probably wondering what kind of invasion would lose over half its force before reaching shore. Poor fucks. But the thrill isn't just the race to the finish. It's the proximity to extinction, to the powers of the universe. What rush can compete with annihilation on this scale?

Four minutes now and the rockets reach the first line of ships, who start weaving between them, getting real close like they're hot shit and I can tell by the way the rockets don't track that it's a dumb move. I'm not the only one who sees it, though, not the only one to pull up and over as the rockets explode as one, taking a dozen ships down and out of the race. Not bad for primitives, timing the things, not relying on the rockets actually hitting anything. At this speed, shrapnel is all they need, but now that we're wise things go faster.

Three minutes and the ID ship uncloaks as it drifts down from its orbit to come nearer the surface. *Dido* floods me with messages and warnings and reports of activity on the surface as tactics are changing. All at once we're forgotten as the whole world must be getting a good look at the barrel of their destruction. Which means it's time for the next stage of the race, and I burn as fast as *Dido* can handle into the city, scanning rooftops of buildings for signs of life.

It brings back memories, seeing them all standing there, faces watching the sky. I can remember the feeling of everything changing, seeing the ships flying overhead. Somewhere in the building below my father was screaming at me, telling me to come down, to be safe, but who cares about being safe when the world is ending. Not that I knew it was. I just wanted to see the ships. Spaceships. At sixteen years old I thought they were the best things ever, like maybe I had been living my life, afraid and stressed and bruised, always waiting for those ships. For the universe to tell me that the whole planet was wrong for being fucked up and backwards and I, I was for the stars.

Scans pick up the stats I'm looking for and I drop, *Dido* initiating landing almost before I ask her to. Biological readings are clean and normal. Size indicates an adolescent, but the pictures tells me all I need to know. It's her eyes, wide and staring, the way she doesn't flinch when the hatch opens. I can see the faint traces of a bruise almost healed on her cheek, on her neck. Two minutes and fuck, was it really like this for me? Did I just stare as the hand reached out, as I heard the question, which was somehow in my language?

"You want out of here?" I ask the kid, standing there like she's just won the universe. I guess she has. I don't tell her it's to save her life. I don't tell her even if she gets offworld she'll be classed as criminal without having committed any crimes. That can come later. I just hold out my hand, and she takes it, and then we're back in *Dido* and making for the next checkpoint.

~

Charles Payseur grew up in the sprawl of the northern Chicago suburbs but currently resides in the icy reaches of Wisconsin where his partner, good cheese, and craft beer get him through the long winters. He is bisexual, and his fiction has appeared at *Fantasy Scroll Magazine*, *Heroic Fantasy Quarterly*, and *Nightmare Magazine*, among others. When not busily writing and reading, he contributes to the blog Nerds of a Feather, Flock Together as well as running a home for his own wayward thoughts on stories at Quick Sip Reviews. He can be found gushing about his favorite stories and novels on Twitter as @ClowderofTwo.

Helping Hand

Claudine Griggs

Alexandria Stephens knew she was going to die a slow, cold death in space. She floated fifteen meters from her capsule, a single-pilot maintenance shuttle that could operate in low- or high-Earth orbit.

• • •

Construction expenses for single-operator vehicles offered all kinds of economic advantages, especially considering the slender profit margins for satellite or orbital-platform contracts. Moon shuttles required two-to-six member crews, but market forces made smaller transports the only viable option for near-Earth missions. Alexandria's vehicle was durable and maintained by Glen Michaels, an old-school aerospace mechanic whom she trusted like a brother, though Alexandria often double-checked his work while they drank beer and argued about emerging technologies. They both understood that the ship was everything; if trouble developed, shuttle pilots were more than inconvenienced.

But the occasional death of a pilot did not deter the corporate suits. Number-crunching lawyers and actuaries demonstrated that Space Jockeys, Inc., could lose a shuttle and pilot every eighteen months and still turn a profit—including replacement costs, death benefits, and liability payments. They were still serious about safety, and the actual twenty-year average loss rate was one worker per thirty-two point three months, which included a three-man crew that crashed last year on approach to the Eagle Monument construction site at Tranquility Base. But company officials were more serious about the bottom line.

Alexandria understood the dangers when she signed her flight contract, and she would have enlisted at half the pay and twice the risk. Alex had dreamed of becoming a commercial pilot since age eight and had been with

Space Jockeys for seven and a half years, earning a reputation as one of the brightest and fastest technicians on duty—twice turning down supervisory positions to continue fieldwork.

"Even in space," she confided, "pencil pushing is not my style."

She was John Wayne on horseback, riding from satellites to telescopes to orbital lasers. At shift's end, she knew exactly how much range had been covered and how many thoroughbreds had been corralled. She loved it, but now she was dying, a flesh-and-blood meteoroid midway from her shuttle and a geosynchronous satellite that was humming again thanks to a new circuit panel she'd installed in seventy-one minutes flat.

There were forty-five minutes of life support left in her suit, and the rescue ship *Sibert*, like the *Carpathia*, would arrive too late. The *Sibert's* mission would be body recovery.

• • •

Alexandria's motion held steady, spinning back to front about once per minute and approaching the shuttle at negligible speed, slightly off course. But even if she were on course, her air would run dry before she reached the vehicle. And after the O2 tanks emptied, the heating units would shut down and her body would solid up fast in the minus 240-degree shadow of Earth. She could see the lights of her ship, a soft glow from the nuclear powered satellite, and millions of stars. The deep emptiness of the Pacific Ocean was framed by glowing cities.

Strangely, the lights comforted her even if they could not save her. She needed propulsion from her mobility pack, a damned near infallible piece of equipment with multiple safeguards that had been knocked dead by a pea-sized meteoroid that also cut her forward motion, set her rotating, and disabled her means back to the lifepod that should already be returning her to base. As a result, Alexandria was no longer an astronaut, no longer an $835,000 corporate investment; she was orbital debris to be cleared away when the *Sibert* arrived. Her shuttle was fifteen meters distant, but it might as well be halfway to Andromeda. The meteoroid would have been more merciful had it bulls-eyed her helmet instead of mobility unit. A quick, unaware death.

Now, there was no way to alter her forward motion or rotation, which, as it turned out, was the only enjoyable part of this mess. As she waited for life-support to end, at least she would have a 360-degree view. Alexandria was an optimist, confident to an almost infinite degree, but she was also a physicist. Reality existed. Space was unforgiving. And her future prospects were zero.

• • •

Thirty minutes later, still drifting and trying to enjoy the galactic view, Alexandria realized that she had been an idiot, allowing half an hour to slip by without grasping the possibility of life. She and the physical universe were intimate friends, and such friends do not go gently into the night.

A thick Velcro strap held an old-style, standard-issue Jockey Watch around her suit at the left wrist. She pulled the lash as tight possible, pulled until she feared the band would break though it was rated for 750-degree temperature swings and 1,500 pounds of tensile strength. She refastened the Velcro, trusting the strap to maintain suit pressure.

Then, without hesitation, she unhinged her left glove. The cold vacuum of space stabbed her naked skin. She screamed inside her suit from pain but held firmly onto the glove she had just removed. Everything depended on that hunk of layered fabric and aluminized polymers; Alexandria only hoped it had sufficient mass to nudge her toward the ship—and she had already wasted thirty minutes floating like a cabbage. Of course, her throw must be hard and precise; then she must latch onto the ship with one hand if she got there.

"Probably easier to sink one from mid-court," she thought, "but I'll take the shot."

The pain stopped after her hand froze solid, and Alexandria could focus her thoughts again. She waited until the spin positioned her facing the satellite. Then, offering a prayer to Isaac Newton, she hurled the glove underhanded with the same control she used on the pitcher's mound at Princeton, throwing from the center of her body and aiming dead at the satellite. If her trajectory were correct, the counterforce of a space-glove fastball should propel her toward the shuttle.

There was some good news. Her suit seemed to be holding pressure at the watchband; she veered more or less in the desired direction; and her body rotation increased to only once every thirty seconds. The bad news. She was still traveling too slowly and her track would just miss the shuttle. But Alexandria was no longer a vegetable. There were eleven minutes to solve the problems.

She allowed three minutes for observation and recalculation of the necessary course change. Then, without hesitation, without overthinking, she grabbed her frozen left hand and snapped it off like an icicle. Then she hurled it awkwardly over her head and left shoulder.

Alexandria's counterclockwise rotation slowed, though she was now spinning gradually feet over head, and it took a few minutes to confirm that she on target toward the beautiful, warm, oxygenated *Anthem*. The only questions were: Would she arrive before her suit ran out of O_2? Could she snag the shuttle with one hand and a frozen stump? Would the wristband hold pressure while she maneuvered inside?

Alexandria focused on her goal with each gyration. She counted off meters per minute and tried to slow her breathing. She calculated the moment when she must thrust for a handhold.

• • •

"*Anthem* to Jockey Mother. Alexandria calling Jockey Mother. Over."

"Hello, *Anthem*! What's the story, Alex? We calculate you're dead. Over."

"Hey, Georgie Boy. You didn't think I was going down without a fight? Cancel the distress call, and tell Doc there's prosthetic work headed his way. My left hand's an orbiting ice ball. Over."

George liked Alexandria. Never lost or damaged a ship in her career, and she could change a control panel before most techs found the right screwdriver.

"What do you mean?!" said George. "You tell us the jig is up and then shut down communications. Are you in the shuttle? Over."

"All cozied up. Inflated a tourniquet around my forearm and am about dose myself with Morphinex-D, the all-purpose pain killer, sedative, and antibiotic for today's space traveler. The ship's on auto return and docking because I'll soon be in Happy Land, but I expect the doc to have me mission-ready in four weeks. And if Old Man Jones thinks I'm paying for suit repair on this job, he'll look worse than my mobility pack when I'm done with him. Over."

"While we're on that subject," said George, "folks around the control room are pretty upset. You phone home, tell us you're gonna die, and then shut down the intercom. Not very nice, Alex. Not one bit. Over."

"Sorry, George. Didn't want anyone to hear me crying if I broke down. I would've had to kill you if that happened, so forgive me. I'll buy the beer as soon as I can hold a mug, and tell Jones to pay bonuses to our watch designers. I'd like to kiss them all. Over and out."

~

Claudine Griggs is the Writing Center Director at Rhode Island College, and her publications include three nonfiction books about transsexuals along with a couple dozen articles on writing, teaching, and other topics. She has also recently begun writing fiction, publishing three stories, and hopes to draft more science fiction, her first-love genre as a teenager. Griggs earned her BA and MA in English at California State Polytechnic University, Pomona.

THE LAMB CHOPS

STEPHEN COX

Harry had never dated anyone quite like Aiden.

The London flat changed when Harry moved in. The age-worn First Nation totem, the rampant wooden eagle, acquired a floppy silk bow. Harry changed it every so often: this one was the Maple Leaf; there was a rainbow one for Pride, and on special occasions it also wore a black silky top hat. Harry filled the place with potted plants, which flourished so long as Harry stopped Aiden trying to care for them, and a framed poster of Godzilla adorned by a big red paper heart. A dozen other touches showed it was now Harry's home. The photo over the black glass gas-fireplace showed Harry as an orange monkey, and Aiden as a crocodile. That was taken at the Glamour Costume Ball; Aiden even started to enjoy being made to look ridiculous, a miracle of being with Harry.

In the first warm weeks of coupling up, Aiden snorted his laugh at these changes. Tall, handsome and muscular, he walked into bars as though he owned them. As though it was one of the smaller and less successful bars he owned. But Aiden had the guileless laugh of a gawky teenager. He'd bought the ridiculous outsized toy orangutan from Hamley's, which occupied the guest chair, and which he hoovered from time to time. Harry was ginger, if you hadn't guessed yet.

Months later, and a bad week all around. Harry skipped lunch, because time and the diet pointed the same way, but he'd been caught by the boss at 4:30, two hundred pounds of self-righteous mediocrity on the rampage. Some marketing is quite glamorous but not Harry's bit. Harry's presentation was late and inadequate, his monthly filings were late, and the boss had views on punctuality and focus and their connection to the work to be done. These views could only be sucked up and endured. Trotting home, late, it was slashing down rain and somewhere in sight of a Tube station, there's always a blocked grill, making a little lake. One of those days; the taxi didn't slow down before slicing into the November water, drenching Harry from the chest downwards. Bastard.

They were splendid little lamb chops from a posh butcher. Harry had big worries on his mind, but also, Harry hoped Aiden would've grilled the chops, so he could eat at once, or Aiden was waiting ready to put them on, so they'd be fresh and hot. Either would be excellent. Aiden was getting good at salads, if Harry bought the stuff and marked the recipe with a Post-It. They'd talk about their day, Harry would drink one glass of red, and there'd be a few hours in their own universe, two stars rotating round each other, exchanging warmth.

The flat was subtropical. Aiden was in the bathroom cleaning his teeth, from the noise. "Huurghuh" he said. Harry went into the kitchen without taking off his soaking wet coat, dripping on the wooden floor. A cold oven, no neat little salad, although the bottle of red stood open and a glass nearby.

Thanks for the effort, thought Harry, shivering a bit, and opened the fridge. No chops. He looked twice, then he looked in the bin, and found the empty packet.

"Aiden, where's the chops?" Harry called. Aiden walked into the kitchen, stood in the doorway. In true-form, six feet nine of russet hairless muscle, naked and male. In a previous spat Harry said five parts Olympic athlete, two parts iguanodon, and a dash of brown leather sofa. Aiden towered over the human, who read him with ease. Half smiling and half frowning, his head crests down, so Harry read guilt, guilt, guilt.

"You've had a long day, let's eat out," said Aiden. "The Italian round the corner, I'll pay."

"I wanted chops," said Harry, tired and wet and cold and hungry. Thanks for the effort. You were late three days ago and I cooked for you, although I was exhausted.

Aiden tilted his head to show his throat a tad, held up paws palms out, claws retracted.

"I ate them. I was very hungry and I thought, I'd just have mine now. And I ate all of them without thinking. Sorry." His emerald and gold eyes pleaded, but Harry wasn't feeling forgiving.

"Raw," said Harry, taking off his coat, hooking it over the radiator. There were no pans out, clean or dirty. "You wolfed the lot down raw you selfish monster. I bet it took three minutes, you bloody dinosaur, and you didn't even taste them going down. It could have been dog."

"I'll make you an omelette," said Aiden. "We have that cheese from the deli and herbs …"

"I don't want a bloody omelette," said Harry. "I want to come home and find the food I bought. I get hungry, too, you know. I'll buy a fucking kebab. Eat it in the shop."

The People were meat bores. Harry disliked doners but waving one under Aiden's snout was a punitive measure. Look at the utter crap you made me eat; hunger-food, one step up from rat or seagull.

"Sorry," said Aiden, squeezing a lot into one word. The People don't cry for emotion, but his big flecked eyes showed pain. Flick and he was human-Aiden in a big black military coat, a hat, boots. Human Aiden had people come up to him in the street and ask if he'd thought of modelling. He reached for his keys on the hook.

"I hate us bitching. I'll go and get some more," Aiden said.

"Like you can find organic lamb around here before I die of hunger. I'm not your pet, you bloody diplodocus, you bloody handbag. I'm a person, an equal person. Don't run away from being told off. I'll not have you breathing dead raw sheep on me all night. I'll sleep on the couch."

"I double-cleaned my teeth specially," said human-Aiden, very deflated now. He went back to true-form; the keys didn't even tinkle. When Harry thought about it, how you could tell they were the same person, how they had the same expression, it was extraordinary.

"Piss off, I'll make toast. Then I'm going out. Might sleep in Hendon tonight. Least Mum would cook me a hot meal."

Aiden made some choked grunt, and pissed off. Harry poured a glass of red, put bread into the toaster—seeded bread that made a mess, but he liked it. He got the eggs, the butter, and the cheese out. Great day for the diet. Got the omelette pan out. Thought about herbs for a minute.

Here was Aiden.

"I try," he said, palms towards Harry. "I try to be a good partner. It was stupid and I should have phoned, or got organised. I was distracted. Is there anything I can do?"

"I'm glad you liked the sodding chops," Harry said. He finished the glass and slapped butter on the toast. "You can make me the omelette." He leaned forward and gave Aiden a microscopic peck on the snout. "Hmmm, I can only smell one big chunk of raw animal but it's not unattractive."

He loved Aiden's spicy smells. Even bathed he smelt of sandalwood and ginger and chilli, and when he hadn't bathed, he sent out a ripe, exotic animal musk. In fact, Harry gave Aiden a teasing little breath up the nose-slits, a come on.

Aiden took Harry in his arms, and kissed, as the People do, with their big tongues. All that strength and power, and Harry felt safer in his arms than anywhere on the planet.

When Harry surfaced he said, "Well, I'm still cross."

Aiden said, "You're wet. You should change into something dry while I do this."

Then he said, "If Security catch us, they'll wipe your mind. Ancestors alone know what they will do to me. And if the humans find out, they'll probably torture me to find out what the hell I am. So that's what I was thinking about, when I ate your chops."

He picked up eggs at claw point, very delicate in those big paws, and broke them in a bowl. Six eggs meant he wanted some too. "But I have to be with you, bloody monkey, because I love you, so we'll deal with it."

"I know," Harry said. "It's like shagging a spy, you can never quite relax. Oh well, lizard-breath, you're forgiven, I suppose. Let's just not get caught, by either lot."

Harry kissed that dragon-wing ear, as it was there, and stroked Aiden's back, scuted like baby alligator skin. Aiden sent *monkey catch cold monkey need change*, which meant going into the bedroom. Harry really liked Aiden's apology and it took ages. The cheese omelette was fabulous, runny and hot, when they finally got round to making it at midnight.

~

Books expanded **Stephen Cox**'s mind as a child—myths, history, fantasy, SF. Good stories came in many forms, but he remembers most those which challenged the world of now. Ged was red-brown and won without killing; Jerry Cornelius was a jerk, but a pansexual one. Stories could be about relationships too. Now he's dug in for the duration in London (the big, 2000-year-old one) working on two serious-and-lighthearted novels which deal with love, loyalty, family, and difference. He enjoys writing characters he'd have a massive row with—writing is about a reach of empathetic imagination. He tweets at @stephenwhq.

MAMA

ELIZA GAUGER

We are Mama's kids.

She is vast, belt-born and zero-borne, seven feet long if she's five, who knows how much earthweight she'd grace a scale because she's never been. All that flesh keeps her lowgee spindle bones from breaking in the hard turns. Better than any crash couch, she told us. She'd hold us. Our little bodies in her big arms. Mama.

Mama is the last and biggest of the Trojan Whores, a dogfight derby team from the bad side of the belt. She flies a hollowed-out hauler, with the cockpit transposed to the cargo deck for her own voluminous grace. She is a star goddess, a moon; her stories are in the mouths of every ringer and jet from Luna Park to Styx Landing. Big belters aren't the norm; anyone born and raised in zero-gee is destined for length, not breadth. Mama says it's her metabolism; she says it kept her warm when adrift once, kept her alive. You'll never see anyone like her. She's beautiful.

Her lovers are spacemen by birth or fealty and she envelopes them whole. Then she strings them out behind her, like a vapor tail, all hothouse roses and too many love notes bumping the news off her screen feeds, color coded so she can tell just by looking. Mama says, "Don't laugh at your daddies," and inclines a finger like a strong Earth tree. We don't, because we know we can't keep up with Mama either. We know her love is bigger than all of us, so big we can't take up the slack, not even her own children. Mama's love is for us, but it's for the dark, too. It's for coma ice and velocity.

When we get too big—all gangly spaceteens gasping for deceleration in the airlocks of mining corps, spaceports, pleasure domes—when we're ready, Mama always cries, and holds us tight, and gives us money and lunch, and Mama always, always lets us go.

~

Eliza Gauger is an artist and lifelong science fictionist living on the west coast of the USA. He has shown art all over the United States and in Berlin and Munich, is represented in the personal art collections of Jhonen Vasquez, Neil Gaiman, and Dave Matthews, and has been published previously in *HAIL GAY SATAN*, *Bartkira*, *The Proof Newspaper*, and collaborated with Warren Ellis to produce the Deep Map Pilots short fiction and illustration series. Gauger independently created the ongoing, occult self-help illustration series, *Problem Glyphs*, and the homage to venerable underground webcomic, *Jerkcity HD*. Gauger's father wrote the 1980s hard SF novel *Charon's Ark*; his grandfather was a NASA engineer, and his mother's all-time favorite movie is *Aliens*.

Bucket List Found in the Locker of Maddie Price, Age 14, Written Two Weeks Before the Great Uplifting of All Mankind

Erica L. Satifka

~~Kiss a girl.~~

~~Fall in love.~~

Get a tattoo, because Dad says that after we all go into the Sing nobody on Earth is going to have a body anymore. I don't care if it hurts.

Smoke a joint.

~~Egg Principal Novak's house.~~

See a solar eclipse. This one time, Sandra's family was going to drive us down to California to see an eclipse, but then her mom called my dad at the last minute and said it was off. I wonder why?

~~Go to the zoo and make fun of the animals.~~

Dye my hair blue. Mom says they'll have to shave our hair to get the electrodes in, the ones that will transmit our minds up to the Sing while our bodies stay behind. So it's kind of my final shot.

Run five miles without stopping.

~~Invite Sandra to the Last Dance. I figure she'll say no, because she's been kind of weird around me ever since we kissed behind the bleachers that one time, but I hope she'll say yes.~~

Finish watching every episode of *Star Trek*. I don't know if they have *Star Trek* in the Sing, so I better do it now while I have the chance.

~~Eat sushi.~~

~~Sit at the cool kids' table.~~

Wear that awesome old dress I got at Goodwill to the Last Dance.

Learn to speak French. Mom says that in the Sing there aren't going to be any languages, everyone just thinks at each other all the time. I don't care if it's not useful. I want to learn it anyway.

Help out at a homeless shelter (I don't *really* want to do this, but it feels like something I should say).

~~Learn to ride a skateboard.~~

Take a trip out to the Coast. We were supposed to do that last month, but when Mom started going over the travel plans she just wouldn't stop crying, and Dad said no trips anymore. I bet I can get Aunt Alice to take me.

~~Break a bone. (Just a little one, to see how it feels.)~~

Get retweeted by a famous person.

~~Tell Sandra how much I hate her stupid face for standing me up.~~

Go to see the servers where they're transmitting all of us into the Sing. I heard they're like these big needles with bulbs on the end of them, and they roast your body to cinders and beam your mind onto these satellites or something. Dad says this one's impossible because there's so much security around the servers. I guess I'll see them soon enough.

Read *Moby Dick* even though it's probably really boring.

~~See a bald eagle.~~

Write a novel. Although it might have to be a short story now.

Go camping, even if it's only in the backyard. Mom says you can recreate this kind of stuff in the Sing, but I know it can't be the same.

~~Tell Grandma I love her (and mean it).~~

Make up with Sandra and tell her I hope I see her in the Sing.

Get to the highest level on Candy Crush.

~~Take my cat for a walk.~~

~~Paint my fingernails ten different colors.~~

Skype with someone on another continent. Dad thinks this one is silly, because the Sing is kind of like a giant Skype with everyone in the world on it, but I want to do it now. I don't think I'm going to care about the things on this list so much when I get to the Sing. I don't think any of us will.

Fly a kite.

Take my roller blades out of the closet and skate around and around the reservoir, no matter how much it hurts, until the sun goes down.

Go one whole day without being scared of anything.

Forgive Sandra for not loving me back.

~

Erica L. Satifka's fiction has appeared in *Lady Churchill's Rosebud Wristlet, Shimmer, Daily Science Fiction,* and *Clarkesworld.* When not writing, she works as a freelance editor and teaches classes on SF/F writing at Portland Community College. She identifies as a bisexual woman and lives in beautiful Portland, Oregon with her genderqueer spouse Rob and three needy cats. Follow her on Twitter @ericasatifka or visit her website at ericasatifka.com.

Deep/Dark Space

Gabrielle Friesen

In space, there should never be the baying of a dog.

She was sure she'd heard it, no matter what the other crew said. A deep barking bouncing off the hull of the ship, so deep it rattled her gold premolar straight out of her jaw. She held the burning tooth in her hand now, as she peered out a starboard window.

The stars were gone. Not a single pinprick. The barking continued.

Pressing against the window, she strained her eyes, praying under her breath, clutching her tooth like a rosary.

There was a dog, the outline of a black dog in the dark of space. It was a deeper darkness than everything surrounding it. The void of space looked almost bright in contrast, spots of color bleeding at the edges of her vision. The great black dog turned its head to her, a massive thing even at a great distance.

Its eyes were dying suns, its mouth a black hole.

She could only manage to blink, and the absence of the dog burned a vivid corona on the backs of her eyelids.

It opened its mouth to howl, and she could just see the missing stars frozen in the beast's event horizon of a throat, swallowed up. Its mouth was the size of the earth's curve, last seen months ago by the crew.

She dropped her tooth, a single star on the gleaming white floor of the ship.

The dog bounded towards her. Its mouth was open, and there was no more light.

~

Gabrielle Friesen's favorite monsters are Scylla and Charybdis, with the alien from *Alien* as a close runner-up. Her work has been featured in *Hello Horror*, *Devilfish Review*, *Theme of Absence*, and *The First Line*, as well as in 18thWall's anthology *Those Who Live Long Forgotten*. She definitely does not believe in Bigfoot, but will talk about it for hours if prompted (and oftentimes when not prompted as well). You can follow her on Twitter @GaelleFriesen.

A Brief History of Whaling with Remarks Upon Ancient Practices

Gabby Reed

It is my absolute pleasure to welcome you to the Bakunawan Whaling Fleet. You now find yourself engaged in an endeavor whose pursuit has spanned the lifetime of humanity, has swallowed whole our lives and bodies from time immemorial, and that has possessed us to our very souls. You stand at the head of a history half-scientific, half-savage. Your hands will taste blood as your hearts know true elation. You will find that the whale is as necessary as the shore. Without rocks to dash itself upon, the water is never a sea, nor is outer space a cosmos. Without a leviathan we are never sailors.

Whales can be divided into three categories: oceanic, interplanetary, and interstellar. The existence of intergalactic whales has been theorized, but up to this date never confirmed. Among these, only the oceanic whales are cetaceans; the remaining two categories, making up the majority of known whale species, fall variously into the orders *Astrozoa* and *Dictyotales*, and more generally to the phylum and class *Mollusca Aplacophora*.

And there we have an end to my knowledge of taxonomy! I can offer no ideas as to the significance of these classifications, except to emphasize that the beasts of the heavens are vastly divorced from the creatures of the Earth. So much so that one feels compelled to ask why they are both termed *whales*. To my unscientific mind, the variations between and among whale species merit three classifications at a minimum, upwards of ten more liberally. My mistake, you'll note, is in seeking pure logic in the never-ending human endeavor to give a name to all the flora and fauna of the universe. In names there is found whimsy and poetry enough to betray the human heart. Consider the tasseled wobbegong or the strange-tailed tyrant. The monkeyface prickleback and the velvetbelly shark. Say to yourself katydid, bumblebee, and ladybird. And then, letting it push apart your lips, pronounce the name of the *whale*.

Sabrina de la Fuente is credited with the first discovery of an interplanetary whale, a coma whale, in 2259. The creatures had been previously observed, but were not thought alive. The coma whale, it's commonly known, traverses a regular route through solar systems, returning at constant intervals to its home gravity well in order to spawn. Coma whales spawning in the well of the Earth's sun were often spotted in ancient skies, where observers fancifully imagined their jettisoned excreta to be tails. For a dozen centuries or more we crouched below these beasts. Seeing them, sometimes even with our bare eyes, but with no real notion of them. It was not until de la Fuente, observing a particular whale (designated *Swift-Tuttle*) on a near-Earth approach, mistakenly switched on a cognitive discriminator and detected a positive reading: that indelible fingerprint of life.

Can we, looking back from our lofty present, possibly conjure the awe of that moment? In a spare second a life was discovered. And such a life! A presence so titanic and for so long invisible. As if discovering that, all this time, the mountains were alive. Peering into the rushing Arve and seeing within it the slow-blinking, dreadful eye of Mont Blanc. Is it any wonder what she named such an animal?

A whale is a whale; not by virtue of its physiology but as a result of its profundity.

Where there were found whales, there was endeavored whaling. Oh, to have been among the crazed crews who first cracked the charred skin of the coma whale! For a pair of eyes below that sky to see the dissected bodies of the beasts as they were towed, and then fell, and then broke against the Earth's very roof and blazed across the savage horizon, alight as angel feathers rent from heaven. To bear witness as the crab-clawed mechanical engines dug their pincers beneath the crust of the coma. As they levered it apart to let spill the sulfur-sweet meat of the thing. To feel the world turn anew.

Cetacean whales were a largely homogenous lot in comparison to their celestial siblings. Uniformly sea-going vertebrate mammals possessing of fins, spouts, and tails, they registered between a 3 and a 10 on the Kei scale of sentience. The organized slaughter of such creatures was as reckless and desperate an endeavor as any interstellar pursuit. Sea-sailors cast themselves out upon frail, bare-timber boats, lashed themselves to the whale, and endeavored to prick at the beast with hairpin harpoons. To prick, and prick him again, to scratch the behemoth to its death. Man after man was flung, crushed, or drowned to his own end in such pursuits. All to scrape the whale of its blubber and abandon the bulk of the carcass to the open water.

Primitive it sounds, and primitive it was: gory decks above the waves and flayed remains sinking below. Consider, though, the ends. The sperm whale slain off the coast of Japan served to banish the night from Kent to Kentucky. Humanity, huddled in spheres of oil lamplight, put their backs to the darkness and feared not. For this security, for this power, the ancient sailors strove. And so too do we strive. So too do we turn, for the sake and the thanks of the interstellar pitch whale whose rich inner liquors light our long trails through the dark.

A century elapsed between the first sighting of a pitch whale and its first capture. It was spotted by that loyal ancient mariner, the *Voyager 1*. Its dense center appeared as black on black, and its hundred filmy filaments as if a spider web caught on *Voyager*'s lens. A spectral vision, a deep-space phantom. Even then, with nothing but this shadow in the dark to its person, even then it was pronounced: a whale.

It is the pitch that you now seek, the pitch that will be your great infatuation and your intimate foe. Know that it is worthy of your obsession. In the vast emptiness it opens its great maw and sifts dark matter for light from suns so distant that they seem merely stars. Its tendrils, at their thinnest as dainty as a human wrist, reach from its center like florets from a dandelion. Among them crackles a web of exquisite power. At their center is the colossal body, the sieve-self. It is the abattoir of the neutrino. Planet-large and ever-expanding with age, the pitch whale wanders the between spaces alone. No kin has been found, no predators, prey, nor peers. It is an ecosystem unto itself. A shadow passing through the night with a beating heart the size of Olympus Mons.

What is the greatest of us to such a thing? What matters our intellect, our desire? Who are we that we should lash ourselves to such a body and prick at its fantastic hide? Where is it allowed that we may dare to extinguish the pitch whale's fire, part its delicate coils, and penetrate into the treasure of its body? We are whalers, I tell you. I declare it here. I allow it. I join my voice to Jonah's. And you, now. You must declare it. You must sail out and seek the whale.

~

Gabby Reed is a queer, bisexual, Filipin@-American writer who hails variously from Cavite, Philadelphia, Seattle, Milwaukee, and Madison, Wisconsin. Her fiction has appeared in *Paren-thesis* from Comma Press, her poetry is Rhysling-nominated, and she's scripted a story in the upcoming *Beyond* anthology of queer science fiction and fantasy comics. Gabby's focus are the things that obsess her: the vast, the minuscule, meetings between the divine and the mundane, diaspora, post-colonial narratives, and queerness throughout history. And whales, obviously. Gabby really likes whales.

NOTHING GOES TO WASTE

SHANNON PEAVEY

I am being abducted in slow-motion.

They're careful and cautious. Nothing changes but this: a feeling I'm no longer the person I once was. Something else has crept in and made itself at home in my skin and it was too quiet, too gradual for me to notice the difference. But things are difficult now that weren't before. I can't trust myself.

They abduct me piece-by-piece. Overnight, they take my left arm and leave me with this dead strange thing, a lump of flesh attached to my shoulder that looks like my arm and moves like my arm but isn't, isn't it at all. Might as well be a cat's paw or a carburetor. An alien thing.

It's one of those Theseus's ship questions. Is that boat the same vessel, after such a careful restoration? I don't think so, no.

• • •

A normal alien abduction goes something like this. A sad woman in a flyover state is called from her bed by a mysterious force. She goes to stand outside, peering up at the heavens—and what a light! She's beamed up to the mothership in a haze of glory like Christ ascending into heaven. Then, a set of scrawny grey men with big heads and long fingers strap her down and perform strange and sexually charged tests on her before sending her back to her bed with nary a scratch. Maybe they forget to button her pajamas correctly, ha ha. Those aliens, what characters. Mystified by our strange Earth garments.

• • •

The doctor's thirty minutes late, and I'm sitting in a jungle-green waiting room alongside a tower of pamphlets on genital herpes. At some point, the nurse calls me back to a small white room and takes my vitals, my temperature and all that. She tells me I have very good blood pressure.

I wait ten minutes more for the doctor, staring at a poster of an ear. How the inner parts twist into the skull in a tight snailshell curl.

Then footsteps click down the hall, slowing to a stop in front of my door. I fold my hands in my lap and think about how sound travels, each of those footsteps tap-tapping past my stirrup bone and my cochlea and down into my brain, telling me: *Careful, now. Don't look crazy.*

The doctor's a pretty woman with green-rimmed bifocals who knocks and then enters without waiting for an answer. She introduces herself and sits across from me; she asks me what's the problem. She listens attentively, though it's a little ruined by the way she jogs her knee and squints through her glasses.

I tell her my symptoms. I show her my dead arm and foot and my three dead fingers. They feel rusty, like they'll crumble into bits when she touches them.

The doctor squints again. Finally she says, "You might need to take more B vitamins."

"Okay," I say.

She gives me a pair of surveys to fill out. The first question says merely: SADNESS. 0, I do not feel sad. 1, I feel sad much of the time. 2, I am sad all of the time. 3, I am so sad or unhappy I can't stand it.

I look up at her, pen in my hand. She won't meet my eyes.

• • •

People who are prone to dark circles under their eyes have unusually delicate, thin skin there. I think the aliens must love that—to come down, scalpel away those triangles of gossamer tissue, and stitch them all together to make the most beautiful art projects. Tapestries and tiny human dolls, so small and fragile that when they're held up to the light, the light shines right through them.

It's not so bad. You see? They take these things for a reason, even if we don't understand it. And at least you know—some part of you, even just that small part, was wanted.

• • •

I want to feel called. I want to understand why this is happening to me. I'll stand in a field at night with my arms held up, saying *take me to your leader.* Please, you can do all the tests you want. Just make it stop, give me my life back.

I hang my elbows out the apartment window at three in the morning and look for lights in the sky. Fireballs, maybe, lit discs or darting spheres—but there's only streetlamps and a flicker of neon at the twenty-four hour laundromat.

So I take my B vitamins. The next night, they abduct the right side of my skull. It gives me a strange buzz in that ear, or a sudden deafness if I turn my head too quickly.

• • •

"You're looking great," my roommate says. "Have you lost weight or something?"

I shrug and say, "Yeah, I guess," because it's too much effort to explain. My roommate is the kind of person who likes to be helpful, which is lovely. She would say, well, my friend's sister in Arkansas has fibromyalgia and she cured herself by drinking herbal teas and thinking about the cosmic balance of the universe.

Instead, she says, "Will you get more paper towels when you're out today? The cat puked in the kitchen again and I had to use, like, the whole roll to clean it up."

I say I will and then go take a nap instead. I lie in bed, looking at the ceiling and I say, "Hurry up," because if they're going to take me I'm ready to go. And I only wonder: What will I find on the mothership? Will I be reunited with all my missing parts, or have they been used for some other purpose? Maybe I'll wake up and the first face I see opposite me will be my own, the face I used to wear before they made me a stranger.

Sometimes I think that's all I'll find there. A hundred versions of me—a hundred stitched-up, beautiful dolls. We'll wander the decks all together, touching each other's faces and wondering: Did this part come from me? Was this mine? Was this?

~

Shannon Peavey is a native of Seattle, Washington. When not writing, she works as a horse trainer and battles rain, mud, and horse-eating plastic bags on a near-daily basis. A graduate of the Clarion West writer's workshop, her fiction has also appeared in *Apex*, *Writers of the Future*, and *The Masters Review*. Find her online at shannonpeavey.com, or on Twitter @shannonpv.

In the Dawns Between Hours

Sarah Pinsker

Tess's first kiss with another woman takes place behind the roller rink in Oak Ridge. She's twenty years old and the kiss sets her heart beating swing time, which never happened with her boyfriend Louie back home. There's no place safe for a kiss like that in 1943, so the only thing she can think of is another time. She starts working on her theory of time travel the next day.

The equations take her ten years; building the machine another two. She's worked out the mathematics for one date, in 2015. Sixty years in the future, one-way. Things have to be better then.

• • •

She's about to step into the machine, that irreversible step, when there's a knock at the front door.

"June got beaten up," says Alice, barging past her. "Again."

Tess looks at June, and June shrugs and steps inside. Tess follows them into her kitchen, where Alice helps herself to a rag from the drawer and runs it under the faucet. Alice is a pint-sized fury, but Tess can't tell if she's mad at June or whoever gave the beating. June's white shirt is stained with blood. Her nose has a new hitch, and both eyes are swelling shut.

"Who did it?" Tess asks. June's been knocked around by other butches before for dancing with their girls, but this looks worse.

"A cop. He said if I could pretend to be a man, I could take a punch like a man."

Alice cleans June up, and Tess gives her a steak to put on her eyes. She had planned on leaving without telling anyone, but now that doesn't seem right.

People would worry. She shows June and Alice the machine.

"Come with me," she says. "In sixty years things have got to be better."

June shakes her head. "Unless they're worse."

"What could be worse?" Tess asks, but that's a silly question. It could always be worse.

Still, the more she thinks about it, the more it makes sense to bring some other people along. She's got time. She hangs around, trying to sell other friends on the idea. Interesting things are happening. Del and Phyllis start the Daughters of Bilitis. Tess is one of the first to join.

"Come with me," she says, sitting around with the other members, but everyone is either skeptical or scared.

"You're scared here, too," Tess points out, but they all prefer the dangers they know to the dangers they don't.

She shows the machine to every woman she brings home; they all change the subject, and she lets them, because there are other ways to transcend time. She haunts the bars, offering a one-way trip to the future. Does the same when they're all squeezed onto the benches of a police van after getting picked up for dancing.

"Fuck that," says a tall Negro drag queen, Dulcinea, spitting out a tooth. She'd swung at a cop. "Stay here and fight."

It's hard to argue with that. She doesn't mean to stay, but she does. They call her Time Machine Tess. She tells herself if she could just find one more person to save, she'd go. One more person, one more couple. Plus the more of the past she lives through, the more she'll know about the future she'll be arriving in when she finally gets there. She'd been rushing into things; better to take her time, make investments.

She's there for the first D.O.B. conference. Still there when the Tay-Bush is raided. There when the first calls for civil rights are made.

"Who would have imagined?" Alice asks on the phone. She and June had moved to New York together in 1967.

Tess is in San Francisco still when the Stonewall riots go down, but Alice calls to tell her what happened. She spends her days at the university, her nights plotting revolution. She helps organize San Francisco's first Gay Pride march. When she finally leaves, she wants to arrive in a better time. It makes sense to put in some of the work.

She volunteers on the campaign of a young gay politician. A gay politician! He doesn't do well, but it's heartening just the same. When he finally wins in 1977, she celebrates with the rest of the Castro.

They still call her Time Machine Tess, but most people don't remember why. It's only after Harvey Milk is killed that she realizes she never even offered him the chance to leave with her. She knows he wouldn't have taken it.

She thinks now maybe she'll go; she's seen enough, she's done enough, but there are protests to be organized. A national march, in Washington. And then her friends start dying, and she can't leave them.

"About that time machine?" asks Dulcinea when Tess visits her in the hospice. "Do you think there's a cure in 2015?"

This is it, Tess thinks, we're going, but Dulcinea doesn't make it to her house.

She breaks, again and again. By the time she's made the last funeral arrangement, she doesn't believe in a better time anymore. She thinks she's made a difference, maybe. She leaves a note explaining how to use the machine in case anyone wants to join her, and she steps through.

• • •

Alice is waiting for her, in a chair by the window. It's very definitely Alice, an ancient Alice, thirty years' worth of lines etched in her face.

"I took the long way," Alice says, "but I figured you could use a welcome wagon."

"June?" Tess looks around.

"She passed two years ago. Not before we got married, though."

It's barely even a word in Tess's vocabulary. "Married."

Alice smiles. "You have no idea."

Tess helps her friend to her feet. Alice links an arm through hers, and together they step outside to see what's changed.

~

Sarah Pinsker is the author of the novelette "In Joy, Knowing the Abyss Behind," winner of the 2014 Sturgeon Award and 2013 Nebula Award finalist, and 2014 Nebula finalist, "A Stretch of Highway Two Lanes Wide." Her fiction has appeared in *Asimov's*, *Strange Horizons*, *Fantasy & Science Fiction*, and *Lightspeed*, and in anthologies including *Long Hidden*, *Fierce Family*, and *The Future Embodied*. She is also a singer/songwriter and has toured nationally behind three albums; a fourth is forthcoming. In the best of all timelines, she lives with her wife and dog in Baltimore, Maryland. She can be found online at sarahpinsker.com and on Twitter @sarahpinsker.

INCREASING POLICE VISIBILITY

BOGI TAKÁCS

Manned detector gates will be installed at border crossings, including Ferihegy Airport, and at major pedestrian thoroughfares in Budapest. No illegally present extraterrestrial will evade detection, government spokesperson Júlia Berenyi claimed at today's press conference ...

• • •

Kari scribbles wildly in a pocket notebook. How to explain? It's impossible to explain anything to government bureaucrats, let alone science.

Kari writes:

To describe a measurement—

Sensitivity: True positives / Positives = True positives / (True positives + False negatives)

Specificity: True negatives / Negatives = True negatives / (False positives + True negatives)

Kari decides even this is too complicated, tears out the page, starts over.

To describe a measurement—

• • •

Janó grits his teeth, fingers the pistol in its holster. The man in front of him is on the verge of tears, but who knows when suffering will turn into assault, without another outlet.

"I have to charge you with the use of forged documents," Janó says.

"How many times do I have to say? I'm. Not. An. Alien," the man yells and raises his hands, more in desperation than in preparation to attack.

"Assault on police officers in the line of duty carries an additional penalty," Janó says.

The man breaks down crying.

• • •

Kari paces the small office, practices the presentation. *They will not understand because they don't want to understand,* e thinks. Out loud, e says:

"To describe any kind of measurement, statisticians have devised two metrics we're going to use. Sensitivity shows us how good the measurement is at finding true positives. In this situation, a person identified as an E.T. who is genuinely an E.T."

The term *E.T.* still makes em think of the Spielberg movie from eir childhood. E sighs and goes on. "Whereas specificity shows us how good the measurement is at finding true negatives." How much repetition is too much? "Here, a person identified as an Earth human who's really an Earth human."

The whole thing is just about keeping the police busy and visible. Elections are coming next year, Kari thinks. *Right-wing voters eat up this authoritarian nonsense.*

"So if we know the values of sensitivity and specificity, and know how frequent are E.T.s in our population, we can calculate a lot. We can determine how likely it is for a person who was detected at a gate to be a real extraterrestrial."

Alien is a slur, e reminds emself.

Eir officemate comes in, banging the door open. He glances at eir slide and yells. "Are they still nagging you with that alien crap?"

• • •

The young, curly-haired woman is wearing an ankle-length skirt and glaring down at Janó—she must be at least twenty centimeters taller than him, he estimates. She is the seventh person that day who objects to a full-body scan.

"This goes against my religious observance," she says, nodding and grimacing. "I request a pat-down by a female officer." She sounds practiced at this.

Janó sighs. "A pat-down cannot detect whether you are truly an extraterrestrial."

"I will sue you!"

"Sue the state, you're welcome," he groans and pushes her through, disgusted with himself all the while.

• • •

Kari is giving the presentation to a roomful of government bureaucrats. E's trying to put on a magician's airs. *Pull the rabbit out of the hat with a flourish.*

"So let's see! No measurement is perfect. How good do you think your gates are at detecting E.T.s? Ninety percent? Ninety-five percent? You know what, let's make it ninety-nine percent just for the sake of our argument." *They would probably be happy with eighty*, e thinks.

E scribbles on the whiteboard—they couldn't get the office smartboard working, nor the projector. Eir marker squeaks.

SENSITIVITY = 99%

SPECIFICITY = 99%

"And now, how many people are actually E.T.s in disguise? Let's say half percent." *That's probably a huge overestimate still*, e thinks.

"So for a person who tests as an E.T., the probability that they truly are an E.T. can be calculated with Bayes' theorem …" E fills the whiteboard with eir energetic scrawl.

E pauses once finished. The calculations are relatively easy to follow, but e hopes even those who did not pay attention can interpret the result.

Someone in the back hisses, bites back a curse. Some people whisper.

"Yes, it's around thirty-three percent," Kari says. "In this scenario, two-thirds of people who test as E.T.s will be Earth humans. And this gets even worse the rarer the E.T.s are."

And the worse your sensitivity and specificity, e thinks but doesn't add. E isn't here to slam the detection gate technology. "This, by the way, is why general-population terrorist screenings after 9/11 were such abysmal failures." Americans are a safe target here; the current crop of apparatchiks is pro-Russian.

This is math. There is nothing to argue with here. Some of the men still try.

Kari spends over an hour on discussion, eir perkiness already worn off by the half-hour mark.

"We can't just stop the program," a middle-aged man finally says. "It increases police visibility in the community."

Kari wishes e could just walk out on them, but what would that accomplish?

• • •

"I had a horrible day," Kari and Janó say simultaneously, staring at each other: their rumpled, red-eyed, rattled selves.

"I hate myself," Janó says.

"I'm useless," Kari says.

Then they hug. Then they kiss.

Below their second-story window, on Klauzál Square, an extraterrestrial materializes out of thin air, dodging the gates.

• • •

Endnotes:

For those interested in the actual calculations, the Bayes' Theorem page on Wikipedia demonstrates them with the numbers used in the story, in the context of drug testing.

I first heard the terrorism comparison from Prof. Floyd Webster Rudmin at the University of Tromsø, Norway.

~

Bogi Takács is a neutrally gendered Hungarian Jewish person who's recently moved to the US. Eir speculative fiction and poetry has been published in venues like *Strange Horizons*, *Apex*, *Scigentasy*, and *GigaNotoSaurus*, among others. You can visit eir website, prezzey.net, or find em on Twitter as @bogiperson, where e also posts diverse story and poem recommendations five times a week.

Letter From an Artist to a Thousand Future Versions of Her Wife

JY Yang

My dearest Anatolia:

Before you left this world, you asked me to celebrate the dissolution of your body. And I have. Are you proud of me? It has been seventy-two days since you left Earth. Fifteen since we were told the ansibles don't work. Fifteen days to mourn broken promises. Fifteen days to realize that without instantaneous transmissions across the gulfs of space, your voice and mind are lost to me forever. You are not dead, my dearest, but it feels like you are. I have held ceremonies and read poetry and lit candles with friends and family. Your belongings we gave to the needy, your flesh we fed to lions and eagles. Tomorrow, I distribute your bones.

I have been putting this off, but people keep asking, and I am the last of the ship-folk's kin not to have held a bone-wishing ceremony. So I must. There'll be a luncheon at the old church where took our vows, attended by all our family and friends, and I'll give your bones away. You didn't leave a list of who gets what, so I've made one up.

But my ceremony won't be like the other bone-wishings, grim and dreary and spartan. I have been to those and they left a bad taste in my mouth, like ashes and charcoal. I refuse to give your bones away in little boxes, for them to sit on shelves and gather dust. What a terrible waste that would be.

So I've taken your bones, my love, and made them functional and beautiful. I've strung them up and wrapped them in velvet and platinum and precious stones. They served you well in this lifetime and they will continue to serve your loved ones well. I have made spoons of your scapulas and a dinner bowl from your skull; I have threaded your teeth into a bracelet for your youngest grand-niece.

Your vertebra, strung with pearls, will make a fine necklace for your sister, so she can carry the weight of your bones around her neck. Your ribcage, adorned with lace and sequins, shall grace the lobby of the institution, so that all the scientists passing by will never forget their founder.

If I could imagine you reading this, I'd imagine you laughing and saying something like "This is why I married an artist," in whatever passes for laughing and speaking in your version of existence. But I'll never know the truth.

I'm not good at math, never was, so your sister explained how this letter will work. I hope I've got this right: Radio transmissions travel at the speed of light. But your ship is headed to the edge of our galaxy in jumps a thousand light-years apart. Your first stop will be in the vicinity of Delta Orionis, and it'll take my letter a thousand years to get there. But that's okay, because each stop will be a little more than a thousand years long, because the hydrogen fuel takes that much time to gather, because you ship-folk can afford to wait, immortal as you are in a bunch of ones and zeros created out of brain patterns. Then your ship will jump another thousand light-years, while my letter continues outwards at the mere speed of light. We'll be leapfrogging our way across the universe: Ship, letter, ship, letter, ship. Over and over again.

So this could be the first time you're listening to this. Or the seventieth. Or the thousandth, far past the edge of the Milky Way.

I feel like I should be writing to a thousand different Anatolias, all the Anatolias of the future, but I don't know any of them. I don't know what wonders the universe will peel back before you, and how that new awe will change you. By the time you've gotten this I'd have been dead for hundreds of years. And it's only the beginning. At a hundred thousand years I will have been nothing but a tiny blip, an organic aberration in the long path of your life. I've remained flesh-bound and heavy while you sprint light through the heavens, having shed your blood and bones.

How much does the iron in your blood and the calcium in your bones remember of the heart of the star in which they were born? And if they can forget that terrible, magnificent heat and light, what hope do I have of being more than an unremarkable footnote to you?

I've been thinking of that beach in Seattle, the place where we first made love on the soft sand, the waves murmuring at our feet as pleasure took us, over and over again. In my memory I held your sweat-glazed body and kissed it while you pointed to the glittering night sky and talked about the birth and life and death of stars over scales of time I couldn't grasp. You talked about how our galaxy would merge with the Andromeda in a hundred billion years, described in glowing terms the spectacular light show that those around to witness it would see.

A hundred billion years. I could not even imagine what the planet would look like in one of those billions. What humanity's children would look like. All I saw were strange, distant flickers in the sky.

At that moment I knew that I would lose you, long before the idea of mindships were proposed, long before you tried convincing me that ansible technology would keep us in contact in jump-space, long before the ashen-faced project director told the auditorium full of relatives, "We can still track their progress, but send/receive is not working." Way back then, on the beach, I already knew you would one day slip from my grasp.

After all, you were the brilliant professor with her gaze forever tilted to the heavens, and I was only the silly little girl with her feet anchored to the sand.

Science is about taking risks, you once said. So is love, I countered.

I have saved your right femur for myself. It's not that I treasure it more than the two hundred and five other bones you left behind. But I looked at it and I saw a flute, thin and hollow and metal tipped, and where I saw flute I saw endless potential. A way, my love, that the remnants of your earthbound existence can bring me joy. Your grand-nieces, in your family's grand tradition of being brighter than suns, are building their own radio-transmitter to send messages to big Aunt Anatolia. When it is done, we will bring it to that Seattle beach, together with the flute I have made your bones. And there I shall play. I shall send your boneflute song soaring over the bowl of the sky, out to the edge of the Milky Way, where in a hundred thousand years it will whistle past you, gentle as a butterfly's whisper over a forest.

~

JY Yang is a lapsed scientist, a former journalist, and a short story writer. She lives in Singapore, in a bubble populated by her imagination and an indeterminate number of succulent plants named Lars. A graduate of the 2013 class of Clarion West, her fiction has appeared or is forthcoming in *Clarkesworld*, *Strange Horizons*, and *Apex*, among others. A list of her publications can be found at misshallelujah.net, and she can be found on Twitter as @halleluyang, grumbling about Scandinavian languages and making displeased noises about the state of the world.

BLACK HOLES

RJ EDWARDS

Art by Elizabeth Leggett

You have butterflies on your skin, welcoming me in.

"What do you think it would feel like to die in a black hole?" Joey asked, then immediately added, "Not being morbid."

Kant laughed. He had a loud belly laugh that made the bare bedroom feel full and bright. The mattress they were lying on had no bed frame, and, at the moment, no sheets. The only set not being used as makeshift curtains were drying in the basement. The only decorations on the walls were a handful of postcards. One was from Joey, one was from a high school friend living in Argentina, and two were from no one at all. Kant bought them himself, because he liked them.

Joey turned zer head to give Kant a wildly serious glare. When his laughs subsided, Kant said, "It probably feels like dying."

Joey sat up. "But what kind of dying? You know—maybe it would crush you, or maybe you would suffocate."

"Jo! This *is* morbid." Kant said.

"What if it didn't kill you?" Joey went on. "When I was a kid, I thought black holes just brought you to other places. New worlds. That's what they did in TV. Or maybe the worlds that pass through them change."

Joey was too embarrassed to tell Kant why ze had a sudden morbid interest in black holes. Kant always seemed completely open to telling Joey any strange, spiritual or superstitious thought that ran through his head. He told his roommate those things, too. He talked about them with people he bummed cigarettes from at the bus stop, if it was the right sort of day. Joey was still practically a stranger when Kant opened up to zer about his kinks.

• • •

They had met by chance three times—first, they were introduced to each other by a mutual friend at a birthday party. Then they sat together at the transmasculine spectrum support group that neither of them ever attended again. After running into each other at the Eric Carle picture book art museum, they decided to make a real intentional appointment to spend time together. They met up one week later in a cafe called the Purple Kitty for brunch.

"Is it a latex thing?" Joey asked.

"No, it's not latex, and it's not just balloons," Kant replied, digging the side of his fork into his eggs benedict. They had a crab cake in the middle instead of a slice of ham, and the menu called it Kitty's Seafood Delight. Kant did have a knife, but neglected to use it even once. "It's more specific than that."

"I don't know what you mean." Joey said. Ze worked hard to get good at saying that. It used to be a terrifying thing for zer to admit.

"It's—I think it's the moment that they pop." Kant said, bringing a big gooey forkful to his mouth.

"I hate that noise." Joey said. Ze had finished zer modest plate of single egg over hard and wheat toast, and sat with zer hands folded on zer lap. Ze looked around at all the cat-themed photographs, paintings, clocks, and trinkets littering the walls. There was one blue porcelain kitten with a white tip at the end of its tail on a shelf in the corner of the room, facing the wall.

"It's not the noise," Kant said tentatively, as if he was going to launch into a delicate explanation, but then smiled and shook his head. "I don't think I can explain it. But it just fills me up with heat. People just have those things, you know?"

"Yeah." Joey said.

"Do you?" Kant asked.

"Do I what?"

"Have one of those things?"

• • •

Across the Atlantic Ocean and underground, Jean-Michel Gregory was speaking to Dr. Benedicta Goeppert about the end of the universe. She felt very strongly about the nature of existence being cyclical, that all matter would eventually return to the state that stimulated the beginning of the universe as we know it—long after humans were extinct and our sun was dead, expanding space would shrink until it was conducive to a big bang and everything that ever was would be again in its earliest, most basic form. Gregory wanted to know whether or not it would lead to another planet like ours, with creatures like ours, with he and Dr. Goeppert here, having this conversation again. She told him that this cycle would happen an infinite number of times, and since they were currently proving that this conversation was already a possible outcome, yes, someday, they would have this chat again. Gregory was more indifferent. He told Dr. Goeppert that he felt the same way about the end of the universe that he did about God: he could never know for certain, so venturing guesses felt arrogant.

Dr. Benedicta Goeppert smiled at him with her tight, pained smile that made him regret whatever he had just said. She excused herself, as she had a lot more work to do before she went home. They were actually going *home* soon—they had been working on site at the collider in Switzerland for a few weeks now. She would finally go to her home in Berlin and see her sister and her nephew, and he would go to his home in Lyon and see his wife, Anna, and their two daughters, Nadene and Anne. He was looking forward to it, but he already knew it would very difficult going back. He had fallen in love with Dr. Goeppert during the third day they worked together. That was the day that a miscalculation about the placement of a magnet committed by someone they had never met and would never meet set them nearly a month behind where they thought they would be. Gregory had glanced over at Dr. Goeppert, and could see that she was flushed and trying very hard not to cry from frustration, and at once he felt it all. Her angst, his angst over her angst, a need to keep her safe and close to him, a need to run his fingers through her dark hair, sweat, blood, idealism and dopamine. He loved her, oh, very much.

• • •

You know that I could kiss you forever and ever?

Joey had started writing bad love poems on any spare bit of paper ze found in Kant's apartment. Receipts, grocery lists, junk mail envelopes. Ze put them right back where they were before, and remained unsure if Kant accidentally threw them in the trash until he quoted them back to zer. On top of the polka-dot sheets that had been in the dryer the night before, Joey ran zer hands over Kant's bare shoulder.

"They say hi." Kant said with a tired smile, referring to his tattoo there. "Welcoming committee. Welcome inside, Joey."

He had gotten the ink when he was eighteen, before he started transitioning, and even before he thought about being a boy. It was a very pretty cluster of black, orange and yellow butterflies. Kant only started to get questions about what they meant when he was twenty four, after he started passing as a man and his chest surgery scars had healed. It drew attention any time he wore tank tops or went topless at the beach (or more often, at the little swimming holes he and his friends found while exploring the woods of western Massachusetts). He had once very much liked trying to explain what the tattoo meant. On the rare occasion someone asked, he used to talk about growth, rebirth, and not changing, but becoming something you already are. Now that someone asked pretty much any time it was visible, he just said that it was pretty. He didn't like that people needed a justification for him to put something beautiful on his body.

"Can I stay this time?" Joey asked.

"You can stay as long as you'd like," Kant said. He shifted in the dark and kissed Joey's neck, then across zer shoulder.

"Can I live here?" Joey asked. "I'll live right here, in the bed. I can come in and out of the window. I won't make any noise."

"Jo, what are you talking about?"

"I want to live with you, Kant. I hate going home all the time. I hate being alone in my apartment. It's making me nuts."

"We'll get you a cat," Kant assured zer, and pressed his mouth on zer skin again.

"I'm allergic," Joey said, but Kant's kisses were trailing down onto zer chest. If he heard zer, he pretended he hadn't.

• • •

On July nineteenth, Jean-Michel Gregory was one of the last people to leave. He was unsure if he was even allowed to be alone anywhere inside the thing, but he took advantage of the quiet time in this underground city. The endless walls of metal began to seem less harsh and more majestic as he wandered undisturbed. It must have been past midnight. Everyone lost track of time pretty easily down in the Large Hadron Collider. He lay down on his back. The floor was cold, and he closed his eyes and imagined everything as it would be soon, bright and humming, full of possibility. He flushed with pride just thinking about it, even though he had no role in its inception and only a small role in its construction. He thought about Benedicta, about her tense smile. He hadn't seen her since their end-of-the-world talk. He knew she was probably busy, just as busy as he was, but it still made him nervous. He wasn't sure if he'd see her again after they went home. He wasn't anticipating making love to her on the floor next to part of a particle accelerator, but the thought of never getting to say goodbye filled him with a deep, cold loneliness.

• • •

"Eight, nine …" Kant counted. Joey was lying on zer back, and Kant gently pulled back zer lips to inspect zer teeth. "You know you have a funny wisdom tooth back here?"

"Yesh," Joey mumbled. Kant released zer lips and ze swallowed some saliva. "I know."

"It's almost sideways," Kant said, "Why didn't you get it pulled?"

"Because there's only one," Joey replied. "My dentist didn't think it was a big deal. I like being a mutant."

Kant smiled. "Do you want to get brunch?"

Joey breathed deeply. "Yeah, okay. How late are they open? Can I trim my hair first?"

"Sure, whatever. It's barely eight."

Joey cut zer own hair, so ze was in a state of constant trimming and adjustments. Ze stepped into Kant's bathroom and regarded zer reflection. Zer hair was currently in what ze thought of as a Safe For Work state, meaning that none of it was shaved or dyed, and the asymmetry came off as trendy instead of jarring. Zer summer job had ended a week and a half ago, however, and ze could use a change. Ze pulled open the cabinet behind the mirror and pulled out a pair of scissors. Ze grabbed a handful of wavy brown hair and chopped it off.

When ze closed the cabinet to take a look in the mirror, ze found light dancing in zer peripheral vision. Suddenly disoriented, Joey sat down on the toilet and closed zer eyes. When ze opened them, the phenomenon was still happening. It seemed like the trick of light ze used to experience as a child, when ze could see tiny micro-organisms floating on the surface of zer eyes. These, however, moved much more swiftly, and were distinctly opaque and silver. It was just as likely a new trick of light, but Joey was consumed with anxiety. The complete foreignness of the sensation made zer feel like these were tiny silver slices in the universe; reality seemed punctured and these were fragments of something else leaking out.

Eventually both the phenomena and the anxiety subsided. Still seated, Joey opened the cabinet underneath the sink and pulled out Kant's razor.

"Buzzcuts all around, then." Ze said to zerself.

• • •

He saw her as soon as he walked in. Dr. Benedicta Goeppert was wearing a bright green dress with white buttons down the front. It wasn't the kind of thing he thought she would wear at all, but he was thoroughly charmed. He reminded himself that he didn't actually know her that well, that he was a ridiculous human being with a ridiculous fantasy life. He crossed the floor of well-dressed scientists and engineers sipping wine and stopped just before reaching her. Suddenly self-conscious about how he would greet her, he turned to a nearby table of food and pretended to consider its contents. She approached him and touched his arm, which thrilled him briefly. They talked about what they had done between leaving the collider and this reception. Then she asked a question that surprised him: Have you received any hate mail?

He gave a flustered no and asked if she knew of some enemy he had made. She told him about all the press around the world that the Large Hadron Collider was getting as the first run approached, and that some people thought they might create tiny black holes and effectively destroy the world. He laughed at the suggestion, and asked if she had received anything. She said she had, one letter. She did not laugh.

After some drinks, they wandered out of the ballroom and down one of the halls of the hotel hosting the event. Dr. Goeppert went into a restroom, and asked Gregory to wait for her. He leaned against the wall next to the door and his mind wandered. He thought about his wife, and wondered if Dr. Goeppert was right, if there had been some incarnation of the universe in which he never met Anna and married her. He loved Anna very much, but he thought that if he didn't, tonight would be the night he would make love to Benedicta the first time. In some other incarnation of existence she would come out of the bathroom and kiss him and ask him to stay here in the hotel with her tonight. When they were at the front desk, they would pretend they were married. They would hold hands like newlyweds, and in the morning they would plan to move here to Geneva together. If she was right, if the universe was born and died infinite times, then it had already happened, or it would happen, someday.

This time, she came out of the bathroom, walked straight to him and put her hand in his. She looked up and asked him, using his first name: Jean-Michel, will I ever see you again after tonight?

He told her that she would, of course. They did not kiss this time.

• • •

I love your hips like mine, I love your body and I love my body less alone. Your body draws me into my body, because I know your body so well, and I know it to be beautiful.

When Joey finally emerged from the bathroom, head freshly shorn, Kant jumped.

"Wow," He said, "I was wondering what was taking you so long."

They went back to the Purple Kitty. Joey still had bits of hair scattered all over zer shoulders. They were especially noticeable against the kelly green of zer current t-shirt, the same one ze had worn to Kant's place the evening before. Joey wore brown and black pretty much exclusively until ze dropped out of college.

"Joey," Kant started hesitantly, tracing a line on his cup of coffee with his index finger, "Have you been okay lately?"

"Is this because I shaved my head?" Joey asked.

"Of course not." Kant said. "It just seems like you've been … somewhere else lately."

Joey adjusted zer fork and knife nervously. "I want to move in with you."

"Is that really all?" Kant said. "Because we talked about that, and I thought …"

He trailed off. The first time they had talked about it, it had actually gone alright, but Kant's current roommate, Ariana, was opposed.

"But she doesn't like me." Joey said.

"She likes you. She doesn't want to live with you. Or live with me *and* you. It's different. She wants her space."

"Why don't we move somewhere else?" Joey asked.

"And leave Ariana to pay the rent on her own? Or fill my room with a stranger?"

"Yeah." Joey said with an uncharacteristic firmness.

Kant paused, then said, "No."

His French toast and zer eggs came, and they both ate quietly for a while. Kant reached for the powdered sugar and picked up the conversation again.

"Just give her a while, alright?"

Joey felt a fluttering in zer chest. "September tenth."

"What?"

"Kant, that's all I can do." Zer throat was growing dry and ze felt humiliated.

"That's five days. This is so random," Kant said indignantly.

"It's the … ok, listen." Joey said. Starting by demanding attention that way made zer feel like what ze was going to say was less ridiculous. "That's the day they're turning on the Large Hadron Collider. And I—I don't think the world is going to end, necessarily, but I feel like—there's no way we can know what it's going to do. And what the world is going to be afterwards."

"This is why you've been so weird lately." Kant said in disbelief. "A science experiment in Europe?"

"Don't make it sound stupid." Joey said quietly. "I just—I need to know that I'm—that I'm worth this much to you. That I can spend my days and nights with you even if your roommate will be annoyed, or resentful. That you can deal with something so, so fucking small, because I'm worth it. Before September tenth. Because, yeah, I'm scared."

Kant thought, then said, "I've known Ariana for years."

"Right." Joey said. Ze got up and fiddled with zer wallet.

"Jo, come on. I'm sorry. It's not stupid."

"Prove it." Joey put a ten dollar bill on the table and walked away.

• • •

You have butterflies on your skin, welcoming me in; I can't tell your skin from mine, but that's just fine.

On September tenth, when the LHC was awake and circulating proton beams for the first time underground in Switzerland, Jean-Michel Gregory was in France, tucking his youngest daughter, Anne, into bed. His older girl, Nadene, was also in bed, but sat up typing. An open laptop rested on the white cotton of her nightgown, and she tried in vain to find her father's name mentioned somewhere in news about the collider. Jean-Michel walked up behind his wife, who was standing on the small balcony outside their bedroom, and gently kissed her shoulder. He told her he loved her.

In Germany, Dr. Benedicta Goeppert was talking to her mother on the phone. She told her about the reception in Geneva without mentioning Jean-Michel at all.

And in the United States, in Joey's one-room efficiency apartment, the phone was not ringing. It had not rung. Ze listened to sad songs and looked online for a new job. The sun set and Joey's melancholy soundtrack began to repeat itself. Ze turned it off and started searching for a new world.

~

RJ Edwards is a writer and library wizard. They are the curator of the LGBTQ literature blog Queer Book Club, co-host of the year-round holiday music podcast HARK, and creator of *Riot Nrrd* (riotnrrdcomics.com), a webcomic at the crossroads of geek culture, social justice, and queer romance. RJ currently resides in Vancouver, BC with their partner and their ridiculous cat, Kurt.

RED RUN

AMJ HUDSON

Art by Elizabeth Leggett

Hinahon didn't belong in that hotel.

On that Monday, she should have been at her apartment on East Bradford Street preparing to meet Natalie at a cozy restaurant downtown. It was their two year anniversary, and she was expected in a few hours. But instead of trying on potential outfits for the evening's dinner, she boarded the elevator of the Red Run Hotel, a single overnight suitcase in hand, and jammed the button for the fourth floor with her thumb. The elevator doors slid closed, and the numbers above the door blinked as the elevator ascended. When it stopped, she retrieved a keycard from her pocket and exited. She hesitated right outside the doors, glancing right and then left with a frown. The suitcase in her hand felt heavy, even though there wasn't anything substantial inside, and she readjusted the handle in her hand, gathering the energy needed to force her legs to move.

Taking one trembling step right, Hinahon proceeded. Checking the numbers as she went past, she eventually reached the door of the appointed room, but just to be sure, she reached into her pants pocket for a familiar business card. Sure enough, the same room number was written in black on the upper right of the well-worn cream card. She'd made it.

With clammy hands, she slid the keycard through the door's card reader, and the light on the mechanism blinked from red to green. The door clicked open, and Hinahon turned the knob and pushed open the door.

The room she entered was done in pale pinks and oranges, and the cream-colored comforter on the bed looked plush and soft, reminding her of the handmade paper Natalie kept stocked in seemingly every place she occupied. The sheer curtains shifted in the breeze. The tiny, square window was cracked just enough to let in a tiny stream of humid Georgia air. There was even a vase of flowers, fresh-cut tulips, on a small table near the window, and altogether, the aspects of the room made for a lavish scene.

It wasn't a bad place to die.

Hinahon removed her simple black heels, placing them beside the door. The sunlight filtering in illuminated the whole space, coming in through the curtains, and somehow, the brightness of the room amplified the uncomfortable feeling that had settled throughout Hinahon's entire body. Still, she pressed on, forcing herself to unzip the suitcase. It was too late to stop now, she reminded herself over and over. Inside her case, there was a navy blue dress in a clear garment bag, a plain black purse, and a zipped travel bag. She ignored those items in favor a small, stab-stitched journal tucked into the side pocket of the suitcase.

Leaving the case, she went and sat on the bed, flipping the book open. Almost every page was full of notations, all in her own barely-legible, slanted handwriting. The scale of the notes varied from page to page, and some pages were completely filled with runny black ink while others were done in pencil. Every now and then, she caught a glimpse of writing done in bright red or ugly, faded violet. Some were a horrible, mismatched combination of multiple pen inks and pencil, and in some parts, lines of text were scratched out so thoroughly that there were little trenches in the paper. The organization, Perennial, had offered a data pad to hold all her personal information, since that was the easiest and fastest way to do things, but Hinahon had refused.

Natalie had given her the book for their six-month anniversary, and almost every element of the book bore evidence of her girlfriend's touch, from the pressed violet blossoms embedded in the heavy paper cover to the handmade paper within. Sometimes Natalie ordered her papers from another paper-maker, to save time, but for Hinahon, she had done them herself. She had even sprayed each individual page with her preferred brand of perfume, some celebrity-inspired scent Hinahon couldn't hope to pronounce, and even after all the writing she had done in the past year, the scent of Natalie lingered, heavy and real on each sheet.

Hinahon loved the gift, even if writing in it sometimes made her sick with guilt, and she felt the least she could do was put it to good use before the end.

Now each of the two-hundred some pages was full to the brim with every fact Hinahon could think of about herself. Perennial had sent over a rough list of things to include, and thus, the first few pages were filled with the basics—facts about her family, her schooling, her childhood. From there, the focus was less concrete, more about Hinahon's personal relationships and feelings than the facts. There were anecdotes from her childhood, and stories her parents had told her numerous times. She spent pages and pages talking about Natalie, carefully detailing all the things she loved about her. All the fights they'd ever had. They were all necessary to know, and she had carried the book with her almost everywhere, never knowing when she'd think of something that might be important. Thirty pages, front and back, and she'd forgotten how to be shy. For this to succeed, the book had to be an extension of herself. It had been painful to carry a reminder of what she intended to do, but it was worse to do nothing at all and continue on.

Hinahon flipped through the pages, never pausing long enough to read a complete thought. In truth, she'd never really gone back to reread any part of the book. Each word made her feel raw and embarrassed, and she hated the look of her writing, all the mistakes crossed out in black. In all her other journals, she'd try to keep the journals perfect. She tried to sound deep, tried to make her letters small and uniform. Whenever she made a mistake or complained about something she later thought was trivial, she'd tear the page out. But the rough edge of the paper inside the journal she could never fully remove, the evidence she always screwed up and never had anything interesting to say, always kept her from continuing a journal through to the end. Instead, she'd buy another journal, and the cycle would repeat. Natalie had admitted, four months after gifting the book to Hinahon, that she was a little upset that Hinahon wasn't using the book after all the hard work she'd poured into it. But it had been too beautiful to screw up, and Hinahon still hadn't had anything interesting to say. It had seemed wrong to use such a beautiful gift when she didn't have anything important to put in it.

She sifted through the pages until she heard the click of the door unlocking. Hinahon closed the book, and her eyes turned to the opening door. Ford, their representative, entered wearing a charcoal suit with no tie, and he carried a stocky brown case, though its weight didn't appear to be a burden for him at all. Ford's dark hair was short and neat, and he walked and smiled without a care. He and Hinahon had spoken on the phone a few times, discussing terms and procedures, and it had been clear by his laidback demeanor and their conversations that Ford had been in the game for a while. He had anticipated each of her questions, and Ford always seemed patient when answering her nervous questions.

Leigh, a grey-haired woman, walked through after Ford, her steps slow and careful, and her brown eyes darted about the room as soon as she entered, cataloging each detail. She was a head shorter than Hinahon, but she stood tall and straight. Her gaze became stuck on Hinahon when she first caught sight of her, and Hinahon stared, unable to summon a smile.

"You're here," Leigh blurted out. She flushed and looked embarrassed as soon as the words left her mouth. "I'm sorry. It's just, on the phone …" She let out a frustrated breath. "You sounded like you were reconsidering." Leigh wrung her hands as she spoke, a nervous smile spread across her face.

Hinahon was trembling, so much that it was noticeable in almost every line of her body. She wanted to lie; it would have been easier—probably nicer, too—to deny any of her doubt, but it didn't seem fair to Leigh. "I was," she admitted. "I've never really been great at making decisions." Hinahon smiled, feeling the sudden beginnings of an urge to cry bubble up in her chest. Her fingernails dug into the cover of the book in her hand to anchor herself.

Leigh's mouth opened, the smallest of noises exiting before she closed it again. She swallowed. "But you're here," she said. Hinahon knew what she probably wanted to ask but felt that Leigh was afraid what her answer might be. Ford had relayed a bit about Leigh's background to Hinahon and more importantly, her enthusiasm at the idea of starting over on a-not-quite-blank slate. Wealth couldn't cure old age, and Leigh was a driven woman. One lifetime hadn't afforded her enough opportunities, but this was her chance to start again, in a world that Leigh described as more "progressive" than her own.

"Yeah," Hinahon said. "Yeah, I'm here; I'm still in." Leigh looked even more uncomfortable with that lukewarm answer, and she shifted her stance and pursed her lip. Her eyes darted to Ford as if seeking guidance; however, the man was taking the lamp down off of the bedside table to make room for his case and didn't seem to be paying attention to the women's conversation.

"Are you?" Leigh asked, her eyes tired but not unkind. Her words were patient, but there was an edge of disappointment to them, as if she was waiting for Hinahon to chicken out. Ford had admitted, without much pressing, that close to fifty percent of their clients didn't follow through. Perennial, therefore, refused to touch a client's payment until the full service was rendered. They refunded up to sixty-five percent, depending on the reason for the failed transition.

Hinahon was tempted. She could go home to her apartment, could even go to dinner with Natalie and celebrate the past two years. She could pretend everything was fine. Apparently, she hadn't done such a terrible job. No one suspected anything was seriously wrong with her. She could forget about the Red Run, Leigh, and Ford. Despite everything, Hinahon could leave, but she had the book, and even if she got rid of it, she'd still have *those* mornings, the ones where she felt so sick of herself that she couldn't bear to get out of bed. She'd have those days where she cried over nothing, days where Hinahon'd tell Natalie she was too sick or too busy to see her because she couldn't deal with anyone seeing her. There was no reason for it. No explanation. She had fantastic parents and a close circle of supportive friends. Natalie was far from perfect, but she was wonderful. They were happy together, on Hinahon's really good days. Hinahon had done well in college. Her job at the Customer Service department at the local phone company sucked, but it paid the bills. All and all, there was nothing. But sometimes, that made it feel even worse.

"Hinahon," Leigh said, stepping closer. "It's okay." The tone of Leigh's voice suggested it wasn't okay at all, but Leigh didn't sound angry. It was almost as if she was expecting this outcome. "This is a little crazy to begin with, and you're still really youn—"

Ford butted in: "What's this? You thinking of opting out, Miss Bird?" The man had opened his case, but after hearing their line of conversation, he stopped his set-up process and turned to Hinahon. He still smiled, even though Hinahon might be seconds away from telling them she was too scared, too guilt-ridden to continue.

Swallowing with a grimace, Hinahon tried to calm her breathing and *think*. It occurred to her that Leigh should be pissed at her for doing this, for being indecisive at such a critical point. Leigh had paid, and it was obvious she really wanted her second chance, one she would only get through Hinahon. They had an agreement, and Leigh, from the very beginning, had been very accommodating. She had promised to move in with Natalie, to continue her monthly visits to her parents in South Carolina. Hell, the woman had promised to continue her tutoring gig at one of the local middle schools early each Saturday morning at least for another quarter.

"No," she said, forcing the word out before she could talk herself out of it. Leigh jumped at the volume of the word, and Ford stared, eyes examining her face hard for a few minutes, before he turned back to his case. He began working again.

Leigh stared, too. She still appeared unsettled, but she was no longer wringing her hands. "If you're sure," she said. "This is really what you want?"

"Yeah," Hinahon replied, speaking before Leigh could finish her question. Leigh's eyes narrowed, and she clasped her hands in front of her. She looked as if she wanted to argue, but Hinahon shut her down. When she continued, she tried to sound decisive and confident. "I *want* this." She took a deep breath, fussing with her hair absently. "I mean, I'm not jumping for joy about this or anything. This is way beyond screwed up. But I want it." She took a shuddering breath, feeling a little of the tension leave her body. "I don't want to be like this anymore." Hinahon covered her face with one of her hands, disgusted that she had started to cry, and turned her face away from Leigh.

"You won't be like *anything* anymore," Leigh whispered.

"Why're you trying to talk me out of it?" Hinahon muttered, smearing the tears into her skin in an attempt to wipe them away. "If I back out, you lose everything. Shouldn't you be trying to convince me rather than—"

Leigh took a half-step back. "I'm not going to talk someone into committing suicide!" She shook her head, the gray strands swaying at the movement, and began to wring her hands again. She looked pale, and there were drops of sweat on her face and neck. Hinahon, in turn, scrubbed at her face with her palm. She didn't trust her voice. Hinahon suspected that if she tried to speak at all, she'd probably start to cry for real, and she had promised herself she wouldn't let anyone see that, especially not before she died.

Ford clucked his tongue, interrupting their emotional debate, "We avoid that word."

"What do you call it then?" Leigh asked, frustrated. There were splotches of ugly red coloring her face.

Ford answered, "Consensual body snatching." He sounded serious.

To Hinahon's surprise, Leigh laughed. But it was a short, shocked thing that suggested Leigh didn't find the comment humorous. Still, Ford continued on despite Leigh's reaction, more playful now, "Well, I call it that anyway. Company policy is to call it a 'substitution' or a 'switch,' but those always make me think of the *Parent Trap*."

"What difference does it make what you call it?" Leigh said, hands sweeping her hair up above her ears. She took a deep breath, eyes fluttering closed. "I'm encouraging someone to commit suicide for me. That's what this is."

Ford shrugged, "This was never a very *moral* arrangement, just a consensual one." He was now taking a set of headpieces from inside the case. "Hinahon wants to die. You want a new life. That's it." He turned from his work and smiled at Leigh, his white teeth visible. "It would be best for both of you to stop thinking beyond that. You'll be a lot happier if you do."

"I imagine the money has nothing to do with it either," Leigh said, disgust permeating each word.

Hinahon shuddered and cut in, "Stop. Let's just get on with it. Leigh, we've been talking about this for over a year—"

"We never discussed *why* you were doing this," Leigh said. "I was told I could only ask you in person, and even then, Perennial ... advised against it."

Hinahon wiped at her eyes and patted the dampness from her cheeks. She was exhausted; she wasn't supposed to have to explain this. "What's the point?" she interrupted. "It'll just make you feel shitty about the whole thing, and there's no point." She took a deep, shuddered breath. "Worry about tonight. You'll be having dinner with Natalie at seven-thirty. Please don't ruin this. I mean, how many chances are you going to get to be twenty-seven again?"

The room went silent save for the sound of Ford shifting his machinery.

Finally, Leigh spoke, sounding ashamed, "Y-yes. You're right." She exhaled. Inhaled. Her eyes did not meet Hinahon's.

"Why don't you tell Hinahon what you're going to do for dinner," Ford prompted. "I'm almost ready."

So Leigh laid out the scene. Hinahon would arrive right on time to find Natalie seated, smiling in their favorite booth in the back of the restaurant right under that god-awful neon sunset painting. There'd be a kiss, a slight clasp of hands, fingers soothing Natalie's tired hands. Then they'd sit, side-by-side in the booth, legs touching and hands entwined until the food came. Hinahon would order her usual, the restaurant's specialty soup, a seafood dish that came piled high with fresh cilantro and hot peppers. Natalie would order something new but would take her peppers since Hinahon had always refused to eat them. They'd eat and talk, and because it was their two year anniversary, they'd talk about themselves—Hinahon and Natalie. One happy little unit.

At the end of dinner, Hinahon would give her gift and finally say "yes." She had danced around answering the question of sharing an apartment for a long time, citing one excuse or another. There was no way she could have kept the switch a secret while sharing a living space, and the idea of being in such an intimate arrangement with anyone—even Natalie—made her sick with nervousness. Natalie had seemed put off by Hinahon's reluctance to give a straight answer, but also seemed to understand how important the idea of living together was to Hinahon. Lately, she barely mentioned the notion at all, leaving it up to Hinahon to bring up the subject again. And tonight, she would.

Or rather, Leigh would.

While Leigh described dinner, Ford set up his workstation. The brown case he'd brought in was open on the nightstand, and inside was a mess of wires and lights with tiny, almost illegible labels beneath them. The wires were all coiled around a central mechanical structure—a small silver dome with a slot at the top for a memory disc.

Hinahon never glanced at Ford's case; her attention was fixed on Leigh, on the way she described the night ahead of her. The more Leigh talked, the faster and easier the words came. She looked more at ease, and she wore a small smile now. There was no more trembling, and Leigh's bubbling excitement for her new life made most of the cold dread flee from Hinahon.

"Sounds like it'll be a charming night," Ford said. The man was still smiling. "Are you ready, Hinahon? You're up first." He had removed his suit jacket and had rolled up his sleeves. He was still in high spirits despite the near-meltdowns he'd almost witnessed, and his casual, almost playful attitude made it easier for Hinahon to proceed, to push past any lingering negativity that still existed inside her. She glanced away from Leigh and turned to Ford.

"How do you want me?" Hinahon said.

Ford let out a snort of a laugh before replying. "Lie on the bed—but keep your head close to the edge. The cords they give me are always too damn short." Hinahon did as she was told, and as if entranced, Leigh moved to the other side of the bed, hesitating before sitting at the other edge. She reached forward, her movements sluggish, before resting her hand on Hinahon's shoulder. The headpiece Ford had in hand were not unlike the old style headphones. Instead of speakers, however, flat stems curled outwards, and each stem had a tiny metal pieces attached at the end of one side.

From his pants pocket, Ford retrieved a bottle filled with translucent fluid, and he loaded the syringe neither woman had noticed on the nightstand. Without speaking, Hinahon offered her arm. She didn't need to know what it was. In a little while, it would be Leigh's problem.

"We used to do this without medication," Ford said, massaging the area he intended to inject with calloused fingers. He paused and tilted his head, as if thinking about how to continue. With a brief smile, a flash of almost menacing teeth, he let out a huff and shook his head. "Let's just say things go much smoother with meds," he finally said.

"How long does it last?" Hinahon eyes flickered to Leigh, concerned. There wasn't a large window of time for mistakes.

"If all goes well, she'll make the dinner," Ford soothed.

Hinahon nodded once and turned her head towards Leigh. "Please, don't screw this up," she begged, grabbing Leigh's arm and squeezing with all her might. "I know I'm asking a lot—especially since you're the one paying—but … please. Just stick to what you promised." She stared up at Leigh, her eyes wide and keen, and her nails bit into the old woman's flesh even through the sleeve of her plum-colored jacket.

"I will," Leigh said, patting the young woman's hand. "I don't break my promises." Hinahon stared at her for a few moments before drawing her hand back. Her other hand, which had never stopped clutching her book, stretched out to Leigh.

Hinahon smiled. "It's everything," she said. "Don't know if it'll make sense, but hopefully it'll help, at least a little." She laughed as Leigh took it into her hands, her eyes bright. The drugs had kicked in. "Sorry 'bout the later stuff. I tried to write so you'd understand, but my thoughts were all over the place. I just wanted to get as much down as possible, you know? I couldn't really keep up with my head so it's all very messy. Sorry." Hinahon didn't sound sorry, but Leigh nodded, her smile disappearing and reappearing. The wrinkles on her forehead seemed to multiply, and she squeezed the book in her hand.

Ford spoke, "We're clear to start. Say when, Hinahon."

"Leigh," Hinahon began before pausing. Her eyes closed, and her mouth crinkled with glee. "*Hinahon,*" she amended. "Happy anniversary."

Ford laughed, "That all? I'd hate for her to miss her dinner because you wanted to chit-chat all night." His fingers hovered over the main switch that would start the process of downloading Hinahon's memories onto the disc.

A pink-faced Hinahon nodded and the switch fell. The three were silent as the machine began its work. From what Hinahon understood of the process (which wasn't much), it downloaded from the brain in sections. Sight memories, audio memories, tactile memories. The device downloaded them to a disc to make way for Leigh. Lights flashed on and off, too quick to keep track of. One green light fell steady. Hinahon's body seemed to sink further into the bed, and her eyes ceased moving, glazing over.

She drifted through thoughts of those education films in high school, the ones that went through the signs of depression. One sign, she had always remembered. *Someone who's suicidal might say something like, "I want to sleep forever."* Hinahon had laughed with friends about that one, at the campy actors and overdramatic reading of the line. The actor, a boy around fourteen or so, had worn a red and white striped shirt, and his eyes were downcast. He had clung to his book bag as he admitted to his mom that he was tired. *"I just want to go to sleep and never wake up,"* he had said, his lip trembling. It was so blunt and obvious; Hinahon had never understood.

Another light stopped blinking—then another.

Hinahon knew the feeling at twenty-seven. There was heaviness in her limbs when she went to bed nowadays, and she dreaded closing her eyes sometimes because it seemed like she could never sleep enough to keep her body and her mind satisfied. There was too much to worry about when she was awake. But now, despite the guilt lingering, she felt something like peace settle over her mind. She was aware, in an abstract way, of her breathing—its steady, constant rhythm. The worries that plagued her disappeared into the fog, and Hinahon found herself lulled to sleep by the quiet, by the expanding emptiness.

Eventually, there wasn't enough in her head anymore; she didn't think or feel anything. Instead, she slept, knowing there wasn't anything to worry about. There would be no painful mornings spent wondering if she could find the strength to get up. Finally, it was done.

The last few lights took twenty minutes to calm, and at last, there was a high-pitched mechanical beep that signified the download was done.

Leigh broke the quiet, "She's gone?"

"Not yet," Ford answered. He pressed the release on the memory disc slot at the top of the dome. "I have to destroy the disc first." Leigh nodded and waited for him to do so. Instead, he gestured for her to come to his side of the bed, and he took a second headpiece into hand. "It's best to do this fresh. You understand how this works, right? Same initial procedure—but I upload your disc into her body." He tilted his head in the direction of Hinahon's empty shell as he spoke. "Then, dinner." Leigh nodded more times than necessary, and Ford's amusement seemed to intensify.

"No injections, doctor?"

Ford shook his head, "If I was a doctor, we wouldn't be doing this in a damn hotel." Leigh started but didn't speak. "Now just sit there next to Hinahon and make sure you lean *away* from her. This should go rather quickly." He set the headpiece on Leigh's head, and they went through the same sequence. The lights went solid, and the old woman went still. Then, she pitched sideways, her body falling away from Hinahon, onto the bed. Ford prepared, in blissful silence, for the second phase.

~

AMJ Hudson is a senior undergraduate student at Columbus State University preparing to dive into a creative nonfiction thesis. She won first place at the 2015 Southern Literary Festival for "Motherland," a piece that showcases her interest in dissecting identity and familial ties, and her poetry has been incorporated into the Memory's Cabinets exhibit in the Columbus Museum. She currently works on CSU's literary and arts journal *Arden* as its executive editor and serves as the vice president of the Alpha Kappa Upsilon Chapter of Sigma Tau Delta. She can drink a pot of coffee a day and has a weakness for anything sweet.

CyberFruit Swamp

Raven Kaldera

Don't you hate it when the phone rings right as soon as you've climbed into the shower? I mean, it's like they *know*. Hiss of hot water over your shoulders, your body relaxes, and you've just dumped a handful of shampoo onto your head when they *do* it to you. *Ringggg*, like a demon's screech, and you curse, and try to leap out, and trip on the wet floor, and end up sliding through the filth in the hallway, and hit the phone stand with your shoulder, and grab the thing just before it cracks you in the skull, and scream "What!!" into the receiver. Whereupon a taped voice informs you that you are behind on your insurance payments, and to disregard this notice if you have already sent your payment.

What do you mean that's never happened to you!

Of course it wouldn't have happened to me either, if I hadn't been waiting for Chakti to call. I'd have just let the machine get it otherwise, but I wanted to hear her pretty voice in my ear in realtime. I was pretty sure we had a date, but I'd called her the day before and her roommate said she was out of town with someone named Pito. Never heard of him. "Well, I'm supposed to get together with her tomorrow; do you think she'll be back by then?"

"I have no fucking idea," said her roommate angrily and hung up on me. Not a good omen, O Great Chief. Let's maybe disembowel a couple more to be sure of the intestinal portent. I dialed her beeper and left a message. "Chakti, honey, maybe I made a mistake, but I thought…" Well, it's the next day and I'm sliding around on the floor to get the phone and she still hasn't called back. Okay, sweetie. There are other winktis in the world. Effing Hangouts full. Time to change my plans, definitely.

I finish my shower, dry off and dress to Hunt. The age-old ritual—are you watching, class of Anthro 502? The native shaman clothes themself for the possibility of mate attraction. I have to have a sense of humor about my hobbies, or I'll start taking them seriously, including the rejection part. Which is the road to madness.

I almost wish there was a class of students watching me. I've gotten myself to the point where I like my body, finally, after so many years. Oh, yes, according to the Cynthaians, you're supposed to get to like your body the way it is, part of all their love yourself chickenshit. Well, I hated being a round weak little genfem. I love my flesh now—hard, muscled, drifts of golden hair over my arms and legs that catch the light. I can sit and watch my body hair glisten, and it doesn't matter that my car blew out a hoverjet last week. I can touch my firm pectoral muscle, trace the curving snake tattoo that covers where the lasers carved my tits off, and it doesn't matter that I can't replace the hoverjet till next month and I'll have to ride in to work on the skybus. I can stroke the beard on my chin and cheeks—beards are a great toy to play with and chew on, I've discovered—and it doesn't matter that I still have the huge bill for my surgery and testosterone implants because I've been blowing all my money on APPles. When you're at home with yourself, everything else can be dealt with.

I slide into my pants. Black and malachite green deadleather—meaning it's constructed to be indistinguishable from the real stuff, which is so expensive as to be out of my reach. Hundreds of slashes decorate them, with puffs of green deadsilk. When the fashion tommyhaws started borrowing from Renaissance German mercenaries, I knew that for once I'd been born into the right era. I leave my torso bare, throw on the doublet-cut deadleather jacket with its matching slashes and puffs, my black spacer's boots (Okay, I've never been off the planet, but they look good) and transfer my wallet, credit chips, and Paki blade from my other jacket. I also detach the chain and fasten it around my shoulder, through one of the slashes.

The chain is what's really important. Gold means you're looking for a gen-guy—a genetic male—and silver is for a genfem. Rose gold or copper means a winkti—used to be genguy, now girl—and black iron means a kurami, like me. I used to wear gold and silver chains twined together, even before I Tranzed, but not any more. Gave them away. I just can't seem to trust people who are onlymen or onlywomyn. I mean, they can be nice people, and most of my friends are male or female, as well as most of my ex-lovers, but they just don't get it like a nachtlei does.

We nachtlei—winktis and kuramis and a few nonspecific folk right in the middle—we didn't used to date each other. We were supposed to date gens, to prove we weren't freaks. But it's been fifty years since Dis Sybil was assassinated and the TranzPride movement got underway. Now my chain is copper-and-black twisted, with my antique TranzPride pendant and my nachtlei basket-and-bow charm. Mind you, it's not just about solidarity or politics. If you're both, like me, my head snaps around so fast my neck almost breaks and my

APPle flares up like a magic charm. I used to call myself pansex, but men and womyn, they think you're great at first, and then they get to thinking. Thinking. Wondering what they are in relation to you. Queer. Straight. Husband. Wife. Then they get uncomfortable. So when I fill out the forms for the Net personals now, I check off NQ—Nachtlei Queer. I only sleep with my own kind. It's safer that way.

Time for the final touch. I open the drawer where I keep my precious APPles, all seven of them. "Why don't you just hang them on the wall, you love them so much," my last genguy lover had said nastily. Yeah, yeah, but some things are too blatant even for me. Why seven of them? Different moods, different lovers, different orifices. Besides, since I can't afford the rare transplant surgery to get a natural-flesh cock, why shouldn't I have the next best thing—and have a variety as well? I mean, it's one of the few bennies about Artificial Penile Prosthetics, also known as APPles, CyberCocks, Freudbusters, and some other less flattering terms.

Which one for tonight...hmm. Puck, small and thumb-size, no balls, really an enlarged clit, for virgin assholes. Mjollnir, realistic but small, four inches or so (song cue: Thor had a hammer that was a hand too small!) for slightly larger assholes. Legba, shiny and plum-black, bought on a whim to match a dark-skinned genguy lover. (He wasn't amused.) Coyote, with a special trick, an inlaid vibrator. Wapiti, nested in fur and feathers, masturbation only. Pan, perfect and realistic, about eight thick uncut inches when hard. And finally, Asmodeus. Nine cut inches hard, glinting with gold piercings—the Prince Albert at the tip, three dydoe rings along the back of the head, an ampallang, several jingling hafadas in the scrotum. People have been known to fall to their knees at the first glance at it. They've also been known to run, so if I pack Asmodeus I usually bring another just in case.

I think that'll be that plan tonight. I tuck Pan into the inside pocket of my jacket and undo my codpiece. The base of Asmodeus fits up against my pubic bone, and I find the implanted metal socket among the coarse blond hair, just above my clit. Asmodeus is warm, pulsing, alive-feeling in my hand. I guide the plug in; there's that moment of grinding sensation that I hate and then all I feel is my own hand on my cock, stroking it.

No matter how many times I've done it, it's still magick. What is it about cocks that they should be so feared and so valued, so hoarded and so desired? I've stopped wondering about it. To find out might make me crazy.

So I go out and kick my bike into gear and hit the streets. It's raining, but only a mist. Not hard enough for the Public Works to send up the Precipitation Dome. Which is fine, because I'm too chicken to ride all this leather through an unDomed rain and the Nachtlei Hangout that I like best, the Black Sun, is outside metro lines.

My luck doesn't hold. The rain steepens and I pull off under a store awning of fragrant bioengineered plantstuff to watch the pearly curve of the Dome rise. Damn. Do I try for Black Sun even in the wet—damn that busted car!—or go for something in town, an unknown quantity? A gleam of violet/periwinkle light catches my eye and I see a Hangout I've driven by before; the Camshaft. Supposed to be mostly pansex, but my winkti coworker Alphonsine said it's mostly overrun by the male type. Wait, didn't she say that she also picked someone up there? Maybe it's worth a try.

They have a cheap bike rack, which is good. If your bike isn't racked and guarded in this town, it'll be gone in two minutes flat. Which is why I have to take the hoverbus to work. Inside, it's the usual low light for flattering aging looks, music, cubbies with people talking, bar for drinks. A few winktis—oh, how I love the little winktis, drool drool—but they all seem to be with someone. The only loner looks at me, smiles, then sees the TranzPride logo and looks away. Shopping for a gen tonight, eh, honey? Fine, your loss.

I take a seat next to a genfem with crescent eyebrow pendants and order fizz'n'citrus. No booze; I have a bad reaction to deintoxicants. The genfem looks at me, is just about to dismiss me as a genguy when she sees my advertising too. Then she looks disgusted. Probably a Cynthaian, by the preponderance of crescents. They think what we do is unnatural, especially kuramis. By her lights I've committed a crime of mutilation against a woman's body, never mind that it's my body and I'm no woman. She's probably also pissed because she's just realized that if I hadn't Tranzed, I might be someone worth picking up to her. Life's a bitch, sweet thang.

Maybe it wasn't worth it to come here after all.

That's when I see the Boy. No, not a guy, a Boy. She's staring at me like I was—what? No, now, she's ducked her head and is looking away. I can smell her desire from here, see it in the curve of her shoulders under that androgynous jacket and ripped pants, baggy to hide the hips under them. She shuffles her feet in their scuffed runner's shoes and tries desperately not to look at me again. No genfem dresses that grungy in a bar these days unless they're dipping a toe into the kurami sea.

She gives in for a second and glances my way again. This time I'm staring at her over my fizz and she draws in her breath sharply, reaching too fast for her drink and inadvertently knocking it over. Someone next to her snarls something and she turns to apologize, face scarlet. I keep studying her. Let her turn and see me, see that her clumsiness is irrelevant to me, that I'm more interested in her ass. I know when I was just starting out, first wondering whether this was the path I wanted to take, I would have paid anything for an older, experienced kurami to accost me in a bar and say, "Okay, kid, this is what you're gonna look like, and this is what it's gonna be like, and your sex life will be better than ever. Now bend over."

No chain, no pendants, no signs, but I'm sure she can see mine from here, and she'll know what I'm looking for, and be able to guess what I am. I expect this will be a kind of formal initiation for her. If I'm an NQ, and she goes with me, it'll mean she's one of us, she's taking the first step from the silver to the black. Which'll it be, Boy? I ask her silently. I can't hang out here all day staring at you. I'll get bored, or maybe that cute winkti in the amethyst skinsuit will get bored first. You never know. Better make up your mind, kid.

Five minutes crawl by as she hunches over her drink. I'm just about to give up and order another fizz when she slowly turns. This time, when our eyes lock, I don't let her look away. (I mastered that trick a while back.) Go to her? Nah. She made me wait. Let her come to me. I jerk my head toward the empty stool next to me that the Cynthaian has evacuated. Get your ass over here. She does, oh thank you gods below. Phew.

"You know what I am," I snap at her as soon as her ass touches the seat. Small talk is for people with time to kill.

Her eyes widen and she doesn't speak for a moment. "Kur-kurami?" she squeaks, finally. "I wasn't sure...You can't tell, looking at you. You look just like..."

"A genguy," I say, relieving her of having to say it. "That's the way it works. You might work for one of us, and if he's not political, you'd never know." Kuramis are a little luckier than winktis in this regard, but I don't mention that. Then I zoom in. No sense in wasting my time. "And how many souls do you have?" I ask her, the somewhat stereotypical line.

She looks caught, like a moth fluttering on a pin. "If I said … two … what would it …?" She trails off in a whisper.

"Entail?" I ask.

"Mean," she says quietly.

"I've asked myself that a lot," I say. "We all do, and we all come to the conclusion that nobody would claim to be one of us if they weren't. I can usually smell my kin, anyway." I'm leaning closer to her as I say this.

She draws in her breath again, nostrils flaring. It's a neat habit, sexy. "And am I your kin?" the Boy asks.

"Do you want to be?" I return, almost in her ear.

She closes her eyes and a shiver runs down her spine. "I think I'd kill for that." Her eyes open and she looks at me, worried. "But I'm not sure I'm ready to commit to any … changes."

"Neither of those," I assure the back of her neck, "are necessary to letting me fuck you. That is, if the idea appeals."

I swear she almost faints. I get the Boy around the waist, shove them up against the counter (I think this Boy deserves the plural Nachtlei pronoun now) and press Asmodeus, rapidly hardening, into that shapely chicken-kurami ass that I've been lusting after. The Boy is not fainting now, but is pressing hard against me. I reach around and grab, opening the seal of a fly, find a cheap silicon pants-filler prosthesis and a wet boy-cunt. I get a little carried away at this point, and I'm glad the Boy's head is now down on the bar because the people staring might give them an attack of stage fright. I yank their pants down, undo my codpiece, and am just about to release a straining Asmodeus when there's a tap on my shoulder.

It's the bouncer. "Not in here," she says. "There's a stall in the john for that kind of thing." Gestures over her shoulder toward the back. No point in arguing. I grab the Boy by the back of their jacket and yank them toward the bathroom.

Stall, eh? She must have meant the one without the door, I guess. Oh well, life is short. The Boy gets slammed up against the wall and kissed, brutally, thoroughly. Their teeth finds my lip, gnaws momentarily on my beard, my throat, the collar of my jacket, and sinks lower until they're chewing on the front of my pants. Not wanting them to wreck the leather, I pull their head away by the hair and get the last sticking point on my codpiece. Asmodeus slides out into my waiting hand, piercings glinting in the bright, bald lighting. The Boy opens their mouth reflexively, and takes me without even commenting on size. Manages to take nearly the whole thing, almost to where it form-fits to my upper vulva. Manages to get fingers up where fingers shouldn't be without explicit permission.

I grab the Boy's wrist, digging a nail between the tendons as a warning. They make a muted sound around my cock and glance upwards, brow furrowed. I yank the hand out and check the manicure. Good. Back to the quick. "All right," I growl, letting them know that this is a privilege. "But you better be good at it."

The Boy's eyes get that I'm-going-to-faint expression again, but they don't stop sucking my cock. Three fingers slide up behind my balls, into wetness, and it takes about two minutes for me to come. (OK, so one of the nasty truths I learned about myself within twenty-four hours of getting my first APPle is that I'm a premature ejaculator.) My cock contracts, shooting come right down that pulsing throat.

There is stuff that you can buy, four bucks a can, to fill the reservoir in the cyber/testes that completely mimics human semen in looks, taste, and smell. At least that's what they say, but I find it has a faint metallic odor that just isn't quite right. I did have a girl complain about it, the only time I used it, so I don't bother. Besides, one-hundred-twenty proof vodka keeps it cleaner internally and is much more of a surprise.

• • •

Minutes later, we curl up in one of the cubbies together. I order a felissium inhaler, thumb on the heater, and take a hit. The Boy is telling me about the last scene they did with their last lover. "It was a big party, all these people watching, and she had me tied to a support beam, and got this branding iron really hot with a blowtorch. All I could do was stare—I mean, we'd never done anything that heavy before. Just some light whipping, and one pretty heavy caning once ... Anyway, she went around behind me. I don't think anyone in the place made one sound at that point. And then I felt it."

I stare at them, half mesmerized trying to picture it. "The brand?"

Their shoulders droop. "No. Cold. She had a second brand back there, in a bucket of frozen nitrogen. It hurt for a second, and then I realized it was all just a mindfuck. I started to cry, in front of everyone."

"In relief?" I ask.

"In disappointment. I had really wanted her to do it. She was embarrassed and got really pissed off, and we broke up two weeks later."

"In other words," I say, thumbing on the heater in the inhaler and keeping it on until it glows cherry red—which burns up the last of my felissium, but what the hell—"in other words," I say, holding the flame half an inch away from her forearm, "don't threaten you with anything unless I'm willing to come through on it. Is that it?"

The Boy flushes, but their eyes are on the flame. "I didn't mean it to be ... impertinent, sir."

I turn the inhaler off and leave it on the table. "But you hate being whip-teased. Or cock-teased, I take it. And I did say I was going to fuck you, didn't I?"

The Boy is wary, searching my face, unsure of what I want. My hand goes out like a striking snake (it's a trick I learned a while back) and closes on her throat, pressing just hard enough so that they can't move their head. "I always keep my word," I tell them. "But I do it in my own damn time, and I won't be rushed. Understand?"

Tries to nod, can't, says "Yes, sir," in a whisper.

I let go of them and stand up. "Come with me, Boy."

• • •

The underground parking garage—cities are so much nicer now that all the parking is underground—contains cars and racked bikes from several shops above. I'm just about to get my bike when I notice the car parked next to the rack. Large, expensive, covered in stickers from retro-conservative groups, one of them Nature's Front. My jaw immediately clenches. The Nature's Front goons are pushing for legislation to make prenatal hormone blockers mandatory. You know, the implants that block the variable fetal hormone showers that create people like me. Something evil boils up in me and I grab the back of the Boy's jacket again. "Bend over on the hood of that car, Boy."

It takes only one look at the stickers for the Boy to realize that it isn't mine. "The cameras are on," they remind me, not sounding as if they care much.

"I'm counting on it," I mutter, slamming them down on the expensive silver finish. I undo my pants again, and realize I have to change dicks to fuck this boy properly. It's one thing to deepthroat Asmodeus, but quite another to take it up the ass. Besides, Pan is specially built to ooze lube when squeezed. I make the change in full view of the cameras—go ahead, let the guy in the booth have some jollies—albeit wincing a bit at the replugging. The Boy is watching sideways from under their fringe of bangs, wide-eyed. I can almost hear the wheels turning in their head. This is one who'll go home and cry over their bank balance tomorrow, unless that retro grunge garb is an affectation.

I yank down those ragged pants and slide a few fingers up underneath into that wet boy-cunt and its owner moans, humping my hand vigorously. "Hold still," I say sternly, pressing down on their tailbone with my hand. The Boy tries, valiantly, but it's no use. The squirming starts again, and I make a snort of disapproval and withdraw my hand, wiping it on the torn pants. An inarticulate sound of disappointment comes from the other end, muffled slightly against the silver car hood. Pan is hard and ready, throbbing in my other hand; I press against the Boy's asshole and release some lube, slowly inching my way in. My little chicken-kurami pants and makes muted howling noises, trying desperately to hold their ass still and not hump my cock, fingernails scraping the gleaming enamel. (Good.)

I get the knife out of my pocket and give it the flick that makes the blade appear like a flash of red-and-white light. I like the way it runs along their shoulder, their scapula. The Boy turns their head obediently so that my knife can slide a hair's breadth above the fine skin over the carotid artery. My cock is pounding hard into their ass, and I'm just about ready to come when a voice sounds through a portable police loudspeaker. "All right, don't move. There are three K38A2's pointed at you. Step away and put your hands behind your head."

Oh, crap, crap, crap. Me and my stupid ideas. The guy in the parking booth probably called the cops. Well, it would be really stupid not to do as I'm told at this point. It's a serious effort to pull my throbbing cock out of the Boy's ass, but I do it. As I lift my arms, a hand grabs my wrist and relieves me of the knife. Shit. That one was a gift from an ex. Now I'll probably never get it back. My arms are twisted behind me by the two cops I can now see by turning my head. "Hey," I protest. "At least let me get my pants up!" The cops ignore me and snap on the restraints. They're filming everything; I can see the small cameras on their hats.

The Boy is hustled out of my field of vision; their face is white, but the last glance at me is worried, not accusing. Then I can't see them and there's a yell. "No! Not at all! No! Stop!" Then my attention focuses on the medcop in front of me, brandishing a cotton swab as if it were a deadly weapon. Huh? He takes a sample from my bobbing dick, which is rapidly going soft. I'm a little confused. All this for at best a vandalism arrest? Then, as he takes out his medscanner, pointing it at me to check for drugs in my system, it dawns on me and I start to laugh near-hysterically. The idiots think it's a rape arrest! The booth worker must have seen the knife and misinterpreted. Big time.

I laugh even harder when I see the expression of the guy holding the medscanner. My flesh will show up in shades of red, but my APPle will look bright green. Cyberflesh. His eyes leap to my face, and I sag in the cops' grip, I'm laughing so hard. "Shut up or we'll have to slap you," snarls the guy locked onto my left arm, and that manages to sober me up a little, but I'm still shaking silently.

There's a two-hundred-year-old law in this state that nobody's gotten around to changing yet. It isn't rape unless it's done with a real penis. Of course, it's all made irrelevant in a moment as the Boy comes hurtling back around and flings their arms around me, yelling wildly, "Don't! Don't you hurt him!" The medcop rolls his eyes and heaves a big sigh.

• • •

Two hours later, I'm released from the cell I'm in, sitting alone on my ass. The jerks decided to charge me with the vandalism act so as not to have wasted their time, but they confiscated both my APPles anyway. Maybe they thought I'd sit here in my cell and masturbate. Hell, I might have. The look on that one cop's face when he got Asmodeus out of my jacket pocket was enough to put me into another spasm of laughter, which didn't do much for my case.

The Boy is waiting for me by the desk when I'm led out. They look worried; I'm touched. I guess I'd expected that when the cops chose not to arrest them that they'd hightail it home faster than a jackrabbit, but instead the kid runs over and throws their arms around me. "You okay?" they ask. "They didn't put you in a cell with real rapists or anything, did they?"

I gently disengage them from my neck. "Nah, nachtlei get separate cells. It's policy. I'm okay. It was a stupid stunt anyway. I'm sorry I dragged you into all this, kid."

The kid grins. "It's all right. I called Mom and got your charges dropped. It won't even be on your record. And I got back your stuff." They hold up a clear sealed bag with my wallet, keys, two lovely curved cocks, and, wonder of wonders, my knife. The kid's eyes are twinkling, and I notice the sullen expressions of the cops behind the desk as they glare at me. "It was the least I could do," the Boy is saying.

I blink. "Who the hell is your mother?" I ask, almost afraid of the answer.

"County commissioner." Complete innocence in those big eyes. "Sir."

Shit. The kid must have raised one gargantuan stink to spring me. Now I'm going to have to deal with gratitude and obligations. The police station suddenly feels terribly oppressive, and the force of those glares pushes me right out the front door, the kid at my heels. I find I really don't know what to say. I mean, a one-nighter is a one-nighter, but ... I owe this kid big, and it makes me vaguely uncomfortable.

My bike is in front of the cop station. I take a step back in surprise. "What—How?"

"I had it towed here, sir."

"That must have cost a lot."

The Boy shrugs. "No big deal, sir." The honorific helps. I glance over. Those eyes are still on me.

"Thanks," I say. "I appreciate everything. Really. A lot."

The eyes drop. "I ... I hoped you wouldn't consider it too impertinent, sir. I mean, I know you can handle your own problems. I didn't want it to seem ... interfering."

The kid is trying really hard not to smile throughout this self-effacing speech, and that breaks through my shell of discomfort and makes me chuckle. Okay, so I've been dumb more that once tonight. One more test, and then they're off the hook. I rip open the bag and pull my keys out. "Guess it's time to go," I say. The Boy doesn't say anything. The way-too-new sneakers scuff the ground.

I straddle my bike and start it. Then I look up, scrutinizing the figure who stands there, hands jammed into pockets. "Well?" I say, jerking my head in a command. "Do I have to tell you to do everything?"

The Boy's face breaks into a big grin, relief and joy and—something else? I don't know. They scramble behind me onto the bike. I freeze them with a noise, and hold out the plastic bag, holding everything I value inside it. "Think you can take care of this on the ride home?" I ask. "Keep it safe in your coat, not drop it on the highway? 'Cause if you lose my dicks, I'll have to kill you. Not to mention that you won't get fucked."

The kid takes the bag gingerly, as if it's a treasure, which it is, and tucks it inside their coat like a baby. Then their arms go around me, just as gingerly, as if it might not be allowed. I chuckle again as I put on my helmet. "You'll have to hold on tighter than that. I wouldn't want to lose my valuable cargo." The arms tighten into a bear hug, and the kid puts their head on my shoulder. Valuable cargo. As I kick the hoverbike into gear and roar off, I wonder for a moment exactly what I was referring to.

~

Raven Kaldera is a Northern-Tradition Pagan shaman, herbalist, astrologer, transgendered inter-sexual activist, homesteader, and founding member of the First Kingdom Church of Asphodel. He is the author of too many books to list here, including the Northern-Tradition Shamanism series, *Leather Spirit Stallion*, *Neolithic Shamanism* (with Galina Krasskova), *Pagan Astrology*, and *Hermaphrodeities: The Transgender Spirituality Workbook*.

THE SOUND OF HIS WINGS

RAND B. LEE

On that very last morning, the alarm woke Hugh Mabary out of the most beautiful dream of his life. Enraged, he struck out at the clock, and it flew through the air, hit the pine wall of the cabin with a thud, and clattered to the floorboards. The old man clutched the sheet to him and tried to recapture the vision that had been stolen from him. The last wisps of the dream were fading, all the complexities of character and circumstance losing substance, dwindling to the image of the white gull flying over a dark city and sluggish river. Moonlight gleamed off wing, gemming the murk. Mabary's heart leaped. Then the image retreated and was stored, flat, in his memory. "Rise and shine," said a deep voice.

"Go to hell," said Mabary. Something furry brushed his cheek. He batted at it; it persisted; there was a moment of mouth and sweat. Mabary broke away spluttering. Joe Braga grinned down at him through his forest of grey beard.

"Good morning," Braga said.

"What time is it?"

"At the time of the murder, the clock's hands were set at half-past seven."

"What murder?"

"You have slain our loyal timepiece. Even now it spills its guts out on the floor." Braga kissed him again. Rapidly the kiss began to turn into something more complicated. Mabary groaned and struggled into sitting position. "Come back," said Braga.

"There isn't time."

His lover caught his wrist. "Part of you, at least, seems in no hurry to go."

"I can't control my reptilian hindbrain," Mabary said. "And stop flexing those muscles at me." The bigger man pulled him back down to the bed. All at once, Mabary clung to him, fiercely, and Braga held him while Mabary shivered and wept.

"Tell me," Braga said gently.

"I had a dream."

"About?"

"I don't remember very much of it. There was a seagull flying through it. Everything below was old and corrupt." He buried his face in the crook of Braga's arm. "That came at the end. There was a lot more. You were in it, and Dorothy, and the people from the camp. The gull came at the end."

"And?"

"It was the only beautiful thing in the world."

He wept again, from a sense of loss that he could not put a name to, and Braga wondered. After a while they made love. Gradually Mabary felt his tension loosen. His mind, however, was racing, unwilling to give itself to the pleasure. He tried to relax and rejoin his body. Braga helped him, being tender, loving him, telling him so. Still, when Mabary reached climax, it was merely emission and nothing else, and afterwards they dressed without a word.

The compound was cool with the early morning. The mess hall was nearly full despite the hour. First-shifters were herding one another away from the tables to make room for second-shifters who had not yet eaten. Everywhere people were holding hands: couples, triples, waiting their turns in line, singing or talking softly. Mabary noted automatically and with satisfaction that the groupings were not according to Talent. In the early days of the Refuge, a good many cliques had formed along such lines. Dorothy Laturno had discouraged this loudly and Braga and Mabary's pairing had set a powerful example. The two men were still called "the sike and the simp," although there were now many such couplings around the camp. In the beginning their partnership had shocked nearly everyone, but that had been during the war. "My God, Joe," said Mabary as they moved toward the food line, "who are all these youngsters?"

"They're asking themselves who the two doddering old fools are."

Mabary grimaced. "How old was I last birthday?"

"Sixty-four."

"That's what I thought. And you were seventy." He patted Braga's absurdly flat stomach through the cotton tunic. "How improbable that seems. But then, I always went in for older men."

"That we're alive at all seems improbable," said Braga. He touched the scar on Mabary's forehead. "I'm glad you're talking to me. When you decide to tell me what's really wrong, I'll be even more glad."

"I told you. The dream upset me."

"You said it was beautiful."

"Losing it upset me."

"So deeply?" Braga murmured. "You're the psychologist, my friend, not I; but it doesn't take a mind trained to map the convolutions of the human psyche to tell the difference between irritation and despair."

They were hailed. Eula Chan threaded her way through the throng toward them. Her food-tray floated several feet behind her, like an Old Chinese wife following her husband at a respectful distance. For anybody else it would have been considered an arrogant show of power. Compound etiquette condemned as ostentatious the doing with one's mind what one could do with one's hands. But Chan was a mental hyperactive, the sort of sike whom in ages past had caused poltergeist phenomena.

Laturno, Mabary, Braga, and the other few who had founded the Refuge were the sort of people who are horrified by bureaucratic minds, which tend to reduce persons to personnel and names to numbers. However, in cataloguing days, Chan would have been classified a Top Secret, A-1, Telekinete First Class, Emergency Deployment Only. As things stood now she was just Aunt Eulie. "Jeez me beads," she said, coming abreast of them, "but don't you two look like little lovebirds. Skip the dofu; it's watery as hell. Any bad dreams, Hugh?"

The men exchanged glances. "You sure you're just a kinny, Auntie?" asked Braga.

"Yeah," said the old woman, "but Mabbitt woke up yelling, said he'd had a vision; kept me awake till three in the morning calming him down." She gave Mabary the eye. "So you did?"

"Not what you'd call *bad*, and not what you'd call a *vision*," Mabary said cautiously. "Nothing apocalyptic or anything like that."

"What then?" She folded her arms and stood there waiting.

"A private dream, that's all, Eula."

"Don't evade me, boy, or you'll be waving your sorry saggy butt to the breeze in front of all these impressionable youngsters."

"How is Mabbitt feeling now?" Braga asked hastily. Chan shrugged.

"Foolish. Said being around sikes is driving him batty. Fact is, he registers slightly below lead-head average on every sike test imaginable, but the way he described his dream was so much like stuff I've heard from claires it bugged me. I'm going around asking all the simps whether they've experienced anything similar."

"One dream," began Mabary.

"Mabbitt *never* remembers his dreams."

Braga stroked his beard. "The conform theory. Auntie's pet."

"Laugh all you like," said Chan, with amusement in her small black sharp eyes, "but one day you'll come around to seeing it my way. *Everybody's* a sike,

Joe. The ones we call simps just block it." She reached up and tapped Mabary's skull. "Even you, leadhead. Your dream have a seagull in it like Mabbitt's?"

Mabary started so violently that the person next to him in line turned around and raised an eyebrow. Chan looked satisfied. "That makes five so far," she said, and walked off. Her tray floated up to Braga and deposited itself in his hands, then sagged as the woman's mind let it go.

"Conform theory," said Braga thoughtfully. "I wonder if it's true."

"What, Joe? That being around sikes long enough will bring out a nontalent's talent? Hasn't done it for me so far, has it?" He said it lightly, but Braga gave him a look.

"Hugh. You *know* your being a simp lessens no one here's love and respect for you and your other gifts. You *do* know that, don't you? Hugh?" For Mabary found himself turning away, unable to meet Braga's eyes. *What in hell's come over me?* Mabary thought.

"All right," whispered Mabary. "All right, Joe. I'll talk to you. I *hate* it." Two lines over, one of the empies picked up his distress and gave a cry of pain. Mabary drew his lover out of line and walked away from the breakfast area to an open spot near the mess hall exit. Then he faced the Russian, shaking a finger under his nose. "You want honesty? Here's some honesty, Joe. There are times when I *hate* being a nontalent in a sike community. There are days when I feel like an outsider here. 'There goes Uncle Hugh. He's really nice for a *simp*." He made a retching noise. "Simp. I hate that term most of all. Short for 'simpleminded,' of course, a sike pejorative right up there with 'fag' and 'retard' and 'nigger.' Or 'deadhead,' another put-down term folks around here throw around as though it were nothing." His lover opened his mouth to interject. Mabary stopped him with a raised palm.

"No, Joe. I know what you're going to say: nobody means any harm; we've used those terms so long nobody thinks twice about them or their etymology; we *love* our simps, we love and protect them and would be terribly, *terribly* sad if anything bad happened to any of them, because they're our little *friends*." His breath was coming so hard in his lungs that he thought he was going to faint. "The fact is, Joe, you people use those terms because you forget not everybody around here isn't like you. How many simps to how many sikes? Let's see." He made a show of counting on his fingers. "Three hundred eighty-six talents to fifteen deadheads. A ratio of nearly twenty-six to one. I don't blame you for forgetting we're here."

"Are you through?"

"Yes." Mabary turned to leave.

"Where are you going?" asked Braga.

"I'm going to talk to Mabbitt."

"You're not going to eat with me?"

"Joe." Mabary turned back, managing a small smile. "There are nearly 400 people, most of them much younger, much more handsome, and much more *talented* than I, who would give their left arms to sit at your side, given the opportunity. I'm sure you won't lack for company in my absence."

"We have not concluded this conversation."

"We have for now."

"Will you meet me for supper?"

"I'll think about it. Give me Eulie's tray."

He deposited Chan's tray in the rack by the kitchen door, pretending not to notice the anxious faces turned in their direction. He kissed a child he knew, but otherwise avoided his friends on the way to the exit. Outside, he heaved a sigh of relief. The sun had not yet risen, and the morning mists swirled about the street, making white dimnesses out of the buildings. First shift had departed already for bed; second shift had not finished eating. He had the street to himself. He hesitated, wondering whether Mabbitt would be awake after his difficult night. Then he thought, *Only one way to find out,* and moved down the street away from the mess hall.

He could not help remembering.

• • •

The revolutionaries had attacked on the third of May at eight o'clock in the morning, just as the salvage team was preparing to take the top off the ruined armory. Fortunately, there were a few seconds of warning: the team claire gave a yell, and all the sensitives suddenly shuddered as invisible scalpels scraped their minds. Then the sensitives were down, in various postures of discomfort, the ground was erupting, and the crane was doing odd things in the billowing dust. By the time things had settled, five workers had been hurt, three of them seriously. One, the claire, was dead, his skull crushed by a flailing cable. Everyone became very busy. A crevice had opened up beneath the crane, which stuck out of the hole at a crazy angle, like a grasshopper in the mouth of a bullfrog.

Dorothy Laturno arrived on the scene almost at once, reining her horse dramatically, swearing a blue streak, demanding why the camp precogs had not foreseen the incident, and holding about three dozen people responsible. Mabary, who was public relations director for the project, followed in her wake, saying nothing. "Where the hell is Joe?" said Laturno.

"Here." Braga stood up to his thighs in rubble. Some distance in front of him, sand and stone swirled lazily, piling themselves. Laturno dismounted and stood at his side. They watched the piles grow, the huge man and the huge woman. *Well-matched,* thought Mabary. He had known them both for several years, since he had been transferred to the Midwest bureau of the National Bureau of Health and Education. He was already in love with Braga, and that was painful. But Mabary was twenty-two, and everything was painful.

The sands stopped swirling and finally settled. Braga had dug a pit. He and Laturno squatted, poked the ground. Laturno yelled. "What have you found?" Mabary called.

"A piece of a wendy. A goddamn piece of a wendy."

They stomped to the lip of the excavation, Laturno brandishing the thing, which turned out to be a hand, messily severed at the wrist. Mabary stared at it in fascination. He had never seen a dead hand before. "They tunnelled," said Braga. "They set the charge. It went off prematurely. One of them was caught in the blast. At least one. There is more detritus below."

"If they had gotten any closer to the armory," Mabary said.

"They wouldn't have dared," said Laturno. "They don't know what's down there any more than we do." She whistled into her chest mike. The orders she gave were short and to the point, but good-natured; the discovery had sweetened her mood. She brandished the hand as she talked.

Sickened, Mabary surveyed the ruins of the excavation. The medics were removing the claire's corpse and fussing with the wounded. One of the excavators had been pinned under a mound of earth that had come away from the side of the pit during the explosion. Someone was hurrying over; he recognized the new kinny, Chan. He had never met her, but she was said to show great promise. He watched her squat near the moaning worker. Chan was tiny in her green coveralls. Dirt began to flow. A medic stuck a needle in the wounded worker's arm, and she stopped moaning.

Mabary turned his attention back to the project boss. "How long do you estimate?" Laturno was saying into her mike. "Too slow, Schure, goddammit! These things have to be tracked fresh. I don't care. *Do* it." She tapped the mike into silence and said, "Give me a hand, Hugh." He helped her up to his level ground, and she grinned at her choice of words. Holding the severed member between her thumb and forefinger and giving a moue of distaste, Laturno went over to her horse and dropped the hand into a pouch in her saddlebag. She came back wiping her fingers on her trousers. "How many kinnies would it take to lay our people low like that?" she asked Braga.

"It is not how many. It is how powerful," said Braga.

"We're talking about *wendies,*" said Laturno. "Untrained talents."

"Unlicensed," corrected Mabary. Laturno frowned. Mabary added, "There have been talents near the end of their training who have gone wendy before official licensure." Laturno grunted.

"It does seem as though this attack, like the others, was executed with unusual deftness," rumbled Braga. "The fire at the St. Louis offices; the mindburning in New York. The fact that no serious damage has been done is beside the point. We can attribute that to the quality of our people's training, not to any clumsiness on the part of the revolutionaries."

"Mindburn," said Laturno. She chewed her lower lip. "Chan told me they tried to mindburn you all just before the blast."

"Juan warned us just in time for us to throw up our shields."

"Shit," Laturno said. "A coordinated nationwide wendy effort? It's inconceivable. It would be like trying to teach a family of schizophrenics to square dance. I suppose it would be possible, but only if a BHE-trained talent coordinated it. But what BHE-trained talent would? It isn't as though we're running some sort of Orwellian society here. This is still the United States of America. The secret police do not knock on doors in the dead of night; the BHE is not conducting secret genetic experiments, weeding out the inferior talents in order to build some master race! I can understand somebody from the street swallowing wendy propaganda but not somebody who'd been on the inside with us. What would she have to *gain* by going over?"

"Who said that he would rather rule in hell than serve in heaven?" said Braga. He said it softly, so that only Mabary heard him.

"What I want to know is *why* the presence of the saboteurs and their goddam tunnel wasn't sensed earlier," said the boss.

"We know this area of Old Chicago is honeycombed with tunnels," pointed out Mabary. "Old streets, ceilinged with rubble. They wouldn't have had to dig far to join up with the armory complex."

"This area was swept for cave-in hazards before we set up camp," said Laturno. "No tunnels were reported."

Braga said, "A finder cannot tell the difference between a tunnel that has been filled in and a layer of stable rubble."

"So they burrowed in last night when nobody was looking?" said Laturno. "I want to know *why* nobody was looking! Who was on guard duty?"

"Nicolaisen and Poag were up," said Braga.

"Where are they now?"

"Nicolaisen never made it to watch last night," said Mabary. They stared at him. "I went by the infirmary last night to pick up some aspirin. He'd reported in at 2000 hours with a severe migraine. The medics had put him under by the time I got there."

"Who was next on duty roster?" asked Laturno.

"Keenoy," said Braga.

"And where," said Laturno calmly, "are Keenoy and Poag now?"

Nobody seemed to know. The boss stood at the edge of the dig with her hands in her pockets. Mabary was glad that he was not a telepath. Even to his untalented senses Laturno's anger was so great it hurt him to look at her. Eula Chan had finished her sifting work; the unconscious victim was being loaded onto a stretcher. "Tell me what I'm thinking is impossible," barked Laturno without turning around.

"Improbable," said Mabary. "But."

"But *Keenoy*," said Laturno. They had been lovers. When the finder team arrived, the big woman turned to it with blood in her eye. The owner of the hand was traced. Their search led the BHE sikes to a wendy hideaway in the bowels of the old city. There were several hours of fighting, in the course of which Dorothy Laturno mindburned Jonna Keenoy and was nearly killed herself when Keenoy brought half the roof down on their heads.

Keenoy proved to have been a top kinny, equal perhaps to Eula Chan. Keenoy had hidden her extra talent for years, masquerading as a finder. She was the first multiple talent on record to have evaded classification by the Bureau of Health and Education. She was also a major link in the remarkably well-organized network that, the following year, set into motion what came to be known as the Wendy War.

• • •

Mabary found the old cobbler in front of his cabin. Mabbitt's black hands moved quickly, plying a needle; he was sewing two pieces of leather together. As usual, he was naked, and though his body was withered, his muscles ropey, his skin gleamed with the same rich ebony it had held for all the years Mabary had known him. Chan liked to say that Mabbitt had the most beautiful skin she had ever seen. *How long has it been?* thought Mabary. *Mabbitt was the last refugee in, before the barrier was put up. Was that '44? Mabbitt and that water-witching kinny. Wallens.* The memory of Wallens's dying face moved him to Mabbitt's side. "Hello, Mab," he said.

"Hughie!" The old man jerked up his head. "Didn't hear ya comin'. Take a load off, boy." He patted the chair beside him. Mabary settled into it. "Been a while since you came by. To what do I owe the pleasure?"

"Auntie told me about your dream," Mabary said.

The cobbler stiffened, then relaxed and continued his sewing. "So what do you think?"

"I had one, too."

"Yeah?"

"Yeah," said Mabary.

"About a seagull?"

"Yes."

Mabbitt sighed. He did not raise his chin, but the set of his shoulders told of his attention. "Tell me," he said.

"I don't remember much of it now. The alarm clock woke me before I could see how it turned out. You were in it, I think."

"What was I doing?"

"I don't remember. There were a lot of people from the camp: Dorothy, Joe. We were in the city again, and it was dying. It had been plague-bombed or something. I remember the river was already dead. Water like glue, things that stank. We were all arguing about something, some plan for cleaning up the river. The seagull came in at the end."

"Yeah?"

"It was like a song."

"Like the song of a jewel," said Mabbitt quietly. "Whiter than snow. Like light. Like I remember light."

For a moment, Mabary thought the cobbler was speaking figuratively. "Mab," he said, "you mean you *saw* your gull?"

"Saw as in eyes," said Mabbitt.

"I thought you dreamed in smells and touch and temperature."

"This is the first goddam dream I've had in years that was visual. Christ, I went blind when I was six; I can barely remember what a seagull looks like." He dropped his voice. "But that gull, now. That was no dream, Hughie. That was real. That was a true seeing."

"What do you mean?"

"I mean," said Mabbitt, "it was a vision."

"I thought you believed religion was the opium of the people."

"Who said anything about religion?" snapped the cobbler. "And don't start thinkin' I'm goin' senile. It was the *quality* of the dream that impressed me. It was completely vivid."

"So was mine," said Mabary.

"There you are."

Where are we? thought Mabary. "We're not the only ones, Mab. Eulie says three others have had dreams like ours. All simps."

"Holy Kennedy," breathed Mabbitt. "Who?"

"I don't know. She didn't say. But she's asking all around camp."

"See? Eulie knows," the cobbler said. He chuckled deep in his throat. "*She* knows it was really something."

"She thinks this may support her conform theory, Mab. What do you think? Do you think we simps have got talent, and it's finally starting to show?"

"If it is, then it's sure taken its own sweet time about showin'," said Mabbitt.

"I don't know, Hughie. Maybe. All I know is we saw *something*."

"Mab," Mabary said.

"What, Hughie?"

"I hope Auntie's right. I've always wanted to be a talent. I've never told anybody but Joe that before."

"Ever been checked out properly?"

"Of course. You forget how old I am. My mother brought me to the clinic at St. Louis University Hospital when I was eight, and every year after that till I was sixteen."

"Good old Bureau of Health and Ed," said Mabbitt. "So they told your ma you were a bright boy but no dice, huh?"

"That's right," Mabary said. *Dear Mother,* he thought. She had wanted it for him, and she had been so relieved when he had tested normal. "What about you?"

"I never got tested before I came here."

"What?" Mabary sat up. "How old are you, anyway?"

"It's no secret. I'll be ninety-eight in August."

"Ninety-eight." Mabary figured. "You were born in the second decade of testing, then. Why didn't they get around to you?"

"Ghetto," said Mabbitt.

"I see."

"Remember Miami, Hughie?"

"Miami? You grew up in *Miami?*"

"Born there, just before the supertyphus came in from Cuba. We got out fast. Daddy took us up to Atlanta, and from there to Chicago. We moved into a building that was practically in the shadow of the old Moody Bible Institute. The Christians United For a Free America turned it into their headquarters. They made a lot of noise at night, I recollect." Mabbitt chuckled.

"Daddy had bad luck in choosin' his abodes. They started the bombing, and that's how I got blind. Damned if he didn't get us out, though, the three of us. I had two sisters. He marched us up the steps of the Institute singing 'When the Roll Is Called up Yonder' like our lives depended on it, which they did. We thought he was crazy: bombs goin' off all over the city and he's singin' hymns. But Daddy told me they looked at me with my face bandaged up and looked at him lookin' at their guns like they were the loaves and fishes, and by God, they let us in."

"That was twenty-five years before I was born."

"Is that a fact." Mabbitt's face dropped. "That was Chicago in my dream last night, Hughie. I felt it plain as rock, smelled the stink. Now, how long has it been since you smelled a gasoline engine?"

"Tell me about your dream," said Mabary.

Mabbitt's hands kept sewing. "Too beautiful," he said. "Too hard to keep sharp in your head. We were walking down State Street, Eulie and I, out to take the air. It's nonsense, of course; I didn't even meet Eulie till I came here. I'd heard of her, though, from the revolutionaries: Yooliechan the Chink Vampire. God, we were scared of her. She was the Establishment's top bitch, all right, and everybody knew it. They said she could raze a building with her mind. I wish I had a twenty for every fancy plan we came up with to get rid of her.

"So we were walking, ambling, like, with the noise of cars and their stink, actin' like there was no war, no Health and Ed, all the time in the world. There was this preacher on the corner. There were always boys from Moody preaching on State, real nice, all shot to hell during the Chicago Revolution, of course. And that's a funny thing, because in my dream we were both *in* the war and *not* in it, sort of. Anyhow, we were walkin' down State, and there were some air-raid sirens goin' off, but they didn't bother us; we just kept walkin'. And there was this preacher on the street corner talking out of Second Samuel. You know your Bible, Hughie?"

"Some."

"Second Samuel tells about King Saul and King David and what they did," Mabbitt said. "The preacher was preachin' on the part in Second Samuel when King David is going to fight a battle against the heathen, and the Angel of the Lord comes to him invisible with his army. And the sign the Lord gives that He's shown up," and here Mabbitt began to sound a little like a preacher himself, "is the sound of His army in the treetops. In my dream, the preacher preached on that. Only he got it different. He said the Lord was near, and if we listened hard we could hear the sound of His *wings* in the treetops. When we heard the sound of His *wings* in the treetops, it would be time to change our minds about our sins and turn to Jesus. I remember that perfect."

"The sound of His wings," said Mabary. A shiver went up his spine. "And the seagull?"

"It came pretty soon after that," said the cobbler. His voice was hushed; he was experiencing it again. "The sirens got louder and drowned out the preacher. Then they stopped, and everything was so quiet.

"Now up to this point my dream had been a blind man's dream, Hughie. After this it changed. I started *seeing*: a light. Far off in the distance at first, a moving light, moving toward me. I grabbed Eulie and started yelling I can see. Then I could see *everything*: the city and the preacher, and Eulie, kind of blurred, but there. You and Joe, too. He's real big."

"He is that," said Mabary. "And the gull?"

"It came out of the light," said Mabbitt. "It was hovering, Hughie, hovering above us like I don't know what, like a father protecting his children."

"Shit," said Mabary. Their eyes were wet.

"It flew away," said the cobbler. "And I wanted to fly away with it."

"I know," said Mabary. "So did I."

• • •

Chicago had gone, and so had St. Louis, but there was Kansas City, and the Provisional Government of the Midwestern United States of America set up headquarters there, in the same complex that had once housed the Midwest Bureau of Health and Education. The Bureau, owing to its superior foresight, had moved some months previously. The government had been slower to act. What had begun as the Wendy War had grown into something much greater. Radical groups that would not have dreamed of joining forces fifty years earlier had suspended their differences in an unprecedented show of cooperative terrorism. And the plagues had returned.

They had come the first time a hundred and fifty years before. The United States had been in the grip of one of its periodic economic depressions. An extremely conservative government had been in power; the death toll had been high, and the Chinese had been blamed. Then the *Washington Post* had come out with the most sensational exposé since the Watergate scandals of the previous century: the viruses had escaped from an American military testing laboratory in northern Michigan, and they represented a new strain, recently developed, despite government insistence that disease warfare projects had been abandoned. The next government was dominated by liberals. The National Bureau of Health and Education was formed in those years to disseminate information about the plagues and to teach people how to care for their dying.

Twenty years later, the first sikes had shown themselves. The Bureau had pricked up its ears. The first wave of plagues had abated, yet the appearance of the espers and the disappearance of the disease seemed an interesting coincidence. The Bureau set quietly to work amidst the political, military, and ecclesiastical excitement. No conclusive evidence was put forth linking the lab-mutated disease and the mutated humans. Nevertheless, the Bureau was placed in charge of studying the new talents.

It was the *National Enquirer* that coined what came to be known as siketalk: *sike* from *psychic*, *patty* from *telepath*, *kinny* from *telekinetic*, *claire* from *clairvoyant*, *simp* from *simple-minded*. And later, when the Bureau began licensing some talents and surgically putting the damper on others, it was the unlicensed talents who came up with their own self-designation: *wendies*, after Wendy, the little girl who left Never Never Land for adulthood and yearned to return in vain.

Sikes kept being born, at first in North America, then westward around the globe. The National Bureau of Health and Education suggested to Congress that all children be tested for talent as a matter of course. It was about the fifteenth year of such testing that the plagues returned. A mutated typhoid fever swept into the Florida Keys from the Caribbean, spread to Miami and thence into the Deep South. Two years later, a new bubonic erupted in the Southwest, at first among cattle, then among humans. Talent and non-talent alike died, but it was found that talents, particularly kinnies, seemed somewhat less susceptible.

Certain politicians accused the Bureau of Health and Education of trying to reproduce the conditions in which the first sikes had appeared, hoping thereby to weight the surviving population in favor of the talented. There was rioting in Miami and Chicago; large sections of both cities were destroyed. By the time Hugh Mabary was transferred to the Midwest Bureau of Health and Education, Chicago was a mixture of ruins and ghetto, a center for underground wendy activity.

So the Wendy War came, and the Bureau and the government both fled to Kansas City, and there Mabary found himself in the spring of his twenty-seventh year. He and Joe Braga had been lovers for six months. There was no real place for Mabary in the complex; his old public relations job had collapsed with the public communications systems. So they made him a psychologist and assigned him to interview captured wendies. For three years he put his stamp of approval on the official Bureau license-withholding certificates.

The day he quit was the day Eula Chan dragged in the arsonist.

The guards stripped the prisoner, burned his clothing, checked his rectum for bombs and such, sonicked his body clean, and shoved him into the room where Mabary was sitting. Then the guards moved behind Mabary and stayed there, trying to look simultaneously menacing and inconspicuous. The arsonist sat down on the cement floor. Mabary looked him over. He was fifteen years old; Navajo: bronze-skinned, flat-nosed, high-cheeked. His straight black hair fell into his eyes, and he stared balefully at Mabary through it. He had tried very hard to set fire to the Health and Education Emergency Relief Facilities.

"What's the matter?" the boy said after a while. His voice trembled. "Ain't you never seen a wendy before?"

"Never one so stupid," said Mabary. The boy flinched. "How could you have expected to get away with a stunt like that?"

"I almost got away with it."

"You could never have gotten away with it. Trained sikes had you pinpointed practically from the moment you entered camp. It was just a matter of time."

He shrugged. "So okay," he said. "Now what are you going to do with me?"

"I don't know," said Mabary. "I'm just a psychologist. Give me one good reason why we shouldn't sterilize you."

This scared him. He stood up and started yelling. The guards grew tense; Mabary shouted the boy down. "If it's anybody who should be namecalling, it's me! Who tried to poison the water supply to the training camp? Who mindburned Dominica Juarez, our pregnant patty? And what about the charming bonfire your people made of your hostages? Say it was retaliatory."

"It *was* retaliatory!" said the boy.

"Pig shit. It was the most cowardly piece of terrorism I've ever seen, and it didn't work. We're not terrorized; we're plenty pissed. You blew your last chances of peaceful settlement to this whole mess."

"Peaceful settlement! Putting us on a reservation? Carving up our brains?"

"Testing your kids and training those who are trainable for full sike status. Giving you decent medical care, decent food. Education, too, ever hear the word? And a chance at reintegration."

He settled back onto the floor. "You lie well," he said.

"And you're just a walking cliché, wendy." He let this sink in while he scribbled notes on his pad. The boy was a very low grade kinny; he could barely open locks and could only fan flames with his mind, not start them. Mabary said, without looking up, "How badly do you want to stay free and fertile?"

"Screw you," said the boy, but he was listening.

Mabary looked him in the eye. "Help us and we'll license you."

The boy hung his head, his hair falling over his face. When he raised his head again, his eyes were moist. "I wanted to be a licensed sike more than anything else. I really did. I wanted to be an Indian super-hero, see? When I was first tested I was nine. They said I showed promise. I couldn't believe it!" His voice turned bitter. "They disqualified me."

"It appears they were right to do so."

"I was just a kid!" The boy leaned forward, eyes sharp. "I was scared. For years I'd gotten telepathic flashes and not known what they were. The BHE guy in our neck of the woods knew about V.D. and alcoholism and bubo, period. He wasn't equipped to handle multitalents. What could the people from the city do with me? They only saw me once a year. But they decided I wasn't worth working with, see? And whose fault was that?" He wrung his hands. "I was getting *good,* I tell you. I could have been a top sike! But there was this war on, and I wasn't straight enough for them."

"So you joined the Revolution." *Paranoid schizophrenic,* the file read. *Delusions of grandeur; delusions of persecution.* The boy had had so little talent that he had not been judged to need suppression-surgery. "Look, kid," said

Mabary, leaning across his desk. "Every wendy has the same story. Every wendy claims to have been classified unsuitable because of racial or class prejudice, a psychologist's whim, bureaucratic stupidity, quota ratios, you name it. None of you seems willing to entertain for a second the notion that you were just plain unsuited to licensure. It's no shame; it's a fact. We all have things we're good at and things we're not; I'm unsuited to professional athletics, for instance. So you accept it, and move on. Learn to use your other talents."

"It's not the same," said the boy. "Siking is magical! Everybody wants to be a real sike! Who wants to be a wendy? They cut you so you can't use your talent any more. They turn you into a *simp*." He was trembling again.

"They didn't cut *you*."

"Is that what my records say?" The boy sneered. "I'll bet they do."

"Hardly anyone ever gets surgery," Mabary said. "Only criminals, violently insane people, people whose Talents would be used to hurt themselves or others."

"Liar," said the boy. "They cut me. They cut people all the time. How would *you* feel?"

"I don't know," said Mabary. "I'm not Talented."

He did not know why he had said it, and once again he was unprepared for the boy's reaction. "You poor shit. They got you by the short hairs, don't they?"

"Watch your language," snapped a guard.

The boy ignored her. "You get a kick out of working with your little superheroes? Get a kick out of hunting wendies because you don't want anybody to have what you *can't* have?"

It hurt Mabary more than he had imagined it would. "You're right, kid. I'm just a woebegone sadist. Now that you've seen through me, I suppose there's just no point in talking any further." He finished writing, folded the paper, and handed it to a guard.

"What are you going to do?" said the boy. He was very frightened.

"What do you want us to do?" Mabary asked.

"What do you mean?" He was trembling again. A guard moved in. The boy leaped to his feet. "Don't touch me!"

"Easy," said Mabary. The guard threw him a questioning glance. "I told you. Decide to join us, and we'll license you. You'll be classified as one of the lower grades, but you'll be a real sike, and we'll train you to open locks quicker than any safecracker and help put out fires instead of make them worse." The guard moved in.

"No!" The boy darted just out of reach. His face was drained of blood and empty of reason. *He's having an episode*, Mabary thought. The guard caught the boy. He began screaming, largely incoherently, kicking and punching.

The guard and Mabary held him down while a second guard prepared a hypodermic. Gradually Mabary became aware that the boy's screaming was making sense to him, that the boy was screaming, *Cut me, cut me*, and that it was warm in the room, too warm for a Midwest April. The boy's frothing mouth and thrashing body flashed before him. *Something's wrong*, thought Mabary. *Cut me!* screamed the boy. The guard prepared to administer the sedative.

The boy burst into flame.

• • •

The mist rose at last, and the Refuge stood glittering. Folk filled the streets. Mabbitt was hailed by several, but he returned their greetings only cursorily. He and Mabary had woven a tight cocoon of memory about one another, and they did not want it pierced. "Come inside," the cobbler said, so they went inside his little cottage and talked the morning down at his pine table. They spoke of the dreams, and of the War, and of the people they had known, and of the very odd thing that was the Refuge, and of the barrier.

"Were we Hitlers, Mab?" Mabary asked at one point. "Was it like Hitler and the Jews?"

"You're askin' the wrong person," said the blind man. "I was on the other side, remember? Sure as shit Health and Ed didn't have folks' *welfare* in mind."

"It got so muddied," said Mabary. "Too many elements had entered the picture. It was no longer a question of who was fit for licensure as a sike and who wasn't. It was political. The BHE became a tool of the government." He put a hand on Mabbitt's shoulder. "Did I tell you why I finally quit?"

"Braga was thinkin' of quittin', wasn't he?"

"Yes, but that's not all it was," said Mabary. The edge in his tone was lost on neither of them. "They caught a kid in the middle of trying to commit arson. His file read that he was a nut. Young kid, fifteen, Talented but not very. That's what the file said." Mabbitt shuddered. "The file was wrong. He freaked out and set himself on fire. He died before we could get it out. I watched him burn; I beat him with my hands. He'd claimed to have been a potential Class One, denied proper licensure, surgically suppressed. The files said no. The files lied."

"Oh?" said Mabbitt.

"I found a surgery order on an old disk. The kid *was* suppressed. But it was wartime, and they did a lousy job. Some other cells took over the Talent functions. I found out he'd lived with his mother till their house had burned down. She'd burned to death."

"He wanted you to finish the job," Mabbitt said.

"That's right. To make him pay. It was uncovering the conflicting reports that did it, Mab. I was such a naive little bastard; I'd really believed we'd given these people a fair shake. That's when I quit."

"And came here."

"Eventually." Mabary smoothed the table-top with his hand, then stared at his hand. *Christ, I'm old,* he thought. "The Refuge makes up for some of it, don't you think, Mab?"

"Sure does, Hughie." Mabbitt chuckled. "I'll never forget old Wallens's voice the day we walked into camp and found all of you here. We knew Laturno and Chan and Braga from our Most Wanted lists. We hadn't known where they were; all we'd really known was that there was this Refuge for people who the wendies and the sikes both didn't want. We sure as hell didn't know who we'd be showerin' with the first day."

Mabary laughed. "I remember you, too. You were how old in '44? Sixty-three or sixty-four? Walked right in, bold as brass, Wallens right behind you. You came right up to Auntie and said, 'I want a lay and a bath, not necessarily in that order.' Then you found out who she was, and you almost fainted."

"The next day you put up the barrier," said the cobbler. "Wallens and me, we were the last lucky ones." He shook his head. "Now that spooked me, all of them kinnies and patties standing around in a circle holding hands, getting into each other's heads. It was like a funeral. After it was over, I turned to Wallens and said, 'What the hell? I don't feel no barrier,' and he said, 'Just listen,' and he walked over to the edge of the camp and made a run at the air. It was like paper crackling."

"He lit up like a Christmas tree," said Mabary.

"How we laughed. And it wasn't two years before he was gone."

"That was a long time ago," said Mabary.

They continued to chat until the noon whistle blew. Mabary excused himself, saying he wanted to get lunch. "You want me to bring you something?" he asked Mabbitt.

"Nah. I'm good."

"I'll be back to let you know what I find out about the others."

The cobbler nodded. "Maybe all us deadheads should get together. Compare notes."

"I'll see to it," said Mabary, and left.

On the way to the mess hall he passed a group of children sitting in the grass, practicing the mindtouch. They took no notice of him. Even the youngest, eight-year-old September Miriamson, was so absorbed in concentration that Mabary could have shouted in his ear and would have received no response. A little farther on, Mabary came upon a girl sitting in a sand-pile digging savagely with a stick. Something in her dark face stopped him. He squatted opposite her and said, "Hi, Manuela. I'm Hugh. May I speak with you?"

"It's no use; I can't hear," she replied. She did not look up from her digging.

"You just did," said Mabary. Manuela glared at him. He saw that her dark face was streaked with tears.

"Don't make fun of me," she said, shaking her brown curls. "I meant *that* kind of hear," and she pointed to the quiet circle of children.

"Oh, *that* kind," said Mabary. "I can't hear either."

Her eyes narrowed. "You can't?"

"No."

She considered him. "But you're old."

"Yes, I am."

"Even September can hear," she said. "And he's just a baby."

"How old are you?" asked Mabary. She caught the amusement in his tone and frowned again.

"Nine and a half," she answered. "I'll be ten in March." She resumed her digging.

"Manuela," said Mabary. She glanced at him. "Did you have a big dream last night?"

The girl's shoulders slumped, and she knuckled her right eye. "Yes," she said, in a small voice.

"I did, too," said Mabary. "A lot of people did who can't hear mindspeak. Do you know what mine was about?" She shook her head again. "A beautiful big white bird."

The child stopped her digging, and sat, her face struggling with some great emotion, trying to decide how much of it to reveal before this wrinkled ancient, deciding at last to show nothing. "Go away," she said. "I called to it, and it wouldn't answer me. Go away."

"Did you love it a lot?" asked Mabary.

"*Go away.*"

He had just gotten to his feet when the attack came.

The children in the mindspeak circle began to scream. Mabary's first thought was for September; he whirled and started forward. The young sensitives were slapping themselves and dancing about, as though they had stumbled into a bees' nest. One of them began to beat her head slowly and methodically against the earth. The youngest sensitive lay still, curled into fetal position. His eyes were open, and he was not breathing.

Mabary knelt beside him, felt his pulse, started administering CPR. The boy's mouth smelled of milk. Manuela was tugging at his sleeve. "He's dead," said Mabary, to nobody in particular. He got up, shrugged off the girl, and moved to the sensitive who was trying to beat in her own brains. He caught her head and held it in his arms. She bit him, then slumped. The other children were dropping. He felt for her pulse, felt it flutter, then surge. The girl who had dreamed tugged his sleeve again.

• • •

Dimly he had been aware of other cries. Now he looked up and saw what the girl had wanted him to see. The mess hall was burning. People stumbled out of it, alarmingly few people. "Go ring the fire bell," he told Manuela. "Run and ring it." She ran. He picked up September, then put him down again, and headed towards the flames. There was nothing in the sky but white clouds. *Thirty-four years,* he thought. *It took thirty-four years, but they've found us at last.* A man collided with him; they went down, the man flailing. Mabary pushed the man off and got up, then saw who it was. "Manuelita," said the man. "Have you seen my daughter?"

"I sent her to ring the fire bell," said Mabary. "Go help her." He pulled the man to his feet and sent him stumbling off, then thought, *Joe. He was waiting to have lunch with me.*

The quadrangle looked like a battlefield, but the battle had been one-sided. Everywhere sensitives lay, moaning and thrashing or curled and silent. Braga was not among them. The fire bell began to ring. The calm June summer noon seemed to absorb the claxon, drain it of urgency.

The roof and sides of the mess hall were burning. Smoke poured from the doors and windows. Mabary pulled his tunic up over his mouth and nose and rushed into the smoke. The heat struck him like a fist. He dropped to the floor and crawled. It was difficult to breathe. The miasma filling the mess hall was very thick, as though there were more to it than simple smoke. There were dozens of bodies everywhere, tumbled trays, overturned chairs, food splatters. *Mindburn,* he thought. *Burn mind, burn body.* It fit. He crawled. *I was late,* he thought. *Joe would have gotten my tray for me, as he always does when I'm late, and he would have taken our usual spot by the east window.*

He crawled until he felt flesh beneath him, then kept crawling. The heat grew worse and he felt his forehead begin to blister. He crawled under a table. *Our spot,* he thought. He could not see. He felt with his hands, with his mouth: a child; a woman; a man with a bushy moustache; a man with a beard and a big, big chest. His heart dropped into dark. He pressed close to the bearded man, and clung to him. *You can always tell by the teeth,* he thought, and then he wondered why he had thought it. Then he remembered. *The bunker. Were we like the Nazis, Mab? Was it like Hitler and the Jews?* And he clung to the big-chested lifeless body in the tunic and jeans, while the smoke filled his lungs at last.

It was then that he saw the gull. It was flying against a night from which the stars were missing. There was a roaring in his ears, so that he could not hear the beat of the long bright wings or catch the knife-edged cry. But the gull's glory lifted him up with it, out of the smoke, above the flame, out into the free air.

It was night, but it was day also. He looked down, and he could see the Refuge spread out over the hilltop far below him. There were the cottages, set out like so many cloches on a mound of green. There the greenhouses sparkled and the solar collectors winked. There the wind turbines turned in slow majesty. Down the terraced hillside, the fields stood in strips, lush with beans and corn. At the base of the hill sat the girdle of fence that physically represented the psi-barrier that had kept the Outside outside for so many years. Beyond the fence, the virgin forest stretched off into the far distance, where mountains rose to nibble on the edges of the endless sky.

Hughie! someone cried in his head. Mabary's vision was full of gull and sky, so he did not see the cobbler, but he felt him and heard him. *Hughie! It's happened! Eulie was right!*

You! Man! It was Manuela, the child who had dreamed, the one he had sent to ring the fire bell.

Mabary!

Mabbitt!

Hugh!

He felt them all around him now, all of the simpleminds. *What's happened?* someone cried.

They attacked us, Mabary said. It was effortless. He simply thought, and felt his thought go out from him in waves.

Who? asked Manuela.

Folks from Outside, said Mabbitt. *The ones who've been hunting Eulie and Joe and the other sikes all these years. A lot of 'em must have got together, pierced the barrier.*

They mindburned Joe, said Mabary.

Eulie, too.

They killed September! cried Manuela.

But what's happened to us? someone asked. Mabary recognized, as distinctive as scent, the thought of Manuela's father. The gull burned in the darkness. They encircled it, danced around it. It sang to them. *Are you God?* Mabbitt cried. *If so, You got a shitload of explainin' to do.*

It never answers, said the girl.

Not in words, said Mabary. *Look.*

The army was coming out of the woods toward the fence at the bottom of the hill. Mabary could not count the number of people, but it was enough to capture a camp of four hundred stricken and confused. The army wore camouflage and carried weapons. It did not march so much as flow. *The ones in front are the sikes,* said Mabbitt. *They're the ones as did the burning. The others are simps like we used to be. They're along in case of retaliation, because leadheads can't be mindburned.*

Can they see us? asked a woman. *Can they see her?*

Does it matter? asked Mabary. They were the planets, and the gull their sun. They began to fall inward toward the gull, and one by one it drew them beneath its wings. Mabary did not lose sense of himself. He merely ceased to be concerned. Light filled him, all of them. They wheeled, and cried, and the mountain shuddered.

Then David asked the LORD,
Shall I march against the Philistines?
Wilt thou give them into my hand?
And the LORD said,
March! For I shall certainly give
The Philistines into thy hand.
It shalt be, when thou hearest the sound of
Marching in the treetops,
Act at once,
For I shall have gone out before thee
To strike down the army of
The Philistines.

The gull around and within them struck. And a great light came, and scoured, and when it had passed, there was no army, no flow of cloth and metal, nothing but a green summer day and the hysterical crying of jays.

The great gull wheeled in a blue, blue sky. *Why a seagull?* Mabary asked the cobbler.

I read an old book once, the blind man replied. *A stupid old book, we used to make fun of it. The image stuck, though, I guess.*

The mess hall had stopped burning. The alarm bell was still clanging. They touched it together with their thoughts, and it stopped. *The attack must have done it,* said Mabary. *Triggered something inside us. There was so much power. It unblocked us. That was your dream we all dreamed, Mab, your storybook gull, or maybe one you saw in Miami when you were a kid. Eulie must have been working on you all these years, hoping to stir up your Talent to prove her theory. She must have been making some headway when they attacked.*

An upwelling of voices from the messhall and the quad: weeping, cursing, questions.

They're awake! cried Manuela. *Papa, come on! Come on!* The group of minds began to disperse, flowing back towards the camp.

The cobbler said, *You coming, Hughie?*

You go on, Mab, Mabary replied.

Hasta la vista, then, boy, said Mabbitt, and melted into the summer air. Above them the seagull wheeled, flicked its wings, darted off high and away. For a long time Mabary watched it, until it was a speck of light; then the speck merged with the higher light and was lost to his sight.

If you're going to go back, you'd best go now, someone said to him. *Your body's not dead. You stopped the fire in time.* Mabary turned. Braga stood, wrapped in light and fur. *Hello, dear heart,* Braga said.

You were working on me, too, weren't you? asked Mabary.

For years and years, said Braga. *It was very tiresome. You reached me just before I died, and you moved into mindtouch like a pro.* Braga smiled. *Go back to your body, Hugh. You'll live to be a hundred.*

Mabary walked up to Braga and kissed him. They went on kissing for a very long time.

~

Rand B. Lee's science fiction has appeared in *Amazing Science Fiction Stories, Isaac Asimov's Science Fiction Magazine, The Magazine of Fantasy & Science Fiction,* and several anthologies, including *The Year's Best Science Fiction: First Annual Collection* (1984); *The 1984 Annual World's Best SF; Worlds Apart: An Anthology of Lesbian and Gay Science Fiction and Fantasy* (1986); and *Things Invisible To See: Gay and Lesbian Tales of Magic Realism* (1998). His father was Manfred B. Lee, co-author of the "Ellery Queen" detective novels, radio scripts, and short stories. Rand lives in Santa Fe, New Mexico.

O Happy Day!

Geoff Ryman

They're fooled by history. They think they won't be killed until they get into camps. So when we load them onto a different train, they go willingly. They see an old country railroad station with a big red hill behind it, and they think it's just a stop along the way.

They slip down from the cars and can't keep their feet on the sharp-edged rubble of the track. They're all on testosterone specifics, a really massive dose.

They're passive and confused, and their skin has a yellow taint to it, and their eyes stare out of patches of darkness, and they need a shave. They smell. They look like a trainload of derelicts. It must be easier to kill people who look like that, easier to call them Stiffs, as if they were already dead.

We're probably on specifics, too, but a very mild dose. We have to work, after all.

We load the Stiffs into cars, the Cars with the special features, and the second train goes off, and ten minutes later it comes back, and we unload them, dead, and that is life under what we call the Grils.

We are the Boys. We get up each morning and we shave. We're male, so we shave. Some of us do our make-up then, a bit of lipstick and slap, and an earring maybe. Big Lou always wore an earring and a tight short-sleeved T-shirt that showed off his arms. It was very strange, all those muscles with his pudding basin haircut and hatchet face, all pressed and prim around the lips.

Big Lou thought what was happening was good. I remember him explaining it to me my first day, the day he recruited me. "Men are violent," he said. "All through history, you look at violence, and it's male. That was okay in the jungle, but not now, with the gangs and the bombs and everything else. What is happening here is simple evolutionary necessity. It's the most liberating event in human history. And we're part of it." Then he kissed me. It was a political kiss, wet and cold. Then he introduced me to the work.

After we unload the trains, we strip the corpses. There are still shortages, so we tie up the clothes in bundles and save everything else of value—money, watches, cigarette lighters—and send them back on the train. It would be a terrible job for anyone, but it's worse for a faggot. Most of the bodies are young. You feel tender toward them. You want them to wake up again and move, and you think, surely there must be something better to do with this young brown body than kill it? We work very quickly, like ants on a hill.

I don't think we're mad. I think the work has become normal for us, and so we're normal within it. We have overwhelming reasons for doing it. As long as we do this work, as long as there is this work to do, we stay alive. Most of the Boys volunteered, but not for this. At first, it was just going to be internal deportation, work camps for the revolution. They were just going to be guards. Me, I was put on that train to die, and I don't know why. They dope whole areas, and collect the people they want. Lou saw me on the platform, and pulled me in. Recruited me, he called it. I slept with him, out of gratitude and fear. I still remember sleeping with him.

I was the one who recruited Royce. He saw me first. He walked up to me on the gravel between the trains, nothing out of the ordinary, just a tall black man in rumpled khaki. He was jingling the keys in his pockets, housekeys, as if he was going to need them again. He was shaking, and he kept blinking, and swaying where he stood, and he asked in a sick and panicky voice, "It's cold. It's cold. Isn't there any food?"

The information that he was good-looking got through slowly. The reaction was neutral, like you'd get from looking at a model on a billboard. Then I thought: in ten minutes' time, he's going to be dead.

You always promise yourself "just once." Just once, you'll tell the boss off; just once, you'll phone in sick and go out to the lakes. Just once. So here, I thought, is my just once: I'm going to save one of them.

"Are you gay?" I asked him. I did it without moving my lips. The cameras were always on us.

"What?" Incomprehension.

Oh God, I thought, he's going to be difficult, this is dumb. I got scared.

"What did you ask me?"

"Nothing. Go on." I nodded toward the second train.

"Am I gay?" He said it quickly, glancing around him. I just nodded.

The last of the other Stiffs were being loaded on, the old ones, who had to be lifted up. I saw Big Lou look at us and start walking toward us, sauntering, amiable, with a diamanté earring.

"Yes," said Royce. "Why?"

"Make like you know me. My name's Richard."

"Royce," he said, but I couldn't catch it.

Then Lou was standing next to us. "A little tête-à-tête?" he asked.

"Hi Lou," I said. I leaned back on my heels, away from him. "We got ourselves a new recruit."

"Don't need one, Rich," he said, still smiling.

"Lou, look. We were lovers. We lived together for two years. We did a lot of work for the movement together. He's okay, really."

Lou was looking at Royce, at Royce's face. Being black was in Royce's favor, ideologically. All the other Boys were white. No one wanted the Station to be accused of racism.

"I don't believe a word of it," said Lou. "But okay."

Lou walked toward one of the cameras. "Hey!" he shouted up to it. The camera was armed. It turned toward him, slowly. "We've got a new recruit."

"What was that?" asked the camera, or rather the voice of the Gril behind it. The sound was flat and mechanical, the tone offhand and bored.

"A new recruit. A new Boy. He's with us, so don't burn him, okay?"

"Okay, okay," said the camera. Lou turned back, and patted Royce's bare, goose-pimpled arm. Royce lurched after him, and I grabbed hold of his shirt to stop him. I was frightened he was going to get back onto the train. I waited until it was pulling out, creaking and crashing, so that the noise would cover what I said.

"It's terrible here," I told Royce. "But it's better than dying. Watch what you say. The cameras don't always hear, but usually they can. It's all right to look disgusted. They don't mind if you look a bit sick. They like us to do the job with distaste. Just don't ever say you think it's wrong."

"What's wrong?" he asked, and I thought: Oh God, he doesn't know. He doesn't know what's going on here. And I thought: now what do I do with him?

I showed him around the Station. It's a small, old-fashioned building made of yellow and black brick, with no sign on it to tell us where we are. One hundred years ago women in long dresses with children would have waited on its platform for the train to take them shopping in the city. There would have been a ticket-seller behind the counter who knew all the women by their last name, and who kept a girlie calendar pinned on the wall. His booth still has ornate iron bars across it, the word "Tickets" in art nouveau scrolling, still slightly gilded. The waiting room is full of temporary metal beds. The walls are painted a musty pistachio, and the varnish on the wooden floor has gone black. There are games machines in the corner, and behind the ticket counter is an electric cooker. We eat sitting on our beds. There are cold showers, outside by the wall, and there are flower boxes in the windows. James the Tape Head—he's one of the Boys—keeps them full of petunias and geraniums. All around it and the hill behind are concentric rows of wire mesh, thirty feet high and thirty feet deep, to keep the Stiffs controlled, and us in. It isn't a Station, it's a mass graveyard, for them and probably for us.

I tried to get Royce to go to bed, but he wouldn't. He was frightened to be left alone. He followed me out onto the platform where we were unloading the Stiffs, rolling them out. Sometimes the bodies sigh when they hit the concrete.

Royce's eyes went as wide as a rabbit's that's been run over by a car.

"What are you doing? What are you doing?" he yelped, over and over.

"What the fuck does it look like?" I said.

We strip them on the platform, and load them into trolleys. We shake them out of their trousers, and go through the pockets. Getting them out of their shirts is worse; their arms flop, and their heads loll. We're allowed to leave them in their underwear.

"They're doing it. Oh God, oh Jesus, they're killing them! Nobody knows that! Nobody believes that!"

"Help me carry them," I said. I said it for his sake. He shook his head, and stepped back, and stumbled over arms and legs and fell into a tangle of them.

Only the worst, we're told, only the most violent of men. That means the poor bastards who had to pick up a gun, or join a gang, or sign up for the police or the army. In other words, most of the people we kill are either black or Latino. I tried to tell them, I tried to tell the women that would happen.

Royce was suddenly sick. It was partly the drugs wearing off. Charlie and I hoisted him up and dragged him, as limp as a Stiff, into the showers. We got him cleaned up and into bed—my bed, there wasn't any other—and after that he was very quiet. Everybody was interested in him. New dog in the pound. Harry offered him one of his peppermints. Harry came up smiling, but then Harry is always smiling like the Man who Laughed, yellow teeth in a red beard. He'd got the peppermints off a Stiff. Royce didn't know how precious they were. He just shook his head, and lay there staring under the blanket, as one by one we all came back from the platform. Lou was last, thumping in and sighing, like he was satisfied with something. He slumped down on my bed next to Royce's knees, and I thought: uh-oh, Lou likes him too.

"Bad day, huh," Lou said. "Listen, I know, the first day is poison. But you got to ask yourself why it's happening."

"Why is it?" asked Royce, his face and mouth muffled in the crook of his elbow. He sounded like he was going to be sick again.

"Why?" Lou sounded shocked. "Royce, you remember how bad things got. The assassinations, the military build-up, the bombs?"

Only in America: the gangs got hold of tactical nuclear weapons. They punched out their rivals' turf: parts of Detroit, Miami, Houston, Chicago and then the big DC.

"I know," said Royce. "I used to live in Los Angeles."

Los Angeles came later. I sometimes wonder now if Los Angeles wasn't a special case. Ever hear of the Reichstag fire? Lou went respectful and silent, and he sat back, head bowed. "I am really sick at heart to hear that. I am so sorry. It must be like your whole past life has been blown away. What can I say? You probably know what I'm talking about better than anyone else here. It just had to be stopped, didn't it?"

"It did stop," said Royce.

"Yeah, I know, and that was because of the testosterone specifics. The women gave us that. Do you remember how great that felt, Royce? How calm you felt. That's because you'd been released from your masculinity, the specifics set men free from themselves. It was a beautiful thing to do."

Lou rocked back on the bed, and recited the old doggerel slogan. "TSI, in the water supply, a year-round high. I remember the first day I could leave my gun at home, man. I got on the subway, and there was this big Kahuna, all beads and tattoos, and he just smiled at me and passed me a joint. I really thought the specifics were the answer. But they hurt women, not many, but that's enough. So the specifics were withdrawn, and look what happened. Six months later, Los Angeles went up. The violence had to stop. And that's what we're going for here, Royce. Not men per se, but violence: the military, the police, criminals, gangsters, pornographers. Once they go, this whole thing here stops. It's like a surgical operation."

"Could you let me sleep?" Royce asked.

"Yeah sure," said Lou gently, and leaned forward and kissed him. "Don't worry, Royce, we take care of our own here. These guys are a really great bunch of people. Welcome home."

The Boys went back to playing computer games in the waiting room. Bleep bleep bleep. One of the guys started yelling because a jack was missing from his deck of cards. James the Tape Head sat on his bed, Mozart hissing at him through his headphones. I looked at Royce, and I thought of him: you are a good person.

That's when I began to have the fantasy. We all have the fantasy, of someone good and kind and strong, who sees who we really are when we're not messed up. Without knowing I was doing it, I began to make Royce my fantasy, my beautiful, kind, good man. The strange thing was that in a way the fantasy was true. So was it a fantasy at all?

The next day—it was the very next day—Royce began his campaign.

I volunteered us both to get the food. The food comes down the tracks very early in a little automatic car. Someone has to unload it and take it into the kitchen. I wanted to get Royce and me away from the Boys to talk. He was unsure of me; he pulled on his socks and looked at me, solemnly, in the eye. Fair enough, I thought, he doesn't know me. Lou loaned him a big duffle coat, and Royce led us both out through the turnstiles and onto the platform.

We didn't have our talk. Like he was stepping out onto a stage, under the cameras, Royce started to play a part. I don't like to say this, but he started to play the part of a black man. It was an act, designed to disarm. He grinned and did a Joe Cool kind of movement. "Hey! How are you?" he said to one particular camera.

The camera stayed still, and silent.

"You can't fool me, I know there's someone there. What's your name?" he asked it. Silence, of course.

"Aw, come on, you can tell me that, can't you? Listen, I have got a terrible name. It's Royce. How would you like to be called after a car? Your name can't be as bad as that. What is it? Grizelda? Hortensia? My favorite aunt's called Hortensia. How about Gertrude? Ever read Hamlet? What about … Lurleen?"

There was a hollow sound, like in a transatlantic phone call, when you talk over someone and it cuts out what they're saying for a couple of seconds afterwards. The camera did that. It had turned off its voice. And I thought, I didn't know it could do that; and I thought, why did it do it?

"Look. I have to call you something. My sister is called Alice. You don't mind if I call you Alice? Like in Wonderland?" Royce stepped forward. The camera did not have to bristle; its warm-up light went on.

"You see, Alice. I—uh—have a personal question."

The camera spoke. "What is it?" the voice was sharp and wary. I had the feeling that he had actually found her real name.

"Alice—uh—I don't want to embarrass anyone, but, um, you see, I got this little emergency, and everywhere I look there are cameras, so, um, where can I go?"

A pause from the camera. "I'm sorry," it said. "there are toilet facilities, but I'm afraid we have to keep you under observation. "

"Really, I don't do anything that much different from anyone else."

"I'm sure you don't. "

"I mean sometimes I try it standing on the seat or in a yoga position."

"Fine, but I'm afraid you'll still have to put up with the cameras."

"Well I hope you're recording it for posterity, 'cause if you get rid of all the men, it'll have real historical interest."

There was a click from the camera again. I stepped out of the line of fire. Royce presented himself at the turnstiles, and they buzzed to let him through. He made his way toward the john singing "That's Entertainment."

All the cameras turned to watch him.

Just before he went into the shed, he pulled out his pecker and waggled it at them. "Wave bye-bye," he said.

He'll get us all killed, I thought. The john was a trench with a plywood shed around it, open all along one side. I went to the wire mesh behind it, to listen.

"Alice?" I heard him ask through the plywood.

"I'm not Alice," said another voice from another camera. She meant in more ways than one, she was not Alice. "Uh—Hortensia? Uh. There's no toilet paper, Hortensia."

"I know."

"Gee, I wish you'd told me first."

"There are some old clothes on the floor. Use some of them and throw them over the side."

Dead men's shirts. I heard a kind of rustle and saw a line of shadow under the boards, waddling forward, crouched.

"I must look like a duck, huh?"

"A roast one in a minute."

Royce was quiet for a while after that. Finally he said, grumbling, "Trust me to pick tweed."

He kept it up, all morning long, talking to the Grils. During breakfast, he talked about home cooking and how to make tostadas and enchiladas. He talked about a summer job he'd had in Los Angeles, working in a diner that specialized in Kosher Mexican Food. Except for Royce, everyone who worked there including the owners was Japanese. That, said Royce, shaking his head, was LA. He and his mother had to move back east, to get away from the gang wars.

As the bodies were being unloaded, Royce talked about his grandmother. He'd lived with her when he was a child, and his father was dying. His grandmother made ice cream in the bathtub. She filled it full of ice and spun tubs of cream in it. Then she put one of the tubs in a basket with an umbrella over it on the front of her bicycle. She cycled through the neighborhood, selling ice cream and singing "Rock of Ages." She kept chickens, which was against the zoning regulations, and threw them at people who annoyed her, especially policemen. Royce had a cat, and it and a chicken fell in love. They would mew and cluck for each other, and sit for contented hours at a time, the chicken's neck snugly and safely inside the cat's mouth.

It was embarrassing, hearing someone talk. Usually we worked in silence. And the talk was confusing; we didn't think about things like summer jobs or household pets anymore. As the bodies were dumped and stripped, Royce's face was hard and shiny with sweat, like polished wood.

That afternoon, we had our talk. Since we'd gotten the food, it was our turn to cook lunch. So I got him away from the Boys.

We took our soup and crackers up to the top of the mound. The mound is dug out of a small hill behind the Station. James makes it in his bulldozer, listening to Mozart. He pulls the trolleys up a long dirt ramp, and empties them, and smoothes the sandstone soil over each day's addition of Stiffs. I get the feeling he thinks he works like Mozart. The mound rises up in terraces, each terrace perfectly level, its slope at the same angle as the one below it. The dirt is brick red and there are seven levels. It looks like Babylon.

There are cameras on top, but you can see over the fence. You can see the New England forest. It looks tired and small, maybe even dusty, as if it needed someone to clean the leaves. There's another small hill. You can hear birds. Royce and I climbed up to the top, and I gathered up my nerve and said, "I really like you."

"Uh-huh," he said, balancing his soup, and I knew it wasn't going to work. Leave it, I thought, don't push, it's hard for him, he doesn't know you.

"You come here a lot," he said. It was a statement.

"I come here to get away."

Royce blew out through his nostrils: a kind of a laugh. "Get away? You know what's under your feet?"

"Yes," I said, looking at the forest. Neither one of us wanted to sit on that red soil, even to eat the soup. I passed him his crackers, from my coat pocket.

"So why did you pick me? Out of all the other Stiffs?"

"I guess I just liked what I saw."

"Why?"

I smiled with embarrassment at being forced to say it; it was as if there were no words for it that were not slightly wrong. "Because I guess you're kind of good-looking and I … just thought I would like you a lot. "

"Because I'm black?"

"You are black, yes."

"Are most of your boyfriends black?"

Bull's-eye. That was scary. "I, uh, did go through a phase where I guess I was kind of fixated on black people. But I stopped that, I mean, I realized that what I was actually doing was depersonalizing the people I was with, which wasn't very flattering to them. But that is all over. It really isn't important to me now."

"So you went out and made yourself sleep with white people." He does not, I thought, even remotely like me.

"I found white people I liked. It didn't take much."

"You toe the line all the way down the line, don't you?" he said.

I thought I didn't understand.

"Is that why you're here?" A blank from me. "You toe the line, the right line, so you're here."

"Yes," I said. "In a way. Big Lou saw me on the platform, and knew me from politics. I guess you don't take much interest in politics." I was beginning to feel like hitting back.

"Depends on the politics," he said, briskly.

"Well you're okay, I guess. You made it out."

"Out of where?"

I just looked back at him. "Los Angeles."

He gave a long and very bitter sigh, mixed with a kind of chortle. "Whenever I am in this … situation, there is the conversation. I always end up having the same conversation. I reckon you're going to tell me I'm not black enough."

"You do kind of shriek I am middle class."

"Uh-huh. You use that word class, so that means it's not racist, right?"

"I mean, you're being loyal to your class, to which most black people do not belong."

"Hey, bro', you can't fool me, we're from the same neighborhood. That sort of thing?" It was imitation ghetto. "You want somebody with beads in his hair and a beret and a semi who hates white people, but likes you because you're so upfront movement? Is that your little dream? A big bad black man?"

I turned away from him completely.

He said, in a very cold still voice. "Do you get off on corpses, too?"

"This was a mistake," I said. "Let's go back."

"I thought you wanted to talk."

"Why are you doing this?"

"Because," he said, "you are someone who takes off dead men's watches, and you look like you could have been a nice person. "

"I am," I said, and nearly wept, "a nice person."

"That's what scares the shit out of me."

"You think I want this? You think I don't hate this?" I think that's when I threw down the soup. I grabbed him by the shirt sleeves and held him. I remember being worried about the cameras, so I kept my voice low and rapid, like it was scuttling.

"Look, I was on the train, I was going to die, and Lou said, you can live. You can help here and live. So I did it. And I'm here. And so are you."

"I know," he said, softly.

"So okay, you don't like me, I can live with that, fine, no problem, you're under no obligation, so let's just go back."

"You come up here because of the forest," he said.

"Yes! Brilliant!"

"Even mass murderers need love too, right?"

"Yes! Brilliant!"

"And you want me to love you? When you bear the same relation to me, as Lou does to you?"

"I don't know. I don't care." I was sitting down now, hugging myself. The bowl of soup was on the ground by my foot, tomato sludge creeping out of it. I kicked it. "Sorry I hassled you."

"You didn't hassle me."

"All I want is one little part of my life to have a tiny corner of goodness in it. Just one little place. I probably won't, but I feel like if I don't find it soon, I will bust up into a million pieces. Not love. Not necessarily. Just someone nice to talk to, who I really like. Otherwise I think one day I will climb back into one of those trains." When I said it, I realized it was true. I hadn't known I was that far gone. I thought I had been making a play for sympathy.

Royce was leaning in front of me, looking me in the face. "Listen, I love you."

"Bullshit." What kind of mind-fuck now?

He grabbed my chin, and turned my head back round. "No. True. Not maybe in the way you want, but true. You really do look, right now, like one of those people on the train. Like someone I just unloaded."

I didn't know quite what he was saying, and I wasn't sure I trusted him, but I did know one thing. "I don't want to go back to that bunkhouse, not this afternoon."

"Okay. We'll stay up here and talk."

I felt like I was stepping out onto ice. "But can we talk nicely? A little bit less heavy duty?"

"Nicely. Sounds sweet, doesn't mean anything. Like the birds?"

"Yes," I said. "Like the birds."

I reckon that, altogether, we had two weeks. A Lullaby in Birdland. Hum along if you want to. You don't need to know the words.

Every afternoon after the work, Royce and I went up the mound and talked. I think he liked talking to me, I'll go as far as that. I remember one afternoon he showed me photographs from his wallet. He still had a wallet, full of people.

He showed me his mother. She was extremely thin, with dark limp flesh under her eyes. She was trying to smile. Her arms were folded across her stomach. She looked extremely kind, but tired.

There was a photograph of a large red brick house. It had white window sills and a huge white front door, and it sagged in the way that only very old houses do.

"Whose is that?" I asked.

"Ours. Well, my family's. Not my mother's. My uncle lives there now."

"It's got a Confederate flag over it!"

Royce grinned and folded up quietly; his laughter was almost always silent. "Well, my great-grandfather didn't want to lose all his slaves, did he?"

One half of Royce's family were black, one half were white. There were terrible wedding receptions divided in half where no one spoke. "The white people are all so embarrassed, particularly the ones who want to be friendly. There's only one way a black family gets a house like that: Grandfather messed around a whole bunch. He hated his white family, so he left the house to us. My uncle and aunt want to open it up as a Civil War museum and put their picture on the leaflet." Royce folded up again. "I mean, this is in Georgia. Can you imagine all those rednecks showing up and finding a nice black couple owning it, and all this history about black regiments?"

"Who's that?"

"My cousin. She came to live with us for a while. "

"She's from the white half."

"Nope. She's black." Royce was enjoying himself. The photograph showed a rather plump, very determined teenage girl with orange hair, slightly wavy, and freckles.

"Oh." I was getting uncomfortable, all this talk of black and white.

"It's really terrible. Everything Cyndi likes, I mean everything, is black, but her father married a white woman, and she ended up like that. She wanted to be black so bad. Every time she met anyone, she'd start explaining how she was black, really. She'd go up to black kids and start explaining, and you could see them thinking 'Who is this white girl and is she out of her mind?' We were both on this program, so we ended up in a white high school and that was worse because no one knew they'd been integrated when she was around. The first day this white girl asked her if she'd seen any of the new black kids. Then her sister went and became a top black fashion model, you know, features in Ebony, and that was it. It got so bad, that whenever Cyndi meant white, she'd say 'the half of me I hate.'"

"What happened to her?"

"I think she gave up and became white. She wanted to be a lawyer. I don't know what happened to her. She got caught in LA."

I flipped over the plastic. There was a photograph of a mother and a small child. "Who's that?"

"My son," said Royce. "That's his mother. Now she thinks she's a witch." An ordinary looking girl stared sullenly out at the camera. She had long frizzy hair and some sort of ethnic dress. "She'll go up to waiters she doesn't like in restaurants and whisper spells at them in their ears."

"How long ago was this?" I felt an ache, as if I'd lost him, as if I had ever had him.

"Oh ten years ago, before I knew anything. I mean, I wouldn't do it now. I'd like any kid of mine to have me around, but his mother and I don't get on. She told my aunt that she'd turned me gay by magic to get revenge."

"Were they in LA too?"

Royce went very still, and nodded yes.

"I'm sorry," I said.

He passed me back the wallet. "Here. That's all of them. Last time we got together."

There was a tiny photograph, full of people. The black half. On the far right was a very tall, gangling fifteen-year-old, looking bristly and unformed, shy and sweet. Three of the four people around him were looking at him, bursting with suppressed smiles. I wish I'd known him then, as well. I wanted to know him all his life.

"I got a crazy, crazy family," he said, shaking his head with affection. "I hope they're all still okay." It was best not to think about what was happening outside. Or inside, here.

It was autumn, and the sun would come slanting through the leaves of the woods. It would make a kind of corona around them, especially if the Boys were burning garbage and there was smoke in the air. The light would come in shafts, like God was hiding behind the leaves. The leaves were dropping one by one.

There was nothing in the Station that was anything to do with Royce. Everything that made him Royce, that made him interesting, is separate. It is the small real things that get obliterated in a holocaust, forgotten. The horrors are distinct and do not connect with the people, but it is the horrors that get remembered in history.

When it got dark, we would go back down, and I hated it because each day it was getting dark earlier and earlier. We'd get back and find that there had been—oh—a macaroni fight over lunch, great handprints of it over the windows and on the beds, that had been left to dry. Once we got back to the waiting room, and there had been a fight, a real one. Lou had given one of the Boys a bloody nose, to stop it. There was blood on the floor. Lou lectured us all about male violence, saying anyone who used violence in the Station would get violence back.

He took away all of Tom's clothes. Tom was beautiful, and very quiet, but sometimes he got mad. Lou kicked him out of the building in punishment. It was going to be a cold night. Long after the Grils had turned out the lights, we could hear Tom whimpering, just outside the door. "Please, Lou. It's cold.

Lou, I'm sorry. Lou? I just got carried away. Please?"

I felt Royce jump up and throw the blanket aside. Oh God, I thought, don't get Lou mad at us. Royce padded across the dark room, and I heard the door open, and I heard him say, "Okay, come in."

"Sorry, Lou," Royce said. "But we all need to get to sleep." Lou only grunted. "Okay," he said, in a voice that was biding its time.

And Royce came back to my bed.

I would hold him, and he would hold me, but only, I think, to stop falling out of the bed. It was so narrow and cold. Royce's body was always taut, like each individual strand of muscle had been pulled back, tightly, from the shoulder. It was as tense through the night as if it were carrying something, and nothing I could do would soothe it. What I am trying to say, and I have to say it, is that Royce was impotent, at least with me, at least in the Station. "As long as I can't do it," he told me once on the mound, "I know I haven't forgotten where I am." Maybe that was just an excuse. The Boys knew about it, of course. They listened in the dark and knew what was and was not happening.

And the day would begin at dawn. The little automatic car, the porridge and the bread, the icy showers, and the wait for the first train. James the Tape Head, Harry with his constant grin, Gary who was tall and ropey, and who kept tugging at his pigtail. He'd been a trader in books, and he talked books and politics and thought he was Lou's lieutenant. Lou wasn't saying. And Bill the Brylcreem, and Charlie with his still, and Tom. The Boys. Hating each other, with no one else to talk to, waiting for the day when the Grils would burn us, or the food in the cart would have an added secret ingredient. When they were done with us.

Royce talked, learning who the cameras were.

There were only four Grils, dividing the day into two shifts. Royce gave them names. There was Alice and Hortensia, and Miss Scarlett who turned out to be from Atlanta. Only one of the Grils took a while to find a name, and she got it the first day one of the cameras laughed.

She'd been called Greta, I think because she had such a low, deep voice. Sometimes Royce called her Sir. Then one morning, Lou was late, and as he came, Royce said. "Uh-oh. Here comes the Rear Admiral."

Lou was very sanctimonious about always taking what he assumed was the female role in sex. The cameras knew that; they watched all the time. The camera laughed. It was a terrible laugh; a thin, high, wailing, helpless shriek.

"Hey, Sir, that's really Butch," said Royce, and the name Butch stuck.

So did Rear Admiral. God bless all who sail in him.

"Hiya, Admiral," gasped the camera, and even some of the Boys laughed too.

Lou looked confused, a stiff and awkward smile on his face. "It's better than being some macho prick," he said.

That night, he took me to one side, by the showers.

"Look," he said. "I think maybe you should get your friend to ease up a bit."

"Oh Lou, come on, it's just jokes."

"You think all of this is a joke!" yelped Lou.

"No."

"Don't think I don't understand what's going on." The light caught in his eyes, pinprick bright.

"What do you think is going on, Lou?"

I saw him appraising me. I saw him give me the benefit of the doubt. "What you've done, Rich, and maybe it isn't your fault, is to import an ideological wild card into this station."

"Oh Lou," I groaned. I groaned for him, for his mind.

"He's not with us. I don't know what these games are that he's playing with the women, but he's putting us all in danger. Yeah, sure, they're laughing now, but sooner or later he'll say the wrong thing, and some of us will get burned. Cooked. And another thing. These little heart to heart talks you have with each other. Very nice. But that's just the sort of thing the Station cannot tolerate. We are a team, we are a family, we've broken with all of that nuclear family shit, and you guys have re-imported it. You're breaking us up, into little compartments. You, Royce, James, even Harry, you're all going off into little corners away from the rest of us. We have got to work together. Now I want to see you guys with the rest of us. No more withdrawing."

"Lou," I said, helpless to reply. "Lou. Fuck off."

His eyes had the light again. "Careful, Rich. "

"Lou. We are with you guys twenty-two hours a day. Can you really not do without us for the other two? What is wrong with a little privacy, Lou?"

"There is no privacy here," he said. "The cameras pick up just about every word. Now look. I took on a responsibility. I took on the responsibility of getting all of us through this together, show that there is a place in the revolution for good gay men. I have to know what is going on in the Station. I don't know what you guys are saying to each other up there, I don't know what the cameras are hearing. Now you lied to me, Rich. You didn't know Royce before he came here, did you. We don't know who he is, what he is. Rich, is Royce even gay?"

"Yes! Of course!"

"Then how does he fuck?"

"That's none of your business."

"Everything here is my business. You don't fuck him, he doesn't fuck you, so what goes on?"

I was too horrified to speak.

"Look," said Lou, relenting. "I can understand it. You love the guy. You think I don't feel that pull, too, that pull to save them? We wouldn't be gay if we didn't. So you see him on the platform, and he is very nice, and you think, Dear God, why does he have to die?"

"Yes. "

"I feel it! I feel it too!" Lou made a good show of doing so. "It's not the people themselves, but what they are that we have to hold onto. Remember, Rich, this is just a program of containment. What we get here are the worst, Rich, the very worst—the sex criminals, the transsexuals, the media freaks. So what you have to ask yourself, Rich, is this: what was Royce doing on that train?"

"Same thing I was. He got pulled in by mistake."

Lou looked at me with a kind of blank pity. Then he looked down at the ground. "There are no mistakes, Rich. They've got the police files."

"Then what was I doing on the train?"

Lou looked back up at me and sighed. "I think you probably got some of the women very angry with you. There's a lot of infighting, particularly where gay men fit in. I don't like it. It's why I got you out. It may be something similar with Royce."

"On the train because I disagreed with them?" Everything felt weak, my knees, my stomach.

"It's possible, only possible. This is a revolution, Rich. Things are pretty fluid."

"Oh God, Lou, what's happening?"

"You see why we have to be careful? People have been burned in this station, Rich. Not lately, because I've been in charge. And I intend to stay in charge. Look."

Lou took me in his arms. "This must be really terrible for you, I know. All of us were really happy for you, when you and Royce started. But we have to protect ourselves. Now let's just go back in, and ask Royce who and what he is."

"What do you mean?"

"Just ask him. In front of the others. What he was. And not take no for an answer." He was stroking my hair.

"He'll hate me if I do that!" I tried to push him away. He grabbed hold of my hair, and pulled it, smiling, almost as if he were still being sexy and affectionate.

"Then he'll just have to get over that kind of mentality. What has he got to hide if he needs privacy? Come on, Rich. Let's just get it over with." He pulled me back, into the waiting room.

Royce took one look at us together as we came in, and his face went still, as if to say, "Uh-huh. This is coming now, is it?" His eyes looked hard into mine, and said, "Are you going to put up with it?" I was ashamed. I was powerless.

"Rich has a confession to make," said Lou, a friendly hand still on the back of my neck. "Don't you, Rich?"

They all seemed to sit up and close in, an inquisition, and I stood there thinking, Dear God, what do I do? What do I do?

"Rich," Lou reminded me. "We have to go through this. We need to talk this through."

Royce sat there, on our bed, reclining, waiting.

Well, I had lied. "I don't really know who Royce is. We weren't lovers before. We are lovers now."

"But you don't know what he was doing, or who he was, do you, Rich?"

I just shook my head.

"Don't you want to know that, Rich? Don't you want to know who your lover was? Doesn't it seem strange to you that he's never told you?"

"No," I replied. "We all did what we had to do before the revolution. What we did back then is not who we are." See, I wanted to say to Royce, I'm fighting, see I'm fighting.

"But there are different ways of knuckling under, aren't there, Rich? You taught history. You showed people where the old system had gone wrong. You were a good, gay man."

Royce stood up, abruptly, and said, "I was a prison guard."

The room went cold and Lou's eyes gleamed.

"And there are different ways of being a prison guard. It was a detention center for juveniles, young guys who might have had a chance. Not surprisingly, most of them were black. I don't suppose you know what happens to black juvenile prisoners now, do you? I'd like to know."

"Their records are looked at," said Lou. "So. You were a gay prison guard in charge of young men."

"Is that so impossible?"

"So, you were a closet case for a start."

"No. I told my immediate superior. "

"Immediate superior. You went along with the hierarchy. Patriarchy, I should say. Did you have a good time with the boys?"

"This camp is a hierarchy, in case you hadn't noticed. And no, I kept my hands off the boys. I was there to help them, not make things worse."

"Helping them to be gay would be worse?" Every word was a trap door that could fall open. The latch was hatred. "Did you ever beat one of the boys up? Did you deal dope on the side?"

Royce was still for a moment, his eyes narrow. Then he spoke.

"About four years ago, me and the kids put on a show. We put on a show for the girls' center. The girls came in a bus, and they'd all put their hair in ringlets, and they walked into the gym with too much make-up on, holding each other's hands, clutching each other's forearms, like this, because they were so nervous. And the kids, the boys, they'd been rehearsing, oh, for weeks. They'd built and painted a set. It was a street, with lights in the windows, and a big yellow moon. There was this one kid, Jonesy. Jonesy kept sticking his head through the curtain before we started. 'Hey everybody! I'm a star!'"

Royce said it again, softly. "Hey everybody, I'm a star. And I had to yell at him, Jonesy, get your ass off that stage. The girls sat on one side of the gym, and the boys on the other, and they smiled and waved and threw things at each other, like gum wrappers. It was all they had."

Royce started to cry. He glared at Lou and let the tears slide down his face. "They didn't have anything else to give each other. The show started and one of the kids did his announcing routine. He'd made a bow tie out of a white paper napkin, and it looked so sharp. And then the music came up and one of the girls just shouted. 'Oh, they're going to dance!' And those girls screamed. They just screamed. The boys did their dance on the stage, no mistaking what those moves meant. The record was 'It's a Shame.'"

His face contorted suddenly, perhaps with anger. "And I had to keep this god-damned aisle between them, the whole time. "

"So?" said Lou, unmoved.

"So," said Royce, and gathered himself in. He wiped the moisture from his face. "So I know a lot about prisons. So, some of those kids are dead now. The boys and the girls wanted each other. That must be an ideological quandary for you, Lou. Here's a big bad guard stopping people doing what they want, but what they want to do is het-ero-sex-u-ality." He turned it into a mock dirty word, his eyes round.

"No problem," said Lou. "All women are really lesbians."

Royce stared at him for a moment. Then he began to laugh.

"I wouldn't expect you to understand. But the first experience of physical tenderness that any woman has is with her mother."

"Gee, I'm sure glad my old aunt Hortensia didn't know that. She would be surprised. Hey, Alice. Are you a dyke?"

Lou went pale, and lines of shadow encircled his mouth.

"Yes," said Alice, the camera.

"Well, I'm a faggot, but it doesn't mean everyone else is."

Lou launched himself from the bed, in a fury. He was on his feet, and shouting, flecks of spit propelled from his mouth.

"You do not use demeaning language here!" His voice cracked.

Alice had been working nine hours, and now she was alone, on the night shift. She had been watching, silently, for nine hours. Now, she wanted to talk.

"I had a girlfriend once who was straight," she said. "No matter how hard she tried, women just didn't bring her off. Mind you, that's better than those lust lesbians. They just want your body. Me, I'm totally dedicated to women, but it's a political commitment. It's something I decided. I don't let my body make my decisions for me."

"Yeah, I know what you mean," said Royce. "It's these lust faggots, I can't stand." He cast his eyes about him at the Boys, and they chuckled.

"We do not use the word 'dyke' in this station," said Lou.

Royce looked rather sad and affectionate, and shook his head. "Lou. You are such a prig. Not only are you a prig. You are a dumb prig."

The floor seemed to open up under my feet with admiration. Only Royce could have said that to Lou. I loved him, even though I did not love myself. The Boys chuckled again, because it was funny, and because it was true, and because it was a little bit of a shock.

"Alice," said Lou. "He has just insulted women."

"Funny," said Alice. "I thought he'd just insulted you."

Lou looked like he was in the middle of a nightmare; you could see it in his face. "Alice is being very tolerant, Royce. But from now on, you talk to and about the women with respect. If you want to live here with us, there are a few ground rules."

"Like what?"

"No more jokes."

Royce was leaning against the bar at the foot of our bed, and he was calm, and his ankles were crossed. He closed his eyes, and smiled. "No more jokes?" he asked, amused.

"You mess around with the women, you put us all in danger. You keep putting us in danger, you got to go."

"Lou," said Alice. "Can I remind you of something? You don't decide who goes on the trains. We do."

"I understand that, Alice." He slumped from the shoulders and his breath seeped out of him. He seemed to shrink.

"Lou," said Royce. "I think you and I are on the same side?" It was a question.

"We'd better be," said Lou.

"Then you do know why I talk to the women."

"Yeah," said Lou. "You want to show off. You want to be the center of attention. You don't want to take responsibility for anything."

He didn't understand. Lou was dangerous because he was stupid.

"I've been a prison guard," said Royce, carefully. "I know what it's like. You're trapped, even worse than the prisoners."

"So?" He was going to make Royce say it, in front of a camera. He was going to make him say that he was talking to the Grils so that they would find it hard to kill us when the time came.

"I'm talking to the women, so that they'll get to know us," said Royce, "and see that there is a place for gay men within the revolution. They can't know that unless we talk to them. Can they?"

Bull's-eye again. That was the only formulation Lou was ever likely to accept.

"I mean, can they, Lou? I think we're working with the women on this thing together. There's no need for silence between us, not if we're on the same side. Okay, so maybe I do it wrong. I don't want to be the only one who does all the talking. We all should talk to them, Lou, you, me, all of us. And the women should feel that they can talk with us as well."

"Oh yeah, I am so bored keeping schtum," said Alice.

Lou went still, and he drew in a deep breath. "Okay," he said. "We can proceed on that basis. We all communicate, with each other and with the cameras. But Royce. That means no more withdrawing. No more going off in a corner. No more little heart to hearts on the mound."

"I didn't know that was a problem, Lou. There will be no more of those."

"Okay, then," said Lou, murmurous in defeat. Royce strode toward him, both hands outstretched, and took Lou's hand in both of his.

"This is really good, Lou. I'm really glad we talked."

Lou looked back at him, looking worn and heavy, but he was touched. Big Lou was moved, as well, and he gave a slightly forlorn flicker of a smile.

So Royce became head of the Station.

He gave me a friendly little nod, and moved his things away from our bed. He slept in Tom's; Tom never did. It didn't matter, because I still had my little corner of goodness, even if we didn't talk. Royce was still there, telling jokes. I was happy with that because I knew that I had deserted him before he had deserted me; and I understood that I was to be the visible victory he gave to Lou. None of that mattered. Royce had survived. I didn't cry the first night alone; I stopped myself. I didn't want the Boys to hear.

Things started to change. The cameras stopped looking at us on the john. We could see them turn and look away. Then one morning, they were just hanging, dead.

"Hey, Rich!" Harry called me. It was me and Harry, unloading the food cart, as winter finally came. Harry was hopping up and down in front of the camera. He leapt up and tapped it, and the warm-up light did not even go on.

"They've turned it off, Rich! the camera's off. It's dead!"

He grabbed my arms, and spun me around, and started doing a little dance, and I started to hoot with laughter along with him. It was like someone had handed you back part of your pride. It was like we were human enough to be accorded that again.

"Hey Royce, the camera in the john's off!" shouted Harry, as we burst through the canteen doors with the trolley.

"Maybe they're just broken," said Gary, who was still loyal to Lou.

"Naw, man, they'd be telling us to fix it by now. They've turned it off!"

"That so, Alice?" Royce asked the camera in the canteen.

"Oh. Yeah," said Alice. Odd how a mechanical voice could sound so much more personal than a real one, closer somehow, as if in the middle of your ear.

"Thanks, Alice."

"'S okay," said Alice, embarrassed. "We explained it to the Wigs. We told them it was like pornography, you know, demeaning to us. They bought it. Believe me, you guys are not a lovely sight first thing in the morning."

I could see Royce go all alert at that word "Wig," like an animal raising its ears. He didn't mention the Wigs again until later that afternoon.

"Alice, is our talking ever a problem for you?"

"How d'you mean?"

"Well, if one of the Wigs walked in …"

Alice kind of laughed. "Huh. They don't get down this far. What do you know about them, anyhow?"

"Nothing. Who are they?"

"Mind your own business. The people who run things."

"Well if someone does show up and you want us to shut up, just sneeze, and we'll stop talking."

"Sneeze?"

"Well, you could always come right out and say cool it guys, there's someone here."

"Hey Scarlett," said Alice. "Can you sneeze?"

"Ach-ooo," said Miss Scarlett, delicately.

"Just testing, guys," said Alice.

Big Lou hung around, trying to smile, trying to look like somehow all this was going on under his auspices. Nobody was paying attention.

The next day, the train didn't show.

It was very cold, and we stood on the platform, thumping our feet, as the day grew more sparkling, and the shadows shorter.

"Hey, Butch, what's up?" Royce asked.

"I'll check, okay?" said the camera. There was a long silence.

"The train's broken down. It's in a siding. It'll be a while yet. You might as well go back in, have the day off."

That's how it would begin, of course. No train today, fellas, sorry. No need for you, fellas, not today, not ever, and with what you know, can you blame us? What are ten more bodies to us?

Trains did break down, of course. It had happened before. We'd had a holiday then, too, and the long drunken afternoon became a long drunken day.

"Well let's have some fun for a change," said Lou. "Charlie, you got any stuff ready? Let's have a blow-out, man."

"Lou," said Royce, "I was kind of thinking we could get to work on the hot water tank."

"Hot water tank?" said Lou. "Are we going to need it, Royce?" there was a horrified silence. "So much for talking. Go on, Charlie, get your booze."

Then Lou came for me. "How about a little sex and romance, Rich?" Hand on neck again.

"No thanks, Lou."

"You won't get it from him, you know."

"That's my problem. Lou, lay off."

"At least I can do it." Grin.

"Surprise, surprise," I said. His face and body were right up against mine, and I turned away. "You can't get at him through me, you know, Lou. You just can't do it."

Lou relented. He pulled back, but he was still smiling. "You're right," he said. "For that, he'd have to like you. Sucker." He flicked the tip of my nose with his fingers, and walked away.

I went and sat down beside Royce. I needed him to make everything seem normal and ordinary. He was leaning on his elbows, plucking at the grass. "Hi," I said. It was the first time we'd spoken since the inquisition.

"Hi," he said, affectionate and distant.

"Royce, what do you think's going to happen?"

"The train will come in tomorrow," he said.

"I hate it when it comes in," I said, my breath rattling out of me in a kind of chuckle, "and I hate it when it doesn't. I just hate it. Royce, do you think we could go to work on the tank?"

He considered the implications. "Okay," he said. "Charlie? Want to come work with us on the tank?"

Charlie was plump with a gray beard, and had a degree in engineering, a coffee tin and a copper coil. He was a sort of Santa Claus of the booze. "Not today," he said, cheerily. "I made all of this, I might as well get to drink some of it myself." It was clear and greasy-looking and came in white plastic screw-top bottles.

Charlie had sacrificed one of the showers to plumb in a hot water tank. We'd hammered the tank together out of an old train door. It was more like a basin, really, balanced in the loft of the Station. There were cameras there, too.

Royce sat looking helplessly at an electric hot plate purloined from the kitchen stove. We'd pushed wiring through from the floor below. "Charlie should be here," he said.

"I really love you, Royce."

He went very still for a moment. "I know," he said. "Rich, don't be scared. You're afraid all the time."

"I know," I said, and felt my hand tremble as I ran it across my forehead.

"You gotta stop it. One day, you'll die of fear. "

"It's this place," I said, and broke down, and sat in a heap. "I want to get out!"

He held me, gently. "Someday we'll get out," he said, and the hopelessness of it made me worse. "Someday it'll be all right. "

"No, it won't. "

"Hi, guys," said Alice. "They're really acting like pigs down there. "

"They're scared," said Royce. "We're all scared, Alice. Is that train going to come in tomorrow?"

"Yup," she said brightly.

"Good. You know anything about electricity?"

"Plenty. I used to work for Bell Telephone. "

Royce disengaged himself from me. "Okay. Do I put the plate inside the tank or underneath it?"

"Inside? Good Lord no!"

So Royce went back to work again, and said to me, "You better go back down, Rich."

"The agreement?" I asked, and he nodded yes. The agreement between him and Lou.

When I got down, the Boys looked like discarded rags. There was piss everywhere, and blood on Lou's penis.

I went up to the top of the mound. All the leaves were gone now. For about the first time in my life, I prayed. Dear God, get me out of here. Dear God, please, please, make it end. But there wasn't any answer. There never is. There was just an avalanche inside my head.

I could shut it out for a while. I could forget that every day I saw piles of corpses bulldozed and mangled, and that I had to chase the birds away from them, and that I peeled off their clothes and looked with inevitable curiosity at the little pouch of genitals in their brightly colored underwear. And the leaking and the sudden hemorrhaging and the supple warmth of the dead, with their marble eyes full of seeming questions. How many had we killed? Was anybody keeping count? Did anyone know their names? Even their names had been taken from them, along with their wallets and watches.

Harry had found his policeman father among them, and had never stopped smiling afterwards, saying "Hi!" like a cartoon chipmunk without a tail.

I listened to the roaring in my head as long as I could and then I went back down to the Boys. "Is there any booze left, Charlie?" I asked, and he passed me up a full plastic bottle, and I drank myself into a stupor.

It got dark and cold, and I woke up alone, and I pulled myself up, and walked back into the waiting room, and it was poison inside. It was as poison as the stuff going sour in our stomachs and brains and breath. We sat in twitchy silence, listening to the wind and our own farts. Nobody could be bothered to cook. Royce was not there, and my stomach twisted around itself like a bag full of snakes. Where was he? What would happen when he got back?

"You look sick," said Lou in disgust. "Go outside if you have to throw up."

"I'm fine, Lou," I said, but I could feel a thin slime of sweat on my forehead.

"You make me sick just looking at you," he said.

"Funny. I was just thinking the same about you." Our eyes locked, and there was no disguising it. We hated each other.

It was then that Royce came back in, rubbing his head with a towel. "Well, there are now hot showers," he announced. "Well, tepid showers. You guys can go clean up. "

The Boys looked up to him, smiling. The grins were bleary, but they were glad to see him.

"Phew-wee!" he said, and waved his hand in front of his face. "That's some stuff you come up with, Charlie, what do you make it out of, burnt tires?"

Charlie beamed. "Orange peel and grass," he said proudly. I thought it was going to be all right.

Then Lou stood up out of his bed, and flopped naked toward Royce. "You missed all the fun," he said.

"Yeah, I know, I can smell it."

"Now who's being a prig?" said Lou. "Come on, man, I got something nice to show you." He grabbed hold of Royce's forearm, and pulled him toward his own bed. Tom was in it, lying face down, like a ruin, and Lou pulled back the blanket. "Go on, man."

Tom was bleeding. Royce's face and voice went very hard, and he pulled the blanket back up. "He's got an anal fissure, Lou. He needs to be left alone. It could get badly infected."

Lou barked, like a dog, a kind of laugh. "He's going to die anyway!"

Royce moved away from his bed. With Tom in it, he had no place to sit down. Lou followed him. "Come on, Royce. Come on. No more pussyfooting." He tried to put his hand down the front of Royce's shirt. Royce shrugged it away, with sudden annoyance. "Not tonight."

"Not ever?" asked Lou, amused.

"Come on, Royce, give it up man," said Harry. He grabbed Royce playfully, about the waist. "You can't hold out on us forever." He started fumbling with the belt buckle. "Hell, I haven't eaten all day."

"Oh yes you have," said Lou, and chuckled.

"Harry, please let go," said Royce, wearily.

The belt was undone, and Lou started pulling out his shirt. "Let go," warned Royce. "I said let go," and he moved very suddenly. His elbow hit Harry in the mouth, and he yelped.

"Hey, you fucker!"

"You turkey," said Lou.

And all the poison rose up like a wave. Oh, this was going to be fun, pulling off all of Royce's clothes. Gary, and Charlie, they all came, smiling. There was a sound of cloth tearing and suddenly Royce was fighting, fighting very hard, and suddenly the Boys were fighting too, grimly. They pulled him down, and he tried to hit them, and they held his arms, and they launched themselves on him like it was a game of tackle football. I thought, there is a word for this. The word is rape.

"Alice!" I shouted up to the camera. "Alice, stop them! Alice? Burn one of them, stop it!"

Then something slammed into the back of my head, and I fell, the floor scraping the skin of my wrists and slapping me across the cheeks. Then I was pulled over, and Lou was on top of me, forearm across my throat.

"Booby booby booby booby," he said, all blubbery lips, and then he kissed me. Well, he bit my upper lip. He bit it to hold me there; he nearly bit through it with his canine teeth, and my mouth was full of the taste of something metallic: blood.

The sounds the Boys made were conversational, with the odd laugh. Royce squealed like a pig. It always hurts beyond everything the first time. It finally came to me that Royce wasn't gay, at least not in any sense that we would understand. I looked up at the camera, at its blank, glossy eye, and I could feel it thinking: these are men; this is what men do; we are right. We are right to do this to them. For just that moment, I almost agreed.

Lou got up, and Charlie nestled in next to me, fat and naked, white hairs on his chest and ass, and he was still beaming like a baby, and I thought: Don't you know what you've done? I tried to sit up, and he went no, no, no and waggled a finger at me. It was Lou's turn to go through him. "Rear Admiral, am I?" asked Lou.

When he was through, Charlie helped me to my feet. "You might as well have a piece," he said, with a friendly chuckle. Lou laughed very loudly, pulling on his T-shirt. The others were shuffling back to their beds in a kind of embarrassment. Royce lay on the floor.

I knelt next to him. My blood splashed onto the floor. "Can you get up, Royce?" I asked him. He didn't answer. "Royce, let's go outside, get you cleaned up." He didn't move. "Royce, are you hurt? Are you hurt badly?" Then I called them all bastards.

"It was just fun, man," said Harry.

"Fun!"

"It started out that way. He shouldn't have hit people."

"He didn't want to do it. Royce, please. Do you want anything? Is anything especially painful?"

"Just his ass," said Lou, and laughed.

"He'll be okay," said Charlie, a shadow of confusion on his face.

"Like fuck he will. That was some way to say thanks for all he's done. Well? Are any of you going to give me a hand?"

Harry did. He helped me to get Royce up. Royce hung between us like a sack.

"It's that fucking poison you make, man," said Harry to Charlie.

"Don't blame me. You were the first, remember."

"I was just playing."

They began to realize what they'd done. He was all angles, like a doll that didn't work anymore.

"What the fuck did you do?" I shouted at them. He didn't seem to be bruised anywhere. "Jesus Christ!" I began to cry because I thought he was dead. "You fucking killed him!"

"Uh-uh, no," said Gary. "We didn't."

"Pisshead!"

Charlie came to help too, and we got him outside, and into the showers, and he slumped down in the dark. I couldn't find a rag, so we just let the lukewarm water trickle down over him. All we did was get him wet on an evening in November.

"It's cold out here, we got to get him back in," said Harry.

Royce rolled himself up onto his knees, and looked at me. "You were there."

"I wasn't part of it. I tried to stop it. "

"You were there. You didn't help. "

"I couldn't!"

He grunted and stood up. We tried to help him, but he knocked our hands away. He sagged a bit at the knees, but kept on walking, unsteadily. He walked back into the waiting room. Silently, people were tidying up, straightening beds. Royce scooped up his clothes with almost his usual deftness. He went back to his bed, and dropped down onto it, next to Tom, and began to inspect his shirt and trousers for damage.

"The least you could have done!" I said. I don't know what I meant.

Lou was leaning back on his bed. He looked pleased, elbows sticking out from the side of his head. "Look at it this way," he said. "It might do him some good. He shouldn't be so worried about his little problem. He just needs to relax a bit more, try it on for size. The worst thing you can do with a problem like that is hide from it."

If I'd had an axe, I would have killed him. He knew that. He smiled.

Then the lights went out, without warning as always, but two hours early.

There was snow on the ground in the morning, a light dusting of it on the roof and on the ground. There was no patter. Royce did not talk to the cameras. He came out, wearing his jacket; there was a tear in his shirt, under the armpit. He ate his breakfast without looking at anyone, his face closed and still. Hardly anyone spoke. Big Lou walked around with a little half-grin. He was so pleased, he was stretched tight with it. He'd won; he was Boss again. No one used the showers.

Then we went out, and waited for the train.

We could see its brilliant headlight shining like a star on the track.

We could see the layers of wire-mesh gates pulling back for it, like curtains, and close behind it. We began to hear a noise coming from it.

It was a regular, steady drumming against metal, a bit like the sound of marching feet, a sound in unison.

"Yup," said Charlie. "the drugs have worn off."

"It's going to be a bastard," said Gary.

Lou walked calmly toward the cameras. "Alice? What do we do?" No answer. "We can't unload them, Alice. Do we just leave them on the train, or what?" Silence. "Alice. We need to know what you want done."

"Don't call me Alice," said the camera.

"Could you let us back in, then?" asked Lou.

No answer.

The train came grinding into the platform, clattering and banging and smelling of piss. We all stood back from it, well back. Away from us, at the far end of the platform, James stood looking at the silver sky and the snow in the woods, his back to us, his headphones on. We could hear the thin whisper of Mozart from where we stood. Still looking at the woods, James sauntered toward the nearest carriage.

"James!" wailed Charlie. "Don't open the door!"

"Jim! Jimmy! Stop!"

"James! Don't!"

He waved. All he heard was Mozart, and a banging from the train not much louder than usual. With a practiced, muscular motion, he snapped up the bolt, and pulled it back, and began to swing open the door.

It burst free from his grasp, and was slammed back, and a torrent of people poured down out of the carriage, onto him. His headphones were only the first thing to be torn from him. The Stiffs were all green and mottled, like leaves. Oh Christ, oh Jesus. Uniforms. Army.

We turned and ran for the turnstile. "Alice! God-damn it, let us in!" raged Lou. The turnstile buzzed, angrily, and we scrambled through it, caught up in its turning arms, crammed ourselves into its embrace four at a time, and we could hear feet running behind us. I squeezed through with Gary, and heard Charlie behind us cry out. Hands held him, clawed at his forehead. Gary and I pulled him out, and Lou leapt in after us, and pulled the emergency gate shut.

They prowled just the other side of a wire mesh fence, thick necked, as mad as bulls, with asses as broad as our shoulders. "We'll get you fuckers," one of them promised me, looking dead into my eyes. They trotted from door to door of the train, springing them. They began to rock the turnstile back and forth. "Not electric!" one of them called. They began to pull at the wire mesh. We had no weapons.

"Hey! Hey, help!" we shouted. "Alice, Scarlett. Help!"

No answer. As if in contempt, the warm-up lights went on. "We're using gas," said Alice, her voice hard. "Get your masks. "

The masks were in the waiting room. We turned and ran, but the cameras didn't give us time. Suddenly there was a gush of something like steam, in the icy morning, out from under the platform. I must have caught a whiff of it. It was like a blow on the head, and my feet crossed in front of each other instead of running. I managed to hold my breath, and Royce's face was suddenly in front of me, as still as a stone, and he pushed a mask at me, and pulled on his own, walking toward the gate. I fumbled with mine. Harry, or someone, all inhuman in green, helped me. I saw Royce walking like an angel into white, a blistering white that caught the winter sunlight in a blaze. He walked right up to the fence, and stood in the middle of the poison, and watched.

The gas billowed, and the people billowed too, in waves. They climbed up over each other, in shifting pyramids, to get away, piling up against the fence. Those on top balanced, waving their arms like surfers, and there were sudden flashes of red light through the mist, and bars of rumpled flesh appeared across their eyes. One of them had fine light hair that burst into flame about his head. He wore a crown of fire.

The faces of those on the bottom of the heap were pressed against the fence into diamond shapes, and they twitched and jittered. The whole wave began to twitch and jitter, and shake, against the fence.

It must have been the gas in my head. I was suddenly convinced that it was nerve gas, and that meant that the nerves of the dead people were still working, even though they were dead. Even though they were dead, they would shake and judder against the fence until it fell, and then they would walk toward us, and take us into their arms, and talk to us in whispers, and pull off the masks.

I spun around, and looked at the mound, because I thought the dead inside it would wake. It did seem to swim and move, and I thought that Babylon would crack, and what had been hidden would come marching out. The dead were angry, because they had been forgotten.

Then the mist began to clear, blown. I thought of dandelion seeds that I had blown like magic across the fields when I was a child.

"Hockey games," I said. I thought there had been a game of hockey. The bodies were piled up, in uniforms. They were still. We waited. Harry practiced throwing stones.

"What a mess," said Gary.

There were still wafts of gas around the bottom of the platform. We didn't know how long we would have to wait before it was safe.

Suddenly Lou stepped forward. "Come on, let's start," he said, his voice muffled by the mask. He pulled back the emergency gate. "We've got masks," he said.

None of us moved. We just didn't have the heart.

"We can't leave them there!" Lou shouted. Still none of us moved.

Then Royce sat down on the grass, and pulled off his mask, and took two deep breaths. He looked at the faces in front of him, a few feet away, purple against the mesh.

"Alice," he said. "Why are we doing this?"

No answer.

"It's horrible. It's the worst thing in the world. Horrible for us, horrible for you. That's why what happened last night happened, Alice. Because this is so terrible. You cage people up, you make them do things like this, and something goes, something inside. Something will give with you, too, Alice. You can't keep this up either. Do you have dreams, Alice? Do you have dreams at night about this? While the Wigs are at their parties, making big decisions and debating ideology? I don't believe anyone could look at this and not feel sick."

"You need to hear any more?" Lou asked the cameras, with a swagger.

"I mean. How did it happen?" Royce was crying. "How did we get so far apart? There were problems, sure, but there was love, too. Men and women loved each other. People love each other, so why do we end up doing things like this? Can you give me a reason, Alice?"

"You do realize what he's saying, don't you?" asked Lou. He pulled off his mask, and folded his arms. "Just listen to what is coming out of his closet."

"I am not going to move those bodies, Alice," said Royce. "I can't. I literally cannot move another body. I don't think any of us can. You can kill us all if you want to. But then, you'd have to come and do it yourselves, wouldn't you?"

Lou waited. We all waited. Nothing happened.

"They'll—uh—start to stink if we don't move them," said Gary, and coughed, and looked to Lou.

"If we don't move them," said Harry, and for once he wasn't smiling, "another train can't come in."

"Alice?" said Lou. "Alice?" Louder, outraged. "You hear what is happening here?"

There was a click, and a rumbling sound, a sort of shunting. A gate at the far end of the platform rolled back. Then another, and another, all of them opening at once.

"Go on," said Alice.

We all just stood there. We weren't sure what it meant, we didn't even know that all those gates could open at once.

"Go on. Get out. Hurry. Before one of the Wigs comes."

"You mean it?" Harry asked. We were frightened. We were frightened to leave.

"We'll say you got killed in the riot, that you were gassed or something. They'll never know the difference. Now move!"

"Alice, god-damn it, what are you doing, are you crazy?" Lou was wild.

"No. She ain't crazy. You are." That was Royce. He stood up. "Well you heard her, haul some ass. Charlie, Harry, you go and get all the food there is left in the canteen. The rest of you, go get all the blankets and clothes, big coats that haven't been shipped back. And Harry, fill some jugs with water."

Lou didn't say anything. He pulled out a kitchen knife and he ran toward Royce. Royce just stood there. I don't think he would have done anything. I think he was tired, tired of the whole thing. I mean he was tired of death. Lou came for him.

The Grils burned him. They burned Lou. He fell in a heap at Royce's feet, his long, strong arms all twisted. "Aw hell," said Royce, sad and angry. "Aw hell."

And a voice came cutting into my head, clear and blaring. I was crazy. The voice said, "This is radio station KERB broadcasting live from the First Baptist Church of Christ the Redeemer with the Reverend Thomas Wallace Robertson and the Inglewood Youth Choir, singing O Happy Day."

And I heard it. I heard the music. I just walked out onto the platform, reeling with the sound, the mass of voices inside my head, and I didn't need any blankets. O Happy Day! When Jesus wash! And Los Angeles might be gone, and Detroit and Miami, a lot of things might be gone, but that Sunday night music was still kicking shit, and if there wasn't a God, there was always other people, and they surprised you. Maybe I'd been fooled by history too. I said goodbye to the cameras as I passed them. Goodbye Alice. Goodbye Hortensia. See ya, Scarlet. Butch, I'm sorry about the name.

They were making funny noises. The cameras were weeping.

I walked on toward the open gate.

—*For America*

~

Geoff Ryman is the author of the novels *The Warrior Who Carried Life, The Unconquered Country, The Child Garden, Was, 253, Lust, Air,* and *The King's Last Song.* His short fiction has appeared in *The Magazine of Fantasy & Science Fiction, Interzone, Tor.com, New Worlds,* and has frequently been reprinted in Gardner Dozois' *Year's Best Science Fiction* series. Most of his short work can be found in the collections *Unconquered Countries* and the recent *Paradise Tales and Other Stories.* He is a winner of the World Fantasy Award, the John W. Campbell Memorial Award, the Arthur C. Clarke Award, the Philip K. Dick Award, the Tiptree Award, and the British Science Fiction Award. He is also the editor of the anthology *When It Changed.*

Skin Folk

(from "Something to Hitch Meat To")

An Excerpt Presented by Open Road Media

Nalo Hopkinson

Artho picked up a bone lying in the street. No reason, just one of those irrational things you do when your brain is busy with something else, like whether you remembered to buy avocados or not. The alligator-tail chain of a day care snaked past him, each toddler hanging on dutifully to one of the knots in the rope by which they were being led. One of the young, gum-popping nannies said:

"So then little Zukie draws herself up real tall, and she says, 'No, silly. The purpose of the skeleton is something to hitch meat to.' Really! I swear, I nearly died laughing, she sounded so serious."

The woman eyed him as she walked past, smiled a little, glanced down. She played with her long hair and stage-whispered to her co-worker, "God, Latino men are just so hot, don't you think?" They giggled and moved on, trailing children.

The gears of Artho's brain kicked back into realtime. He was standing at the southwest corner of King and Bay, holding a chicken thighbone. Fleshless and parched, it felt dusty between his fingers. He dropped it and wiped his hand off on his jeans. Latino? What the hell?

Streetcar coming. Artho got on, elbowing himself some rush hour standing room between an old man with a bound live chicken that lay gasping in his market basket and three loud, hormonal young women, all politics and piercings. Artho reached for a steady strap. Traffic was gridlocked. He stared blankly out the window as the streetcar inched its way past a woman struggling with two huge dogs on leashes. Bergers des Pyrenées, they were; giant, woolly animals bred for rescuing skiers trapped under alpine avalanches. They were so furry that Artho could barely make out their legs. They lumbered along in a smooth, four-on-the-floor gait. The dogs' handler tugged futilely at their leashes, barely able to keep up. The beasts could probably cover miles in effortless minutes, snowshoeing on their woolly feet. Artho fancied that they would move even faster, smoother, if you changed them to have six legs, or eight. They would glide along like enormous tarantulas. Artho looked at their handler's legs and had the oddest feeling, like when an old film skips a frame, and for an instant, you can see the hole-punched edges of the film strip, black and chitinous on the screen, and then it jerks back into place, but now you're looking at a different scene than you were before. It was like that, Artho looking at this woman walking on ordinary woman legs, then reality skipped frames, and he was seeing instead a being whose natural four-legged stance had been twisted and warped so that all it could manage was this ungainly two-legged jerking from foot to foot. Made into something it wasn't.

Alarmed, Artho blinked. He made himself relax. Tired. Too many hours at work in front of a computer screen, staring at all that skin. He leaned his head against the streetcar window and dozed, thinking hungrily of the stewed chicken and rice he would have for dinner, with avocado—his dad always called them alligator pears—on the side. He could see the fleshy avocado in his mind's eye: slit free of its bumpy rind; pegged and sitting on a plate; beads of salt melting on the sweating, creamy skin. He imagined biting into a slice, his teeth meeting in its spineless centre. His mouth watered.

It wasn't until he reached his stop that he realized he really had forgotten to buy the damned avocados. He found some tired, wrinkly ones in the corner store near his apartment. The man behind the counter, who served Artho at least twice a week when he came in for cigarettes or munchies, grumbled at the fifty dollar bill that Artho gave him, and made a big show over holding it up to the light to see if it was counterfeit. Artho had seen the same man cheerfully make change from bills that large for old women or guys in suits. He handed Artho a couple of twenties and some coins, scowling. Artho held each twenty up to the light before putting it into his pocket. "Thank you," he said sweetly to the guy, who glared. Artho took his avocados and went home. When he sliced into them, one of them was hard and black inside. He threw it out.

• • •

"So," Artho's brother said, "I'm out with the guys the other night, and …"

"Huh? What'd you say?" Artho asked. Something was obscuring Aziman's voice in the phone, making rubbing and clicking sounds over and around his speech. "What's that noise?" Artho asked the receiver. "Like dice rolling together or something."

"One dice, two die. Or is it the other way around? Anyway, so I'm …"

"What're you eating? I can't make out what you're saying."

"Hold on." Silence. Then Aziman came on again. "This any better?"

"Yeah. What was that?"

"This hard candy the kids brought home. Got me hooked on it. These little round white thingies, y'know? I had a mouthful of them."

"Did you spit them out?"

"Well, not round exactly. Kinda egg-shaped, but squarer than that. Is 'squarer' a word?"

"Did you spit them out?" Artho was just being pissy, and he knew it. He could tell that Aziman had gotten rid of the candies somehow. His voice was coming through clearly now.

"Yeah, Artho. Can I tell my story now?"

"Where'd you spit them?"

"What's up with you today? Down the kitchen sink."

And Aziman started in with his story again, but Artho was distracted, thinking on the tiny white candies disappearing into the drain, perhaps washed down with water.

" … so this man walks up to us, a kid really, y'know? Smart-ass yuppie cornfed kid with naturally blond hair and a polo shirt on. Probably an MBA. And he says to me, 's up, man?' only he says it 'mon.' I mean, I guess he's decided I'm from Jamaica or something, you know?"

"Yeah," said Artho. "I know."

"He gives me this weird handshake; grabs my thumb and then makes a fist and I'm supposed to touch my fist to his, I think, I dunno if I did it right. But he says, 's up' again, and I realize I didn't answer him, so I just say, 'Uh, nothing much,' which I guess isn't the lingo, right? But I dunno what I'm supposed to say; I mean, you and me, we're freaking north Toronto niggers, right? And this white guy's got Toronto suburbs written all over him, too. Probably never been any farther than Buffalo. So what's he trying to pull with that fake ghetto street shit anyway, you know? And he leans in close, kinda chummy like, and whispers, 'Think you could sell me some shit, man?' And I'm thinking, *Like the kind you're trying to sell me on right now?* I mean, he's asking me for dope, or something."

Artho laughed. "Yeah, happens to me, too. It's always the same lame-ass question, never changes. I just point out the meanest-looking, blackest motherfucker in the joint and say, 'Not me, man, but I bet that guy'll be able to help you out.'"

"Shit. I'll try that next time."

"Though I guess it isn't fair, you know, my doing that. It's like I'm picking on guys just 'cause they're blacker than me."

"Heh. I guess, if you want to look at things that way. You going to Mom's for Easter?"

"Is Aunt Dee going to be there?"

But Aziman's only reply was a rustling, shucking type of noise. Then, "Shit!"

"What?"

"I stuck my hand into the bag for more candy, y'know? Just figured out what these things are."

"What?"

"Skulls. Little sugar skulls, f' chrissake."

Dead people bits. That's what the candy was. It was all in the way you looked at it.

"No," said Artho. "It'll be just like last year. I'm not going to Mom's for Easter."

• • •

A few days later it happened again, a weird unfamiliarity when Artho looked at human bodies. He was in the mall food court on his lunch hour. When he went back to work, it would be to spend the rest of the day updating the Tit for Twat site: *Horny Vixens in Heat! No Holes Barred!*

The food court was crowded. People in business suits wolfed down Jolly Meals, barked on cell phones. The buzz of conversation was a formless noise, almost soothing.

Not many empty spaces. Artho had to share a table for two with a thirtyish man in fine beige wool, engrossed in the financial pages of the Globe & Mail newspaper. The man had shaved his head completely. Artho liked it. There was something sensuous about the baldness, like the domed heads of penises. Cute. Artho was thinking of something to say to him, some kind of opener, when the man's ears caught his gaze. They jutted out from the side of his head like knurls of deformed cartilage. There really was nothing odd about the guy's ears—that's just how ears were—but they still gave Artho a queasy feeling. With one hand, he worried at his own ear. He looked around at other people in the food court. All their ears seemed like twisted carbuncles of flesh sprouting from the sides of their heads, odd excrescenses. Nausea and doubt squirmed like larvae in Artho's chest. His fingers twitched, the ones that he would use a few minutes from now to point, click, and drag his mouse as he smoothed out the cellulite and firmed up the pecs of the perfect naked models on the screen, making them even more perfect. He closed his eyes to block out the sight of all those ugly ears.

Someone was singing. A child's voice, tuneless and repetitive, threaded its whiny way through the rumble of lunchtime chatter:

"Tain't no sin,
Take off your skin,
And dance around in your bones.
Tain't no sin…"

Artho opened his eyes. Wriggly as only seven-year-olds can be, a little girl slouched beside her father at a table for four, sitting on her spine so she could kick at the centre pole supporting the table welded to its four seats. Her wiry black hair was braided into thousands of dark medusa strands. The brown bumps of her knees were ashy with dry skin. The lumpy edge of a brightly coloured Spider Man knapsack jutted out from behind her back.

"Tain't no sin…" She kicked and kicked at the pole. An old man who'd been forced to share the table with them looked up from his chow mein and gave her a strained nice-little-girl smile.

"Quit it, Nancy." Not even glancing at his daughter—was she his daughter?—her father reached out with one hand and stilled the thin, kicking legs. With his other hand he hurriedly stuffed a burger into his mouth. Green relish oozed between his fingers.

The little girl stopped kicking, but all that energy had to have some outlet. She immediately started swaying her upper body from side to side, jerking her knapsack about so that something thumped around inside it. She bobbed her head in time to her little song. Her braids flowed like cilia. She looked around her. Her gaze connected with Artho's. "Daddy," she said loudly to the man beside her, "can you see me?" She wore glasses with jam-jar-thick lenses, which refracted and multiplied her eyes. She didn't look up at her father.

And he didn't look down at her, just kept gnawing on his burger. "Can't see you at all, little girl," he mumbled. "I only think I can. You're nowhere to be seen."

She smiled at that. "I'm everywhere, though, Daddy."

Must be some kind of weird game they had between the two of them. Then she started singing again. Artho found himself swaying slightly from side to side in time with her song. He looked away. He'd always hated Spider Man. As a kid, the comic book character had frightened him. His costume made him look like a skeleton, a clattery skin-and-bone man that someone had painted red as blood.

" ... dance around in your bones!" the little girl shouted, glaring at him from the depths of her specs.

Artho leapt to his feet and dumped the remainder of his lunch in the garbage, fled the girl's irritating ditty. His table partner still had his nose buried in his paper.

As Artho walked the last few feet to the elevator of his office building, he suddenly became aware of the movement of his legs: push off with left leg, bending toes for leverage; contract right knee to extend right leg, heel first; shift weight; step onto right foot; bend right knee; repeat on the other side. For a ludicrous moment, he nearly tripped over his own feet. It was like some kind of weird jig. He stumbled into the elevator, smiled I'm-fine-really at a plump young woman in a business suit who was gazing at him curiously. She looked away. Then he did. They stared politely at the opaque white numbers, knobbled as vertebrae, that indicated each floor. The numbers clicked over, lighting up one at a time: 10 ... 11 ... 12 ... *Roll the bones*, thought Artho.

~

Nalo Hopkinson is a Jamaican-born Canadian whose taproots extend to Trinidad and Guyana. She has published numerous novels and short stories and occasionally edits anthologies. Her writing has received the John W. Campbell Memorial Award, the Locus Award, the World Fantasy Award, the Sunburst Award for Excellence in Canadian Literature of the Fantastic, and the Andre Norton Award. Hopkinson is a professor of creative writing at the University of California, Riverside. She has taught numerous times at both the Clarion Writers' Workshop and the Clarion West Writers' Workshop. Hopkinson's short story collection *Falling in Love With Hominids* will appear in 2015.

Author Spotlight: John Chu

Kate M. Galey

Your QDSF story centers around the cyborg subjects of a peace treaty which classifies them as weapons. How did those characters start for you?

Matters of trust are really interesting, especially in the context of a relationship. Here, I wanted a relationship where neither Jake nor Tyler are ever really sure whether they are friends or enemies. but they keep at it anyway. To some degree, that ambiguity is reflected in who they are. Neither of them are exactly human, but they aren't not-human either. Making the secrets they keep military in nature gave everything a life-or-death aspect. It's the one clear thing that's necessary to drive the story when everything else is ambiguous.

The Chinese strategy game Go plays a significant part in the relationship between Jake and Tyler. Why did you choose that symbol for the larger machinations at work in the story?

Go suggested itself at first because, unlike chess, modern day computers don't play it very well. (I should point out here that I play even worse.) This is, in part, because Go has a huge state space. To me, plays in Go can feel rather subtle. Placing a stone off by a point can have drastic ramifications. A fight on one side of the board may affect the situation on the other side of the board. There's a lot to keep track of. Some of the techniques that work for computer chess don't work for computer Go because computers don't have the capacity. At a mundane level, this points out just how technologically advanced Jake is that he plays effectively a perfect game.

Given full information, Jake can think his way out of any situation. Of course, he's hamstrung because at no point in this story does he ever have full information. Most of this story is him trying to puzzle where he stands in both the matter of life-and-death and his relationship with Tyler. Using Go also got across the fact that even though the story focused on this one relationship, their actions have wider ramifications. The local interactions between Jake and Tyler have an effect on things much larger than their personal lives.

It wasn't until after I finished the story that I realized that Jake was behaving as a classic Go proverb suggested. Once I realized that, the story named itself.

By the end, it's clear that Tyler is several steps ahead of everyone in his plans. Yet many of those schemes hinge upon trust he puts in Jake. Was he able to predict Jake's actions to that degree, or was trusting Jake a leap of faith for him?

This is where I put on an enigmatic smile and say, "What do *you* think?"

Seriously, one of the things I love about short stories is that I can play with ambiguity. This story has a bunch of different readings and as the writer I don't like to privilege any of them.

However, personally, I think if the cyborgs were that predictable, they wouldn't have been all that useful during the war and wouldn't be such a problem for the government now that the war is over. To me, it's not obvious that Tyler is several steps ahead or if he has plunged ahead trusting that Jake will somehow figure things out because that's what Jake does. He spends much of the story not exactly sure where he stands with Jake.

The final scene has more than one reading. I think you can also read it as Jake proposing a deal to Tyler that allows them to be together taking the leap of faith that Tyler will agree. However you read the story, I think they are both taking leaps of faith. Ultimately, they will always have secrets they can't tell each other.

I enjoyed this story immensely. Do you have any upcoming work for us to look forward to?

Thank you! I'm glad you liked it.

I have a story called "Restore the Heart into Love" in the May/June issue of *Uncanny Magazine*. "Hold-time Violations" is forthcoming at Tor.com. Also, I have a story called "Selected Afterimages of the Fading" acquired for the anthology *Defying Doomsday*, to be published in 2016 by Twelve Planet Press. (This is assuming the Pozible campaign, which will be over by the time this spotlight is published, has succeeded.)

Author Spotlight:
Kate M. Galey

Robyn Lupo

How did this story emerge? Were there any unexpected challenges along the way?

This story actually started about five years ago in a community college creative writing class. Our instructor had us each grab something from our cars and swap items—I ended up with a replacement car thermostat with this list of instructions on the packaging. That became the story's structure, and I built around that. It took me four years to actually finish it, mostly because at the time I didn't have the chops to write the story I wanted to tell. The viewpoint presented certain challenges—first person present tense using no pronouns isn't a perspective I'm used to writing. But the structure and the voice were challenges I set myself, so I'm happy with the result.

What struck me forcibly about this story was that even though the technology is beyond anything we have now, people in the future will still be in these terrible accidents, there will still be those moments of not knowing if the treatment will work, and probably times it won't work at all. Can you tell us what sort of experiences you pulled on to show that?

I studied to be an EMT in college and spent a short time working in that field, and especially on an ambulance, that's a daily reality. There are well-known interventions—like C.P.R. or defibrillation—that, despite what we see on TV, aren't usually successful. It's a hard situation to be in, because you can do everything perfectly and still lose someone. And even if it works, it doesn't always work for long, and sometimes the damage you do trying to save someone isn't worth it to them. It's a real downer, but that's where I pulled from. Humans are fragile. Technology helps, but it can't change that. Yet.

What drew you to use the Frankenstein motif to frame a story about resuscitation?

That actually came late in the process, once I really got to know the protagonist. They started as a noble scientist whose work has been perverted for evil, but that didn't make for a very interesting story. So they got more megalomaniacal, more mad scientist, and with that came the grandiose comparisons to Einstein and Curie. This character is constitutionally incapable of seeing themselves as unimportant. So when their attempt to save the world turns into an attempt to bring back the dead, they naturally go to Frankenstein as a new way to frame their actions.

What's next for you?

I'm not quite sure! This is my first publication, so I'm hoping to follow it up soon. I hope to continue destroying science fiction in whatever way I can!

Author Spotlight: Bonnie Jo Stufflebeam

Jill Seidenstein

What does it mean to you to destroy science fiction? What do you think still needs destroying in science fiction?

For me what needed and still needs destroying are these ideas that to focus on or promote diversity in science fiction ruins the integrity of the genre. There are so many stories out there; some focus on plot, others on language, and still others on characters of all kinds. What's wrong with that? The whole idea that emphasizing diversity will destroy a genre is preposterous. The truth of the matter is that there isn't an easily accessible queer presence in science fiction. We need to emphasize queer voices until their absence becomes a healthy abundance. Science fiction is a huge playing field. There's room for everyone.

How does your queer identity and experience inform your storytelling?

I spent my adolescence struggling to give myself a label. Not because I wanted one, but because it seemed to make people uncomfortable for me not to have one. When I entered into my first long-term relationship with my first love, a woman, it was easiest to say that I was a lesbian. When we broke up after two years, I felt free to once more explore my sexuality. This made some people uncomfortable. They'd spent a long time thinking of me as one thing. I was told there was no such thing as "straddling the fence," that I would eventually choose. I was warned about the dangers of men as though

I was wholly naïve, which, to be fair, I mostly was. I spent a troubled first few years of college going back and forth between lesbian and bisexual, trying to fall in love with a man, to see if I could do it. Then I did it. I fell in love with my partner, and it was every bit as real as the first time.

All of this experience impacts my fiction. When I write about adolescence, I write about characters who are struggling the way I struggled, trying to come to terms with complicated issues of self in homes where complicated topics aren't readily discussed. As someone very interested in sex and sexuality, I write about sex a lot and try to do so in an open, honest way. When I tackle issues of sexuality, I tackle them without emphasizing the labeling process that fucked me up for so many years. Because sexuality doesn't have to be a complicated thing; it can be fluid and can shift, purposefully or accidentally. I'm an exploratory writer, and I've always loved like I write: without knowing what's coming next, or what gender they'll identify with.

What was the hardest thing about writing this story?

The hardest part of writing this story was the inspiration itself. For years now I've had recurring dreams in which I was with my first love. Most of the time, in these dreams, I'm unhappy. Both because I feel as though we have gone through all this already, that this period of my life has ended, and also because I always know in the back of my mind that I'm in love with someone else, someone I can't remember. I always wake frightened but relieved to remember. In a way, the story was easy, as the process of sculpting the dreams into something constructive proved therapeutic.

What surprised you in the writing of this story?

All of it. I don't plan before I write, so from the beginning I had no idea what was going to happen. I knew only that it was going to be a superhero story where the superpowers came from a bacterial infection that could be cured. I also knew that somehow the main character would be going back and forth in time from her first love to her second love. I didn't know Archer would be part of it until he showed up. I didn't know how it would resolve until it was over.

I love the idea of superpowers, and I thought your idea of their superpowers coming from a bacterial infection was really cool. What was the spark or seed from which this story grew?

I've always been into the idea of inserting practicality into superhero stories. I like messing with expectations and forcing everyday life into stories of the fantastic. I hate antibiotics and was reading some articles about their dangers. So the idea started with the antidote.

Was there anything you wanted to say in this story that didn't fit?

I would've liked to include more of the good times between Rosa and Archer. Friendship is such a complicated thing, especially for someone as thick-skinned as me, and I feel like some of that had to give way to let in the more pressing love stuff.

What advice do you have for other queer folks wanting to write in genre?

Don't pay heed to assholes. I'm often disheartened by assholes. Don't follow my lead. Instead, reach out to other queer writers. Form support groups and communities that you can reach out to when things get rough.

Is there anything you wish I had asked you but I didn't?

The age-old superpower question, maybe? Mine would be flight, which is boring but would give me complete control over my transportation capabilities (I'm afraid of planes). Also, since there aren't, to my knowledge, any other superheroes flying around up there, traffic would be a breeze. Though I expect I'd have some wicked pressure clogging my ears.

Author Spotlight:
Chaz Brenchley

Rahul Kanakia

Not sure how much you want to reveal about the story in your interview, but your story involves the startling juxtaposition of a historical figure into a Victorian-era Martian colony. What inspired this? And can you describe the process of writing the story?

A couple of years back, there was a conversation going on about diversity in steampunk, how it didn't all have to be set in some alternate British Empire. Which of course is so true it really shouldn't need saying, though unhappily it does. But in the way of such conversations, it did start me thinking about, yup, the British Empire, and how thoroughly my own life and reading has been saturated with it (my mother is a classic daughter of empire, born in Rangoon and grew up in Kuala Lumpur and Singapore, where her father was stationed with the Scots Guards between the wars; and I had a classic middle-class English education, built around the British Eng-Lit canon), but I really hadn't written about it at all. All my work was either contemporary Britain or far-flung historical fantasy.

At the same time, I'd recently moved from the U.K. to California, so I had something of that expatriate mindset going on; and we live a short walk from a NASA base and the SETI HQ, where I was going to a lot of talks about planetary science and space exploration. Curiosity had just touched down on Mars, so there was a preponderance of Red Planet science in my head; and all of this stuff kind of fell together in a rush, the way things do: steampunk, Mars, empire—oohhhh …

Since then, "if Mars were a province of the British Empire" has been the constant theme running through my head like an earworm. How it could have happened, what it might have meant, what it might imply for science, for politics, for international relations, for empire on two planets (or three, in fact, because the Russians have Venus).

One of the consequences is that I keep interrupting myself with new revelations—"Oh, hey, if Mars were a province of the British Empire, T.E. Lawrence would so have gone there," and like that, over and over. So many damaged people, looking for a chance to reinvent themselves.

And of course Oscar Wilde would be one. (Hint: not a spoiler. The giveaway is in line one. It used to be earlier; I almost gave the story a subtitle, "The Ballad of Reading Wilde.") After Reading Gaol, after Italy and Paris, he would totally have gone to Mars if the chance were there.

After that, I just followed my usual process: start with a title and a first line, and see what happens. My fiction is always character- and situation-driven; plot is just what people do, in given circumstances. So I put the people in the circumstances, and stand back to see what happens. It's a process of discovery, for me as much as the reader.

In reading the story, I was particularly struck by the tone and the language, and how evocative they were of the Victorian adventure story. How did you find this voice? Was there research involved? Was it difficult to write an explicitly queer character in an era which is mostly familiar to us from books in which same-sex desire is hidden or absent?

The voice emerges from childhood saturation; honestly, no more research needed. I grew up reading Robert Louis Stevenson and Rider Haggard and Sax Rohmer and Conan Doyle; that voice is embedded. And then there was all the fun of writing about Oscar in a voice that Oscar would have deprecated …

And I don't think queerness is really absent from the literature of the time, so much as unacknowledged. Look at E.W. Hornung's stories about Raffles and Bunny; Graham Greene made that relationship explicit in his later play "The Return of A.J. Raffles," but he was only pulling aside the curtain on what was already and absolutely inherent in the canon.

And I grew up in an atmosphere where gay sex had only recently and barely been made legal ("between consenting adults in private" was the rubric; you could still be arrested for holding hands in public, and gay pubs were raided as a matter of course), where coming out called for genuine physical courage, and custom and practice was still to keep it hidden; the kind of rendezvous the men are having in this story is something I absolutely recognize from England in the '70s.

Throughout the story, there's an undercurrent of shame and bitterness that seeps out of the narration. Your narrator, like the rest of the group, seems to have come to some understanding of his sexuality, but it's uneasy, and that uneasiness seems, to me, to be what bursts out at the end and leads to some level of communication with the alien creature. What's the parallel being drawn here between queerness and alien sexuality? What led you to this analogy?

See all of the above, I guess. The shame and the bitterness both were inculcated early. Gay sex was legalised in England in my childhood, but only for over-twenty-ones; which meant that all my adolescent sexual experience was criminal. I went to college in Scotland, where it was still illegal altogether. There was a gay liberation movement, but most gay men didn't participate; the culture was to keep your head down, keep quiet, be discreet and hope that no one noticed. Unease was inherent, in any understanding of same-sex desire. (The legal experience was different for lesbians—the story we all believed at the time was that lesbian sex was never criminalised because Queen Victoria just couldn't understand what women might do together—but the social and cultural experience I think was much the same.) If there's an analogy being drawn here between what's queer and what's alien, I think it stems absolutely from the world I inhabited and the influences that shaped my thinking. I used to feel astonished that my grandfather was born into a world where as a child he never saw a motor-car, but before he died men had walked on the moon; these days I feel almost the same way about my own experience, where I was born into a world where gay sex was an imprisonable offence, and now even the prime minister is obliged to support gay marriage.

Finally, I noticed on your website that you're planning a novel in this setting. Would you care to tell us anything about that or about other upcoming works?

Oh, I am planning so much, so very much in this setting. The novel is essentially Kipling on Mars (because of course he would have gone there; Kipling went everywhere), and it's a sort of exploration of what colonialism means when the creatures whose land you're colonising really don't recognise the concept, and have very much their own agenda for bringing you there; while at the same time it's a Big Dumb Object story, and a Vanished Race story, and another of those Edwardian adventures.

And there are more short stories, out already (the first is "The Burial of Sir John Mawe at Cassini," which was published in *Subterranean* and will be reprinted in Gardner Dozois' *Year's Best Science Fiction*) or else forthcoming. And stepping away from Mars, there's a collection of queer short stories, *Bitter Waters* from Lethe Press, which is currently shortlisted for a Lambda award; and there's a short novel recently out, *Being Small*, which is about coming of age with a dead twin and a mad mother, and falling in with AIDS caregivers, and all that then ensues …

Author Spotlight:
Felicia Davin

Robyn Lupo

What was the initial thing that made this story happen? What made you consider writing about technology used to oppress people?

I had been reading a lot about the history of reading itself. People in power have historically perceived the literacy of the masses as dangerous. As more and more women and workers learn to read in, say, eighteenth- and nineteenth-century France, you get more and more critics warning against the dangers of reading. According to these critics, the practice of reading is harmful, but the content of the books is harmful as well. Those critics were joining a long conversation about the social and moral role of art, one that stretches as far back as Plato kicking poets out of the republic and that is still going on today.

Oppressive regimes ban and burn books, even books that might not—at first glance—directly threaten their existence. And since this is the Queers Destroy Science Fiction! issue, I was thinking about how often queer stories have been censored, and how those stories have survived in subtext and in margins and in readers' imaginations. The Kickstarter campaign for this issue included so many moving essays by queer fans and writers about their relationship with science fiction. We connect intimately with our favorite books. Reading is powerful. That's what I wanted to write about.

The description of Alice struggling to read was particularly vivid to me. What did you draw on to make that scene work?

I love languages. I have studied many of them, including Hindi and Biblical

Hebrew, and both of those languages required me to learn to read other writing systems. When you learn to read a new script, the characters always look tiny at first. The first time you try to read a full page of normal-size text in another script, it looks impenetrable. Once you learn to distinguish the characters a little better, the size of the print doesn't matter as much. I had that experience in mind while I was writing.

What's next for you?

I'm working on a fantasy novel.

Author Spotlight: Rose Lemberg

Sandra Odell

"How to Remember to Forget to Remember The Old War" (whew—a great title!) starts with a visceral sensory punch that borders on the intimate. There is also an edge of familiarity with issues involving veterans' mental health and their re-introduction into society. You mention on your website that the story was inspired by "Greyhound therapy." What is it about the practice that inspired you to write this particular story?

I am forever concerned with what happens when the war is over. I keep writing about it. Where others enjoy writing about the shine and splendor of warfare, I am interested, viscerally, in the aftermath, in survivors, in those who are left behind when the glorious leaders are done with their conflicts. In a recent epic fantasy poem in *Strange Horizons* (strangehorizons.com/2015/20150309/lemberg-p.shtml), I write about the effects of war upon children, and how the devastation and trauma are all too often swept under the rug. The titular child, Long Shadow, says:

> Immortals and mortals alike
> recoil from maimed children. Easier not to see
> the horrors inflicted upon us, easier to pretend
> that nothing bad has happened here.

Greyhound therapy relates to this. It's about trying to erase trauma, especially war-related trauma, from the communal conscience. I am a twice-immigrant and a survivor of some horrible things, so it's something that gnaws at me.

Greyhound therapy, and other practices like it, is about people thrown away, sent away to become someone else's problem; it's about the erosion of care, and of community.

I was so caught up in the opening characterization and seemingly mundane setting that the introduction of speculative elements took me by surprise. Some of the best fiction encourages the reader to find the familiar amongst the strange. How important is creating such a mood to you in your own work?

I write in a variety of speculative genres from magic realism to surrealism to fantasy to SF. In all of my work, I am deeply concerned with the mundane. The weight of simple white dishes, the smell of an old paperback, the feel of hemp rope against one's cheek, the interplay of sunlight and shadows upon the walls of an office. I have sometimes been criticized for this focus, but that's an important part of my voice—the details are real, whether or not they are fantastical.

The use of first person point-of-view allows greater insight into the character's hopes and fears, the loneliness and search for "something." What of your own experiences and sexual identity went into writing this story?

I've written in first, second, and third-person, but I love the first person. A lot of my work is in first person, all of it from different viewpoints. What I love about it is the process of "putting on" other people's viewpoints; it's one of the greatest joys for me as a writer. In this particular story, my experience is very different from the narrator's. I am not physically strong; I don't find breaking things therapeutic in the slightest; I am horrible at repairs and spreadsheets. The narrator is pansexual and non-binary, but there is no overt sexuality in this story. Yet, this story is dedicated to my now-partner, Bogi Takács. I think where my experience and the narrator's overlap is in the very, very general things: pain, survival, survivor's guilt; recognition that it is a privilege to survive as well as the narrator does, scars and all; the belief that survivors can create their own hope, their own support networks in a world that is less than welcoming.

On your website you address your gender and pronoun preference, your partner, and your child's diagnosis of autism. You speak of the importance of diversity in your works, and on being a firm advocate for neurodiversity. Do you have any thoughts on how supporting diversity in one community can benefit other communities as well?

"Diversity" and "community" are loaded concepts, which people have been discussing in the light of the recent fallouts. To what extent can we talk about a single community? To what extent does the word "diversity" help, and to what extent can it be used as a cop-out, as yet another means to check off a to-do item on some list, silencing those who won't be included despite these efforts? I think my practice recently has been focused on understanding how people can still be disenfranchised in our field's movement towards greater diversity—how, for example, new writers who come from a variety of marginalized backgrounds continue to face obstacles, and what we can do as a field, as a community, to help each other thrive, and to help each other see each other as people with valid and worthwhile perspectives. I think that prioritizing these acts of seeing, of recognition, of valuing, of keen compassionate interest in a variety of human experiences without trying to erase or normalize them is something that is not community-specific, but more general.

What authors do you turn to when you want to explore healthy and mindful diversity in fiction?

I seek out up and coming writers, or writers that have been overlooked. I am not sure what "healthy" would mean for me in this context, but I'm following stories from the margins. Instead of naming specific authors, I'd like to name publications that, in my opinion, have a great mix of diverse authors, styles, and genres. In no particular order, *Lackington's*, *Scigentasy*, *Strange Horizons*, *Beneath Ceaseless Skies*, *Clarkesworld*. I am also interested in the new directions *Lightspeed* has been taking, and I am looking forward to reading the new QDSF. I have also been impressed with choices that C.C. Finlay has been making for *F&SF*, and am looking forward to reading more of that magazine.

You are quite prolific in diversity and short fiction. What's next for Rose Lemberg? What can eager readers expect from you in the future?

First of all, *An Alphabet of Embers*, an anthology I've edited, is going to come out this summer. It is a beautiful, striking, and unique collection of very short lyrical works (mostly stories, but also a few prose poems) with cover art by Galen Dara and internal illustrations by M Sereno. It's going to showcase work by many very talented new authors, as well as by established favorites, and I am looking forward to hearing what people think.

I have a number of new stories coming out this year as well. I am really looking forward to sharing the three queer novelettes set in my secondary world fantasy world, Birdverse. "Grandmother-nai-Leylit's Cloth of Winds," forthcoming this summer in *Beneath Ceaseless Skies*, is about queer families, older people—grandmothers, grandparents—and the struggle for acceptance and identity. It's also about carpets. "The Book of How to Live," a story of revolution and academia, is forthcoming in Michael Matheson's anthology *Start a Revolution*. Finally, "Geometries of Belonging," also forthcoming in *Beneath Ceaseless Skies*, is about consent and mind-healing. All three stories have autistic characters: a minimally verbal child in "Grandmother-nai-Leylit's Cloth of Winds," an adult woman who's an Aspie in "The Book of How to Live," and a teen with language and motor difficulties in "Geometries of Belonging." I am very much looking forward to sharing these works with readers.

Finally, I have a new-ish Patreon where I share my Birdverse work in progress—not just fiction, but also poems and drawings.

Author Spotlight: Jessica Yang

Arley Sorg

One thing I love about "Plant Children" is the feeling of authenticity in its characters and the story itself—in moments of humor as well as the tides of emotion. How much of this story reflects your own life? What are the inspirations behind this story?

Aside from the obvious stuff, like the robots and near-sentient plants … a good deal of the story comes from my life. I went to college in an agricultural area (shout out to UC Davis!), and I had good friends who would take me to the conservatory to photograph all the lovely pitcher plants, little green sprouts, and cacti. I had a brilliant time taking Plant Sciences with my housemate, also.

And my mother is always saying contradictory things about family. She warns me that I should have kids so they'll care for me in my old age, but then she'll tell me about an old lady she's been visiting, whose own children abandoned her to a nursing home. Family is complicated, and sometimes the best family is the family you cobble together for yourself.

The portrayal of An and Qiyan's relationship is beautiful, gentle, and careful. It's definitely not the sort of hyper-sexualized content that is more common in contemporary fiction. What were the challenges in presenting their relationship and its development, and how did you meet them?

My biggest challenge was making it a relationship at all! I wanted to show a long-standing bond between friends (who are in unspoken love), but it ended up mostly being about plants. I get embarrassed easily when I write, so I tend to make things as vague as possible. I had to force myself to be more blunt.

"Plant Children" deliberately combines old world and mythic cultural awareness with futurism, while being grounded in a modern sort of sensibility. It really weaves together the past and the present/future. Why is this important to you, and what do you hope readers will take away from this?

Well, culture is what connects us to our past, and will carry us over to the future. Technology's getting pretty intense nowadays, but myth and culture still lend meaning to what we do and who we are. Being Taiwanese American, I feel like I don't have a solid grounding in either Taiwanese or American culture—and, of course, that makes me want it even more!

I really enjoyed this story and I'm looking forward to reading more of your work. What are you working on now, and what can we anticipate seeing from you in the future?

Aw, thanks! This is actually my first SF thing ever. (I clearly don't know what I'm doing.) Right now, I'm working on some fantasy short stories, but I hope to start chipping away at a dragon-length novel someday soon. Maybe it'll be about magic college, or more plants! The future is an unknown creature, you know?

Author Spotlight: K.M. Szpara

Sandra Odell

This is a very in-the-moment, visceral story. Where did you find the inspiration for this story?

This story did not come from one moment of inspiration, but rather a series of my trans experiences. And I say "my" because while I think many other trans people may agree, there is no universal experience.

The Internet, via role-playing and online accounts, message boards wherein no one can see or hear you, acts as an escape for many trans people. You can be your true self there without being questioned. That was the SimGrid portion of the story. When Ash plugs in at a young age, his avatar generates in his self-image. He gets to be "a character who just happens to be gay"—though he is unaware of this, that's how the story begins for readers. That's who I've always written, too, characters for whom their queerness did not impact the plot.

Even while in the SimGrid he faces a longing for more—to unplug and experience physical and emotional sensations in a different body. Body jealousy is overwhelming: this isn't right; this will feel better in a different body; I don't belong here, etc.

Then, there's the shock and disbelief when Ash is forced to face his physical body. Gender dysphoria is admittedly hard to describe to someone who has never questioned their gender before, who has never stared at their naked body in a mirror and felt out of congruence with it. And, for course, the first medical professional he encounters doesn't even know what to say, much less do for him. As someone who generally trusts doctors, I don't trust that they all know what to do with my body. I do feel bad that it all happens at once, for

Ash. I can't imagine dealing with all my dysphoria like a piano being dropped on my head.

When it came to the ending, I recognized the number of depressing arcs for trans people, but also didn't want to tie a tidy rainbow ribbon around it. For a moment, I considered Ash accepting his physical body—Zane too. Trusting doctors. Making it work. Living "real" lives. But why? That's our only option, nowadays: making it work. And lots of trans people have not only made their peace but thoroughly enjoy the bodies they have formed in their true image. But what is real? Trans people talk about "realness" a lot. For Ash, existing in his physical body is too hard—which is not weak to admit. He knows who he is and that person exists in the SimGrid.

Recent developments in virtual reality have brought us one step closer to the reality of your story. How do you envision the implementation of such full VR immersion that have come about in "Nothing is Pixels Here"?

Oh, some big corporation will obviously get a hold of virtual reality once it inevitably becomes as popular as smart phones. They'll have the most high quality version available and they'll offer it as a perk to contractors. In this case, the "work" is glazed over, as it's not vital to the story. I imagine Kinetic, Inc. harvests energy from its contractors, but requires them to exist in a passive but productive state. Being asleep for twenty years doesn't appeal to anyone. Living in your dream world does, especially to vulnerable people: homeless, abused, or rejected queer kids for whom reality is too much to handle.

Some feel that there is no need for a special issue of *Lightspeed Magazine* focusing on the views of the QUILTBAG community, saying that such an issue would be divisive and exclusionary to other writers. If you could speak directly to those concerns, what would you say?

Naysayers don't know what it's like to be queer. Even though I have gained confidence in myself and my writing, I still have doubts about whether my work will be considered "too queer." This story's plot hinges on Ash being trans. Science fiction can be an unforgiving genre. I'm often intimidated out of writing too-queer plots or characters. Will the story or novel be relegated to the LGBT section far away from the science fiction and fantasy audience—its intended readers? QDSF was a safe space, an invitation to authenticity. Even then, I still worried a little, but mostly because of the current emphasis on writing "characters who just happen to be queer." That's important, too, and is often how I write. But queer people will face unique challenges in the future, be it technologically advanced, dystopian, on another planet, or post-apocalyptic. Those stories are also important to tell.

How have your own queer experiences influenced your writing?

Before I knew I was trans, I wrote in order to occupy male head and body space. When friends would ask why I never wrote female protagonists, I didn't know how to answer. I identified (and still do) as feminist and wanted to smash the patriarchy. So, why couldn't I write that? I felt bad, but didn't let that stop me. I continued writing cisgender gay male protagonists because, like Ash, that's how I imagined myself—though I was not fully aware of the implications, yet.

It's only now, after years of facing my identity, that I'm beginning to write trans characters. It's harder than I thought it would be. Even though I've made peace with my body, that doesn't mean I still wouldn't take a new one, if offered by Kinetic, Inc. I'm just starting to think of my body as desirable, again. And since I almost always write sex/bodies/romance alongside my science fiction and fantasy, that matters.

What's next for you? What writerly treats can readers expect in the future?

Hopefully a novel! This short story was my first in several years. I recently finished writing and editing *Docile*, a science fiction romance set in a near-future Baltimore City. It focuses on debt, autonomy, and consent, features lots of queer characters, and lots of plot-relevant sex (!!!). By the time QDSF is in your hands, I'll be nose-deep in querying. Other than that, QDSF has given me hope for the future of queer short fiction and I plan to be a part of that.

Author Spotlight:
Amal El-Mohtar

Wendy N. Wagner

"Madeleine" is crafted around the exploration of psychology and neuro-science, two branches of science not as commonly discussed in SF as, say, astrophysics or genetic engineering. What made you decide to explore these fields?

Honestly, I initially thought I was writing a time-travel story! I found myself imagining a woman with the power to inadvertently travel back in time through sensory triggers, gradually developing the ability to change her past by changing her memories. I knew I wanted her to encounter someone in her memory-space who wasn't actually part of her memories, and for her acquaintance with this stranger to catalyze that memory-changing/shaping skill. But I didn't know where I wanted it to go from there—it was muddled with a lot of different Things I Wanted to Do, and it percolated for a long time before I decided to try and make it my submission to QDSF. When I focused on the relationship I was imagining instead of the time-travel MacGuffin, though, it started coming together—and it was in trying to figure out a frame for that relationship, and figuring out Madeleine's character, loneliness, and motivation, that the story really emerged.

We learn that Madeleine has used the reading of dense, difficult nonfiction as a way of burying her feelings after her mother died, and then we see her using passages from these texts as a way to break out of her unwanted memories. Do you think intellectualism is a kind of emotional armor for her? And is that something you've seen in yourself or in others?

I don't think Madeleine sees it as "intellectualism" per se—in my view she's someone who suddenly has a lot of time on her hands, after her mother's death, and is trying to fill up empty space with as much noise as possible. So it's less outward-facing than armour; in the absence of emotional connections, she fills herself up with theory to structure that empty space inside her.

For myself—by the time this sees print I'll have been living an ocean away from my fiancé for six months. The only thing that's made the separation anywhere near to bearable has been filling every hour of every day with more work than I can feasibly deal with. Some of that work was for a graduate Canadian Literature course taught by Jennifer Henderson, called "Making Settler Colonial Modernity." It was amazing, an utterly brain-breaking revelation of a course, and one of the ways in which I found myself processing the material was through fiction; since it was structuring so many of my own daily thoughts, I found myself using the theory to structure Madeleine's as well.

Since this is a piece about involuntary memories, and you even quote Proust at the beginning, I have to ask: Have you read *In Search of Lost Time*? Also, how do you feel about madeleines?

To my shame, I haven't. The Proust is all Michael Damien Thomas' fault. Back when this was still a time-travel story, I was describing the idea to him, and he said "Oh! Like Proust and the time-travelling madeleine!" When I asked what he meant, he explained about the famous passage. I googled it and stared and stared and stared and decided on my protagonist's name, and the story suddenly had a foundation in text.

I was uncertain about keeping the quote at the beginning of the story, but I'd kept it there as a sort of story-compass during the writing process and the story felt oddly incomplete without it.

You are a reviewer, a scholar, a writer of prose, and a poet. How do you wear all those hats?

With increasing difficulty! The hats are like Tupperware. At first they stack neatly, each has a lid and a space in which it fits. But then they *change*. They warp in the microwave or dishwasher. The lids don't fit. You lose the lids. You start trying to keep the food in with foil and plastic wrap but the plastic wrap won't stick to the sides and meantime your leftovers are going stale outside the fridge or mouldering at the back of the fridge because things no longer stack so stuff hid behind other stuff and you overdid the foil on one and couldn't see inside it so didn't realize it was a week overdue being eaten and the only solution seems to be to buy new containers but the old ones still have food inside them and there's no room there's never any room—

I guess what I'm saying is that I need a bigger fridge for my hats. Which are Tupperware. Sometimes.

Also I don't sleep.

You also participated in Women Destroy Science Fiction!. For you, what does it mean to destroy science fiction?

It means grinding into a fine powder the conviction that I'm not smart or educated enough to write hard SF. It means obliterating the fear that men I respect will roll their eyes at my attempts. It means facing up to the fact that men who would do that don't deserve my respect, and that indeed men for whom I care deeply rooted for and supported me throughout the process. It means standing up, shoulder to shoulder, with women and queer people and people of colour against the fiction that things are fine as they are, that nothing needs to be changed or addressed, that our voices are sufficiently loud at a whisper.

Do you have any up and coming projects we should be looking for?

I'm very excited that M Sereno has turned my very short story, "Wing," into a tiny comic to be included in *An Alphabet of Embers*, edited by Rose Lemberg. I genuinely think that anthology will be one of the most exciting released this year—there are so many new voices in it, and the table of contents puts me in mind of hands heaped with colourful jewels. Those titles!

I'm also very slowly working on a novel set in the same world as "The Green Book," a short story of mine that was nominated for a Nebula—here's hoping there's something like a draft by year's end!

Scott Lynch, Liz M Myles, Michael Damien Thomas, and I are starting up a *Blake 7* podcast, tentatively titled *Down and Safe*. I've never watched *Blake 7* and know literally nothing about it. At the time of this writing it's still possible that the show is about the seventh clone of poet William Blake. I'm really looking forward to it.

Finally, I've got a story coming out in Ann VanderMeer's *The Bestiary* in August. My field notes on the Weialalaleia and insights into cryptohirudology are writ therein. It's also the first book for which I've had to sign book-plates, making it the *fanciest* book production I've had the pleasure of seeing my work in, with the exception of Erzebet YellowBoy's limited hand-bound editions of *The Honey Month*.

Author Spotlight: Tim Susman

Rahul Kanakia

What inspired you to write this story?

I had recently read John Joseph Adams' and Hugh Howey's excellent anthology, *The End Is Nigh*, and a member of my writing group is big into apocalyptic fiction, so that was on my mind. I was thinking about a lot of the post-apocalyptic tropes, one of which is survivors gathering to form a new society, and then asked what might happen if a gay couple's original tolerant society had been eradicated, and they were faced with the choice of joining a less tolerant one—would there be a situation so drastic that someone might choose not to join the survivors? For a novel I'm currently working on, I had already imagined the U.S. splitting along ideological lines, and I borrowed that idea for this story to create two Americas. I'd read an article a while back positing that certain states are attempting to use local state laws to create what is, in effect, a different country, even if they are not politically seceding, and we are seeing those arguments continue today (the furor over Indiana's law took place after I'd written this story, of course, but it's another great example).

The story opens with a long road trip, and before we even know what's happening, we're plunged into the barren landscape of your peri-apocalyptic Earth. It's a world that has, as one character says, been reduced to the Pre-Cambrian, and it's not quite like any other ecological vision I've seen in SF. How did you come by this imagery?

Part of the focus of the story is on the inability of a gay couple to procreate naturally—that's why some of the colony ships don't allow male gay couples, but female gay couples are okay. So there's a kind of matching imagery there with the barren Earth that they have the chance to leave behind if they give up their relationship. The details of the road trip came about from experience; I've driven from the Bay Area to Colorado many times, and a couple years ago there were swaths of dead trees throughout the Rockies as a result of the pine beetle infestation. The patches of grey amid the beautiful green stuck with me, as did the blackened patches from the fires, and I finally worked that into a story.

In the end, the protagonist and his husband decide not to go into space with the Christians. Instead, they pin their hopes on a different spaceship. However, in the world you've created, that seems like a fool's errand. In practice, they're consigning themselves to a foreshortened life on a doomed earth, but the story leaves them with this sliver of hope—maybe they'll find salvation in White Sands. Why give them that? Why not end the story on the doomed note?

Personal preference. I think hope is one of the great qualities of people, that even in the worst circumstances we can still find a sliver to hold onto. In this case I feel like that's the way I would face the situation: hey, this probably won't work, but it's better than doing nothing. They refer earlier in the story to scientists still trying to figure out the problem of declining oxygen; I really do feel that humanity wouldn't go extinct without a fight. So that little sliver of hope at the end is my way of taking that general thought and making it specific to these people.

Internal to the story, I think it's Grandma's way of helping Daniel alleviate his guilt over his decision. She's a woman of action, and it feels to me like a compassionate move on her part, not only because she believes she can get them on the shuttle, but also because it's better than saying, "Well, you wanted to stay here and die, so let's find a place to do that."

You founded Sofawolf Press, which is dedicated to publishing fiction that focuses on anthropomorphic animals. What prompted that? What do you see as the role of this kind of specialty press?

My founding partner Jeff and I had been active in the furry community for probably seven or eight years at that point and had seen the fiction in that community slowly getting better, though it was mostly published in photocopied fanzines. Meanwhile, from the best writers, we heard that larger SF/F presses just weren't interested in that kind of story (in general; there are exceptions too numerous to list). Jeff discovered that it was becoming possible to create professional publications in small runs, and we both thought it was time the community had a publisher willing to do that. In a larger sense, founding Sofawolf contributed to the definition of the furry community as its own entity and encouraged the development of many of the aspiring writers in it, which we've continued to do both as a publisher and by leading panels and workshops at conventions. And we publish stories that this community loves and wants to read, which they can't get anywhere else.

What else are you working on? On your website, you mentioned a novel and a shared-universe that you're working within.

I'm usually juggling half a dozen projects at a time. Currently I'm working on an alternate-history 1815 magic school story that I've been trying to get right for about five years now (third time's the charm!). I've also got a few novel manuscripts in various editing stages (a time-travel gay coming-of-age, a supernatural New Adult story, and a fantasy gay romance) and am writing a few scattered short stories here and there. The shared universe has been dormant for going on a decade now, but I still get asked about it from time to time, so you never know …

Author Spotlight: Susan Jane Bigelow

Jill Seidenstein

What does it mean to you to destroy science fiction? What do you think still needs destroying in science fiction?

For me this means tearing down a lot of the barriers and assumptions around what "should" be in science fiction—specifically, that it should be by, for, and about straight white men from western countries. I want to see science fiction featuring all kinds of people, and I want to see myself reflected there as well. It really isn't destroying science fiction so much as it's destroying an old, noxious stereotype about the genre.

How does your queer identity and experience inform your storytelling?

I'm trans and bisexual, and that often creeps into my stories. I tend to write queer women as protagonists, not for any abstract or political reason or because I want to see myself there, but because those are the stories that I'm interested in and the kinds of characters I care about.

What was the hardest thing about writing this story?

Oh jeez, this story really wrecked me emotionally. That's how I knew I had something good, but it hit me in all the feelings and made it so I couldn't write anything for about a week. Writing about what happens to someone on the receiving end of Internet harassment is not a comfortable thing, because I know people who are going through this, and I feel like most women who are active online are at such risk of this happening to them.

What surprised you in the writing of this story?

The relationship that happens.

How did this story come about? Specifically, I'm curious to hear more about kindness, since it seems too rare on the Internet, where people can hide behind their anonymity.

I really wanted to write a story about a) a living Twitter bot and b) the awful stuff I see going on online all the time, and those two things sort of melded together. I do feel like kindness is underrated. I try to lead with kindness whenever I can, and I know that's in part because I have the mental energy and space afforded by privilege to do so. I don't, for the record, think that kindness works on people who are determined to ruin someone else's life, but in a lot of cases it can make a difference. Is that naïve of me? Probably! But that's where I'm coming from.

Anonymity is so dangerous because people feel like they can do anything. It's sad and horrifying that what so many people decide to do with it is so cruel. In the face of all of that, the rest of us should remember to try and be kind to one another. It's not much of a counterweight, but it's not nothing, either!

Author Spotlight: RJ Edwards

Sandra Odell

"Black Holes" starts with a vividly intimate setting—from the postcards on the walls, to the descriptions of the sheets, to Kant's belly laugh. What inspired this particular tale?

Those details, and several others in the story, were inspired by life—and one person in particular, a friend who was coming out as trans the same time I was. I knew I wanted to write something about the Large Hadron Collider, this inconceivably huge and important thing that might change the world, and relate it back to these small decisions made by individuals. And I wanted to write about a relationship between two trans people. I started with this image that is very much rooted in my relationship with this friend. I borrowed his postcards and his laugh. Though it diverged from there—Kant is definitely *very* different from the real-life person.

Joey and Kant are not only likeable characters, they are believable. Their likes, desires, fears, and transitions: In many ways, they speak of what it means to be queer. What of your own experiences as a queer writer went into writing this story?

A lot came from my own experience. The setting, western Massachusetts, is where I found a lot of important connections to other queer and trans people myself. Not all of it is lifted straight from life, but as the character of Kant grew out of my friend, Joey grew out of myself. Ze is anxious and overwhelmed in a way that I felt in my early twenties when I was figuring myself out. Like me at that time, and I think like a lot of people, Joey tries and fails to find zerself in another person.

The voices of the differing POVs are distinct, lending to the character portrayals. Do you like to take chances with your writing, using different voices, exploring challenging subjects?

I always want to figure out what voice or format works best for the story and try out different things, but I don't think of myself as particularly experimental. I also don't think of myself as liking to explore challenging subjects per say, but I do think that I—and a lot of queer and trans writers—end up doing so because complexity or struggle is the truth of our experience.

QDSF strives to encourage the voices of QUILTBAG writers and their exploration of diversity in genre fiction. What do you see as some of the obstacles queer writers face when it comes to presenting their works to the world?

I struggle with this "hand-holding" issue a lot in writing trans characters: How much knowledge can I assume that my audience has? Do I need to explain this or that about trans people, or can I let the reader figure it out on their own? And of course, these questions assume that the reader *isn't* trans. You want to write for your own community, but when you're trying to get published, there's a fear that a straight or cisgender editor is not going to "get it" even if the work is good. I think there are probably still a lot of QUILTBAG writers who aren't writing or aren't showing their work to anyone because they don't see a place for their stories. But there's certainly people trying to change that—there's projects like Queers Destroy Science Fiction! and the *Beyond* anthology of queer SF comics launched by Sfé R. Monster and Taneka Stotts. There are books like Imogen Binnie's *Nevada* and Casey Plett's *A Safe Girl to Love*, which are literature by trans women for an audience of trans women, and they're incredible. I'm hopeful that it's getting better.

What's next for RJ Edwards? What do eager readers have to look forward to?

I can't speak to anything forthcoming immediately, but I have a lot in the works—more short speculative fiction looking for a home and a young adult novel about a fluffy romance between two girls at a rock camp. More trans characters, always. And having just finished library school this spring, hopefully I'll have much more time to devote to writing!

Author Spotlight: AMJ Hudson

Sandra Odell

"Red Run" begins with a detailed, almost comforting, description of setting and mood, and then delivers a gut punch that drives the story home, seeming to blur the line between science fiction and horror. Do you rely on genre labels when writing a story, or do you prefer to let the characters and situations develop and see where they lead?

I tend to focus more on creating a character-driven narrative. I think it's important to be aware of the genre I'm working within, but I always spend most of my time on the characters and their motivations, letting them guide me through the story.

No matter their gender, self-identification, or preference, many in the queer community suffer from depression. What of your own experiences, if any, went in to writing this story?

Unfortunately, a lot of the experience with depression detailed in "Red Run" is similar to my own. When I began to question my sexuality, I met a lot of resistance from my family. When I came out, they didn't talk about it. No one did. I was met with silence and blank stares, the shrugging of shoulders. Having to internalize so many things that defined who I am destroyed the trust I had in those around me. I questioned my place in my world. I hated myself for not being what everyone expected and wanted. Sadly, all this seems to be a pretty common experience.

Hinahon's relationship with Natalie is almost secondary to the issue of her depression. The story could easily have been written with a heterosexual character, yet your choice to make Hinahon a lesbian lends the story a weight that makes it hard to deny. Do you feel that representation in fiction of any stripe can serve as a stepping stone to push back the weight of depression and the looming shadow of suicide?

I don't know if I want to say that it can do all that, but I'd like to hope visibility helps in some way. I know it's a great comfort for me to hear about queer anything being published. It's wonderful to see ourselves in stories. All representation, I feel, however, isn't good representation. Some stereotypical portrayals of queer characters probably do more harm than good. But I hope, on a whole, representations of queer characters lead others to understand the complexity of sexuality and gender.

When did you first realize you wanted to be a writer? When did you first decide to address issues of queer identity in your work?

I've always wanted to be a writer, but I didn't think I could actually make it work until I was about two years into college, miserably making my way through as an art major. When I started to reevaluate what I was doing, I realized the only thing I really enjoyed in college was the writing, and it was something I'd always enjoyed, something that was always there, so I turned to it completely. I believe the first time I began discussing queer identity in my work was at the end of high school.

Are there any queer writers out there who inspire your readings or writing?

A major inspiration is Benjamin Alire Sáenz. I recently read his collection of short stories, *Everything Begins and Ends at the Kentucky Club*, and I was blown away by the beauty of his language and the emotional impact of narratives.

What's next for AMJ Hudson? What can readers expect from you in the coming year?

I'm working on several creative non-fiction essays at the moment, working with the faculty of my university in preparation for my thesis. Many of these tackle my identity as a queer, bi-racial woman. I'm also in the process of outlining some fiction that further explores the idea of memory and identity.

Author Spotlight: Raven Kaldera

Sandra Odell

"CyberFruit Swamp" has a distinct, immediately accessible voice that captures the reader's attention and carries it through the story. Some writers believe that it is difficult to capture the narrative voice in science fiction and still integrate the fantastical elements of the story. How do you approach creating a believable character in an unfamiliar setting?

Really? They do? I've always preferred the narrative voice myself. It grabs the reader's attention and gets them inside the head of the character. I think that the first step in making that link is to have the character in a situation that is emotionally familiar, even if the technology is different. For example, the character in "CyberFruit Swamp" is waiting be called by a girlfriend, or perhaps someone waiting impatiently for transport to arrive. It doesn't matter what the transport is; we've all been in the situation of "hurry up and wait." The fact that the emotions of the situation are immediately relatable makes it easier for readers to connect to the situation.

I love the color and symbol coding of the chains. Many younger readers of SF/F may not recognize the handkerchief code that was such a vital part of queer culture (and, in some instances, still is today), yet you expertly managed to blend the past with the future in a way that supports the struggle for identity. How do you see the evolution of such symbols having come about in the world of "CyberFruit Swamp"? Do you see them connected at all?

"CyberFruit Swamp" was actually written a couple of decades ago, when the "hanky code" was much more common, which is how I got inspired to write it. At that point, there was a lot of pressure for transfolk not to date each other, but to select a nontrans partner as a way of "proving" that one was accepted as one's chosen gender. As a trans person who is mostly in relationships with other trans people (as in, three of my four partners are trans), I didn't like that at all. I wanted to portray a future where a large trans-oriented pride movement had already happened, and a subculture had arisen from it. Decades later, that hasn't happened (and perhaps that's a good thing) but it's a lot more acceptable now to date each other, which is excellent.

I also wanted to portray a signal system that wasn't about being "gay" or "lesbian" or "bisexual," but merely about which sort of person you're looking for in the moment, without regard to identity. Many of us transfolk have a hard time with monogendered labels—to whom are we the same sex or the opposite one? As someone who is also intersex, that doesn't apply to me.

The story is graphic and does not apologize for its exploration of sexual themes both in terms of body awareness and in the politics and policies that form and challenge our queer identities. Where did you find inspiration to write this particular tale?

Well, Cecilia Tan was having trouble finding anyone to write decent trans erotica, so I did it for her. It's still a problem. Nontrans people don't know what's anatomically real, what's offensive, what's emotionally real. If you don't know what it's like to have changed your body, or to have been seen in public as more than one gender, it's rather difficult to realistically write about it. Well, you could actually do research (gasp!) and talk to real trans people (gasp!) but for some reason most nontrans writers who attempt that don't bother, especially if it's science fiction or fantasy. Yes, one can come up with a situation in a future culture or technology that doesn't exist to be interviewed, but it's still important to put in realistic emotional responses. I'm also aware that if you're going to combine politics with sex in a story, the sex had better be good, because otherwise the irritation of the politics will make people stop reading, and stop listening. If you can get them hot, you can get your message in under their radar more effectively.

You have a rich, varied history in gender and sexual activism, promoting positive gender awareness as well as support for sexual safety issues. What of your own experiences went into this story?

First, the experience of being trans (specifically FTM) and suddenly going to the bottom of the heap as far as sexual market value goes. That was still very new for me as of that writing, and jarring—I'd been used to being seen as normally attractive so long as I hid who I was, and I had to deal with the fact that being myself (as far as current technology could take me) made me a freak. Secondly, the experience of body dysphoria, and how far one will go to get the physical sensation one wants. Third, the boy was based on the "boy" I was dating at the time—I converted them to trans/trans dating and they promptly left me for another trans person! Fourth, there was some political discussion at the time around what was legally considered rape, and how limiting that was.

What authors do you turn to when it comes to getting your queer fiction on?

Well, my friends and colleagues Hanne Blank, Lee Harrington, Cecilia Tan, just offhand. I like queer fiction that doesn't give two shits about being politically correct, and in fact is willing to risk that edge for the sake of hotness. I'm also always on the lookout for trans erotica that doesn't suck, which is an uphill battle, and I wish it wasn't. But at least there is trans erotica now; I remember the days when your choices were either bad forced feminization porn or some nihilistic noir bullshit where the trans character exists to be pathetic and get killed.

If you could speak directly to the readers with the Queers Destroy Science Fiction! issue in hand, what would you say to them about awareness and acceptance of themselves and others?

Find a way to know that you are sexy. If your body and your desires are not represented in a sexy way, change that. Show people how they're sexy. Write if you can write, film if you can film, do something to widen the horizons of erotica. Somewhere out there exist people who are terrified that they're the only ones who like this thing that you also like, who are sexual in the way that you're sexual. They will be incredibly grateful to find your words and images and realize they're not alone.

AUTHOR SPOTLIGHT: RAND B. LEE

ARLEY SORG

What stands out about this story to me, among other things, are the elaborate and well-developed genre elements. They give the reader a sense of a full world. This feels like a place that has been on the author's mind for a long time. How did the story come about and develop?

Most of my stories come to me as an image and a mood. I wrote "The Sound of His Wings" when I was in my thirties, disillusioned by my attempts at intimacy with men and feeling marginalized in the gay culture. The hideaway mutant community in which the story is set was I think an unconscious fantasy of the home I wished I could have found—a safe private world where my differences would be celebrated rather than denigrated. At the same time I knew the hostility with which the outside world treats those who are "different;" hence the menace hanging over the heads of the characters. The community setup itself was loosely based on East Wind Community in Tecumseh, Missouri, where I lived in the very early 1980s.

You bring to life a host of diverse characters. What did you find challenging about writing with diversity? And what do you hope readers will gain from it?

My father's people were Russian Jews, my mother's were Anglo, we had African American friends while I was growing up. I was irritated by the relentlessly monocultural focus of most SF at the time. NOTE: In the original story, the little girl the old man speaks to near the end of the piece was explicitly written as black. When the story appeared in *Asimov's*, the illustrator—without malign intent, I'm sure—drew a very fine picture of her as a little white girl. Unconscious racial bias is hard to quell.

Dreams play a pivotal role in your story and work on many different levels. Even within the piece, they mean different things to different people. How did your relationship to dreams impact the writing and story?

I've been interested in the underpinnings of consensus reality for most of my life. I began reading Tarot cards for fun in college, then converted to Fundamentalist Christianity in order to escape my sexuality. Seven years later, no longer a Christian, I returned to my exploration of mysticism. Gradually I became aware that in some of my dreams, I seemed to connect with truth-with-a-capital-T. I've been working as a professional psychic now for many years.

It's hard to imagine this as a world created solely for a single tale. Where can readers go to revisit these characters and this setting? Will we see a book that builds upon the piece?

Possibly, but unlikely. Since I wrote this story, the whole mutant meme has gone viral and is now considered sort of old hat by fantasy editors.

What are you working on now that fans can look forward to?

I've been laboring for some years on my first full-length science fiction novel, entitled *Centaur Station*. It's set on a space station staffed half by humans and half by a nongendered alien race called the Damánakíppith/fü. All sexual orientations are present in the book; there are some strong female characters; and Karel Van Houten, the Station's new Security Chief, is a body dysphoric seeking haven. I'm about two-thirds through the manuscript and aim to have it finished by the fall of this year.

Author Spotlight:
Geoff Ryman

Robyn Lupo

How did "O Happy Day!" emerge for you? Why do you think people are drawn to read and write about dystopias? What was it for you, in particular? Was there any particular research involved?

"O Happy Day!" came about because of some things that friends reported hearing people say at women-only meetings in the early '80s, some of which sounded a bit alarming. Also the reactions of some radical feminists regarding MtoF transexuals as some kind of invading force to be excluded—it seemed to imply they thought genes determined behaviours and loyalties. I never believed that women are intrinsically less violent than men. It smacks of wishful thinking or sentimentality to me. It also strikes me as deeply sexist in itself. It over estimates the influence that genetically determined sex has on character, and maybe doesn't allow for the bell-shaped curve of differences anyway. It seems unaware of the social construct of gender, which was much more prevalent back then. To emphasize, this piece was inspired by a breathtakingly bold and simple idea of something like gendercide that grew of conversations from that long ago era.

At the time it was considered a very bold and direct idea. Now I think the term "feminazi" is stale and stereotyped, but this story is older than that term.

I was also interested in the box that people put themselves in if they define someone else as being intrinsically violent or intrinsically the problem. We see traces of that all over the world right now—these prisons (if not quite extermination camps) that incarcerate on suspicion or belief. The vast prison building programme for discredited populations also feels still relevant to now.

Finally, of course, the story let me write about race in America, particularly love (or blindness) between white and black at a time when that wasn't as prevalent a theme as it is now.

The structure of the world in the story seems to be violence all the way down: the men sent to die; the men sent to kill; the prison structure of The Station; and there's also the sense that the Grils watching may be captives themselves. What drove you to explore it so thoroughly?

I was grimdark before my time.

Violence besmirches everybody. One of the aspects of the box is that it ends up imprisoning the people who build the actual walls. Just before the gates open at the end, you're right, everybody in the story is in prison. But someone sees sense and opens the gates. I hope that note of optimism sticks.

What draws you to short fiction?

I'm attracted to novellas and novelettes because they give you a chance to build your world and tell a story—but before the novel length reveals that you've only lived in the past and not the future and that you are copying the past onto the future ... a failing of SF that's almost unavoidable. Your characters come from the past. You tweak them to look like they're from the future, but it's a huge effort—like writing in the point of view of someone from another culture.

What's next for you?

I have a Leverhulme International Academic Fellowship, that will buy out my teaching in Manchester, send me to Cape Town, teach an SFF workshop there, and travel in Africa meeting SFF writers. The aim is to set up a centre for the study of African SFF at the University of Cape Town. I run two mainstream African Reading Groups—one in London, one in Manchester—and also an African Fantasy Reading Group that has about 130 members on Facebook. I'm writing a series of reviews and studies of the rise of AfroSF in the content of oral literature and the tsunmai of mainstream fiction coming out of Africa. Way back in the '70s I did a course on African Tribal History at UCLA, so I will be trying to follow that up.

I will write occasional good pieces (I hope) for lovely people who have a knack for pulling fiction out of me, most recently Nisi Shawl and Bill Campbell for the Delany tribute volume. I've written a utopian tale on commission from the BBC.

However, basically, I've lost faith in the entire notion that SFF is literature, at least literature with social impact and a large following—something it shares with literature in general right now. I'm a working girl, and writing literary SF just doesn't make any cash. The worst of it is, my mainstream colleagues at times seem to assume I write it because it's so profitable. Some of them don't get that I do it out of commitment.

Most of SFF's written material is intended to stimulate and amuse, and as such it does a good job—and a superb job if you can get hold of the good stuff. But the books Readercon discusses may not be in the mall bookshop, if there is a mall bookshop left. Culturally we are far less significant than movies from the Marvel studio—and those only take two hours to watch and are so enjoyable.

The current Hugo mess depressed me more than I can be bothered to delineate for many reasons. If you want politics, go join a political movement. If your story is designed to push a political point of view, it violates the reader's freedom and autonomy. It becomes propaganda. "O Happy Day!" is not a political story. It's a love story; it's a story about the power of stories to box people in and that box trapping prisoner and guard.

Artists Gallery

Art by C. Bedford

Art by Odera Igbokwe

Art by Steen

Art by Isabel Collier; Character ©2015 Reaper Miniatures, Inc.

Art by Paige Braddock

Art by Orion Zangara

Art by Elizabeth Leggett

Art by Elizabeth Leggett

Artists Spotlight

Elizabeth Leggett

One of my favorite movies of all time is *Almost Famous*. If you have not seen it, you should; it has some fantastic quotes. When I started writing this, some of Penny Lane's best lines kept popping into my mind: "We are not groupies. [...] We are here because of the music, we inspire the music. We are Band Aids."

I wish there was a phrase for art-loving fans that was as perfect as "Band Aids" is for music, because I would wear that title proudly. I am fascinated and mesmerized by courageous writers and illustrators. They are my rock stars. Everything they do, brings me to my knees. I am in awe.

So when *Lightspeed* asked me to be art director for Queers Destroy Science Fiction!, I had to say yes. This was my chance to ride in the tour bus! No true fan in their right mind misses that chance!

Some of the most innovative and talented queer creators are represented here. The field of speculative fiction is richer because of their contributions. Wait until you see C. Bedford's clean design and evocative imagery; Paige Braddock's powerful visual storytelling; Isabel Collier's compelling, futuristic style; Odera Igbokwe's potent and fluid expressions; Steen's superb line and composition awareness; and Orion Zangara's lush, lush ink work.

Oh, and the stories are pretty amazing, too!

This collection is bringing QUILTBAG artists and writers further and further into the limelight and giving more fans like me a chance to be transported. The future is a better place when there is genuine inclusion, and I think this special issue is a great move in that direction.

Tell me a little about your artistic background and your work in this field.

Paige Braddock, illustrator of "Emergency Repair" by Kate M. Galey: I've been working as an illustrator since 1985. I started out doing feature illustration for newspapers, back in the day, and eventually ended up transitioning to licensing in 1999. I've always been interested in adventure comics and science fiction stories, so this project was particularly fun because it allowed me to blend both of those things. In my day job, I oversee licensing for the *Peanuts* comic strip. My "night" job is writing and illustrating my other graphic novel projects: *Jane's World* and *Stinky Cecil* ... oh, and this comedy sci-fi graphic novel titled *The Martian Confederacy*, written by Jason McNamara.

C. Bedford, illustrator of "The Astrakhan, the Homburg, and the Red Red Coal" by Chaz Brenchley: Like many others, I've started out at a very young age and continued with the drive to get better, to be more awesome next time. There was a lot of trial and error, particularly due to lack of proper study, but it was a fun journey nonetheless. My work itself typically bends toward androgynous types. People insisted I draw other things to "expand my horizons," but I just wasn't that interested. That wasn't part of what I wanted to see or create, or what I had to say.

Steen, illustrator of "Melioration" by E. Saxey: I've been working out of Queens, NY for a few years now and have been in a few anthologies and other publications. I work in ink, then scan the drawing, and do coloring in Photoshop. I love making weird textures on yupo paper and overlaying it on the drawing to get strange effects. Science fiction holds a dear place in my heart; the first show I ever loved was *Star Trek: The Next Generation*.

Isabel Collier, illustrator of "Nothing is Pixels Here" by K.M. Szpara: I've been sketching and drawing in earnest since high school and working as a professional artist since college, although illustration isn't really my specialty. (I try to do a little bit of just about everything creative, however.) I've been working as a concept artist and character designer in the tabletop gaming industry (think *Dungeons & Dragons* and such) for a couple of decades, though. And now, I feel old.

Odera Igbokwe, illustrator of "勢孤取和 (Influence Isolated, Make Peace)" by John Chu: I am a freelance illustrator located in Brooklyn, NY. I started drawing as a child because of my inspired diet of anime, video games, and cartoons (like much of my generation). As a teenager I had my first art classes and found online communities that provided lots of structure and early critiquing. Fast-forward to college, where I graduated from Rhode Island School of Design and studied illustration. And now I am here at the beginning of my *professional* illustration career, and I'm having a blast. My first published illustration was actually the cover of the December 2014 issue of *Lightspeed*, so it is an honor to work with *Lightspeed* again for this very special issue.

Is your illustration for this project reflective of your own life experiences or related more to a larger social statement?

Braddock: I'm not sure it relates directly to my life except that I found the story compelling and would have enjoyed it even if it hadn't been assigned to me for the illustration. I liked the tone of the piece and the sort of gender neutrality of it. Personally, I love post-apocalyptic stories and images … so this was fun for me to imagine. I hope the writer was pleased with the image. I tried to capture the intensity of the moment … life and death … in the story.

Bedford: I don't typically align myself with any large social movement (nor do I actively avoid them either), but I feel I can only speak from my own experiences and therefore can only speak for myself. They're definitely more reflective of my own life experiences. Saying that, being mixed race, along with several other things, I've had a hard time belonging to any "larger social group." It's difficult for me to actually define social groups or who belongs to what or if I belong with them since I don't meet all the requirements for anything.

Steen: More related to a larger social statement. I've been very lucky in that I haven't gotten much hate for who I am and who I love.

Collier: I think my big statement for this illustration was, "Hey, this is an interesting story. You should read it." Terribly unromantic, I know. Hopefully, it has a bit of an introspective feel, because it seems that as individuals, we're often conflicted between other people's perceptions of who we are, and our own internal understanding of ourselves—which is a major theme of the story.

Igbokwe: "勢孤取和 (Influence Isolated, Make Peace)" is a wonderful slice of intersectionality and the transcendent nature of queerness. It isn't simply a story about same-sex romance—it manages to be science fiction, action, slice-of-life, and the beginnings of romance all at once. The story also inhabits this strange space of romantic tension that keeps you turning the page. So for this illustration I opted to strip it down to that moment of tension and connection.

Ultimately, every project and piece of artwork I create is coming from some part of my internal mythos. And my life experiences as a queer child of the afrodiaspora/reincarnated Sailor Senshi/sun goddess are in themselves a social statement. So even though this illustration is meant for "勢孤取和 (Influence

Isolated, Make Peace)," it is impossible to strip it from my identity—it's still an ember coming from my flame.

When you illustrate a story, do you look for a scene or character within the piece or do you approach the art in a broader, thematic sense?

Braddock: I always start with a character, and then I build the scene out from there. If the image of a character feels authentic ... if that character captures the emotion I'm after, then I feel like at that point I can build the rest of the scene. [My colleague] Jose Mari Flores did the color for this image. It's always interesting to see someone's color interpretation of a line drawing.

Bedford: I think I approach things in a broader sense, but it definitely depends on the work in question. I like trying to include as many parts of a work as possible as I tend to think things, stories especially, are fluid. We feel a certain way about a part of a story later on because of the events that have happened beforehand. I want my work to be reflective of that.

Steen: It depends. With this one, I instantly latched on to the idea of Petheridge being huge and pink. What a great visual for this guy who is menacing, but [whom] I pictured as soft as a wad of chewed gum.

Collier: Honestly, it depends on the story. For "Nothing is Pixels Here," I wanted to avoid any major spoilers, so I tried to focus on the characters, and on the recurring theme of the "glitch," while not getting too specific with anything.

Igbokwe: I'm less interested in taking a snapshot of narrative events, and I'm more interested in using symbolism and iconography as metaphor. However I also love character exploration and the personalities that keep us grounded in these fantastical stories.

This dynamic tends to create scenes that don't necessarily occur in the story and ultimately pushes the illustrations toward the underlying mythology and dreamscape of the narrative.

Do you feel the look, mood, and design of science fiction movies influenced the content and look of your illustrations? If so, in what way?

Braddock: Well, as I mentioned, I'm a big fan of post-apocalyptic stories and movies. I definitely think movies and books like *The Road* (a personal favorite) informed this image. I think the thing I like about post-apocalyptic stories is discovering what gets left behind. Every apocalyptic tale is really a meditation on what has meaning. There's almost a spiritual component in those stories that I find compelling.

Bedford: Some works, yes—most definitely yes. There were many great sci-fi films that came out just around the age of the peak of my imagination, and have forever instilled their influences in me. Sometimes I completely forget that until I re-watch an old movie or re-read an old comic book. It's striking how much I've drawn from these things. At the same time I find myself trying to explore more visual themes and follow what feels right rather than sticking to a specific genre.

Steen: I've been really getting into 1970s sci-fi art lately. A lot of it is very strange, some of it bordering on abstract, but there's such emotion that comes out of it. Their bold, unusual color choices really influenced me.

Collier: Undoubtedly. Artists are magpies by nature, and are constantly pulling out and re-purposing shiny objects that they have mentally hoarded in the past. In this story, though, the science fiction elements and influences aren't very apparent—most of it is going on in the layout of the illustration.

Igbokwe: My knowledge of classic science fiction movies is pretty limited, so I can never sense a direct influence on my illustrations. Typically I ingest science fiction when it is fused with something else (e.g. fashion, music, gaming, etc).

So while I love *Metropolis, X-Men*, Octavia Butler, and *Outlaw Star*, the typical sci-fi influence that rises to the top is more along the lines of "I sure do love the subtle Afrofuturistic aesthetic of that Aaliyah music video, 'We Need a Resolution.'"

With this illustration for "勢孤取和 (Influence Isolated, Make Peace)," I think I subconsciously implemented colors and textures from my science fiction memory bank. However for some of the mark-making and brush strokes, I specifically remember thinking "I want this to feel like a cross between the iconic green text of *The Matrix* and the glyphs that float around in *Final Fantasy IX's* Oelivert."

What did you love most about the story you illustrated?

Braddock: One facet of the story I liked was that you get a sense of what these characters meant to each other, even though only one of them is speaking. You understand how strongly this one character feels about the other as she goes through the process of basically performing a radical medical procedure in a battlefield situation. I like stories where character is revealed through extreme survival circumstances. I also like that the story doesn't actually resolve everything for the reader.

Bedford: I really enjoyed the abstract ideas put forward. I liked that the communication between everyone was not just through words, but the entire way everyone was as a being and reacting off of that. There were a lot of feelings involved rather than direct visual cues to describe what was happening, or the sensations that were effecting the characters. I also enjoyed how the narrator was an active observer, but an observer more than anything else.

Steen: I like how none of the characters are good or bad. I sympathize with all of them, and I still don't know who was correct in their actions. All of the characters were justified, save for Petheridge. But does he deserve his fate in the end? Who is right and who is wrong? I love stories like this.

Collier: I think my favorite thing was the repeated use of hands to describe the characters, and as a pivotal part of the narrative. I find hands fascinating, so that was kind of playing to my bias there, anyway.

Igbokwe: I love the metaphor of strategy and gameplay in regards to this romance. The story also occupies this space of desire, where there is a heavy palpable tension that keeps you turning the page.

Furthermore I think it's critical to have a diverse spectrum of visibility for queer romance. "勢孤取和 (Influence Isolated, Make Peace)" captures a subtle shade of queer romance that we don't get to see often. And that in itself is a revolutionary act.

So, uh, welcome to the revolution where any gender can have passionate, primal, agapeic romance.

Where genderqueer telepaths can explore masturbation on the astral plane.

Or, you know, a Taiwanese man and a cyborg start the beginnings of a loving relationship with a simple game of Go.

Book Reviews, June 2015

Friendship, Chosen Family,

and Queer Communities

Amal El-Mohtar

This month, I want to take a look at how queers destroy science fiction through seeking, building, and defending community. The following books are all deeply concerned with the families we choose and the connections we build together, amongst each other, to survive worlds hostile to us.

Archivist Wasp
Nicole Kornher-Stace
Trade Paperback/ Ebook
ISBN 978-1-61873-097-8
Big Mouth House
Small Beer Press, May 2015
250 pages

An Archivist has two jobs. The first is to hunt and catch ghosts in order to learn about the precataclysm past from them; the second is to defend her life and position against "upstarts"—the other girls marked by the goddess Catchkeep's claw-shaped scars at birth—once a year. Wasp has been Archivist for three years, and wants nothing more than to escape a dismal life of killing her sisters and obeying the Catchkeep-priest—so when an unusually powerful ghost asks her to help find his former partner in the underworld, she agrees. But, as is so often the case with the underworld, she finds both more and less than she bargained for.

More than anything else, this book is *sharp*. You could cut yourself on the prose—Wasp's world is one of thorns, knives, edges of thick, broken glass, a constant background-hum of pain that sometimes swells into a shout. Wasp's perspective absolutely thrums with tension and violence, but also aches with a fierce, hollow loneliness to break the heart. The longing and gratitude for the smallest beginnings of true friendship make the betrayals more vicious, and the stakes just keep rising. I burned through this book in about three hours, desperately rooting for her.

It's also a brilliantly constructed narrative and world. The gods are cruel and absent. The underworld is a maze in layers, a twisting, turning palimpsest, one that allows Wasp to descend almost archaeologically through time by literally experiencing her ghost-partner's memories. The pre- and post-apocalyptic worlds reflect each other in shards and fragments, all the more powerful for being subtle, for their resistance to being spelled out.

It was also keenly refreshing—especially in something that's ostensibly YA, where the Love Triangle of Doom is so annoyingly pervasive—to find a book in which *all* of the strongest, primary relationships are friendships; where friendship has the narrative, motive force usually reserved for sexual-ized romance. I very much wanted to see the A in QUILTBAG represented in this column, and this is a fine example: while the connection between the ghost and his (female) partner is intense and loving, it is never represented as sexual, and sex is in fact completely irrelevant.

I've heard rumors of a potential sequel in the works, which I would welcome because I love Wasp, and because the world Kornher-Stace has invented is fas-cinating—but *Archivist Wasp* also stands perfectly, satisfyingly well on its own.

Karen Memory
Elizabeth Bear
Hardcover/ Ebook
ISBN 978-0-7653-7524-7
Tor Books, February 2015
352 pages

It's 1878, the West is Wild, and the Hôtel Mon Cherie is the respectable home of respectable seamstresses, including our narrator, Karen Memery—and so long as she and the other ladies all pay their $50 a week in seamstressing taxes, the city "don't care if your sewing machine's got a foot treadle, if you take my meaning." But everything changes when the Hôtel is crashed by two women escaping Peter Bantle, a nasty piece of work who deals in human trafficking and runs an illegal brothel by the docks, kicking off a many-armed octopus of an adventure plot that includes U. S. Marshall Bass Reeves, mysterious mind-control engines, and more feats of derring-do than you can shake a dime-novel at.

Given how many reviews of this book include the word "rollicking," I was expecting something rather more light-hearted and slight than what I got: truly riveting voice work and a wealth of wrenching detail, the kind of precision and care that makes you feel like you're looking at one of those glass-covered pocket-watches that lets you see all the gears. Karen's perspective is warm, generous, and kind, working hard at being honest with herself and doing right by others, and it's a joy to spend time with her.

I was also fascinated and delighted by the diversity of the cast, including characters who are black, Chinese, East Indian, Comanche, and trans. Karen herself is queer, and her budding romance with another woman is crucial to the story. This diversity never felt forced or unusual; everything about Bear's chosen setting recalls Mary Robinette Kowal's principle of "subtracting homogeneity for the sake of realism." I also never felt that the characters were reduced to those identity-markers, though Karen's first-person narration means that any access to their interiority is necessarily limited and filtered through her perspective.

My experience of reading this was perhaps a bit odd, in that after reading *Archivist Wasp*—with its privation, cold, and pain—I wanted to dwell in the deliciousness of market descriptions, Karen's enjoyment of her community, and the small kindnesses exchanged between her and her fellow seamstresses. I would have happily read a novel's worth of Karen talking about how she stitched her own journal together or braided her own rug, or how much she enjoys Connie the cook's food—but this is an adventure story, and that means threatening those comforts as often as they appear is a feature, not a bug.

Scruffians!
Hal Duncan
Trade Paperback/ Ebook
ISBN 978-1-59021-193-9
Lethe Press, April 2014
197 pages

Orphans, foundlings, latchkey kids. Urchins, changelings, live-by-wits. Rascals, scallywags, ruffians, scamps. Scoundrels, hellions, Scruffians STAMP!

Hal Duncan began his Scruffians project as a form of "story-busking," releasing the stories online for free if donations for them reached a certain threshold. These stories, along with new material, are collected in *Scruffians!* from Lethe Press.

Scruffians are indestructible children of varying ages and backgrounds who've taken "the Stamp," an operation that "fixes" them in place by raising their souls into visible glyphs on their bodies. Once Stamped, a Scruffian can't die or be changed from their Fixed form: cut off a finger, for instance, and it'll grow back. Making Scruffians has proven useful over the ages for Children's Crusades, work houses, factories—but at some point the Scruffians stole the secret of making the Stamp, figured out that changing the Stamp changed their bodies, and fought back. Now, any rag-tag band of rascals could be Scruffians, roaming streets and byways, feral and froward, and inviting you along for the ride.

This is a motley assortment of stories and story-telling methods entirely appropriate to its subject matter. Scruffians have their own rituals, mythologies, gods, and histories, and Duncan whirls among them like a spinning top. Everything queers and is queered, from language to history to mythology. The Scruffians' enemies are principally the groanhuffs (say it out loud), and their tale-telling claims a magpie's treasury of stories, from Biblical to medieval to classical, as they spell out a shadow-history to what's familiar, recorded, accepted, or known.

There is nothing straightforward about this collection: straightness is groanhuff stuff, and therefore anathema to Scruffians. The stories in this collection are sometimes stacked within twisting frames, sometimes looping back to refer to half-mentioned incidents, sometimes a catalogue like "An Alphabetcha of Scruffian Names"—one of my favorite pieces, offering an alphabetised list of Scruffians and snapshots of their backgrounds. What they lack in straightforward narrative, they more than make up for in relentless inventiveness, fierce heart, and filthy humour—and at its core, each Scruffian story contains a compass needle pointing towards community, towards joining hands with the used, the broken, the unbreakable, and defending themselves and each other with a rhyme.

Interview: David Gerrold

Mark Oshiro

When I watched "The Trouble with Tribbles" last year, I was aware that I was watching a piece of science fiction history. This was not my first introduction to David Gerrold's work, however. Years ago, I was ranting to a friend about how hard it seemed to be to find good science fiction or fantasy with main characters who were gay. They recommended that I read *The Martian Child*, not only because it was something I might like, but because it dealt with another issue that was close to my heart: adoption. The novel was a lot more subtle than I expected, which worked to its advantage. It haunted me for years. And yet? Somehow, it wasn't until I began *Star Trek: The Original Series* as a Mark Watches project that I came across David Gerrold's work again.

Well, I suppose that also depends on if you consider his posts online 'work,' because that's actually how I became re-acquainted with Gerrold. I'm lucky that I have friends who understand what sort of rants will make my day, because one of them sent me Gerrold's blistering takedown of Orson Scott Card's attempt to shy away from his own opinions on homosexuality and same-sex marriage. I think, more than anything else, this gave me an insight into Gerrold's mind and the way he could combine wit and fury to make a point that, frankly, needed to be made. (Which is why I've been such a huge fan of his work dissecting the recent disaster surrounding the 2015 Hugo Awards.) David Gerrold is not an apologetic person, nor is he interested in saying or writing anything that's expected from him over the years. From his work with time travel (*The Man Who Folded Himself*) to his numerous contributions to *Star Trek*'s canon (Tribbles! James T. Kirk! *Star Trek: New Voyages*!), and then to his own inventive contributions to the genre (the War

Against the Chtorr and Star Wolf series), that same ethos can be found.

At heart, though, Gerrold was drawn to science fiction much as many of us were—by the promise of a better future.

He said to me:

> When I was nine, science fiction was an amazing discovery—it was an escape from a world I didn't understand into one that was far more interesting. There were spaceships and aliens and robots and time machines.

> And of course, in those days, if you read books—especially science fiction books—you were the dork, the nerd, the geek, the whatever. But you got to hang out (metaphorically) with Heinlein, Clarke, Asimov, Leinster, Andre Norton, and the many others who were reinventing the universe. There was a sense of inevitability that these were genuine reflections of what the world would be someday. I was impatient to get there.

Of course, for many of us who don't fit into dominant cultural and social narratives, we found that this inevitability rarely included us. We waited to find ourselves in these worlds of possibility and promise, often unable to ever do so unless we happened to read the few authors who were breaking boundaries. Such was the case with Gerrold, who began to intentionally break the paradigm of what was considered part of the science fiction canon.

That's not to suggest that getting queer, gay, and non-white characters into fiction was as simple as writing it. In the context of Gerrold's work on *Star Trek*, he knew that the show had to pick its battles, and said:

> *The Original Series* was produced from '66-'69. In those days, just putting a black woman and an Asian man on the bridge was daring. The Stonewall riots didn't happen until June of '69. *Trek* was already over. So there was simply no awareness then of LGBT people. The episode "Turnabout Intruder" was an interesting attempt, but most fans found it too weird for their tastes, and even today it's not held in high regard.

> The time to introduce gay crewmembers would have been at the beginning of *The Next Generation*, and even though Gene

Roddenberry had made that promise, it never happened. It was one of many promises that were broken. And it was one of the main reasons why I left the show.

I loved the original series, I still do. I might argue that there's a lot about it that could have been done better, especially when you look at it with 21st century eyes.

But the heart and soul of the show—that marvelous set of characters, especially Kirk, Spock, and McCoy—who wouldn't want to spend more time with them? We were blessed with the right actors for the crew, every single one of them. And the magic that happened in front of the camera—we fell in love with them because they were the kind of people we wanted to be.

But what happens when you don't feel like those people are the same as you? Even I can admit to falling for the charm, wit, and joy of the holy *Trek* trinity. I came to adore Leonard Nimoy's portrayal of Spock; I looked forward to every bit of cynicism and wry sarcasm from McCoy; I eagerly kept track of every time Captain Kirk's shirt was ripped off. I knew what a *huge* deal it was to see people like Nichelle Nichols and George Takei on the screen. And yet, like many *Trek* fans, I wanted more. That's a sensation that is unfortunately familiar to many queer/LGBT folks; we thirst for anything that confirms that we are part of these worlds. Why is that important, though? Why is that a shared experience between many people who are marginalized along lines of sexual orientation or gender identity? Gerrold knew that this kind of representation mattered because he grew up in a time when LGBT characters weren't just rare; they were *monsters*.

"There's a scene in a Bugs Bunny cartoon where Bugs pretends to be a manicurist working on Gossamer, the big orange monster," Gerrold said. "And he says, 'I think monsters are the most interrrresting people.'"

Gerrold continued:

That's how I feel about human beings. We're all different, we're all interesting, and we're all monsters too, each of us in our own way. I've had the "privilege" of meeting a lot of people, weird, beautiful, sane, crazy, damaged, recovering, sad, ambitious, foolish—and even a couple of sociopaths as well. And that stuff rubs off. (I have no idea what part of me rubs off onto other people, I hope it's the good stuff.)

When I was growing up, LGBT people were considered monsters. And then I discovered I was one of those monsters. In those days, gay people didn't get to have teenage romances until you were in your early twenties—so I'd say that was the decade when I was learning the most about who I was and who other people really were. I learned to appreciate the courage it takes just to get out of bed in the morning and face a world of massive disagreement.

[For me] the influential books of that time were John Rechy's *City of Night*, which was a horrifying picture of what you didn't want to be—and Patricia Nell Warren's *The Front Runner*, which was unashamedly positive. But it was Theodore Sturgeon's *Venus Plus X* that actually addressed the idea that gender-identity was a fluid, evolving construction, not something indelibly stamped into our bodies. When I wrote *The Man Who Folded Himself*, it was really an internal exploration of all the possibilities in the world, including the sexual ones—the last lines of the book, Dan Eakins accepts the responsibility that he has to make wise choices.

So how did the world change and how do we continue to change it for the better? It's very common that demands for an improvement of diversity are met with a single charge: "Well, why don't *you* make it better?" Gerrold has never been one to shy away from speaking openly about his experience trying to do just that, specifically with *Star Trek*. "Gene Roddenberry promised a room full of 3,000 fans that we'd have gay characters on TNG," he told me. "He repeated that promise in a staff meeting. So I put two gay characters in my script for 'Blood And Fire' (unproduced). But the argument was raised that we couldn't put gay people in the show because it would offend viewers. And when I realized that Gene's promise would never be kept, I decided to quit."

That's not an easy decision to make, obviously, but it was also the reality of the time. Since then, Gerrold contends that the television landscape has changed in incredibly visible ways, and that includes the *Star Trek* canon.

He said:

But that was 1987. Times have changed. When James Cawley

asked if we could do "Blood And Fire" for *Star Trek: New Voyages*, we took my original script, gave the story to Kirk, Spock, and McCoy, expanded the gay relationship to have it be much more personal, and came up with an episode that has some very powerful moments.

I think in recent years, television is starting to recognize that LGBT lives are real. We're seeing a lot more LGBT characters as just people who happen to be LGBT without that being the sole focus of their identity. It's progress. I'd like to get to the point where the Captain of the *Enterprise* can be a gay man without someone at the studio saying, "Uh, maybe you might want to rethink that …

This process—of writing works that challenge people's expectations of gender and sexuality—inevitably ends up being a very personal journey. It *has* to be for those of us who are not heterosexual, cisgender, or a combination of those identities. Where do you draw the line between the personal and the political? How do you navigate such a difficult course? "Starting out, you try to write like everything you've read, everything you've been exposed to—and you're channeling yourself into a mold that really doesn't fit that well," Gerrold explained to me. "Every time you break the mold, every time you experiment, every time you get ambitious, you redefine yourself."

There were logistical issues to consider, too. "I stopped worrying about 'What if Mom reads this?' with *The Man Who Folded Himself*," Gerrold said. "There was a moment when I said to myself, if I don't write the gay scene, I'll be copping out. The whole point of this book is to go the distance, to go as far as it's possible to go. And yes, I was asking—what would I do if I had a timebelt, so a lot of the book is about the adventures I would want to have."

He continued:

After *The Man Who Folded Himself*, I didn't worry anymore about how much of myself was in a story.

See, here's the part about any piece of writing that isn't obvious. Whatever you want to write, you have to become the kind of person who can write that story. So if you're going to set yourself an ambitious goal at the keyboard, you're also setting yourself an ambitious goal in your own way of being.

In *Moonstar Odyssey*, I wrote about a society where children choose their sexual identity at adolescence. It's about a gender-fluid world. It was certainly the single most ambitious thing I'd ever attempted at the time. To write it, I had to put myself into the head of Jobe, the heroine. So that meant walking around in her skin, looking at this world through her eyes—after the book was finished, I did not go back to being the person I'd been before. Now I was a person who had looked at this world through different eyes.

So yes, that's liberating.

Such was the case for Gerrold when he wrote *The Martian Child*, published in 1972 and made into a fairly terrible (and decidedly not gay) film in 2007. The work is imbued with personal meaning for him, largely due to the auto-biographical nature of the story. Gerrold himself is a single adoptive parent, and it's hard *not* to see him within the novel. "When I got to *The Martian Child*, all I set out to do was write a story about how much I love my little boy," he said. He continued:

When I finished, I knew it was like nothing else I'd ever written before. It was sloppy, badly structured, and didn't seem to have a real ending—until you realize that it's one long internal conversation about coming to terms with being a parent. The SF element is almost negligible. And 90% of the story is how it actually happened, with only one or two lines of dialog tweaked for dramatic effect.

That the story was so well received by the readers was liber-ating—it showed me that I could go to very personal places in my own life, exploring what I'd learned along the way, and the audience would respond well to that.

In terms of audience response, there's been a longstanding interest in Gerrold's works, from the numerous series he's written to the work he's done in the *Trek* world. It's also been rewarding to watch the response to many of the pieces Gerrold has written on his Facebook account. It's fascinating to see how these posts toe the line between personal screeds, nonfiction works, and social commentary. "I use Facebook as a way of getting out of the house without leaving my chair," he explained.

He added:

> Writing is little more than sitting alone in a room talking
> to yourself. You need to take a break. You need to go out in
> the back yard and look at the flowers. You need to throw
> the ball for the dog. You need to take a walk around the
> block and get a snack from the corner diner. But most of
> all, you need contact with other people, because that's your
> source material.
>
> So Facebook is a momentary break. More than that, it's a
> chance to discuss what you're experiencing. It's a chance to
> share, connect, listen, and learn.

And Gerrold does a whole lot of connecting and teaching through his posts,
which helps foster an environment where he can re-think his perception of
the world.

He said:

> Where I sometimes get frustrated—with myself, as well as
> with others—is that almost-daily discovery of how hard it is to
> listen. When you're writing, you're the author of the conver-
> sation; the only people who are allowed to talk back are your
> own characters.
>
> When you go to Facebook, you don't have that arrogant
> luxury. You have to listen. And after you listen, you have to
> get it. You have to grok it. You have to respond to what was
> said—notice, I said "respond." I didn't say "argue." People do
> not share stuff on FB as an invitation to argue. They share it
> because they want to know they're not alone. They want to
> know that other people understand.
>
> Over here, when I share stuff—half the time, it's because I'm
> sorting it out in my own head. Some people don't do this. They
> speak and they think that settles it. They run their tapes, they
> type their screeds, and they think they're done.
>
> No, that's just the first part of the job. The real job is to reread

what you wrote and see if that's really true for you, or just something convenient to type.

• • •

David Gerrold can be found on his official website (gerrold.com) and his Facebook (facebook.com/david.gerrold).

We've Made It To ... Magrathea?

Why We as QTPOC Need To Hack Science Fiction's Improbability Drive

Jennifer Cross

I was sixteen when I opened Frank Herbert's *Dune* and established a connection with Paul and Alia Atreides. Page after page, I walked with the "outcast" and "abomination" of their world, examining and empathizing with their trials and tribulations while acknowledging that their story was altering how I reflected on all I had been taught up to that point about what it meant to be human, and what repercussions yielded from human power, innovation, unequal interaction, and its resulting accountability. In spite of its problematic elements (e.g., the conflation of homosexuality and pederasty) *Dune* had become my gateway into science fiction, for science fiction had become the sietch for those who do not fit neatly into this white cis- and heteronormative world.

Over the course of almost 200 years, science fiction has grown to include a multiverse that attempts to mirror the different aspects and experiences of humanity. In doing so, science fiction became that optimal medium of escapism by retaining an intimate connection to optimistic realism—a window into how things could be better for those of us who struggle with simply being. This observation is one of the primary reasons why science fiction has acquired a large contingent of queer fans throughout its existence. The genre, however, is not without its flaws, especially in its varying LGBTQ+ representations. Within the multiverse whose very existence is dependent on transcending boundaries, the instances of whitewashing, alienating, destroying, and otherwise shoveling queer folk into white boxes typically perpetrated by mainstream media have been pervasive and disheartening.

However, if we were to take only those negative trends into consideration when positing the evolution of the genre, we would be failing to acknowledge the recent reappearance and surge (in limited forums) of complex, nuanced queer and trans people of color (QTPOC) characters onto the literature scene. Because Octavia Butler's *Lilith Brood* no longer stands alone as the model QTPOC representation in science fiction, does this mean that science fiction has realigned itself with its original modus operandi? Has it reasserted itself as the haven for those who do not belong and who will not be cataloged, categorized, or easily referenced? Have the appearances of characters like Nahadoth from N.K. Jemisin's *Inheritance Trilogy* or Narita from Mary Anne Mohanraj's *The Stars Change* changed the course of the genre by getting it back on track?

The Flow of the Current—The Fans' Perspective

The digital age became the best tool which QTPOC fans could use to allow their voices to be heard. Courtesy of social media platforms like Facebook, Twitter, and Goodreads, fans have more sophisticated methods for gaining access to their favorite creators' works and to the creators themselves. When fans have quicker, more efficient access to the works that they love—especially if those works accurately portray and elaborate their specific experiences and emotions as QTPOC without apology—fans will digest those stories faster and come back for more.

Increased demand usually leads to increased supply, or in more literary terms, increased representation. Increased representation usually leads to increased inspiration for aspiring QTPOC creators to come forth and present their own words and characters to the next round of fans-who-would-be-aspiring writers. Increased QTPOC representation has allowed these fans-who-would-be-aspiring-creators to believe, as shown in Andrea Hairston's *Mindscape*, that a queer couple of color could be presented in print, not as minstrels or Mammies, but as nuanced, complex characters who worked to save the world from being engulfed by an epi-dimensional barrier; and that such a story would sell. If we are to take into account that queer fans now have empathetic options beyond the white, rich, fabulous, able-bodied Heinleinian representations, it would appear that science fiction is continuing to broaden its horizons without any constrictions.

The Stopbank of the Current—The Industry's Perspective

However, the modus operandi behind the science fiction publishing industry ("Industry") must be taken into consideration. As with any business, the Industry's prime objective is to remain as fiscally sound as possible. In basic economic terms, the Industry needs to make sure its income supersedes its costs. To do so, the Industry will more than likely be using the tools of the digital age to its advantage by way of tracking sales, predicting trends, and analyzing factors that may or may not influence the aforementioned. For example, the achievement of accolades is usually a solid factor in determining the trend of a product and the potential success of its creator. Accolades generally lead to acclaim; acclaim leads to increased sales; consistent, increased sales lead to new trends; new trends direct the Industry to where the money needs to be reinvested. If this were not the case, then John Scalzi would not be negotiating TV deals, and the Marvel Movie Universe would have ceased after *Iron Man 2*.

However, no dam is perfect. Throughout the history of the genre, there have been accounts which demonstrate that the complex system by which the Industry operates can be easily manipulated by those with privilege and the prestige in order to minimize the voices of the marginalized and indirectly profit from their oppression. For instance, in spite of his long-standing, public fight against marriage equality, Orson Scott Card enjoyed a $27 million opening weekend of the live-action theatrical release of his renowned work *Ender's Game*. When those with privilege can understand, and therefore potentially alter, the specs that make up the construct of the game, it can become increasingly difficult, if not impossible, for marginalized characters and marginalized voices to receive the attention needed to not just come to life, but also to inspire innovation and keep science fiction from going down the same path as Google Glass.

Cracks in the Stopbank—Fanfiction, Small Press & Self-Publishing

In the wake of the Industry's seemingly homogenous and imposing wave, fanfiction, small presses, and self-publishing have provided alternative avenues for those who wish for their voices to be heard. Small press publishing especially has been noted for providing a niche market to QTPOC fans who might not otherwise be able to find representation of who they are "beyond the trope"; while the existence of fanfiction has provided a community for isolated QTPOC to come together to share and promote their fanfiction as well as celebrated, traditionally published works featuring complex, nuanced QTPOC characters.

The convention scene has also aided in building relations between creator and fan, particularly in local convention circuits at which small press and self-publishers are more likely to attend, and QTPOC fans have the opportunity to meet the people behind the characters that finally acknowledge and respect their existence. Fostering of such relationships on the ground is imperative for the continuation of any genre fiction—something that small press publishing recognizes—as some small press houses have responded in kind by producing engaging works which feature protagonists who don't emulate Sookie Stackhouse.

Conclusion

Science fiction's purpose is to push and eventually transcend the boundaries of the normal realm, regardless of the Industry's systemic flaws or audacious politicking, so it is natural that its fans have lofty expectations regarding how the genre expands and what the genre produces. However, in order for this evolution to happen, the game needs to change. Progress is slowly being made on certain literary fronts; unfortunately, this progress is being bombarded by the privileged few who purport to be more concerned with preserving their own legacies than expanding and challenging the definition of science fiction for the benefit of those who may not have the power to do so. The genre that is the representation of counterculture cannot become antagonized by it. Monopolizing the genre with the cishet, white, able-bodied hero is no longer acceptable. Replacing that cishet, white, able-bodied hero with the Fabulous Magical Negro is unthinkable. At the end of the day, science fiction needs to start failing better for its fans who are fighting harder for their existence.

~

Jennifer Cross is an unapologetic black queer feminist nerd who takes pride in being able to recite the Bene Gesserit Litany Against Fear in her sleep. She is the Lead Organizer of Just Write Chicago, which is currently Chicago's largest writing group dedicated to providing a safe, inclusive and motivational space for writers of all genres and all levels time to "just write." When she's not trying to keep up her blog, Outside The Box, or to finish her first SF/F novel, she's probably speaking at conventions like C2E2 or WisCon about diversity, inclusion and representation within SF/F, or outside spinning fire while cosplaying as Zoe Washburne and other SF/F Women of Color.

Not Android, Not Alien, Not Accident

Asexual and Agender in Science Fiction

Cedar Rae Duke

Science fiction can provide uniquely fertile ground through which to explore the diversity of real-world human gender and sexuality. In the vast creative playground filled with space ships, alien life, and time travel boxes, there should be room for everyone. The genre has made recent progress toward increased visibility of gay, lesbian, and sometimes bisexual characters, yet transgender, asexual, intersex, and agender/neutrois people remain few and far between. We are usually "other": perhaps aliens, androids, or humans who have been "altered" by technological mishap.

Representation matters, both in SF and in the broader culture. Humans are storytelling creatures; we both create and are created by stories. The narratives we grow up with teach us right from wrong, normal from "other," history, culture, how to relate to others, and, fundamentally, who we are—or, at least, who we are supposed to be.

. . .

I knew I was sex-repulsed in my early teens. Though asexuality as an orientation label would not come into use for many years (and not all asexuals are sex-repulsed), I knew early on that my having any sort of genital contact with another person, or penetration, was abhorrent. And the more I learned about sex, the more grossed out I got.

Suddenly, sex was everywhere—on television, on the radio, at the movies, and in nearly every book and story they assigned in school. The future scared me. Was sex inevitable? Was I doomed?

"No one will ever love you if you're not willing to have sex," I was told.

"When you grow up, you'll change your mind. You're too young."

"If you really love someone, you'll want to give them that pleasure. If you really love someone, you'll enjoy it."

As a teen I would envision myself grown up, forced some day to go through the motions of dating and marrying, and killing myself rather than have sex on the honeymoon. I didn't think I could have a romantic relationship and avoid that fate, because all romance had to lead to sex.

• • •

I was six years old when *Star Trek: The Next Generation* debuted, and even before I was old enough to understand it, the show had a deep influence on me. Indeed, my entire childhood and adolescence revolved around my love of science fiction and fantasy.

I started telling stories before I was old enough to write, by talking into a tape recorder. In elementary school, I begged my family to role-play SF stories ("play alien") with me whenever we got in the car. We couldn't just drive to the store—I was from this planet, my family members from some other.

When I was bored by my mundane spelling lists in school, my mother engaged me by slipping in science-fiction-themed words and drawing cartoon aliens on my practice tests. When I played dolls, I also role-played SF stories (and stuck pins in some of their heads to give them antennae).

Yet when I got older, and children's books and shows gave way to "young adult" material, most characters had or wanted sex. Indeed, the hallmark of "young adult" stories always included the main character's development of sexual interests, as if this "defined" growing up. I would hope each new book contained characters like me, but would be disappointed each time.

Puberty itself also brought me new problems. Although I'd hardly questioned gender before then (only to deny puberty would ever happen to me), once I "developed," my body felt *wrong*. And though I was told I would "get used to it," the wrongness remained.

"It's not forever," I was told at the age of eleven or twelve, "in forty years you'll go into menopause."

I was horrified. That was close to *five times* my age.

I resisted. I started switching the genders in song lyrics in my head. I got into countless fights with my family for refusing to shave. I secretly admired breast cancer survivors who had had a double mastectomy and couldn't understand why, after finally being rid of breasts, someone would have reconstructive surgery to put them *back*.

My best friend, with whom I shared a deep and mutual love of *Star Trek*, resisted the forces of romance, sexuality, and femininity together with me. When I was fourteen, I hung a sign on my wall.

WARNING!

[I wrote GENDER in large letters, encircled by a red circle and slash]

Discussion of gender is prohibited in this room.

Actions related to sexuality are prohibited in this room.

Exceptions will be made when necessary only when permission is given by [me] (ex. getting into a dress for a party, a story that has characters talking about sexuality, characters doing gender-related actions in a story, etc.).

Unless an exception is made, the breaking of the above rules will be cause for immediate expulsion from the premises, or any other punishment decided upon by [me] and [my best friend].

I went through several revisions first. I didn't like wearing dresses to parties, but I didn't have any choice. I didn't want to go so far that my parents would reject the new rules, and refusing to wear dresses would have been *way* too far. The compromise didn't work, however—my mom threw a fit and made me take the sign down. Ashamed, I hid it away.

In book after book, *everyone* seemed to eventually have sex with *someone*. The only asexual character I knew was *Star Trek: The Next Generation*'s Lt. Commander Data, but his lack of sexual attraction wasn't a matter of *orientation* so much as lack of "humanity." He didn't feel sexual attraction because he was a machine. And once I saw "The Naked Now," in which Lt. Tasha Yar seduces him, I lost all hope of identifying with him. Why, I wondered, other than the fixation among writers to "pair everyone off" sexually, would *an android* need to have a sex plot?

Literature, too, offered me little representation, at least in those characters who weren't evil. I read *1984* for school, and wanted to be chapter president of the Junior Anti-Sex League. I was no hypocrite like Julia—I was the real deal. (Nor was my asexuality an evil government plot to break the "human spirit.") I boldly placed an asterisk in my Shakespeare text, in the margin next to Lady Macbeth's speech imploring the universe to "unsex [her] here" so she could plot the murder of the king—a transgression of such scope against God and Man that in order to do so, she first had to commit an equally bold transgression against Nature and be "unsexed," relieved of the "gentle nature" of women.

Unsex me here.

Why couldn't someone please unsex *me?* I wondered. Menstruation was hell, physically and mentally. And I was never supposed to have breasts. Everything was *wrong.*

Unsex me here.

Why, even in science fiction, could I still not be "unsexed"?

• • •

Much has already been written, by Keith DeCandido and others, about the *Star Trek: The Next Generation* episode "The Outcast," specifically about its (not wholly successful) allegory to the oppression of gays and lesbians. Though intended as a commentary on queer issues, with a nod to "conversion thera-pies" intended to (try to) turn queer people straight, the episode nonetheless complicates matters by introducing an asexual and androgynous people. Sadly, the story does not paint us flatteringly—rather than embrace us under the queer umbrella, as people also suffer from compulsory cis-heteronormativity, the episode frames us as the "real" oppressors of gender and sexual minorities. Simplistically trying to flip the real-world oppressor and oppressed, the episode suggests there is nothing the Federation culture must unpack when it comes to queer or trans issues (wait, where are the LGBT characters again?)—the problems lie exclusively with an *alien* culture (that oppresses binary-gendered, sexual people).

To Riker, this oppression of people like him and his friends is such an out-rage that he "risks his career" to rescue Soren. Riker and Worf, both straight and cis, "heroically" break their own society's rules (with no consequences) to rescue Soren from a fate worse than death—becoming *like me.*

But they're too late—Soren no longer feels sexual attraction, "she" finds sexual relations abhorrent, and "she" is now genderless. Despite their so-called love, Riker *obviously* cannot have a relationship with someone like *that*. We never see the J'naii again.

Sadly, many gender and sexual minorities still appear in speculative fiction as "thought experiments," i.e. about "human nature," gender in "general," or the oppression of some other group.

I firmly believe that SF has tremendous power to shape the future, both technologically and socially. Stories help us "try on" the lives of other people and explore their points of view. Compelling SF shows us how the "alien," the "other," is not so alien after all.

We need more stories *by* us, *for* us, not merely about "normal" people "encountering" us. Although we're not yet all able to change our legal gender markers and bodies to reflect our authentic selves, and though the current medical, legal, and cultural establishment still balks at the idea of anyone being "unsexed," we're here now. We need to dream, to see ourselves in the future—a future worth living in. Our inclusion in SF offers a compelling reaffirmation of our humanity, our potential, and the value of our contributions to the greater community.

~

In the nineteenth century, **Cedar Rae Dawn** is a bespectacled old maid schoolteacher who writes novels at night under a male pen name. In the twenty-fourth century, Cedar and her alien spouse live and work on a starship, exploring the cosmos. In the twenty-first century, Cedar is somewhere in between.

Diversity in a Ghetto

The Marginalization of Modern Activism in Traditional Fandom

Pablo Miguel Alberto Vazquez

We were ostracized. We were bullied. We were ignored. Now, we're here, louder and prouder than ever.

This seems to always be the rallying call for the mythological origins of "The Fan," the underdog who now made it from the edges of society to the center of pop culture. They've all fought their battles; they are so wonderfully inclusive; and now they can rest on their laurels. However, that's not the case. There is a specter that is haunting fandom: the specter of diversity.

When I first entered traditional fandom, it was like eating the best red velvet cake. Everything was great and nothing hurt and I couldn't stop myself from wanting more! However, as I went down that metaphorically delicious rabbit hole, it became very clear that not only was I visibly a minority, but to some, I was an annoyance. Yes, I was welcome, but I was given either the open or subtle impressions that I should shut up about race issues, gender nonconformity, my queerness (hi Mom, now you know!), and whatever else I wanted to bother this esteemed group about.

Now, don't get me wrong, unlike a lot of other nerdy groups I'm a part of, at least Traditional Fandom visibly tries and sometimes takes a wonderful stand against the injustices of the world. However, publicly racist remarks continue to be ignored from time to time, and us queers feel the direct and piercing-knife stares that come our way whenever we're being out with our actions and/or how we dress. We hear the insults traded at the back of room parties; we hear between the lines of your questions at panels; and we can definitely see as panelists how moderators shut us out.

It is a bothersome and sometimes surreal fact that this community prides itself on international solidarity, true community, openness and acceptance, and all of the other mushy social terms they use to pat themselves on the back. Yet those activists trying to help others feel welcome and accepted and part of the community are constantly shut out as extremists, people (when we're considered that much at least) with an agenda, the comic relief of the otherwise "calm" panel, or your friendly convention token. Now, being any sort of a minority is already nightmare mode in regular society, but can you imagine being a cocktail of oppressions (brown, queer, poly, etc) and then being shut out on what's offensive or not by an old, over-privileged gay cis white man who touts his activist history as to why he's right and you're wrong? Now, imagine that amplified by the drone of happy applause and you've got yourself a convention panel instead of just street harassment. We are marginalized in an already marginalized community. Sometimes, that's even by others who have "made it," yet refuse to listen to their fellow fighters now.

I hear the cries of change, of diversity coming our way to the convention nearest you, but we're so very tired. We're tired of being thrown into a ghetto of specially-tailored panels in a dark section of the meeting space so no one has to accidentally walk into our fourth talk for the day titled on some variation of "Diversity and SF/F." We're tired of seeing the fence sitters claim superiority when they don't get involved, when they claim it's not their problem when we get called fags and dykes and wetbacks and more by yet another face in the crowd. We're tired of not seeing people like us as Guests of Honor or on programming and we're tired of the age-old excuse of, "If you want to change it, volunteer." Then, when we volunteer, we hear things like "no black guests of honor because all they do is talk about being black" and "we're hurting ourselves by having militant queer programming."

However, if there's one thing to be learned from Traditional Fandom (which, don't get me wrong, is still lovely and has lots of great people in it—but the same can be said of southern plantations), it's that we shouldn't hide who we are. We shouldn't stop in making our communities more open and welcoming to others. They did it and we're in their place now. It's our turn to change society for the better, and we can start with our own communities. Traditional

Fandom really *is* a great place to affect change. Sure, there will be those that will try to stop us, shove us in ghettos within ghettos, but all we have to do is remember that old nerd credo:

We were ostracized. We were bullied. We were ignored. Now, we're here, louder and prouder than ever.

~

Pablo M. A. Vazquez III considers himself many things, including performer, poet, wild fanboy, sometimes scholar/always student, agitator, bard-magus, and whatever else he comes up with. A true lover of Freedom and Passion, he champions love and unity, liberty and danger, creativity and aesthetics. He's a cinephile, DC Comics enthusiast, voracious reader, and avid gamer (tabletop/video). Born alongside the Panama Canal, he strangely does not like extreme heat and views his perfect weather to be something akin to Fimbulwinter, but he definitely is a child of the Caribbean, with all of its mystic glory, tropical paradises and delicious culinary trappings. Pablo spends his time traversing various underground and subcultural communities, ranging from magical lodges and mystic circles, unsanctioned parties and kink events to Underground Rap and radical bookstores to, of course, Science-Fiction and Fantasy fandom. He also prefers Social Justice Wizard, thank you very much.

QUEERS IN A STRANGE LAND

AMBER NEKO MEADOR

To say that Robert A. Heinlein is an influential writer would be an understatement. To say he is a controversial writer wouldn't even be scratching the surface. Heinlein is a six-time Hugo winner, a four-time Nebula nominee, and the first person given the title of "Grand Master" by the Science Fiction Writers of America. He was even on hand for the CBS Walter Cronkite interviews during the Apollo 11 moon landing. Throughout his career he wrote thirty-two novels and almost sixty short stories. He started writing over seventy-five years ago, in 1939, and for a man whose work spans decades, he was the first author I ever encountered who had characters that I, as a curious and questioning young queer kid, could identify with.

Heinlein's early novels were a mixed bag of acceptance and understanding of queer characters, but by the time he wrote *Stranger in a Strange Land* in 1961, his ideas had evolved on the subject of same-sex partners and orgies. The book was so prolific that it is often credited as one of the catalysts for the anti-establishment or "free love" movements that began in the 1960s. In this book, we are treated to the character of Valentine Michael Smith, or Mike for short. Mike is a human who was raised on Mars by Martians. Having just arrived on Earth, Mike is puzzled and confused by human behaviors, the understanding they have of their own world, and their odd social constructs. During his acclimation to his new home, Mike becomes water-brethren with many Earthlings, something that is treated as sacred on Mars. His biggest challenge comes when he tries to understand religion. It makes no sense to him, especially religion's sense of worship or religions that cast out those who aren't the same. Eventually, to combat rigid religious policies, Mike creates the

Church of All Worlds, where everyone is welcome and sex with anyone and everyone is not only encouraged, but is a required part of joining the church. Several male characters are disturbed by sexual approaches from Michael. In an exploratory discussion on sex, Michael's lawyer friend Jubal Harshaw and reporter Ben Caxton try to figure out what made Ben recoil from Mike's touch when he tried to join the Church. Eventually they decide that love is love, and it doesn't really matter where it's coming from when you care enough to be with that someone you love. Michael isn't even offended; he explains that he understands the trappings that society and religion have put on the people of Earth. Honestly, if my mother knew what this SF book had in it, I probably wouldn't have been allowed to read it. You grok?

While reading through some of Heinlein's other books, I ran across the next jewel of acceptance and tolerance, and probably one of the best pieces of SF one could ever hope for, *The Moon is a Harsh Mistress* (1966). This tale of rebellion against Earth and its practices, both socially and economically, is probably the centerpiece of Heinlein's way of thinking. The inhabitants of the moon, mostly descended from prisoners, have been forced to live with meager wages based on what the controlling countries of Earth tell them they are worth. They have adopted a new and respectful way of courting women and protect a woman's rights with force when necessary. The majority of the Moon's residents live in group marriages, or line marriages. Not the kind Mormons would have you believe are right, but ones with any number of men or women. Our protagonist, Mannie, in order to try to reason with Earth, heads down to speak with Earth's governments to try to get fair and equal treatment for the inhabitants of the Moon. But while he's visiting the U.S., more specifically the state of Kentucky, he's arrested by a judge for being in the loving marriage that he's been in for years. Sound familiar? Eventually he is released, and the Moon strikes back. There is a revolution, an A.I. takes a stand, and a few cities of Earth are leveled. It is at this point, going forward, that most of the characters in Heinlein's books are bisexual, and several could even be considered pansexual as events unfold. But none of Heinlein's works shook me as hard as the next one did when I read it.

It was in 1973 when we finally met Lazarus Long, the two-thousand-(plus)-year-old main character of what most consider to be Heinlein's most infamous work, *Time Enough for Love*. We've actually known Lazarus for years; we just didn't know it yet. This book is set a great many years in the future, at least until the characters begin traveling through time. Two of the first characters we meet are bio-engineers by the names of Ishtar and Galahad, who find themselves attracted to each other and agree to a contract of a sexual nature. But they've only ever known each other in huge bio work suits and have never actually seen one another. After the reveal, they discuss whether or not each was hoping that the other was of the opposite gender, but neither seems as though they would have cared either way. They more or less fell in "like" with each other's minds. The bulk of the book is told through short stories, though often mis-told, of the adventures of Lazarus Long. During his thousands of years, he's had many lovers, both male and female, though he prefers female. Throughout the progression of the book, his group marriage grows to include a lawyer, the two bio-engineers we met earlier, a family friend, two female clones of Lazarus, a spaceship's A.I. that was transferred to a human body, and Lazarus's own mother, who works as a sexual healer. The primary mantra of the Long family, and of Lazarus himself, is that everyone should be free and should respect anyone and everyone's privacy no matter what they choose to do or how they operate in life.

And yes, while that mantra does include incest, the book managed to take me deep into ideas that I'd never even dreamed could exist. This book was the one that both caused me to hate and to love Robert A. Heinlein. Sex is discussed—rather often—in the book. And while Lazarus finds no ill will toward same-sex couplings, he does think it's harder to achieve oneness than with heterosexual couples. Lazarus is also given the opportunity to become a woman, which at first I found exciting, but then Lazarus goes on to explain that he wouldn't have considered the "monsters" of past generations, who had limited medical science at their disposal, as women; he would only consider it with the current options available that would make him a whole woman, one able to bring children into the world. I honestly cried, but carried on hopefully. Ultimately he decides not to become a woman, but that is where the two female clones of himself come into play.

It was a book later in the Lazarus Long series that made me glad I didn't abandon his works after having the main character call me a monster. In the novel *The Number of the Beast* (wonderful title), a new group of characters going about in their time-traveling spacecar, the *Gay Deceiver*, encounters Lazarus Long and his family. But there is a new member aboard Lazarus's ship, a woman by the name of Elizabeth Andrew Jackson Long, Libby for short. Andrew Jackson Long is a distant relation and thousand-year-old friend of Lazarus. During the process of rejuvenation meant to reunite these old friends, Andrew was given the body of a woman after being asked which he preferred during the process. Now she is part of the group marriage and expecting a child. This character serves as a huge connector for many of Heinlein's other works, once you realize who "Slipstick Libby" actually is, and how many times you've already met her before. It's arguable that she is either transgender or intersex, but she was there all along—we just didn't know it yet.

Time travel, intercourse, and tomfoolery aside, the writings of Heinlein often feature LGBTQ characters and non-traditional marriages. Though admittedly some of his earlier works were not as "progressive" in their expression or wording, for someone who was writing gay, lesbian, bisexual, and trans characters long before I was born, it's quite impressive. As a young, avid lover of science fiction, it was beyond awesome to see characters that I could identify with long before others started doing so. Heinlein inspired me to dream, and to try and get others to do so as well.

> "I think that science fiction, even the corniest of it, even the most outlandish of it, no matter how badly it's written, has a distinct therapeutic value because all of it has as its primary postulate that the world does change. I cannot overemphasize the importance of that idea."
>
> —Robert A. Heinlein

~

Amber Neko Meador is an author, filmmaker, digital artist, and podcast host of *Transition Transmission*. Amber grew up in the fundamentally conservative Southeast, deep in the Bible Belt. A devotee of George Lucas, the Wachowskis, Masamune Shirow, Robert Heinlein, cyberpunk, and science fiction, Amber has made several independently produced films, including *Night of the Living Catgirl*. In 2008, Amber began the process of transitioning from male to female. Last year Amber completed her collection of transgender speculative fiction, *Other Selves: A Journey of Gender, Fiction, Discovery, and Hope*.

PERSONAL ESSAYS

This special double issue of *Lightspeed* was funded by an extraordinary Kickstarter campaign. Our goal was to run an essay every day our Kickstarter ran, with each telling what it really meant to be queer in SF/F. The community's response was tremendous, and we can't thank our writers enough for their brave words.

Here are twenty-seven voices from every shade of the QUILTBAG spectrum, reminding us just why science fiction needs a little destruction.

—Wendy N. Wagner, Managing Editor

Science Fiction
Failed Me

Cory Skerry

I've always been a stubborn little bastard.

I spent my adolescence in a mountain town with interchangeable numbers for elevation and population. Amid the abundance of casually worn camouflage and Motocross-stickered pickups, it was dangerous to be me. This only made me more obstinate about wearing what I wanted and more feisty when people challenged my civil rights. I was lucky that I got off as easy as I did, but even "easy" meant tasting my own blood more than once.

In 2013, my Clarion West class held a reunion. By a colossal coincidence, our classmate's generous parents-in-law owned a cabin in the woods that we could borrow for the occasion—and it just happened to be planted right there in my teenage Hell, in a county that didn't (and still doesn't) have even one traffic light.

I arrived later than most of our classmates. Crickets chirped a symphony around us while we hugged and greeted one another, and then for a moment it was just the crickets. Someone said, "Cory ... we saw that town. How did you *survive*?"

There are so many answers.

And *none* of them are science fiction.

My supportive parents often drove me the three miles into town to visit a house smaller than ours that had been converted into the county library. I'm not exaggerating when I say that I at least cracked open every science fiction and fantasy book there. I was attracted, like most of you, to the incandescent possibility of infinite worlds, these myriad examinations of the human condition, some of which didn't involve chewing tobacco.

I needed to see fantastic writers imagining a future that included me, that *starred* me. I know now that queer work existed, but those stories were so few that they never made it to me out there in the mountains. I would have adored volumes like *Luck in the Shadows, Swordspoint,* and *The Left Hand of Darkness,* but the available fare was exclusively heteronormative, cisgender monogamy. And the future I imagined for myself was haunted by the possibility of ending up like Brandon Teena and Matthew Shepard.

So I survived because hiking alone in the wilderness gave me the confidence of knowing what kind of animal I am. I survived because I found a tiny but strong support network of family and friends. And I survived because I am a stubborn little bastard who wasn't about to let anyone else win the game of Me versus Them.

Now I'm turning my stubborn little bastardry to setting science fiction on fire. Let's make sure that there are so many queer voices in our genre that even tiny rural libraries can't avoid them. If people want to read about the future, they'll read about us, because we're not going to disappear if humanity colonizes Mars or reaches the singularity any more than I disappeared in rural Idaho.

I'm in your future, science fiction, and I'd like to see you stop me.

~

Cory Skerry writes amusing lies and paints what he shouldn't. He lives in a quirky old house with his partner, his other partner, her partner, and their menagerie. When his human meatsuit falls apart, he'd like science to put his brain into a giant octopus body, with which he will be very responsible and not even a little bit shipwrecky. He pinky swears. You can find more of his nonsense at coryskerry.net.

So Say We All

Emma Osborne

I grew up in Chewton, population 403. Somehow, the SF gene that I inherited from my dad flourished in a house without bookshelves and a TV that ran on solar panels. He delighted in taking me to see *Star Trek* movies at *far* too young an age and played me the *2001: A Space Odyssey* soundtrack on his record player. I ransacked the local library on a weekly basis. I didn't have much, but it was enough to get me hooked. But what I lacked, as a sexuality-questioning and isolated teen, was SF with any kind of queer representation. We've come a long way since the early 90s, but a queer lead in a SF movie or book would have allowed me a safe escape, a haven.

Thousands of worlds are created and populated in the realms of science fiction. Often, those worlds are barren of diverse genders or sexualities. It can seem that these imagined universes (whether closely related to our own or strikingly different) are not a place for me or for my extended queer and trans* family. Without a visible queer presence, SF becomes another place where we are not acknowledged, and thus implicitly unwelcome.

In general, heteronormativity is the standard in popular SF. Ever heard of a gay Jedi? I have become so numb to straight worlds that when a complex queer presence does pop up (for example, Admiral Helena Cain in *Battlestar Galactica*), it brings about a palpable sense of relief, validation and happiness. I am suddenly given approval to exist within, and therefore connect with, our imagined universe.

Writing diverse characters and worlds can be intimidating. Even I find it daunting to write queer characters sometimes, because I want to make absolutely certain that I'm getting it right. But I'm excited to try, to experiment. Every story with queer inclusion makes a difference, because there is still not enough diverse representation in this world, let alone the ones we create.

There are many proud queer writers within the science fiction community, but there are also so many people who cannot yet be comfortably or safely out, both within the community and in society at large. Suicide amongst queer and trans* teens and adults is still shockingly high and discrimination is rife. We are in the unique position of writing about change, innovation, the future. We have the power to write inclusive worlds and societies that may lead to real world changes for the better.

As a young, geeky queer writer in country Australia, it would have meant the world to me to see the growing queer presence within SFF, and to know that it would welcome me with open arms—just as it will welcome you, if you are out there and uncertain, looking for a home planet of your own.

So say we all.

~

Emma Osborne is a fiction writer and poet from Melbourne, Australia. Her short stories can be found in *Aurealis, Bastion Science Fiction*, and *Shock Totem*. Her poetry has been featured in *Star*Line* and has appeared in *Apex Magazine*. Emma comes from a long line of dance floor starters and was once engaged in a bear hug so epic that both parties fell over. She can be found on Twitter as @redscribe.

1984 IN 1980

LEE THOMAS

Most of my childhood experience with science fiction came from the screen. On television, I watched *Star Trek* and *The Twilight Zone*. On film, I saw *Planet of the Apes*, *Silent Running*, *2001: A Space Odyssey*, and *Star Wars*.

Though I loved those visual entertainments, I didn't become a serious science fiction reader. I'd discovered horror literature young. Blame my mom for leaving a copy of *The Exorcist* lying around the house for her ten-year-old kid to find.

Later in life I would enjoy the works of Le Guin, Butler, and Delany, authors who directly addressed sexual, gender, and racial issues in their works, but the science fiction literature I read in my youth were those books assigned in middle and high school classes: *On the Beach*, *Fahrenheit 451*, *Earth Abides*, and George Orwell's *1984*.

By the time I was assigned this classic, I was a pubescent kid who found the high school gym teachers far more stimulating than the cheerleaders. As such, my perspective on the novel was likely different from that of my classmates. Orwell had fantasized the world in which I already lived.

For instance, Winston Smith is forced to meet his lover, Julia, at clandestine locations. They must keep their relationship secret, because the government does not authorize their union. At the time I read *1984*, many of the states in this country still had sodomy laws on the books, making sexual contact in "unauthorized" relationships illegal.

The Party rewrote history and current events to enforce its control. Winston was inundated with propaganda from telescreens, including the one in his home. The US media of the day consistently supported and exacerbated the negative perception of gays. The LGBTQ characters the mainstream media allowed through the filter were victims, jokes, and suicidal depressives: characteristics that are not innate. They are the outcomes of a culture that creates psychological damage. Having succeeded in demeaning gays the media exploited the results.

Like shooting a guy in the legs and then ridiculing him for not being able to run, the media threw back images of the problems it helped create and said, "See? We told you so!"

Orwell's Newspeak was designed to limit the ways in which people voiced and even thought about ideas. If you only have one word for the LGBTQ community and that word is deviant, you are successfully limiting the ways people think about this group. Of course, there were more words—faggot, dyke, abomination, pervert, and others, none of which really allowed for a positive spin. When people thought of "those people," the words they had to describe them (us) simply reinforced negative feelings toward the group.

Though I couldn't rationalize all of this then, I could feel it.

My teacher explained that Orwell's novel addressed the dangers of totalitarian governments, warning of encroaching communist oppression. What she overlooked was the fact that many people were already experiencing oppression, paranoia, and fear under the flag of a "free" nation.

~

Lee Thomas is the Bram Stoker Award and two-time Lambda Literary Award-winning author of the books *The Dust of Wonderland, The German, Like Light for Flies,* and *Butcher's Road.*

Speak Up, Speak Out

Sandra Odell

When I came out as a bisexual to my grandmother at the age of seventeen, she patted my hand and said, "Oh, dear. It's only a phase."

. . .

I started writing at the age of six, and submitted my first short story to a professional market at the age of twelve, a story about two young girls in love and their adventures with a horse who wanted to be a unicorn. I received my first personal rejection at the age of sixteen, spelled out in big red letters across the front page: WE DON'T PUBLISH STORIES ABOUT DYKES.

I didn't know dykes from dikes. All I knew was that I liked girls and boys, and figured if I couldn't find a story about girls like me, I would write one. It wasn't until I was well into my thirties that I realized magazines often refused to publish a story outside their perceptions of "the norm."

. . .

What is normal? A complicated question to be sure, and no less so in science fiction, a genre that encourages readers to think outside the box. People who identify somewhere on the QUILTBAG scale have written, explored, and celebrated right along with their hetero-normative, cisgendered peers. You might know some of them: David Gerrold; K.C. Ball; Arthur C. Clarke; Nicola Griffith; Rachel Pollack; Hiromi Goto; Charlie Jane Anders; Samuel R. Delany; Kelley Eskridge; Nisi Shawl; Henry Lien; Mary Anne Mohanraj; Nalo Hopkinson, and, *and*, AND ... The list goes on, yet many risked their lives or more by refusing to keep quiet about their true selves.

For years, QUILTBAG authors have struggled to make their voices heard, and the Queers Destroy Science Fiction! project is a vital step along that steep path to the top of the genre mountain. Some will balk at another special, hoity-toity, why-can't-they-be-happy-with-the-way-things-are? issue. Others will decry this effort as another excuse to make a mountain out of a mole hill. I'll tell you a secret. It doesn't matter what anyone else thinks. We've taken this step, and we'll take the next, and the one after that. We're here, we're queer, and we refuse to keep quiet for the comfort of a close-minded few. Science fiction is all about making people uncomfortable, making them think, explore new ideas, look beyond their own limited perspective to the normal of this world and beyond.

Every step forward on this path is one step closer to our dream of equal representation. The dedication and hard work of those who have come before has lifted future authors who identify by a different norm to the stars. We don't have to hide in silence. We have the freedom to explore our own strange new worlds and others like us to come along.

I'm still here, Grandma; it's not just a phase, and I'll be here tomorrow. Writing. I have too many stories waiting to be heard: *"Don't be afraid. Speak up, speak out. Let me show you what we can be when we see ourselves as more than stereotypes."*

~

Sandra Odell is an avid reader, compulsive writer, and rabid chocoholic. She attended Clarion West in 2010. Her first collection of short stories was released from Hydra House Books in 2012. She is currently hard at work avoiding her first novel.

How Queer Narratives

Beat the False-Consensus Effect, Reminded Me that Diversity Existed, Exploited Human Psychology, Inspired Sex Positivity, and Helped Me Stop Worrying (But Not to Love the Bomb)

An Owomoyela

Here's the thing: I had a great sex-ed program. The Unitarian Universalist Church developed a program called "Our Whole Lives," which tackles sexuality across multiple grade levels in a holistic sense, everything from relationships to communication to safe sex to cultural and social issues around the whole shebang. No abstinence-only for me; I distinctly remember instructional slides and show-and-tells to introduce us to condoms and dental dams.

I don't think the program had much effect on me.

I decided early on that this "sex" thing wasn't interesting, so I brushed off the information as a sort of background radiation. I'd already written sex off; why bother absorbing facts about it? But there was one thing that bothered me: why did so many people fixate on something so (obviously) pointless? Why were sex scenes damn near mandatory in books and movies, and why did everyone think that getting a boyfriend or girlfriend was the only game in town?

There's this thing called the *false consensus effect*, whereby we tend to think that everyone else thinks the way we do. In my case, this led to thinking that since sex itself wasn't interesting, there had to be some other reason everyone was so obsessed with it. A reason … like *conspiracy*.

So in high school I became convinced that sex was unnecessary, pointless, a low-value activity that culture had brainwashed people into demanding. Like pop-fashion shirts, or the latest poster for the latest band.

It lasted until someone pointed me toward the AVEN (Asexual Visibility and Education Network) forums, and said, "Hey… this sounds like you." And so I was introduced to the greatest repository of asexual narratives on the internet.

Suddenly, the ambient culture made *so much more sense*.

The thing was, I had never been shown that my understanding of sex fell somewhere on a spectrum. The narrative I got was that everyone had a sex drive, and I was part of "everyone," so everyone shared my experience. Right?

Humans are hardwired to respond to narratives. If I'd had stories that showed people opting out of sex, I would have been a much less bitter teen. Recognizing that not everyone experienced sex the same way—that the single narrative in the stories surrounding me was false—let me recognize and support the diverse sexual experience of others.

Learning about asexuality made me sex-positive in a way that preaching sex positivity never could have.

But there are other narratives I still don't see—though now I can see that they're missing. Narratives like how the relationships I form can still be intimate and valuable without the sticky glue of sex holding them together. Or how those relationships spring into being, when not propelled by sexual desire. There are people like me out there, who might not have a friend to point them to AVEN—who might be waiting for a story that helps them make sense of it all.

So what do you do, when you don't have the cultural maps you need? When you have to invent a whole mode of intimacy that no one believes in?

You roll up your sleeves and say, "Let's queer things up."

The culture of intimacy we've been sold is abridged. It's time to make some unauthorized amendments. The more we each speak up, the more space exists for all of us.

So grab a pen, and join me.

~

An (pronounce it "On") **Owomoyela** is an asexual neutrois author with a background in web development, linguistics, and weaving chain maille out of stainless steel fencing wire, whose fiction has appeared in a number of venues including *Clarkesworld*, *Asimov's*, *Lightspeed*, and a handful of Year's Bests. An's interests range from pulsars and Cepheid variables to gender studies and nonstandard pronouns, with a plethora of stops in-between. Se can be found online at an.owomoyela.net, and can be funded at patreon.com/an_owomoyela.

SPARK

MARK OSHIRO

My entry into science fiction was through *Star Wars*. This was also the source of my first fictional crush:

Lando Calrissian.

I couldn't process the concept of a crush at the age when I realized that I was attracted to him. I recall feeling electrified when he strolled onto the screen, insulted Han Solo, then feigned an attack only to embrace his friend in a hug. I was mesmerized by his smile, which lit up his entire face. When Leia told C-3PO that Lando felt "too friendly," I disagreed with her whole-heartedly. *This was not possible*, I told myself. How could you think negatively of a man who wore a cape so majestically? How could you criticize someone who so romantically graced Leia's hand with a kiss? How could you question the undeniable tension and affection between Han Solo and Lando when they were finally reunited?

In the midst of this massive space opera, this epic fight between good and evil, I was transfixed by this character, and I wanted so much more. I would often skip over *A New Hope* just so I could get to that city in the clouds, eager to see Lando's cape flutter behind him as he walked up to the *Millennium Falcon*. I began to imagine my own version of this tale. I fantasized what it would be like to have Lando greet me at the foot of that ship, his arms open wide for me. It was a silly, childhood dream at the time, but it was one I fostered for many years.

It was because of my introduction to *Star Wars* at such a young age that I started looking for something more. I turned to books to find more spaceships. More alien races. More galactic terrors and adventures. I found comfort and joy in the work of Ursula Le Guin, particularly *The Left Hand of Darkness*. I fell in love with Genly Ai, and I fell in love with hope. It was my adoration of Lando and Genly that showed me another possibility of the future: I'd be allowed to love who I wanted to.

I met other nerds in school, but it was a sobering experience. They did not share these same views as me, so I learned to keep them to myself. It was only years later, when I started to supplement my obsession with *Ender's Game* by finding out what else Orson Scott Card wrote, that I discovered how he really felt about boys like me. I spent a long time escaping into fiction after that, desperate to find a world where I'd be accepted. I didn't always find it, but I had a better chance within science fiction than practically anything else in the world.

I still believe that science fiction is both a reaction to our world and a narrative form of hope. It gave me Lando Calrissian in that sweeping cape, and it gave a lonely brown queer a spark of desire, enough to keep him alive so that he could one day ignite the world. Here's to that fire.

∼

What if you could re-live the experience of reading a book (or watching a show) for the first time? **Mark Oshiro** provides just such a thing on a daily basis on Mark Reads and Mark Watches, where he chronicles his unspoiled journey through various television and book series. He mixes textual analysis, confessional blogging, and humor to analyze fiction that usually makes him cry and yell on camera. He's been nominated for a Hugo in the Fan Writer category in 2013 and 2014 for his work, and he's nearly done with his first novel.

Science Fiction Has Always Been Queer

Sigrid Ellis

Where and when does science fiction begin?

We know, of course, of course, *of course*, that space is science fiction. We know that Heinlein is science fiction. We know that clones and lasers and genetic engineering are science fiction. Genetic engineering …

So, therefore, Anne McCaffrey's Pern books are science fiction, right? Because they take place on another planet, and there's genetic engineering through selective breeding. And telepathy, which is obviously science fiction! Unless, of course, it's superheroes. Or fantasy. Or paranormal romance.

… Perhaps this is a trickier question than previously suspected. Here's another question, then.

Where and when does queer begin?

Gay Pride parades are queer, of course. The Stonewall Riot is queer. People are queer, and slogans, and gender and sex. I'm told some ideas are queer. I'm told some books, some stories, are queer.

Which ones? Stories with gay people in them? With robots? With minds in spaceship bodies, with alien lives and forms rubbing up against humanity? Does a story need a gay love scene to be queer?

Of course not. There's no such thing as a queer story. That's stereotyping, that's profiling, that's marginalization.

Except, of course, that all sorts of stories are queer.

To be queer is to defy easy definition. Which is also what science fiction does. It defies what is known, what is safe. Science fiction extrapolates and explores. It pushes the edges of the known. Science fiction takes us to live in other people's bodies, in minds and hearts alien to our own.

There is no possible way that queers can destroy science fiction. Science fiction is already, has always been, queer.

~

Sigrid Ellis is co-editor of the Hugo-nominated *Queers Dig Time Lords* and *Chicks Dig Comics* anthologies. She edits the best-selling *Pretty Deadly* from Image Comics. She is the flash-fiction editor of Queers Destroy Science Fiction!, and she edited the Hugo-nominated *Apex Magazine* for 2014. She lives with her partner, their two homeschooled children, her partner's boyfriend, and a host of vertebrate and invertebrate pets in Saint Paul, MN.

Halfway in the Pool

James L. Sutter

I almost didn't write this. Not because I don't believe in this book—I adore the folks putting it together and think it's important for queer voices in SF to be heard. No, I almost passed because my first thought—and indeed my second and third—was "this space isn't for me."

I'm bisexual. That makes me queer. I'm also white, cis-male, middle-class, married to a woman, and about every other quality that puts me right in the middle of the ol' societal bell curve. People generally assume I'm straight, which means that I rarely encounter any sort of prejudice. Nobody questions my marriage. Nobody beats me up or disowns me. I haven't suffered for the cause, so who am I to speak for it?

That halfway-in-the-pool feeling has defined my sexuality for years. Maybe this describes you, too. Feeling like a fake in the straight world, and a poser among the queers. Hell, to some folks, bisexuals don't actually exist—I've had sympathetic gay men explain to me that there's no such thing as a bi man, and I shouldn't be ashamed of being "the straight friend." Despite being attracted to multiple genders, calling myself queer still feels like I'm wrapping myself in someone else's flag.

Which is why representation in science fiction—and everywhere—is important. Because every time a reader comes across a queer character in a story, it reinforces the idea that queers exist, and that they come in a million different shades and configurations. If I had seen myself reflected in the books I read when I was younger—"Hey, that starfighter pilot likes ladies, but sometimes dudes, too!"—maybe it wouldn't have taken me three decades to make sense of my own sexuality.

As writers, we can educate and provide comfort to people we've never even met. We can reach those different from us not only through debate, but through immersion. We can lure people in with a good story and sucker them into tolerance. Prejudice rarely survives in the face of familiarity and friendship, and by making people fall in love with queer characters, we can make the world—the real world—more accepting.

We can also help widen the scope. Queer culture has often been defined by struggle—but only because it had to struggle. At long last, we're starting to see kids growing up queer without stigma. We're racing toward a day when sexual preferences become no more significant than musical ones, and just as varied. A world where it's acceptable not only to be queer, but to be a little queer.

So if you're worried you're not queer enough to speak, that you don't belong here—stop. You are, and you do. You're a part of this, too.

Welcome.

～

James L. Sutter is a co-creator of the Pathfinder Roleplaying Game and the Senior Editor for Paizo Publishing. He is the author of the novels *Death's Heretic* and *The Redemption Engine*, the former of which was ranked #3 on Barnes and Noble's list of the Best Fantasy Releases of 2011, and was a finalist for both the Compton Crook Award for Best First Novel and a 2013 Origins Award. James has written numerous short stories for such publications as *Escape Pod*, *Starship Sofa*, *Apex Magazine*, *Beneath Ceaseless Skies*, *Geek Love*, and the #1 Amazon bestseller *Machine of Death*. His anthology *Before They Were Giants* pairs the first published short stories of science fiction and fantasy luminaries with new interviews and writing advice from the authors themselves. In addition, he's published a wealth of gaming material for both *Dungeons & Dragons* and the *Pathfinder Roleplaying Game*. For more information, visit www.jameslsutter. com or follow him on Twitter at @jameslsutter.

ALL THAT GLITTERS

JILL SEIDENSTEIN

I am a queer nerdy female.

I came to science fiction as a young teen as I was forming my sense of self—to have something to talk about with the smart boys. I had no idea about my own sexuality. I often wished I could be a brain with feet with none of the messy things having a body entailed. From a very young age, I had a sense that I was not like everyone else. It could be due to being an identical twin, or perhaps it was being Jewish in a sea of very vocal Christians. I moved a few times as a child, so was new on the scene. I excelled in school and this set me apart, too.

I studied and observed my peers to learn what was acceptable, and what wasn't. I mastered the skill of fitting in. Fitting in, which meant cutting parts out that I perceived as being unacceptable. I witnessed the calumny heaped upon people who were different and wished to avoid it, as most people do. I learned to segregate the different facets of myself, only revealing each part to people I thought were safe. I learned to pass. Passing means not being seen for your whole self. It means not expressing your whole self. I thought those parts were unacceptable and more than that, meant I was broken. I lurked on the fringe, believing that these aspects of myself put me there. It was incredibly painful.

I loved reading science fiction, because it showed me worlds of possibility. I didn't like my small town, the small world I moved in, dominated by the cult of football and toxic masculinity. My friends and I were outsiders, smart girls who didn't fit in. I tried in every way to make myself as small and unnoticeable as possible. Escaping into other worlds was a relief from the pressures, real or imagined, in my own.

I accompanied Meg and Charles Wallace Murry on their wild adventure with Mrs. Whatsit to save their father. I flew with Lessa on the back of her dragon to fight the Thread. My mind bent in delicious ways as I worked to understand LeGuin's agendered people of Winter.

It wasn't until I got to college that I examined my sexuality. I looked within science fiction to explore this facet of myself, but I don't recall finding anything that connected with my queer identity. I drew the conclusion queerness was a separate universe from the world of SF, despite Le Guin's story. To not see yourself reflected in the larger world is a form of erasure. Nowhere that I looked did I see a representation that contained the entirety of me. There were no mirrors, no reflections, only absence.

I almost never found a place where all the different parts of me fit. I could hang with the nerds, but I had to leave my sexuality at the door, or I could hang with the queers, but they didn't get the nerdy stuff.

In the last several years, I moved from reader to writer, partly because I didn't see myself reflected in the stories I like to read. I searched for writing communities for close to two decades, but it wasn't until I found Clarion West that I found one that felt hospitable to queers *and* writers. Instead of segregating out my various identities, the two could inform each other. I didn't have to erect barriers or leave behind any part of myself.

Last year I learned about *Lightspeed* and the Women Destroy Science Fiction! Kickstarter. I got a physical copy of the issue and read it slowly, visiting it from time to time, because I couldn't bear for these stories written by women *like me* to be over, and because I was afraid I would be disappointed. Each time I picked it up to read another story, a key turned in a lock I didn't know I'd closed. I wanted to yell *YES* with every word I read. I wanted to weep with relief as I recognized myself in story after story.

I welcome the destruction of the few, limited definitions we have of what it means to be human. I want more! More representation, more diversity, more options. As I've integrated my own identities, I want to see the barriers and walls come down in the wider culture. I want to create bridges and extend hands to invite more people in. Instead of relying on word-of-mouth or stumbling across stories that resonate with queer identities, I want them to shine as brightly as a sparkling, glittery disco ball!

~

Jill Seidenstein contains multitudes. In addition to the above, she is a librarian, writer, yogini, traveler, and photographer. She enjoys tea in the coffee-obsessed city of Seattle. You can find her nattering about all of these things on Twitter as @outseide.

When We're Not There, We're Not Here

Jerome Stueart

I used to say I didn't need to see gay characters in novels or TV or movies growing up—but then, I didn't *have* a gay life growing up. Those two are related.

I didn't know I was gay until I was thirty-four.

I grew up in two worlds: the world of religious Southern Baptist culture and the world of '70s and '80s pop culture and science fiction/fantasy. You can say all you want that it was my religion that gave me the smokescreen, that I stayed too much in my faith-filled rural world to know what being gay was, and I'll give you part of that—but I wasn't Amish. I read extensively: fiction, nonfiction, science fiction, fantasy, and comics. I also listened to popular music, watched hours of TV every day, all the movies I could. I can best anyone at *'80s Trivial Pursuit*. The only trivia where "gay" comes up is about Rock Hudson, Freddie Mercury and AIDS.

This is not an indictment of a culture that would not talk about gays. It's a reminder of the power of absence. The absence of gay characters can produce an absence of gay identity. As much as the negative stereotypes that pummeled me from the other side—that "being a homosexual" was a sin—it was also the absence of gay models that helped keep me in a perfect fog of disconnect.

• • •

I remember dreaming of kissing Wojohowitz on *Barney Miller* and waking up feeling as if it were the most amazing experience of my eleven-year-old life and fearing telling anyone. I knew boys weren't supposed to kiss boys—but not what that meant. When, in my twenties, I did confess it, once, to a girl I was dating, she kissed me, and when I didn't react, she said, "I can make that better than Wojo. Just give me a chance."

I remember how important "buddy" shows were to me: Batman and Robin, Kirk, Spock, McCoy, Simon & Simon. I remember writing in my diary when I was maybe eight, "I love Patrick Duffy" in *Man from Atlantis*. I wished Mr. Spock would find me and take me to live with him on the Enterprise. I wanted to be Steve Austin's son. None of this ever woke me up to the fact that I was gay.

I remember in my room, at fourteen, having just finished a drawing of a werewolf, and stopping—staring at it for maybe an hour, and crying, and not knowing why—that this drawing—a werewolf with his arms open—was something important. I said that to myself, "This is something important." I wanted something in that picture—but it wouldn't coalesce in my head. I was clueless.

So perfectly erased from my world were any signs of gay men that I claimed never to have met one till I was in my Masters Degree in college. After a night of sitting across from each other in wingback chairs exchanging stories of our childhoods, he leaned towards me and said, "I think you're telling me a story about growing up gay." I laughed and said, "If I were gay, I would know it." No, I wouldn't. My first "almost" encounter with a real gay man was an "ex-gay" bear working at my church, over at my house for dinner, and all I wanted to do was hug him (without his shirt on) and I was twenty-eight, and he said, "I think you're gay." And this time I burst into tears and said, "*Everyone thinks that.*" Because I still couldn't see.

What did I even think a gay person was? A dirty, thin homosexual in an alleyway behind a bar in the sleaziest part of the city sinning, sinning, sinning, in the grip of Satan's minions? I could not see myself in that. All the data I knew was coming from one biased source. Had I read a story about a *real* gay person? Seen a movie? Anything to counter that?

Absence of truth will make the lies stick.

• • •

I didn't know how to translate these experiences into "being" gay. I had no language, no concepts. All the signals were there, but they were being mistranslated because I didn't have the model. Imagine getting all the parts to a bike, having never seen a bike, or known what a bike was.

Gay role models would not be able to show up in my religious faith until recently (thank you, Ray Boltz), but I *had* my eyes open. I just didn't know what I was looking for. Because I didn't know I was *gay*—only different—I couldn't seek it out by name. I was not in Greenwich Village or San Francisco. I was Midwest. I was Texas rural. I couldn't get to the pockets of that gay culture. Queer would have to come to me—through science fiction and fantasy, through stories and movies—but there just wasn't enough reaching me. (I know, I can hear you say: If only you'd read Samuel R. Delany! He was the one author people would suggest to you when you came out to them as both gay and a science fiction lover.)

I think about that a lot now. When I consider whether or not to have a gay main character—I see me as a fourteen-year-old reader. Who would I like to offer to him as a model—full of courage, mistakes, bad ideas, noble pursuits? Who would I have wanted as a model? Batman, Steve Austin, a big burly Indiana Jones, Dumbledore (yes!).

I don't begrudge the lessons straight male characters taught me (and female characters, lots!). But I wonder if I could have known more about myself with a little help from queer characters.

• • •

Nowadays, at forty-six, I write under a lamp with a lampshade signed by fifty-two queer authors, including Samuel R. Delany (who was my mentor at the 2013 Lambda Literary Retreat for Emerging LGBT Voices). They and many others are writing their truths into the world to counter lies and rumors and half-truths, to spread hope, reach common ground, celebrate joy. There will be no vacuum now for the lies to grow. We won't let that happen.

Writing LGBT characters into fiction helps readers understand who we are and what we can be—not just one way to be a queer person, but thousands. Maybe we also do it so that we exist in the world of story, in the future, in the past. Hold a mirror up to our culture—we *should* be there. Young adults searching for themselves may know something is different inside them, but still be in a fog because they can't find models of that difference where they're already looking, reading, and watching. We have to give them some. Queer has to come to them.

～

Jerome Stueart is a proud graduate of Clarion 2007, San Diego. His work has appeared in *Fantasy, Strange Horizons, Geist, On Spec, Joyland, Geez*, and three of the *Tesseracts* anthology series of Canadian Science Fiction and Fantasy. He's the co-editor of *Tesseracts 18: Wrestling with Gods*, a collection of SF/fantasy storieswhere characters wrestle with Faith, just out from Edge Science Fiction and Fantasy Publishing. His first novel, *One Nation Under Gods*, will be published by ChiZine Publications, late 2015. He learned to live again in Canada's Yukon Territory, and then moved to be with a bear in Dayton, Ohio, which Advocate Magazine calls the 2015 Queerest City in America. He sings with the Dayton Gay Men's Chorus, and teaches science fiction and fantasy writing to teens, *Writing the Spiritual Journey* to older adults, and has ready an LGBT version of both.

A Gay Boy Gets His Genre On

Anthony R. Cardno

The answer: *The Fall of the Kings* by Ellen Kushner and Delia Sherman.

The question: "When did you first recognize yourself in a science fiction or fantasy novel?"

The first genre books I remember reading: Silverberg's long out-of-print *To Open The Sky*, Tolkein's *The Hobbit*, Bradbury's *Something Wicked This Way Comes*, and an Alfred Hitchcock and the Three Investigators mystery. They all captured my imagination far more than anything assigned in those 5th and 6th grade years and set my love for genre fiction firmly in place. I recognized my shy, keep-your-head-down personality in aspects of Bilbo Baggins and William Halloway; my curiosity in Jupiter Jones and his pals; and even though I couldn't put a name to it, my search for a life true to myself in Noel Vorst and Christopher Mondschein. But even after I'd come to terms with my own sexuality, I wasn't looking in the right places to find well-written gay protagonists in my genre fiction or comic books, and my own writing of the time reflected the fact that I wasn't seeing myself in what I was reading.

Until one of the Book-of-the-Month Club offshoots offered *The Fall of the Kings* as a selection. High fantasy, with gay protagonists at the core? I ordered it, devoured it, and only after reading it discovered it was a sequel. But that didn't matter—what mattered was I now realized I could, in fact, write genre stories featuring characters like me not just in temperament (many of my characters are shy, or self-effacing, or searching for who they are) but also in sexuality. Yes, it's only one part of who I am—but it's the part that was missing from my own fiction for so long.

Now, of course, I find genre fiction with QUILTBAG characters all over the place: Lethe Press's books, *Crossed Genres*, and most online specific magazines, including of course our very own *Lightspeed* and *Nightmare* magazines. Each time I find a story or novel in one of these venues, my pulse races a little bit. I'm excited. I'm intrigued. I'm represented. And I'm inspired to keep writing.

So thank you to Delia and Ellen for showing me what I was missing; to Steve Berman, Ellen Datlow, Bryan Thomas Schmidt, Bart Leib, Kay Holt, John Joseph Adams, and all of the other editors who allow us queer writers to destroy SF, fantasy, and horror with such alacrity; and to all my fellow QUILTBAG authors for challenging me to keep up.

~

Anthony R. Cardno's first published work was a "hero history" of Marvel Comics' *The Invaders* for the late, lamented *Amazing Heroes* magazine back in 1986. His short stories have appeared in *Willard & Maple, Sybil, Space Battles: Full Throttle Space Tales Volume 6, Beyond The Sun, OOMPH: A Little Super Goes A Long Way,* and *Tales of the Shadowmen Volume 10.* In 2014 he edited *The Many Tortures of Anthony R. Cardno,* in which 22 authors Tuckerized him to raise money for the American Cancer Society. In addition to a full time job as a corporate trainer, Anthony is a proofreader for *Lightspeed* magazine, writes book reviews, and interviews authors, singers, and other creative types on anthonycardno.com, where you can also find some of his other short stories. In his spare time, Anthony enjoys making silly cover song videos on Youtube. You can find him on Twitter @talekyn.

ALL YOUR FIC ARE
BELONG TO US

RACHEL SWIRSKY

Don't worry. We aren't really going to destroy your science fiction. We're just going to queer it up a bit. Toss a boa on your chiseled space captain, slip some Birkenstocks to your doe-eyed scientist's daughter. We're going to paint this spaceship purple and dip it in glitter. *Heaps* of glitter. *So much* glitter.

As we depart the spaceport, the whole universe will be our disco ball. We'll shimmy and shimmer as we turn the warp drive to fabulous.

This spaceship is fierce.

We're hiring Tim Gunn to design the uniforms. We've commissioned holographic recreations of Ellen Degeneres and Rosie O'Donnell to host twenty-four-solar-hour talk show programming in our entertainment center. The walls of our mess hall are painted with murals dedicated to the great pairings of slash fiction. Careful viewers will discover renderings of Spock and Kirk ravaging each other in two hundred and twenty-seven different ways.

Our first mission? Traveling to a sudden dimensional rift to pick up Captain Jack Harkness.

Now, we don't want you to feel left out, so we want to assure you that heterosexual content may be included on this vessel as background flavor. Snarky, straight best friends are permitted, especially ones with limited inner lives of their own who help the main characters realize their dreams. Breeder-related hanky panky must be kept to a minimum, preferably off-screen.

Don't worry, though. No one's recommending treating y'all straight folks the way you've treated us. We're going to give the violence thing a miss. No executions, no forced castrations, no corrective rape, no mob beatings, and etc.

Hey, even the thing about backgrounding heterosexuality was a joke. Straight, cis people are welcome on Starship Queer. Grab yourselves a sticky-sweet pink beverage with an umbrella in it and come dance to the latest album by the High Queen of All the Universe, RuPaul.

To those of you who are unhappy with this outcome, we apologize. Unfortunately, there's no way back. Once you go gay, you can't turn away. Queers are like Midas. We transmute the things we encounter. Everything we touch turns to glitter.

Sure, the same old stories are still there, with their same old muscle-bound pilots and starry-eyed wenches (ever considered turning that around?). You can still read them. Please do. We all enjoy old favorites along with the new.

But now, as you read them, you'll know that somewhere in the margins, there's a fleck of glitter. Try to ignore it if you want, but that shine will keep on catching the corner of your eye. And in it, there's a genetically engineered race of haploid lesbian scientists, and a pair of star-crossed male lovers watching the decline of their galactic empire, and a colony built on a planet where no one has any gender. They're out there. You can't forget them.

Tonight in the lounge, we've got Rosie the Riveter doing a stand-up routine with Laverne Cox. There's a boa waiting for you at the coat check. We'll keep a seat warm in case you decide to come in.

~

Rachel Swirsky holds a masters degree in fiction from the Iowa Writers Workshop, and graduated from Clarion West in 2005. She's published over fifty short stories in venues including the *New Haven Review*, *Clarkesworld Magazine*, and Tor.com. Her short fiction has been nominated for the Hugo Award, the Locus Award, and the Sturgeon Award, and in 2010, her novella "The Lady Who Plucked Red Flowers Beneath the Queen's Window" won the Nebula. If it were an option, she might choose to replace her hair with feathers, preferably bright macaw feathers.

Go Bisexual Space Rangers, Go!

Cecilia Tan

I feel like bisexuality has a special place in science fiction. Maybe this impression comes partly from growing up with a sole bisexual role model in the 1970s and '80s—David Bowie—whose image was also that of a space alien at the time. I don't think it's a coincidence, though, that Bowie chose both to represent himself as bi and as unearthly, and that I chose science fiction as the genre I liked best. Bowie used both elements of image to establish himself as an outsider and I, as a budding young outsider by dint of both my bisexuality and my bi-racial identity, choose science fiction as "my" genre. I don't think I was aware at the time that I chose it because it gave me the room to imagine worlds where I belonged.

As I grew older and moved from *Star Trek* (the original show) and *Lost in Space* and Madeleine L'Engle and whatever else I could get my hands on at the public library that had a dragon or space ship on it, I discovered that perhaps I wasn't the only person who felt like bisexuality had a special place in science fiction. In 1981, I was in junior high school and I spent my allowance by riding my bicycle to the local indie bookstore to buy the works of Marion Zimmer Bradley, Roger Zelazny, and Anne McCaffrey. At the time I didn't know what I was searching for. I was already writing by that time: Tolkien knockoffs and inventing my own superheroes and dreaming up planetary societies. But by high school I had started to notice that the only books where bisexuals (or pansexuals or omnisexuals) ever appeared in fiction where they were treated as a normal, everyday part of life were science fiction or fantasy books. In regular "real life" literature, if you introduced a bisexual character, it was like putting a gun on the table in the first act. By the end of the book they had to have cheated on someone or gone mad. Sigh. Whereas in science fiction you could have characters who swapped gender and therefore messed with the concept of "hetero" or "homo" sexuality (Samuel R. Delany, John Varley), where there were group marriages (Diane Duane), or line marriages (Robert Heinlein), or other social and gender structures (Ursula K. LeGuin).

It took a while for this all to soak through my consciousness. Sense of wonder is wonderful for disarming one's resistance but sometimes it left me at the end of a book sort of panting and limp, wondering what had just happened? But then again, how else could a 1980s teenager who seemed to be the Only Bisexual On Earth (except maybe for David Bowie, who might have just been pretending) be expected to react to the fact that an element of her core identity, bisexuality, was by then a genuine bog-standard SF genre trope? Sometimes it wasn't even a core element of the book and maybe that was even more exciting, the idea that bisexuality could be part of the status quo.

The almost incidental nature of the bisexuality trope in SF/F meant being ambushed by drive-by sexuality epiphanies. But maybe every teenager feels that way about coming to grips with any form of alternative sexuality while growing up in a sex-negative culture? I certainly didn't mind it and I don't regret reading all that science fiction during my formative years. And I sure as hell don't ever regret writing it or joining the community of writers and editors and fans who embrace diversity and difference in all forms.

~

Cecilia Tan is the award-winning author of many novels and short stories, the founder of Circlet Press, and she wants you to know all her characters are bisexual unless proven otherwise.

DRAMA KID

CECIL BALDWIN

In reflecting on my modest acting career, I can't help but notice a distinct lack of gay characters in the parts I have played. Tartuffe never seduced Orgon in alexandrine couplets while his outraged wife hid underneath their parlor table; Jaques did not get to cuddle up to Orlando beside the Duke's campfire deep in the forest of Arden; and the typically Chekhovian bookish schoolteacher, alas, pined away for Masha and not her brother Andrey as they futilely attempt the journey to Moscow. Even in the contemporary plays I have worked on, there is a dearth of truly unforgettable, strong, and complex queer roles. When auditioning for mainstream television and film, I find myself contending for the "gay best friend" character whose only contribution to the plot are a few très bon mots and a wicked fashion sense. Gay is who they are, what they are, why they are and not much more.

There are only two exceptions to this shortage of queer representation in my body of work—the first is when writing and performing autobiographical work for the Neo-Futurists based on my own life and experiences as a gay man; and the second is for the podcast *Welcome to Night Vale,* as the host of a local community radio show where Cecil (yes, we share the same first name, to much delight and confusion) proudly discusses his love for another man. Just about every aspect of life in the small, desert town of Night Vale is strange and bizarre, everything except the main character's healthy, adult gay relationship. Tiny civilizations under bowling alleys may attack, glowing clouds may drop small-to-moderate sized animals on the population, and librarians run amok with bloodthirsty abandon, but no one thinks twice about a gay man being the mouthpiece for their community. Cecil's love life is not his defining characteristic; it is simply one aspect of his rich and complicated existence.

Mainstream media is slowly catching on to the idea that gay, bisexual, and transgender characters can stand their ground in stories and genres of every kind. Not only can we be the heroes of our world, but also we are just as good at saving the day as our straight counterparts. Maybe some day soon I will get to play Hamlet *and* have a mind-blowing make out scene with Horatio, or maybe that is just my own wishful thinking.

~

Cecil Baldwin is the narrator of the hit podcast *Welcome To Night Vale*. He is an active ensemble member of the New York Neo-Futurists, creating original work for the long-running show *Too Much Light Makes The Baby Go Blind*. Cecil has also performed at The Shakespeare Theatre DC, Studio Theatre (including the world premier production of Neil Labute's *Autobahn*), The Kennedy Center, The National Players, LaMaMa E.T.C., Emerging Artists Theatre, The Assembly, Rorschach Theatre and at the Upright Citizens Brigade. Film credits include The Fool in *Lear* with Paul Sorvino, *Open Cam,* and sundry national commercials.

REWRITING OUR DEFAULT SETTINGS

ELIZABETH LEGGETT

It was not until I was a sophomore in college that I worked up the nerve to tell my mother I was bisexual. I did not want to do it over the phone so I waited until she came to campus for a visit. I was so nervous that I blurted it out almost immediately after she arrived. Her response was perfect. She cocked her head to the side, smiled at me and said, "So? Do you want to go to dinner?"

I am looking forward to a time when more science fiction enthusiasts react similarly about QUILTBAG themes in their films, books and television. Obviously, we are not there yet. That is what this Kickstarter is about.

This Kickstarter is about awareness and change. As visionaries, science fiction creators should feel compelled to fight social censorship and outdated taboos. White and straight may be the default setting, but it does not have to be. The more diversity the imagination industry brings to light, the closer they are to rewriting canon. (*Star Trek* left an indelible imprint that proved that over and over again.)

The social landscape is changing. The non-heterocentric community deserves to find more inclusive characterization and development especially in science fiction. Science fiction writers and artists should courageously push awareness further and further into a brighter future of acceptance. With more of that in our global entertainment and literary industries, who knows how close we can get to the elimination of bigotry and discrimination?

In the words of Gene Roddenberry, "Welcome home. We have a lot of work to do."

~

Elizabeth Leggett has illustrated for Lethe Press, *Spectrum22,* ArtOrder's *INSPIRED, Infected By Art Vol 3,* Quillrunner Publishing, Quiet Thunder Publishing, Little Springs Design, S.J. Tucker, and private collectors. She was cover artist and art director for *Lightspeed*'s special issues Women Destroy Fantasy! and Queers Destroy Science Fiction!. In 2013, she published a full 78 card tarot and successfully Kickstarted the project. In 2015, she was nominated for a Hugo Award in the Fan Artist category. She has her fingers crossed!

CONFESSIONS OF A QUEER CURATOR

LYNNE M. THOMAS

I came out as a bisexual woman in 1992, during my first year at Smith College. I spent much of college doing everything I possibly could to get my hands on queer content of all kinds. I was desperate to see myself represented. Because it was Smith, I had an immediate support network of friends who gave me a roadmap of materials to follow. (Our dorm had an anonymous Porn Fairy: if you mentioned having strong queer attractions, a pile of varied queer porn would appear outside your door, so that you could explore as you needed to, in relative privacy. A note explained that when you were done, you should leave the pile outside your door once more, and it would magically disappear until it was needed again.) This was in the days Before *Ellen*, when LGBT popular culture was still niche and often hard to find.

So I vacuumed up LGBT films, books, and comics. I attended queer dances and meetups. I came out to my parents right before I left for my Junior year abroad in Paris. (It went … poorly, but we eventually reconciled.) As college came to a close, I decided I wanted to pursue a career as a librarian or an editor, with an LGBT focus, if at all possible.

I wasn't a geek growing up or in college. What SF/F I would casually walk by in bookstores, video stores, and movie theaters in the 1990s didn't really seem to be aimed at me. I wasn't seeing a lot of women featured, and even fewer LGBT characters, as in most mainstream entertainment.

While I was earning my library masters' degree, I dated a woman who was a SECRET GEEK. (In the mid-90s, it was sometimes easier to come out as queer than as a nerd.) She introduced me to an an entire world of queer SF/F that I didn't know existed, beginning with the works of Mercedes Lackey. I was deeply grateful to see queer characters like Vanyel and Stefen in The Last Herald-Mage series, and discovered that I really enjoyed speculative literature. We watched *Xena: Warrior Princess* with its not-so-subtle subtext between Xena and Gabrielle. I became rather passionate about that show. After we broke up, and I married Michael, I continued loving *Xena*—we spent part of our honeymoon at a *Xena* convention, my very first—and I became a fan of other shows with queer content (text or subtext) like *Doctor Who* and *Buffy*.

All of this led up to landing my dream job at Northern Illinois University. I became the Curator of a Rare Books and Special Collections department that contains SF/F *and* Gender Studies materials. My geekery and my queerness both became completely central to my professional work, as if my entire life had been leading up to this.

Part of my job is to make up the historical record by selecting the materials that will survive to be studied. I have an unparalleled opportunity to commit the political act of documenting many underrepresented communities—including women writers, writers of color, and queer writers often dismissed as "not important enough" to document. Though many institutions are collecting SF/F or queer materials, few places handle the combination of the two. I found when I began researching a decade ago that quite a few creators from under-represented communities were being overlooked, particularly within SF/F. I made it my mission to find these authors and make sure that their literary papers would be also be saved for posterity, if they so desired. Queer-friendly conventions like Wiscon became my new home. I've spent over a decade building up NIU's collection (libguides.niu.edu/sciencefiction) to include the papers of queer SF/F writers among its ranks.

When I consider younger Lynne, coming out at Smith and desperate to see herself in literature and entertainment, I wish I could hand her books like Ellen Kushner's *Swordspoint,* Elizabeth Bear's Stratford Man duology, Maureen McHugh's *China Mountain Zheng,* Catherynne M. Valente's *Palimpsest,* or Brit Mandelo's *Beyond Binary* anthology so she could see that speculative fiction can and does represent people like her. *This* is why I document these works. (It's also why I edit such works, but that's another essay.)

This is also why I'm asking you to support Queers Destroy Science Fiction! We need future queers to know at first glance that *we exist* in imaginative SF/F works. *And always have.*

The best way to ensure that is to be able to hand them this special issue.

∼

Three-time Hugo Award winner **Lynne M. Thomas** is the Co-Editor-in-Chief and Publisher of *Uncanny Magazine* with her husband Michael Damian Thomas. The former Editor-in-Chief of

Apex Magazine (2011-2013), she co-edited the Hugo Award-winning *Chicks Dig Time Lords*, as well as *Whedonistas* and *Chicks Dig Comics*. She moderates the Hugo-Award winning SF Squeecast, a monthly SF/F podcast, and contributes to the Verity! Podcast. In her day job, she is the Head of Special Collections and Curator of Rare Books and Special Collections at Northern Illinois University, where she is responsible for the papers of over seventy SF/F authors. You can learn more about her shenanigans at lynnemthomas.com.

WHERE NOW
MUST I GO TO
MAKE A HOME?

HAL DUNCAN

5

And came down in Kilwinning, Scotland, 1988, so they did, the spacers of Delany's "Aye and Gomorrah," discovered in his *Driftglass* collection, picked up in a ratty secondhand copy from fuck knows where or when. Came down in the head of a teenager primed with the trad kid's fantasy fare of Narnia and Middle-Earth, a little snottery spit gobbed into the mix via Larrabeiti's *The Borribles*, but no Sodom. Primed further by a copy of Asimov's *I, Robot* foisted on me by a mate, a first sortie into the more cerebral fantastica of Science Fiction. Ready for … something more.

4

There'd been *Star Wars* too, of course, back in the Odeon of 1970s Saltcoats, the Dolby Stereo thunder of that star destroyer overhead, imaginary lightsabers on the playground, a *Millenium Falcon* toy for Christmas; there were the old *Flash Gordon* serials also, on telly during the summer holidays; the old and new *Buck Rogers*; the original *Battlestar Galactica*. But those were a pop culture pervasion, soul fiction so ubiquitous it's less an element of any personal relationship to SF, more the universal substrate shared by all '70s kidsters, a saturation of tropes still requiring some strange/queer catalyst to crystallise.

3

So, although/because in the utter Rationalism of prepubescence, I was an infant Spock, a bespectacled robot alien mostly oblivious to this thing the humans called *desire*, the *Star Trek* series itself spoke less to me than Asimov's calculus of narratives, the way his stories worked the permutations of the Three Laws of Robotics. From Asimov, I turned to Clarke, Heinlein, the Gollancz Classics line of the era—old editions too, *anything* in the library with a yellow cover. Then as the adolescent urges kicked in, I found my way from Golden Age wonders to Delany. Never to look back.

2

In the decade that saw the "Gay Plague" hysteria of HIV's emergence, and Section 28 introduced by Thatcher, the paedophile's PM, to ban the "promotion of homosexuality" lest gay teachers "recruit" my ass, Heinlein's increasingly self-indulgent grandstanding gave me an avenue of escape into futures of polyamorous tolerance, but it was Delany who really rescued me from the shit of small town queerdom that makes one do an It Gets Better video decades later.

It was *Nova* and *Babel-17* and *Dhalgren*.

It was *Driftglass* with its spacers and frelks, and its opening epigraph of lamentation for lost Sodom.

1

A little escapism's no bad thing, but what I found in SF is something better dubbed *rescuism*, I think. Utopias, dystopias and heterotopias exploring the capacities of cultures for glorious deviance from the normative. The cynic's idealism driving satiric autopsies of societal folly. The cryptofascist wank is not to be overlooked, of course, but the idiom is *defined* by its breaches of assumed reality, no? This fiction of the strange is by definition that of the queer.

So those spacers came down in my imagination, and I saw their future—a potential home for me: New Sodom.

And went up.

~

Hal Duncan's debut *Vellum* was published in 2005, garnering nominations for the Crawford, Locus, BFS and World Fantasy Award, and winning the Spectrum, Kurd Lasswitz and Tähtivaeltaja. Along with the sequel, *Ink*, other publications include: the novella *Escape from Hell!*; chapbooks *An A-Z of the Fantastic City* and *Errata*; a poetry collection, *Songs for the Devil and*

Death; and most recently, a short story collection, *Scruffians*, and *Rhapsody*, a book-length essay on strange fiction. An occasional collaborator with bands such as The Dead Man's Waltz, he also wrote the lyrics for Aereogramme's "If You Love Me, You'd Destroy Me," and is responsible for one musical, *Nowhere Town*. Homophobic hatemail once dubbed him "THE … . Sodomite Hal Duncan!!" (sic.) You can find him online at halduncan.com, revelling in that role.

Destruction Is What Creation Needs

Sunny Moraine

For me, there's pretty much always been something intrinsically *queer* about science fiction.

You wouldn't necessarily think that, right? I mean, I wouldn't have, at least not given the yelling that's been done over how much we're destroying it. I wouldn't have except I do, because I know my own history with it; I've seen it in the lives of my friends and colleagues; I've felt it in how powerful these stories are and what I know they're capable of.

My earliest memories of science fiction involve the feeling of expanding borders, of shooting right past them. Technology, the future, the past, the boundaries between people, between human and non-human. What we might become, what we are now, where we've been and how we can make sense of it all. Science fiction for me has always been about the erosion of constraints. It's always been about flexibility, transformation. It's always been about building, but also about *movement* within and outside of that building. It's always been about constructing something and then smashing it apart to see what happens.

It's been about questioning everything. *Changing* everything, if it's possible to do so.

I was learning how to write science fiction at the same time as I was coming into a fuller understanding of what *queer* meant in the context of me. The two grew together, side by side and then fully enmeshed. Creating these worlds and playing within them was profoundly connected to the grappling with identity I was spending so much time doing. The rearranging of concepts and ideas in one place helped make the same rearrangement possible in the other. Which changed daily. It still does. Hour by hour. There's actually no line between the two.

Who am I? What's my relationship with this body? How do I fit into it? What do I want? What does it want? What does any of this mean? I can't imagine trying to answer these questions, for myself, without the tools science fiction provides. Wild thought experiments, exploding frontiers, not only shifting parameters but the absence of any parameters at all. None of this has to be static. None of it *is*.

All these things are true, and none of them are.

I clearly don't think science fiction shouldn't be queer. I *do* think queers are destroying science fiction. I think we should. I think something like science fiction should be in a constant state of destruction. Destruction in this context is inherently creative. How else are we supposed to live there?

I don't know how *I* would, anyway.

~

Sunny Moraine's short fiction has appeared in *Clarkesworld, Strange Horizons, Nightmare,* and *Long Hidden: Speculative Fiction from the Margins of History,* among other places. They are also responsible for the novels *Line and Orbit* (cowritten with Lisa Soem) and the *Casting the Bones* trilogy, as well as *A Brief History of the Future: Collected Essays*. In addition to authoring, Sunny is a doctoral candidate in sociology and a sometimes college instructor; that last may or may not have been a good move on the part of their department. They unfortunately live just outside Washington DC in a creepy house with two cats and a very long-suffering husband. They can be found at sunnymoraine.com.

SHIVA AND OCTAVIA

SAM J. MILLER

In 2007, I got a rejection letter that messed me up. I'd sent a story about a gay couple after the zombie apocalypse, and the pro SF market that I sent it to said: "It becomes too much about gay men and not people in general."

Now, I'm going to own some of this—I'm a better writer now than I was in 2007, and maybe I did fail to make my love story "work" for that editor. And yes, maybe writing a story about the zombie apocalypse was my first mistake. But for years that line haunted me, making me doubt myself, making me feel like even well-intentioned non-homophobic straight readers wouldn't get and didn't want to read about queer characters. It made me steer clear of some stories I wanted to tell, because 90% of readers are supposedly straight, and why write things that 90% of readers are unlikely to get? It made me change the gender of some protagonists to turn gay love stories straight. It made me censor myself. I had to see a lot of queer stories get published—and see a lot of those stories win awards—and I had to go to the Clarion Writer's Workshop and get lots of community support before I felt comfortable writing the stories that spoke most directly to who I was.

And when I did, I realized: the readers I want are the ones who connect with stories—not labels, not boxes, not cookie-cutter THIS IS WHAT A GENRE TALE SHOULD LOOK LIKE stories. And there's a lot of those readers out there. Love is love. People are people—even when they're robots, or aliens, or gods, or monsters. It's why I, a gay man, got such a severe case of The Feels watching hetero romance unfold between Laura Roslin and Bill Adama in *Battlestar Galactica*. It's why Ken Liu's "The Paper Menagerie" made me cry, even though I don't have personal experience of the devastating hidden injuries of immigration and assimilation that his tale turns to metaphor. Tell a story well enough and you'll blow the shackles off the reader's minds. Of course some people cling hard to their assholery. My own *Lightspeed* novelette "We

Are the Cloud" caught a concentrated dosage of hate from a homophobe. But you're not writing for them. You're writing for your people.

Before you can change the world with your words, however, you have to get your words out into the world.

I think it's difficult for writers and readers who carry privilege, whether of class, race, gender, or sexuality, to understand just how crippling it is to look around at the books and magazines that you love, and not see yourself there. How deep the internalized wounds can go, when everyone around you from high school on up is holding up a book that looks nothing like you, and saying "THIS IS GREAT LITERATURE. THIS IS A STORY WORTH TELLING." Every writer faces an uphill battle getting their words in print—my hero Octavia Butler said "everyone who tries to write experiences savage rejection, and it just goes on and on until finally you begin to break through"—but the savagery is compounded when you add in the external obstacles outsider writers face when their stories feature experiences and arcs that white straight middle class college-educated editors have no personal experience of … and the staggering, sometimes crippling, internalized obstacles: the self-doubt and the self-rejection. Brilliant writer of color Lisa Bolekaja tweeted about facing the need to "*work through shit just 2 feel comfortable putting sentences on paper. Somedays 1 sentence is a miracle.*"

This is why queers need to destroy science fiction. It's why women—and people of color—and writers working in languages other than English—and other marginalized communities need to destroy science fiction. We need to undermine the Straight White American Male underpinnings of the genre.

Understand: destruction is a positive force. Destruction is a sweeping change. I'm talking about destruction as embodied in the Death card in the tarot deck, or Shiva the Destroyer God—a creative force that purges bullshit, crushes the cookie cutters, severs our sentimental attachments. Makes us better.

That's why I'm trying to destroy science fiction. And why I'm so happy to support *Lightspeed*'s Queers Destroy Science Fiction! And why you should too. OR BURN IN THE CLEANSING FIRE OF OUR RAGE.

~

Sam J. Miller is a writer and a community organizer. His work has appeared in *Lightspeed*, *Asimov's*, *Shimmer*, *Beneath Ceaseless Skies*, *Electric Velocipede*, *Strange Horizons*, *Interzone*, *The Minnesota Review*, and *The Rumpus*, among others. He is a winner of the Shirley Jackson Award and a graduate of the Clarion Writer's Workshop. Visit him at samjmiller.com.

CREATIVE DESTRUCTION

LISA NOHEALANI MORTON

I spent a long time dancing around the blank page that was destined to become this essay, doing literally anything at all other than committing words to paper.

The upside of that is that now my bathroom is sparkling clean! The downside is that eventually I ran out of Things I Desperately Need To Do Right Away and was forced to confront myself about *why* I was having so much trouble laying down some words on the topics of Queers, Science Fiction, and Destruction. So I decided to break it down.

Part I: Queers

I'm trying to avoid the inevitable throat-clearing that comes at this point in the essay, where I acknowledge that as a woman currently in a (nominally) straight relationship I am maybe not Queer Enough to write it.

But you know what? Screw that. That line of thinking is why bisexuality is invisible, and it leads to too many of us with both a stake and a lived experience keeping our mouths shut. I am (currently, primarily) with a man, but I have and do also date women. I'm here, I'm bi, and I'm going to keep on talking.

Part II: Science Fiction

I think it was Vonda McIntyre who first clued me in, as a young SF-reading person, to the idea that sexuality covered more than just women marrying dudes and having babies. *Starfarers* is a touchstone for me in many ways, but especially in the way it treated queer relationships and alternative relationship structures as just a fact of life, rather than something to be sneered at or exoticized.

And then there was Heinlein. Oh, Heinlein. I clung to the plural, group, and line marriage stuff; I read and reread that one bit about cuddly spouses in *To Sail Beyond the Sunset*; I considered in great detail the gender and queer implications of *I Will Fear No Evil,* and I assiduously ignored the bits that weren't so friendly. Heinlein told me that life could be lived under different rules than the ones my parents taught me. He told me to question everything. I listened (and applied it to him as well).

Part III: Destruction

By now I should have some rousing call to action. Let's destroy science fiction! *But I like science fiction,* I hear you protest, and that's totally legit: I do too.

But check this out: when we say *destroy science fiction,* we mean *let's make it like something you've never seen before.* Which is, if you think about it, the *whole point* of science fiction.

So: let's do it. Let's tear it down and rebuild it even better. Let's pull our stories from the rubble and the shards of broken, clichéd plots. Let's see where we can go with gender and relationships and sexuality, and let's not be afraid of showing the full range of human experience. Let's have every type of character, and every type of relationship. Let's have characters that younger me and older me and right-now me can recognize as themselves. Let's head out into unknown space, turn our afterburners on, and let's not ever look back.

~

Born and raised in Honolulu, **Lisa Nohealani Morton** lives in Washington, DC. By day she is a mild-mannered database wrangler, computer programmer, and all-around data geek, and by night she writes science fiction, fantasy, and combinations of the two. Her short fiction has appeared in publications such as *Lightspeed, Daily Science Fiction*, and the anthology *Hellebore and Rue*. She can be found on Twitter as @lnmorton.

HERE'S HOW
IT GOES

ALYSSA WONG

Here's how it goes.

You are twelve years old and your heart itches with unrealized desire. You feel it every time you write, a new awareness echoing through the people populating your stories.

It will take you nine more years to come out to yourself. It will take another to begin telling others, to wear yourself with some modicum of comfort. But at twelve, with no locks on the doors and no privacy anywhere, your brain hums with duplicity, hard-edged survival, and stories full of feelings you can't contain.

When you are fifteen, your mother will tell you that she's changing hairdressers because she doesn't want to give money to a gay man. When you are seventeen, your own crippled faith cuts your queer friends away because they look too much like you. When you are twenty-one, your mother will cry for months, send you admonishing emails, and refuse to watch your college play because your character is a lesbian.

You hide them in the back of your math notebook so your parents won't find them. You write in code, you never let anyone kiss, but oh, you know. You turn to ultraviolence for skin-to-skin contact, but lack of emotional intimacy and trust fans the spark in you into self-destructive flames.

In your teenage years, you steal books from the library, hoarding them like the nerdiest Smaug. *Swordspoint, The Will of the Empress*—they change your life, the way you read and write about relationships. For the first time, you see that sometimes girls fall in love with girls and boys fall in love with boys. For the first time, you begin to realize that it's okay.

That maybe you're okay, too.

But those are books. In real life, you hide by going to church and ignore the way your face heats when you talk to your best friend, the way your heart lightens, buoyed by a heady mix of excitement and fear, every time she says, "Sure, I'll hang out with you."

Your mother comments on how close you two are and eyes you with suspicion. You laugh it off and watch your back.

Your writing suffers. Your characters are hollow, cored of their identities. You write until your hands and heart bruise, but it doesn't get any easier. Your writing doesn't get better. It feels stunted, and so do you.

It takes until you're twenty-one to excavate that piece of you buried under sedimentary layers of fear, self-hatred, and guilt. You write your first openly queer story, and things begin to slot into place so fast that you can barely keep up.

Slowly, you stop being afraid.

When you stop self-censoring the queerness of your stories—when you stop mangling your writing and yourself trying to fit into a mold that was never, ever tenable—your writing explodes with life and color. When you stop denying your own existence, you finally start telling your stories the way they need to be told. You begin to reclaim their truth, your truth.

You are twenty-three and your heart still itches with desire, but your words are truer now, more focused, more powerful for it. When you write, it's no longer about destruction of identity, but restoration.

~

Alyssa Wong is a 2013 graduate of the Clarion Writers' Workshop. Her fiction has appeared in *The Magazine of Fantasy & Science Fiction*, *Strange Horizons*, *Black Static*, and Tor.com; and her poetry is forthcoming at *Uncanny Magazine*. You can find her on Twitter at @crashwong or at crashwong.tumblr.com.

ACCEPTANCE

ARLEY SORG

I don't want your *acceptance*.

I want more. And science fiction is here to help.

When I hear those words, "I accept you for who you are," my stomach goes queasy. I desperately craved those words in junior high and longed for them in high school. By college, I saw things in a different way.

Acceptance assumes a position of power. As if one person is overcoming distaste on behalf of another. As if they stand in judgment, waving a scepter: I *accept* you, despite what you represent! And just as one character in that conversation assumes a position of power, the other abases themselves, knowingly or not, giving up their agency by wanting or needing *acceptance*.

Power is only part of the problem. The heart of the problem is judgment. Perhaps (arguably) it's natural to judge that which is "other," even when the "otherness" is kind of similar to elements of one's own persona or experience.

I think of my trips to Paris, specifically of the sense of strangeness that I enjoyed. I think of how I loved being overwhelmed by the size of the city. I delighted in the food, with flavors and styles similar-yet-different to where I'm from. I thrilled at the architecture, the shapes similar-yet-different to buildings and monuments that I pass all the time. I lavished in the sounds, the expressions, the exchanges, enjoying every moment.

When we talk about *Queer* and the notion of *acceptance*, the word isn't synonymous with *thrill, love, lavish, enjoy*.

Acceptance is the very problem.

When you meet a new friend, you don't tell them you *accept* them. You tell them how excited you are that you met. Perhaps you're eager to learn from each other. Maybe you anticipate new adventures. You might just long for the challenges a new friend will bring; or bonding through select, shared perspectives.

I call upon you to move beyond *acceptance*, and to understand it as a flawed principle in which neither person really wins.

Science fiction is a well-established venue for the exchange of ideas, and for challenging dominant or popular assumptions. It functions as a safe gateway to the strange; the reader often expects or craves the experience of strangeness. Simultaneously, it creates moments through which individuals find or develop shared perspectives.

At its best, science fiction is dialogue.

I want you to embrace the things that aren't-quite-you. I want you to appreciate the ways in which someone might be different from you. I want you to value them, to get excited in meeting, to enter into discovery. I want you to learn; to edify each other through cultural exchanges.

These works offer a wonderful chance to interact with what you are not. This is an opportunity to participate in a conversation and to truly embrace the Other. From my perspective, it's an invitation into worlds that you just might enjoy.

Don't *accept* it.

Relish it!

~

Arley Sorg grew up in England, Hawaii and Colorado. He went to Pitzer College and studied Asian Religions. He lives in Oakland, and most often writes in local coffee shops. He has a number of short stories out at various markets and is hammering out a novel. A 2014 Odyssey Writing Workshop graduate, he works at *Locus Magazine*. He's soldering together a novel, has thrown a few short stories into orbit, and hopes to launch more.

THE BOOKS THAT READ ME

EVERETT MAROON

I spent copious hours in my childhood trying to find myself in the books I read, often via the weak beam of a dying flashlight. Although I was a fan of some young adult authors in the 1970s and '80s—Judy Blume, Paula Danziger, and Lois Duncan—it was science fiction that grabbed my imagination and where I most wanted to wander. But SF thwarted me; *Stranger in a Strange Land*, I grokked you so hard, I loved what you had to say about shaking our expectations for government and culture, but then there was the endless het-fest, pages and pages of straight people sex. I learned to twist and manipulate myself to remain in the text—reading *Neuromancer*, I pretended Case was planning to merge with Molly instead of combining the AI machines, producing some new combination of gendered human. When I was eleven I evaded most of the activities during a two-week fat kid camp by burying my face in a leather-bound compilation of *The Hitchhiker's Guide to the Galaxy* books, and while they were hilarious—though I still haven't managed to fly by missing the ground—I became increasingly tired of Arthur Dent's innocence and banality.

Then I moved on to feminist SF, with the likes of Joanna Russ and Katherine Forrest, and I sat amazed at the deconstruction of SF tropes, not to mention modernist narrative, that they created. It was a lesbian love fest in *The Female Man* and *Daughters of a Coral Dawn*. I see them now, along with *The Left Hand of Darkness* and *The Handmaid's Tale,* as standard bearers for second wave feminism's influence over the genre. And there are pieces in Russ's work in particular that stand out to me as transphobic, which made me anxious to move on to a different kind of deconstruction of science fiction.

I found an even more imaginative, queer SF world in the work of Samuel

Delany and his protégé, Octavia Butler. I devoured the Lilith's Brood trilogy. I struggled through *Dhalgren* like I was trying to understand a boa constrictor that was in the process of destroying me, fascinated and frightened and committed to the outcome. What these novels did was incorporate the postmodern reconceptualization of narrative, reorient the SF narrative structure away from white male exploration and philosophy, and offer explosive new ideas on society and subjectivity.

Science fiction, in its mirroring of contemporary friction points, needs another transformation that transgender and queer writers of color can continue to push as a vanguard. SF imagines the worst about people and hypothesizes our exit routes toward cultural actualization at the same time. This is why I write science fiction (you know, for what it's worth). I realize I can't keep up with the tsunami of new stories in SF, but I am having a hell of a good time trying. And hello, *Lightspeed* is a terrific place to start. Thanks for making a contribution to this Kickstarter project.

~

Everett Maroon is a memoirist, humorist, and fiction writer. He is a member of the Pacific Northwest Writer's Association and was a finalist in their 2010 literary contest for memoir, and was a 2013 Lambda Literary Foundation Emerging Writer Fellow. Everett is the author of a memoir, *Bumbling into Body Hair*, and a young adult novel, *The Unintentional Time Traveler*, both published by Booktrope Editions. He has written for *Bitch Magazine*, GayYA.org, Amwriting.org, RH RealityCheck, and *Remedy Quarterly*. He has had short stories and essays published here and there.

THE DESPERATE
TASK

MAKING THE INVISIBLE VISIBLE

CHRISTOPHER BARZAK

Growing up, I read fiction to travel in my mind and imagination to other places, real and imagined. I grew up in a small rural town, and my family wasn't the sort that travels extensively. They were the sort that put down roots several generations back and remain to this day firmly rooted. So reading was a way for me to go out into the world, to see new places, different types of people, and to learn about the various possibilities for my own identity.

Out of all the kinds of characters one can encounter in fiction—in speculative fiction in particular, where aliens abound and the human race itself can be transfigured into something quite different from what we know of ourselves now—there was a particular absence that, later, when I was in my early twenties, I couldn't help but notice: characters of queer identities.

Every sort of literature—whether it is grouped by genre, gender, nationality, ethnicity, or what have you—has invisible men populating the shadows of their stories, where they remain unnoticed for one reason or another. Queer characters were the ones I didn't know speculative fiction lacked until I began to understand this part of my own identity in my early twenties, after which I began to look for people like myself in the books I'd already read and loved, only to realize months into this task that I wouldn't find many.

It wasn't until the mid '90s that I started to see queer characters in science fiction. Maureen McHugh's *China Mountain Zhang* introduced me to a science fictional near future where diversity truly existed. Richard Bowes' Kevin Grierson stories, which eventually became the novel *Minions of the Moon*, lifted the veil that hides the demimonde, where those invisible populations often exist in decades where they were not (or possibly will not be) acknowledged or admitted into the greater family of man. These two books—one science fiction, the other a dark fantasy—gave me hope that I might find more reflections of myself and people like me in literature, in stories set in the future, the past, and also in the present day, where those reflections might take root rather than flit between what has been and what may come.

The desperate task of seeking out those reflections eventually gave way to my taking on a different task: creating some of those reflections in my own stories, to put forth for others who so desperately need stories that help them understand themselves within this world and in other, imagined worlds. I'm thrilled to see so many people supporting an endeavor to bring together more and more of these kinds of stories within the literature of speculative fiction, and I hope that even more will join in that support as we attempt to make the invisible visible.

$\sim$

Christopher Barzak is the author of the Crawford Fantasy Award winning novel, *One for Sorrow,* which has been made into the recently released Sundance feature film *Jamie Marks is Dead.* His second novel, *The Love We Share Without Knowing,* was a finalist for the Nebula and Tiptree Awards. He is also the author of two collections: *Birds and Birthdays,* a collection of surrealist fantasy stories, and *Before and Afterlives,* a collection of supernatural fantasies, which won the 2013 Shirley Jackson Award for Best Collection. He grew up in rural Ohio, has lived in a southern California beach town, the capital of Michigan, and has taught English outside of Tokyo, Japan, where he lived for two years. His next novel, *Wonders of the Invisible World,* will be published by Knopf in 2015. Currently he teaches fiction writing in the Northeast Ohio MFA program at Youngstown State University.

A World of Queer Imagination

Bonnie Jo Stufflebeam

My freshman year of high school, I learned a lot from *Buffy the Vampire Slayer*: about human nature, friendship, the strength of metaphor. I learned what was and wasn't allowed in popular depictions of queerness. The arc of Willow's sexuality threw me; I loved that I finally had queer role models in her and Tara. I loved that she had experienced two true loves: one with a man, one with a woman. But the few brief times that she alluded to her sexuality, she didn't acknowledge the dual nature of it. Willow was straight, then gay, and as much as I loved the understated approach to sexual orientation, I longed more for a role model who would let me know that it was okay not to feel an attraction to one gender only. I wanted a metaphor that addressed queerness not as an absolute but as a spectrum upon which I could slide whichever way I needed.

• • •

Imagine a middle school girl, awkward in her skin. She has always, thus far, used her right hand: to draw, to write, to hold her fork. But the muscles in her left hand itch; the itch comes on suddenly, or perhaps it has been there all along but only now does she notice it, only now does it bother her when she tries to sleep.

The awkward girl tries using her left hand. It feels right, more right than anything she has ever done. In a small-town, this is unheard of; for a week after, the girl is approached before each class by a deluge of classmates and their questions. *What does it feel like to use your left hand?* The school nurse calls her parents to tell them what their daughter is up to.

The mother is unhappy. The girl lies: *I'm a righty, look.* The mother backs off. The girl writes with her left hand only in secret. There's always an itch. There's always the urge. "There's no such thing as being ambidextrous," her sister says. "You can be a righty or a lefty, but you've got to choose."

And where is the evidence to the contrary? The awkward girl grows older. There are no ambidextrous people in the books she reads. There are few lefties, even, relegated to side characters, rarely allowed their own agency, and never allowed to show their affection to other lefties. For someone seeking permission to be comfortable with herself, for someone struggling to fill too-rigid shoes, this lack of representation is a blow that bleeds beneath the skin.

Imagine being told, being shown, that you do not exist. Imagine what that does to someone. In *Buffy*, invisibility becomes literal. In our world, invisibility breaks the mind.

• • •

Buffy the Vampire Slayer is not science fiction in the traditional sense. When I sat down to write this essay, I racked my brain for depictions of fluid sexuality in science fiction books, shows, movies, that affected my younger self. These depictions exist; in my adulthood I'm discovering them. Jack from *Doctor Who*. Octavia Butler's *Patternmaster*. Samuel R. Delany's *Dhalgren*. Ursula K. LeGuin's *The Left Hand of Darkness*. "Inventory" by Carmen Maria Marchado in *Strange Horizons*. But these stories are few and far-between and required seeking-out. Some people are not so lucky to uncover them. That I had to use a supernatural show as my example only underscores my point.

Stories matter. Some say that it's not important to depict fluidity of sexuality because love is love. But love is not love, especially not in popular culture's eyes. First love is different from second love. Love, like sexuality, does not come in absolutes. The culturally-validated love of a man and a woman may not feel different in the heart from the culturally-shunned love of a woman and a woman, but it can feel different in the body when you do not belong to the world in which you love.

Science fiction has the power to change things. Already, science fiction has inspired the future in new technologies, new ways of thinking. It's time that science fiction challenges our notion of sexuality as either/or. It's time science fiction grasps not our future view of sexuality but our present view, even. Here science fiction has unfortunately lagged behind.

Imagine a world where queer characters populate popular culture as frequently as they populate the real world. Imagine a world where specialized anthologies are not the only place we see ourselves. Imagine. It's what we're good at, we readers and writers of science fiction.

~

Bonnie Jo Stufflebeam lives in Texas with her partner and two literarily-named cats: Gimli and Don Quixote. Her work has appeared in magazines such as *Clarkesworld*, *Strange Horizons*, and *Interzone*. She holds an MFA in Creative Writing from the University of Southern Maine's Stonecoast program and curates an annual Art & Words Show, profiled in *Poets & Writers*. You can visit her on Twitter @BonnieJoStuffle or through her website: bonniejostufflebeam.com.

The First Rule I Learned about Writing Queer Characters in Science Fiction

Haralambi Markov

The first rule I ever learned about writing queer characters in science fiction is: You don't.

I had an interesting conversation with a close friend, who has always been accepting of my homosexuality and supportive of my writing. Our discussion revolved around whether or not Daryl from *The Walking Dead* was deep in the gay closet—a rumor that seemed too good to be true (painfully so) and that was discussed by both the comics creator and Norman Reedus himself. This had the power to change queer representation in genre TV in a huge way.

What my friend thought about it? He said that it's not all that relevant for the story if Daryl was gay; that in the microcosm of the story, there's no necessity for him to be gay. He did say that the comics have a kick-ass gay character that needs to be brought to the screen, but his first words stuck with me. This seems to be a prevailing attitude in every genre including science fiction. That it's not all that necessary to have gay characters. That it generally does not matter to the story so why not just make everyone straight.

I'll tell you why it does matter. The absence of QUILTBAG characters suggests that we can't survive the apocalypse. That we've been weeded out in the futuristic dystopias. That we've been scrubbed clean from humanity in the glorious future, actually any future, of space explorers and generational ships. We're omitted from these narratives and the adventures never seem to come our way. If we do appear, we're reduced to our sexual orientation, serve as comic relief or get killed. Have your pick. You can be more than one stereotype. The possibilities are endless.

I'm tired of being irrelevant and non-existent in worlds where the human imagination finds no problem giving birth to sentient AIs, god-like technologies and extraterrestrial life forms. I'm also tired of this being the lesson queer writers receive the moment they realize their identity. I never dared writing gay characters while I was learning to write in my teenage years.

I knew I was going to be a writer the first year in high school. I also knew I'd never make it as a writer writing about gay men. I denied myself exploring a most intimate part of my identity even in private, because I honestly believed queer characters would never have a place in science fiction, fantasy, or horror for that matter. I didn't write queer characters, because I was deathly afraid I'd be told I don't belong and a lot of my early work shows that.

Stepping away from this fear is the first step to breaking this cycle of omission, but it's a hard first step. This is why representation matters, folks. Representation stops self-denial and self-rejection. It's about becoming relevant to these stories, without them necessarily being about queer issues. It's about showing that we exist and that the human experience is all the more beautiful for its diversity. It's about reclaiming our humanity.

This brings me to the second rule I recently learned about writing queer characters in science fiction: Fuck Rule №1. That shit is irrelevant.

~

Haralambi Markov is a Bulgarian critic, editor, and writer of things weird and fantastic. A Clarion 2014 graduate, Markov enjoys fairy tales, obscure folkloric monsters, and inventing death rituals (for his stories, not his neighbors ... usually). He blogs at The Alternative Typewriter and tweets at @HaralambiMarkov. His stories have appeared in *Geek Love*, *Tides of Possibility*, *Electric Velocipede* and are slated to appear in *Tor.com*, *The Near Now*, *Genius Loci* and *Exalted*. He's currently working on outdoing his output for the past three years and procrastinating all the way.

QUEERS DIGGING AND DESTROYING

MICHAEL DAMIAN THOMAS

> Just another attempt to gain civilizations approval of their flawed agenda. What does LGBTQ have to do with Sci-Fi and Doctor Who and what is there to celebrate? Kinda desperate to me...
>
> —One-Star Amazon Review of *Queers Dig Time Lords*

Somewhere, there will be people asking why there's a need for *Lightspeed*'s Queers Destroy Science Fiction! issue. The question won't necessarily come from a place of homophobia or negativity. Many will point to all of the marvelous QUILTBAG SF works and queer authors with awards and successes. Some will claim that an issue just focusing on QUILTBAG authors will further "ghettoize" these pieces and creators. Some will ask, "Why create this when the community is already so accepting?"

I can safely say that this magazine issue is still needed, because I recently co-edited Queers Dig Time Lords. I heard all of those things as we prepared the book about a show that has a very vocal queer fandom and many Out production staff members. I know firsthand what happens when you broadcast the voices of QUILTBAG creators—both the marvelous and not-so marvelous things.

I loved working with my co-editor Sigrid Ellis (who is editing the flash fiction for Queers Destroy Science Fiction!). We published some phenomenal essays. The fact that our book which told the experiences of queer *Doctor Who* fans was nominated for a Hugo Award still astounds me. I was even a Guest at Alien Entertainment's Chicago TARDIS convention twice because of this book.

But it wasn't an easy road, and I want to discuss the less than wonderful things that happened to me due to the book, and the prejudices and microaggressions that still occur when creating a queer book as a QUILTBAG creator.

I identify as a genderqueer bisexual person. (Technically pansexual, but I first came out in the early '90s as bi and am still getting used to the different term.) I've been out since college, but I didn't broadcast the information to some people. As many of you know, I'm the primary caregiver to my medically fragile daughter, Caitlin. My wife Lynne and I for years depended on my conservative family for breaks from Caitlin's difficult care. They often watched her as we travelled to SF/F conventions for work. My aunt's husband in particular is extremely homophobic, partially due to some complicated and horrific family history of his own. Lynne (who identifies as bisexual), and I often bit our tongues hard when we would drop Caitlin off and he would make sometimes violent, homophobic comments.

So when Sigrid and the publisher asked me to co-edit *Queers Dig Time Lords*, I hesitated, and then talked to my close friends about it. To say yes risked losing the only family help we had with Caitlin. My friends assured me that if it happened, they would step in. I said yes, and didn't bring it up much with my family.

Sadly, my family was only one source of problems. Only days after I accepted the co-editor duties, I had my first awkward conversation with our publisher. He'd been talking to another editor at the press who claimed that there was already a "backlash" to me co-editing the book due to my marriage to a woman, though at that point I found that "backlash" comment odd and infuriating since the only people who knew about the book's existence were the publisher, Sigrid, me, that editor, and my friends.

I later had the backlash confirmed due to a drunken convention conversation in a hotel lobby. A prominent, tipsy gay Big Name *Doctor Who* fan decided to cross-examine me about my sexuality. He had decided that marriage to a woman meant I couldn't be bisexual, and therefore I shouldn't be involved with the book. He was adamant and belligerent as I basically gave him a bisexuality 101 course. He didn't buy it.

Once released, *Queers Dig Time Lords* collected different microaggressions; this time, in the form of silence. A huge online retailer of *Doctor Who* merchandise that stocked every *Doctor Who* title from our publisher didn't stock *Queers*. A very prominent SF/F magazine which reviewed all of the previous *Doctor Who* titles from our press suddenly couldn't find room for a review of our book, even after the Hugo nomination. A well-known convention book dealer asked my wife Lynne, whose *Chicks Dig Time Lords* is one of their big sellers, about the *Queers Dig Time Lords* backlash they thought must be going on after Lynne asked why they weren't carrying copies of *Queers* at a convention where we were appearing. I opened this essay with a particular Amazon review that vocalized what many seem to have been unfortunately thinking.

As for my family, they decided that they could no longer help with Caitlin. They didn't give *Queers Dig Time Lords* as a reason, but they coincidentally decided to stop watching Caitlin when we asked them to take her for the Wiscon where we were having the *Queers Dig Time Lords* launch party. (The official reason was that it was "too hard to watch her anymore.") We haven't talked to my aunt and uncle since. Our phenomenal friends kept their promises and have helped ever since.

So is this Queers Destroy Science Fiction! issue of *Lightspeed* necessary? Fuck yes. QUILTBAG creators and stories have made significant strides, but we are nowhere near a point where non-heteronormative voices are as accepted as their cis heteronormative counterparts. We need every opportunity to shine a light on these stories and creators.

I am so fucking proud that I co-edited *Queers Dig Time Lords* with Sigrid. It was completely worth it. Those stories needed to be told and not erased. So many reviewers, readers, and *Doctor Who* fans told us about how much they loved the essays. They let us know that the book touched them, and that they felt less alone after reading stories like their own. Others felt it gave them insight into being a QUILTBAG fan. I am so proud to be a part of that. (Hell, it was worth it just to know that copies of *Queers Dig Time Lords* were included in every Hugo Voters' Packet that went to certain Hugo Award campaigners' supporters.)

Thank you for helping *Lightspeed*, Seanan McGuire, Steve Berman, Wendy Wagner, and Sigrid Ellis and all the rest of the QDSF staff create a place where more of these stories can be told in fiction and nonfiction by supporting this project. These creators and stories need this spotlight and chance to sparkle.

~

Michael Damian Thomas is the Co-Publisher and Co-Editor-in-Chief of *Uncanny Magazine* with his wife, Lynne M. Thomas. He was a two-time Hugo Award nominee as the former Managing Editor of *Apex Magazine* (2012-2013), co-edited the Hugo-nominated *Queers Dig Time Lords* (Mad Norwegian Press, 2013) with Sigrid Ellis, and co-edited *Glitter & Mayhem* (Apex Publications, 2013) with John Klima and Lynne M. Thomas. Michael lives in Illinois with Lynne, their daughter Caitlin, and a cat named Marie. Caitlin has a rare congenital disorder called Aicardi syndrome, and Michael works as her primary caregiver. He and Lynne are the "Official Nemeses" of John Joseph Adams and Christie Yant. This is the greatest honor an editorial team can possibly earn.

ACKNOWLEDGMENTS

We could not have put this issue together without the help and support of our wonderful Kickstarter backers—all 2,250 of them!

One of the secondary Kickstarter rewards allowed backers to add their name to a list of donors that would appear in the published issue. This was an opt-in reward, so we only listed folks here who let us know that they would like their names to appear. (So if you were a backer and you don't see your name here, you either opted-out, didn't respond to the survey, or we messed up! If the latter, let us know and we'll try to make it up to you.)

We're excited to recognize our supporters here. Thank you again to all of you!

Note: Because some people did not include a last name, or included a business name, or Twitter handle, we have this sorted by first name.

@Cspokey; @Curiousbiped; @Dperson; @Emaree; @Gavreads; @Greenmichaelc; @Hyoscine; @Jpellerin; @Karenafagan; @Kellylhaworth; @Kinkzombie; @Ladyapplesauce; @Mcpinson; @Nickpheas; @Noahi; @Onlysaysficus; @Overdesigned; @Rachelcotterill; @Southerntamata; @Spiraling; @Unicronq; @Veduncan; @Waywardscutrgrl; @Wedge; A Kotik; A. Doucet & M. Bond; A. Haddix; A. Hamish Macdonald; A. Kwong; A. Lee Sutton; A.D. Roberts; A.F. Brouwer; A.L.L.; A.Miura; A.T. Greenblatt; A'llyn Ettien; Aaron M; Abbey Schultz; Abby Kraft; Abigail Artemis Fiona Crittenden; Adam Hagger; Adam Jury; Adam Ostrowski; Adam Rajski; Adam T Alexander; Adele Dawn; Adrian Stymne; Aeryn Mccann; Agnes Tomorrow; Agnieszka Backman; Al Ewing; Alan Dehaan; Alana Christie; Alex Barsk; Alex Brett/Kaberett; Alex Claman; Alex Conall; Alex Draven; Alex Fitzpatrick; Alex Grindley; Alex Ristea; Alex Whitehall; Alexander The Drake; Alexis "Poetfox" Long; Alfie Kirk; Ali Hawke, St Louis Mo; Ali Muñiz; Alice T.; Alicia Cole; Alison Pentecost; Alison Wilgus; Allan Hurst; Alli Martin; Allie Jones; Alma Vili; Almighty Jessica; Alreadyknowhow; Althea Poteet; Alyc Helms; Alyssa Hillary; Alyssa Peña; Amanda Center (Introvert X); Amanda Cuello Suñol; Amanda Guarino; Amanda Hassitt; Amanda Holling; Amanda M.; Amanda M. Potter; Amanda Van

Tassell; Amandeep Jutla; Amber G.; Amira K. Makansi; Amy Browning; Amy Henry Robinson; Amy Keyes; Amy Lea Mills; Amz; An Owomoyela; Andan Lauber; Ande Murphy; Andi Carrison; Andi Pagowska; Andrea Corbin; Andrea Cox; Andrea Lankin; Andrea Phillips; Andrea Sinclair; Andrea Smith; Andrea Speed; Andres Rosado-Sepulveda; Andrew And Kate Barton; Andrew Barton; Andrew Hedges; Andrew J. Princep; Andrew Leon Hudson; Andrew Tudor; Andrew Zimmerman Jones; Andrija Popovic; Andy Kinzler; Andy Mammel; Angela Blackwell; Angela Hinck; Angela Korra'ti; Angelica Bohle; Angelo; Angie Pettenato; Angus Macdonald; Angus Mcintyre; Ani J. Sharmin; Anika Dane; Ann Lemay; Ann Walker (Just_Ann_Now); Anna Bark Persson; Anna K. Larsson; Anna Marie Stern; Anna Mcduff; Anna O'connell; Anna Sciolino; Anna Svensson; Anne Ominous; Anne Petersen; Anne Springsteen; Annie Mosity; Anniella; Anthony Flores; Anthony Pizzo Iii; Anthony R. Cardno; Anthony Terragna; Antonietta Coccaro; Anu Bajpai; April Alexander; Aquila; Aramina; Ari Harradine; Ariel E Marcy; Arla Lorincz; Ashleigh Macbride; Ashley Hedden; Ashley Krista Furrow; Asymptotic Binary; Audiaurum; Audrey Penven; August; Auroralee; Avner Shanan; Axel Roest; Axiel B. H.; B. Cory; B. Jones; B.A. Lawhead; B.J. Baye; B.K. Wilson; Backoff2069; Badschnoodles; Balazs Oroszlany; Barbara Rogstad; Barney Walsh; Barry Becker; Barry Stanford; Beanside; Becky Allyn Johnson; Becky Youtz; Bekki Callaway; Ben Babcock; Ben H; Ben Nash; Ben Schwartz; Ben Weiss; Ben Whitehouse @Benjiw; Ben Wickens; Benjamin Allen; Benjamin C. Kinney; Benjamin Franklin Sequoyah Craft-Rendon; Benjamin Staffin; Bennouri; Beth Aka Scifibookcat; Beth And Steve Tanner; Beth Doughty; Beth Wodzinski; Bethan Thomas; Betsy Ralston; Bill Bicknell; Bill Carter; Bill Kaszubski; Blair Nicholson; Blake B; Bob Walker; Boguslaw Olszak; Boris Keylwerth; Boyd Stephenson; Bradley Robert Parks; Bran Mydwynter; Brandon Crews; Brandon High; Brandon R. George; Breeanna Sveum; Brent Millis; Brett Bird; Brian Engard; Brian Farrey-Latz; Brian Holder; Brian Johnson; Brian Nisbet; Brian Quirt; Brian T. Hodges; Brittiny Eastin; Brontë Christopher Wieland; Bronwen Fleetwood; Bronzey; Bruce Baugh; Bryan K; Bryan W. Kieft; Bryan White; Bryce Wolfe; Buddy H; C Frey; C Taschuk; C.D. Hale; C.M. Merritt; C.S. Chu; Cadence Jean Morton; Caitlin Mackay Shaw; Caitlyn Duer; Caleb Huitt; Cameron Harris; Camille Griep; Candra K. Gill; Captain Clewell; Cara Averna; Cara Wynn-Jones; Carl Muller; Carla Dugas; Carla H.; Carly Dingman; Carmen Maria Machado; Carol J. Guess; Carol Mammano; Carol Thomas; Carol-Lee Tutch; Caroline Barraco; Caroline Ratajski; Caroline Standish; Carolyn Hartman; Carolyn Livingston; Carolyn Priest-Dorman; Carrie Sessarego; Casey Canfield; Cassandra Rose; Cat Faber; Cat Jones; Cat Langford; Catherine Haines; Catie Coleman; Catie Myers-Wood; Catt Turney;

Céline; Cg Julian; Chad Bunch; Chan Ka Chun Patrick; Chanh Quach; Chanie Beckman; Charles Crapo; Charles Tan; Charlie Rose; Charlotte Ashley; Chazzle Mcbeanpole; Cheryl Rauh; Choco-Berry Princess; Chris C; Chris Clogston; Chris J. Donaker; Chris Meyers; Chris Salter; Chrissy Rewell-Arundel; Christian Hugs-Bois; Christian Steudtner; Christianne Benedict; Christie O. Hall; Christina Stam; Christine Bell; Christopher A. Corradi; Christopher Barzak; Christopher Reed; CJF; Claire Scott; Clara M. Wunschel; Clare Boothby; Confluence; Connie Wilkins; Connor Goldsmith; Cooper Lilith Miller; Corey J. White; Corey Klinzing; Cory Leonard; Cory Skerry; Craig Fotheringham; Craig Nickell; Craig P Miller; Critical Mass Rocketworks; Crm; Cyanlianas; Cynthia Ward; Cyril Simsa; D. Laserbeam; D. Van Gorder; D.A.R. Richards; D.M. Hauser; Dakota Nebula; Damian O'connor; Dan; Dan & Kat; Dan Balgoyen; Dan Conley; Dan Grace; Dan Stokes; Dane Peterson; Danger Stranger; Daniel D; Daniel Joseph Tavares Moore; Daniel R. Allen; Daniel Swensen; Danielle E. Pollock; Danny C; Danny Lee Pegg; Daphne Deadwood; Darcy Conaty; Darryn Bishop; Das Leser; Dave Thompson; David Aaron King; David Bonner; David Chart; David Farnell; David Gillon; David J. Fiander; David K. Simerly; David Laietta; David Mortman; David Owens; David Ring; Dayna Smith; Deanna Knippling; Deanne Fountaine; Debbie Block-Schwenk; Debbie Phillips; Déborah; Declan Waters; Dee Morgan; Deedre Deaton; Denise Ganley; Denise Murray; Denise Schiller; Diana Castillo; Didi Chanoch; Dina Elenbaas; Dino Mascolo; Doctor Horrible; Don Pizarro; Don Tucker; Don Whiteside; Donaithnen; Donna N. Blitzen; Donovan Corrick; Doron Mosenzon; Douglas Turley; Drew Krull; Drew Wright; Dryn; Ds Colburn; Duncan Macgregor; Dylan Otka; Dylan Sara; E. Hollindrake; E. Lynn Frank; E. Michael Kwan; E. Milligan; E. Nicole Lunsford; E.B. Lloyd; E.J. Jones; E.K. Tidey; Ecogrl; Eddy Falconer; Edgard Refinetti; Eileen M.; Eileen Prince; Elaine Chen; Elaine Tindill-Rohr; Eleanor Owicki; Eleanor Russell; Eleanor Smith; Eli Mcilveen; Eli Stevens; Elias F. Combarro; Elise Friedman; Eliza Savage; Elizabeth Brendasdotr; Elizabeth Bridges; Elizabeth K. Wadsworth; Elizabeth Mccoy; Elizabeth P. Birdsall; Elizabeth Synge; Elle Wise; Ellen Badgley; Ellen Datlow; Ellen Denham; Ellen Goodlett; Ellie Lamb; Elliot Jobe; Elliott Mason; Emanuele Vulcano; Emily Colvin; Emily Coon; Emily Goldman; Emily H.; Emirael; Emma Lord; Emma Standiford; Emma Story; Emma Wearmouth; Emmalynn Spark; Emmanuel Eytan; Emy Peters; Eric C. Magnuson; Eric Danielski; Eric Duncan; Eric G; Eric Grivel; Eric Irwin Kuritzky; Eric Plante; Eric Rossing; Erica Pantel; Erin Bellavia; Erin E. Sharp; Erin Golden; Erin Hawley; Erin Subramanian; Erlend Sand Bruer; Ethan Li; Eugene Myers; Eva Forsom; Eve Stein; Everett Maroon; Evil Kitten & Pyctsi; Eytan Zweig; F.Dunne; Fabio Fernandes; Faith; Faye Mitchell; Fflove190;

Fiona Parker; FJ; Flint Hills Sky; Florian Duijsens; Flutepicc; Franck Martin; Fred C. Moulton; French Canadian Moose; Freya Startup; Frode P. B.; G. Hartman; G. Vaaler; Gabriel Cruz; Gabriel White; Gail Z. Martin; Galexmie; Ganymeade; Gareth Pendleton; Garrett Croker; Garrett Pauls; Garrett Weinstein; Garry Haining; Gary D. Henderson; Gary Emmette Chandler; Gary Halpin; Gavran; Gemma & Brandon Renwick; Geoff "Not That Euphonium Guy" Brown; Geoffrey A. Rabe; Geoffrey Lehr; Gera L. Dean; Gerald Sears; Gilberto Galvez; Gini Von Courter; Glennis Leblanc; Glitter Elizabeth Rainbow; Gmark Cole; Grace G.; Greysen Amadeus-Amadeus Colbert; Griffinfire; Gugli; Guy "Couchguy" Mclimore; Gwenhael Le Moine; H.D. Ortlepp; Håkon Gaut; Hannah C.; Hannah Cook; Hannah Elspeth Catterall; Hans Ranke; Haviva Avirom; Hayley E Smith; Hazel Whitley; Heather Foster; Heather Jones; Heather Mayer; Heather Morris; Heather Noel Robinson; Heather Simmons; Heather T.; Heidi Waterhouse; Hel Gibbons; Hilary Rohr; Hisham El-Far; Hope Rudolph; Howard Rachen; Howell Belser; Hugh J. O'donnell; Hugo Camacho; Humbedooh; Huskiebear; Ian Christie; Ian Herold; Ian Magee; Ian Stone; Ido Bar-Av; Imogen Cassidy; Iulian Ionescu; J & M Albert; J Lily Corbie; J Nilsson; J. Cork; J. Lannan; J. Oberholtzer; J. Webb; J.L. Coffey; J.L. Nelson Kemp; J.M. King; J.R. Doddridge; J.R. Murdock; J.S. Gerras; J.Smith; J.V. Ackermann; J.W. Cooper; Jacinta Richardson; Jack Boyum; Jack Vivace; Jaime O'brien; Jake Frondorf; Jali; James Alan Gardner; James Brophy; James Bywater; James Frederick Leach; James H. Murphy Jr.; James L. Holman; James Pereira; Jami Nord; Jamie Bentley; Jamie Culpon; Jamie Gilman Kress; Jammes Luckett; Jane Seaborg; Jane Taylor; Jane Williams; Jasmine Stairs; Jason A. Zwiker; Jason Kimble; Jason Timermanis; Jason Weigel; Jay Mayes; Jay Swanson; Jay Zastrow; Jaydee Cepticon; Jazz Sexton; Jean Tatro; Jean-Philippe Turcotte; Jeanne Kramer-Smyth; Jed Hartman; Jedediah Berry; Jeff Amlin; Jeff Hotchkiss; Jeff Kapustka; Jeff Klenzing; Jeff Plotnikoff; Jeff Pollet; Jeff Tan; Jeff Xilon; Jeffrey C. Erlich; Jen B; Jen C. Hoskins; Jen Lammey; Jen Maguire-Wright; Jen R Albert; Jen Warren; Jen Woods; Jen1701d; Jeni Bowers; Jenmon; Jenn Mercer; Jenn Reese; Jenna Shively; Jennefer Dawn; Jenni Halpin; Jenni Hughes; Jennifer D. Wattley; Jennifer Doyle; Jennifer Lyn Parsons; Jennifer Tifft; Jennifer Woods; Jenny And Owen Blacker; Jenny Barber; Jens Müller; Jerome Hagen; Jerrie The Filkferengi; Jerry Gaiser; Jerry Howard; Jess Kay; Jess Speir; Jess Zibung; Jesse C; Jessica Bay; Jessica Gravitt; Jessica Halbhuber Powell; Jessica Reisman; Jessica Schulze; Jessica Smith; Jessie Cook; Jim Lai; Jim Otermat; Jim Sweeney; Jim Yearnshaw; Jinnapat Treejareonwiwat; Jjleggo; Jjmcgaffey; Jl Jamieson; Jo Lindsay Walton; Jo Miles; Joanna Lowenstein; Joannebb; Jocelyn Brown; Jodie Baker; Jodie Cooper; Joe Beason; Joe Dicker; Joellen Potchen-Webb; Jóhannes Gunnarsson; John

"Millionwordman" Dodd; John A Kusters Jr.; John Burnham; John Charles Mcdevitt; John Devenny; John Frewin; John G. Hartness; John Green; John Liesch; John Pope; John Tobin; Johnny Mayall; Joie Broin; Jolie Gendel; Jon Fetter-Degges; Jon Stutzman; Jon-Paul Lawrence; Jona Fras; Jonathan "Rocky Boy" Pruett; Jonathan Adams; Jonathan Helland; Jonathan Liraz; Jonathon Dyer; Jonathon R Howard; Jonny Ball; Jonny Leahan; Jordan L. Hawk; José Pablo Iriarte; Joseph C. Double; Joseph Hoopman; Joseph Sharmat Rodriguez; Joseph Wiedman; Josh Green; Josh Larios; Josh Medin And Kathleen Fuller; Josh Storey; Joshua I. Hill; Joshua Kirsh; Joshua Ramsey; Joshua Ziegler; Josie Riley; Joy Crelin; Jr Harris; Juan Pablo Hurtado; Jules Jones; Jules Philippe Laurent De Bellefeuille Defoy; Juli; Julia Brown; Julia Madeline Taylor; Julia Patt; Julia Rios; Julia Starkey; Juliane Steiner; Julie Tai; Julie Winningham; Juliet Kemp; Jun; Justin Jones; K. Bissett; K. Schumann; K.A. Banning; K.E. Curran; K.G. Orphanides; K.K. Roe; K.M.V.; K.N. Reynolds-Gier; Kactus; Kaelyn McIvor; Kai Charles; Kaila Y.; Kaitlynn Yoder; Kanane Jones; Karen Maner; Kari Kilgore; Karin Waller; Karin Wellman; Karl F. Maurer; Karl Hailperin; Karyn Heinrick; Kasmir; Kat Fairman; Kat H.; Kat Man; Kate Brenner; Kate Dollarhyde; Kate Heartfield; Kate Jones; Kate Kulig; Kate Larking; Kate Loynes; Kate MacLeod; Kate R.; KateKintail; Katharine (Thiefofcamorr); Katherine Catchpole; Katherine Dolores Haybert; Katherine Fawcett; Katherine Jay; Katherine Malloy; Katherine S.; Katherine Weinstein; Katheryn Bliss; Kathleen Pulver; Kathryn Long; Kathryn McCloskey; Kathryn Taylor; Kathy Trithardt; Katie Nolan; Katrina Lehto; Katrina Reiniers-Jackson; Katy Noe; Katya; Katya Pendill; Keera Takamiyashiro; Keffy R.M. Kehrli; Kellee Isle; Kelley O'Hanlon; Kelly Garbato; Kelly J. Myers; Kelly Kleiser; Kelly Robson and Alyx Dellamonica; Kelsey Collier; Kelsey M. White; Kelsey R. Marquart; KendallPB; Kennita Watson; Kerithwyn; Kermit O.; Kerri; Kerry (Circeramone) Jacobson; Keslynn; Kevin "Wolf" Patti; Kevin Baijens; Kevin F. McCarthy; Kevin Hogan; Kevin Hynds; Kevin J. "Womzilla" Maroney; Kevin Staggers; Kim Kinsella; Kim Nohr; Kimberley Altomere; Kira Lees; Kirsten D.M. Kowalewski; Kirsten M. Berry; Kit N. Stevens; Kitty Merriweather; Kotatsu; Kris and Jaime; Kris Gesling; Kris Mayer; Kris Wilcox; Kristen Fredericksen; Kristian Schmidt; Kristin S.B.H.; Kristina Canales; Kristina VanHeeswijk; Kristyn Willson; Kyle Barger; Kyle Baxter; Kyle Simons; Kyra Freestar; L. Chao; L. Felix; L.C.; L.l. Cunningham; L.M. Ayer; Lacey Rotier; Lala Hulse; Landrum; Lang Thompson; Langston Blank; Lara R. McKusky; Larisa Mikhaylova; Laura Burchard; Laura Clements; Laura Ford; Laura Lam; Laura Thomas; Laura Woods; Lauren Kramer; Lauren Naturale; Lauren Vega; Lauren Wallace; Leah Marcus; Leah Weaver; Leanne C. Taylor-Giles; Leanne Reich; Lee Harris; Lee Salazar; Lee Thomas; Legira; Leigh

Mellor; Leilani Cantu; Leo Zumpetta; Leonie Evans; Leshia-Aimée Doucet; Lesley Mitchell; Lesley Smith; Leslie Winston; Leticia Saoki Lopes; Lia Kawaguchi; Lianne Burwell; Lilian Og; Liliyana Deslacs; Lina Eklund; Lindsay G.; Lindsay Walter; Lindsey Wilson; Link Hughes; Lisa Adler-Golden; Lisa Barmby-Spence; Lisa McCurrach; Lisa Nystrom; Lisa Padol; Lisa Shininger; Lisa Stock; Lixian Ng; Liz; Liz Gorinsky; Liz Patt; Liz S.; Liz Sabin; Llinos Cathryn Thomas; Loki Carbis; Lorena Dinger; Loretta Michaels; Lslines; Lucius Annaeus Seneca; Lucy Adams; Lucy M. Fox; Lucy Perry; Lura McCartney; Luther Siler; Lyda Morehouse; Lydy Nickerson; Lynn E. O'Connacht; Lynne McCullough; Lysithea; M. Connor; M. Darusha Wehm; M. Grazioli; M. Hardy; M. Huebner; M. Remole; M. Russell Cartwright; M. Scuderi; M. Taylor; M.B. Beckett; M.D.; M.E. Gibbs; M.F.; M.J. Fisher; M.J. Paxton; M.W.S; Madison Metricula; Maggie Allen; Magnus Persson; Maija V.; Malcolm Wilson; Malinda Lo; Mallory Caise; Malnpudl; Malon Edwards; Mandy Hopkins; Mandy Stein; Mandy Tonks; Mara H.; Mara Levy; Mara Tree; Marc Rokoff; Marc Tetlow; Marcheto; Marcin Uliński; Marcus Erronius; Marcy Cook; Margaret Colville; Margaret Dunlap; Margaret N. Oliver; Margaret R. Chiavetta; Margaret S. McGraw; Margot Atwell; Maria Högberg; Maria Nygård; Marie H.; Marina Müller; Marion Deeds; Mark Galpin; Mark Gerrits; Mark Helwig Ostler; Mark Pantoja; Mark Robinson-Horejsi; Mark Stickley; Mary Anne Walker; Mary E. Garner; Mary Jo Schimelpfenig; Masanbol; Mathew A. Howell; Mathew Scaletta; Mathieaux; Matt Fitzgerald (@Firstfitz); Matt Lowe; Matt Sell; Matthew Baldwin; Matthew Brodie-Hopkins; Matthew Burkey; Matthew Caulder; Matthew Ellison; Matthew Golden; Matthew Joel Stewart; Matthew R.F. Balousek; Max; Maya T.; Me!; Meg Morley; Meg Osborn; Megan "M5" Matta; Megan E. Daggett; Meghan Ball; Melanie Lamb; Melanie Spitzer; Melissa Shumake; Melissa Tabon; Melodie Hardwick; Memory Scarlett; Merr1dew; Mhutch; Michael "The Mad Hatter" Pye; Michael A. Burstein; Michael Andersson; Michael Berger; Michael Bernardi; Michael Brassell; Michael C. Berch; Michael Fowler; Michael Horniak; Michael J. Madsen; Michael Kahan; Michael Lovell; Michael M. Jones; Michael McDaniel; Michael Mead; Michael Plezbert; Michael S.; Michael S. Manley; Michael Worrall; Michele McCarthy; Michelle Dupler; Michelle Kurrle; Michelle Muenzler; Michelle Murrain; Michi Trota; Miguel A. Romero; Mike Daley; Mike Moser; Mike Rende; Mike Young; Miles Gossett; Mink Rose; Miriah Hetherington; Miriam Krause; Miriam Stark; Misha Dainiak; Miss Violet DeVille; Mo Ranyart; Molli P. Barnes; Montuos; Moonytiger; Morgan R. Levine; Morva Bowman & Alan Pollard; Moshe J. Gordon Radian; Msmeglet; Myranda Sarro; N.B.; N.G.P; N.S. Beranek; Nancy Paulette; Nat Lanza; Natalia Chwialkowski; Natalie; Natasha R. Chisdes; Nathan Burgoine; Nathan Turner;

Nathan Walker; Nathanael Sumrall; Neile Graham; Nelly Geraldine García-Rosas; Nemo Nein; Nia Black; Nicholas Hansen; Nicholas Schiller; Nick Betancourt; Nick Cook; Nick Suffolk; Nickolas E. May; Nicola N.Z.; Nicolás Flowers; Nicole Bennardo; Nicole Degennaro; Nicole McMichael; Nicole Wooden; Nicuvëo; Nightsky; Niki La Teer; Nikki Walters; Nikolas Braren Blanchet; Nina Allan; Nina Kiriki Hoffman; Nissa Campbell; Noam Weiss; Noella Handley; Nolly Mullican; Nomad; Nori Duffy; Norma Krautmeyer; O. Walter Sand; Oliver Lauenstein; Olivia Gillham; Olivia Luna; Olna Jenn Smith; Oona O.; Ori Cupcakes; Oscar Wolfe; Owen Zahorcak; P. Ramirez; P.M.G.; Paige Ashlynn; Paige Kimble; Paige Speed Catotti; Pat Gamblin; Patrick Cahn; Patrick J. Ropp; Patrick Reitz; Paul A. Hamilton; Paul Andinach; Paul Durrant; Paul Herrera; Paul Hurtley; Paul Sabourin-Hertzog; Paul Stevens; Paul Zante; Paula Morehouse; Paula R. Stiles; Pawel Szwarc; Penda Tomlinson; Peter Aidan Byrne; Peter and Eliza Evans; Peter Andersson; Peter Hansen; Peter Niblett; Peter R. Cleghorn; Peter Recore; Petr Opletal; Petri Wessman; Phil Bowman; Philip Barkow; Philip Weiss; Phoenix Madrone; Phosgene; Pickwick; Pienaru Adrian-Teodor; Piia Puranen; Pippa Adams; Pratyeka; Professor Highland Wolland; Qai; Quintana Pearce; R. Jenkins; R. Lenagh-Snow; R. Reay; R.A. Fedde; R.E. Stearns; R.G.; R.J. Whitley; R.K. Bookman; R.K.G. Nystrom; R.L. Eyres; R.L. Floyd; R.S. Crosby; R.S. Hunter; Rachael Headrick; Rachel Coleman; Rachel Voorhies; Rachelle Benken; Rae Knowler; Rafia Mirza; Raja Thiagarajan; Randi Misterka; Random; Ratesjul; Ray Tomlin; Raymond Chan; Rebecca A. Sims; Rebecca Dominguez; Rebecca M.; Rebecca S.; Reesa Graham; Regis M. Donovan; Remy Nakamura; Revek; Rhong Aokami; Ria Campbell; Rich "Raz" Weissler; Richard Eaton; Richard Guion; Richard Isaac; Richard Leaver; Richard Leis; Richard Roper; Richard Scott; Rick Shang; Rigby Bendele; Rita Von Bees; River Vox; Rivka; Rob Easton; Rob Esene; Rob Krum; Rob Lord; Rob Snyder; Rob Weber; Robert "Rev. Bob" Hood; Robert Levy; Robert Maughan; Robin Snyder; Robyn Alexander; Rodney Holmes; Rohan Sinha; Ronald Pyatt; Ronnie J. Darling; Ronnie Sirmans; Ronny Aviram; Rory Hart; Rosandra Cuello Suñol; Rose Fox; Rose Hill; Rose Pascoe; Rosemary; Ross Mandin; Rowie Moss; Rrain Prior; Rufus; Russell Duhon; Ruth Sachter; Ruth Sternglantz; Ruthi; Ryan Forsythe; Ryan Gerlach; Ryan Haack; Ryan P. Adams; S. Aucuparia; S. Eyermann; S. Hudson; S. MacDonnell; S. Olson; S.A. Fluter; S.B.; S.K. Gaski; S.K. Suchak; S.L. Johnston; S.L. Kanning; S.M.D.; S.P. Derr; Sabrina Strauss; Sabrina West; Sam Galey; Sam Kurd; Sam Lynn; Sam Pearce; Sam Waters; Samantha Brock; Samantha Bryant; Samantha Herdman; Samuel Hansen; Samuel Thomasson; Sandor Silverman; Sandry Wilkie; Sandy Macmillan; Sara Casale; Sara D. Watts; Sara Glassman; Sara Harrington; Sara Hoots; Sara M. Samuel;

Sara Mitchell; Sara Puls; Sara R. Levy; Sara Stredulinsky; Sarah Bolland; Sarah Brand; Sarah E. Chislett; Sarah E. Yost; Sarah Edington; Sarah Goldman; Sarah Goslee; Sarah Howes; Sarah J. Faubert; Sarah Kelley; Sarah Mack; Sarah Mendonca; Sarah Milne; Sarah Nelson; Sarennah; Sasquatch; Savanni D'Gerinel; Sazerac; Schondy; Scott King; Scott Madin; Scott Raun; Sean G.; Sean Tilley; Seanmike Whipkey; Sebastian Morden; Selkiechick; Sentath; Serinde; Shadowcub; Shane Derr; Shane Ryan; Shannon Conaty; Shannon Fay; Shannon Nergard; Shannon Pochran; Shara White; Sharla D. Stremski; Sharon Galey; Sharon Paisner; Shaun M. Cote; Shawna Jaquez; Shayna Bettac; Sheila Addison; Sheila Sine; Sherman Dorn; Sheryl R. Hayes; Shiyiya Lecompte; Shoshana Bailar; Sidra M.S. Vitale; Sidsel Pedersen; Sofie Håkansson; Solene Q.; Some Z. Ing; Sonia & Ruth Mills; Sorida; Spacefall; Squirrel Walsh; Stasia Archibald; Stef Maruch; Stefan Buschmann; Stefan Raets; Steph Kelley; Stephane; Stephanie Bussen; Stephanie Carey; Stephanie Charette; Stephanie Cheshire; Stephanie Gunn; Stephanie Livigni; Stephanie Marshik; Stephanie Shero; Stephanie Wood Franklin; Stephen Abel; Stephica the Mighty; Steve Barnett; Steve Foxe; Steve Gooch; Steve Stormoen; Steven A. Berger; Steven B. Wheeler; Steven Cowles; Steven Danielson; Steven Gould; Steven Saus; Steven Tang; Storium.Com; Stuart Chaplin; Su J. Sokol; Suriya; Susan R. Grossman; Susan Rose; Suzanne Forman; Suzie Eisfelder; Svend Andersen; Sylvia Richardson; T. Pollinger; T. Ross; T. Skupin; T.A. Jacobson; T.D. Walker; T.E. Stacy; T.S. Porter; Tad K.; Tal S.; Tamara L. Degray; Tamsin Mehew; Tanya McDonald; Tara Jacob; Tarja Rainio; Tegan Elizabeth; Tehani Wessely; Teresa Telesco; Terry Jackman; Thalita Carvalho; The Apothecary; The Chimerical Collective; The Dude; The Grawlix Podcast; The Sables; The SF Reader; Therese Norén; Thomas S. Vee; Thomas Werner; Thouis R. Jones; Tibicina; Tibs; Tiffany E. Wilson; Tiffany Leigh; Tim Ellis; Tim Luttermoser; Tina Anderson; Tinuviel Montalvo; TJE; TMeuretBooks; Todd V. Ehrenfels; Todd Walton; Toetsie Z.; Tom Gromak; Tommi Mannila; Tommy Sääf; Tony Egan; Tor Andre Wigmostad; Tove Heikkinen; Tracy Graff; Travis Brace; Traylantha; Trey Peden; Trina L. Short; Trystan Rundquist; Tsutako; Turner Docherty; Tyler Gair; Valerie Gillis; Vee Edwards; Veronica Belmont; Vex Hanson; Vic Wayne; Vida Cruz; Vincent Docherty; Violette Paquet; Virginia McCreary; Vladimir Stamenov; W. Scott Meeks; Walter J. Montie; Wanda Jane; Warren Lapworth; Wendy Hammer; Wes Frazier; Wesley Hillen; West Decker; Whitney Johnson; Wilder Snow; Will J. Fawley; William E.J. Doane; William M. Rawls; William Mawdsley; Xavier Ho; Y.S. Germain; Yjgalla; Yotam Kenneth; Yuetiva Deming; Zach Anthony; Zed Lopez; Zeus; Zina Hutton; Ziv Wities; Zoe Aukim; Zoë Barnard.

COMING
ATTRACTIONS

Coming up in July, in *Lightspeed* . . .

We have original science fiction by Carrie Vaughn ("Crazy Rhythm") and Taiyo Fujii ("Collaboration"), along with SF reprints by Tony Daniel ("Life on the Moon") and Mary Robinette Kowal ("The Consciousness Problem").

Plus, we have original fantasy by Andrea Hairston ("Saltwater Railroad") and Sam J. Miller ("Ghosts of Home"), and fantasy reprints by Liz Williams ("Adventures in the Ghost Trade") and William Alexander ("Ana's Tag").

All that, and of course we also have our usual assortment of author and artist spotlights, along with a feature interview and the latest installment of our book review column.

For our ebook readers, we also have reprint of the novella "Dapple," by Eleanor Arnason and a pair of novel excerpts.

It's another great issue, so be sure to check it out. And while you're at it, please tell a friend about *Lightspeed*!

• • •

Looking ahead beyond next month, we've also got MORE DESTRUCTION TO COME. In October, we'll publish Queers Destroy Horror! as a special issue of *Nightmare*, and in December, we'll present Queers Destroy Fantasy! as a special issue of *Fantasy Magazine*. Queers Destroy Horror! is guest-edited by *Lightspeed/Nightmare* associate/managing editor Wendy N. Wagner, and Queers Destroy Fantasy! is guest-edited by award-winning author Christopher Barzak, with Tor Books editor Liz Gorinsky selecting the reprints.

Then, in 2016, stay tuned for...POC DESTROY SCIENCE FICTION!, guest-edited by award-winning author Nalo Hopkinson!

Thanks for reading!

Subscriptions
& Ebooks

Subscriptions: If you enjoy reading *Lightspeed,* please consider subscribing. It's a great way to support the magazine, and you'll get your issues in the convenient ebook format of your choice. All purchases from the *Lightspeed* store are provided in epub, mobi, and pdf format. A 12-month subscription to *Lightspeed* includes 96 stories (about 480,000 words of fiction, plus assorted nonfiction). The cost is just $35.88 ($12 off the cover price)—what a bargain! For more information, visit lightspeedmagazine.com/subscribe.

Ebooks & Bundles: We also have individual ebook issues available at a variety of ebook vendors ($3.99 each), and we now have Ebook Bundles available in the *Lightspeed* ebookstore, where you can buy in bulk and save! We currently have a number of ebook bundles available: Year One (issues 1-12), Year Two (issues 13-24), Year Three (issues 25-36), the Mega Bundle (issues 1-36), and the Supermassive Bundle (issues 1-48). Buying a bundle gets you a copy of every issue published during the named period. So if you need to catch up on *Lightspeed,* that's a great way to do so. Visit lightspeedmagazine.com/store for more information.

All caught up on *Lightspeed*? Good news! We also have lots of ebooks available from our sister-publications *Nightmare* and *Fantasy Magazine.* Visit nightmare-magazine.com or fantasy-magazine.com to learn more.

ABOUT THE SPECIAL ISSUE STAFF

SEANAN MCGUIRE, GUEST EDITOR

Seanan McGuire (who also writes as Mira Grant) is the bestselling author of more than a dozen novels, with her latest releases being *Symbiont, Midnight Blue-Light Special, The Winter Long, Half-Off Ragnarok,* and *Sparrow Hill Road.* She is a ten-time finalist for the Hugo Award, as well as the 2010 winner of the John W. Campbell Award for Best New Writer. Her short fiction has appeared in the magazines *Lightspeed, Apex, Fantasy,* and *Nightmare* and in numerous anthologies, including *Robot Uprisings, The End is Nigh, Wastelands 2, Glitter & Mayhem, Dead Man's Hand, Games Creatures Play,* and *The Mad Scientist's Guide to World Domination,* among others. She is a regular blogger and dissector of media, and one of the contributors to the Hugo Award-winning podcast *SF Squeecast.* Find her on Twitter @seananmcguire.

STEVE BERMAN, REPRINT EDITOR

Steve Berman has edited more than thirty anthologies, including the Shirley Jackson Award finalist, *Where Thy Dark Eye Glances: Queering Edgar Allan Poe* and the annual series *Wilde Stories: The Year's Best Gay Speculative Fiction,* which has been a two-time finalist for the Lambda Literary Award. His gay YA novel, *Vintage,* was a finalist for the Andre Norton Award. He founded Lethe Press, one of the larger LGBT publishers, in 2001. He resides in New Jersey, the only state in the Union with an official devil.

SIGRID ELLIS, FLASH FICTION EDITOR

Sigrid Ellis is co-editor of the Hugo-nominated *Queers Dig Time Lords* and

Chicks Dig Comics anthologies. She edits the best-selling *Pretty Deadly* from Image Comics and edited the Hugo-nominated *Apex Magazine* in 2014. She lives with her partner, their two homeschooled children, her partner's boyfriend, and a host of vertebrate and invertebrate pets in Saint Paul, MN.

MARK OSHIRO, NONFICTION EDITOR

What if you could re-live the experience of reading a book (or watching a show) for the first time? Mark Oshiro provides just such a thing on a daily basis on Mark Reads and Mark Watches, where he chronicles his unspoiled journey through various television and book series. He mixes textual analysis, confessional blogging, and humor to analyze fiction that usually makes him cry and yell on camera. He's been nominated for a Hugo in the Fan Writer category in 2013 and 2014 for his work, and he's nearly done with his first novel.

WENDY N. WAGNER, MANAGING EDITOR

Wendy N. Wagner grew up in a town so small it didn't even have its own post office, and the bookmobile's fortnightly visit was her lifeline to the world. Her short fiction has appeared in magazines and anthologies including *Beneath Ceaseless Skies*, *The Lovecraft eZine*, *Armored*, *The Way of the Wizard*, and *Heiresses of Russ 2013: The Year's Best Lesbian Speculative Fiction*. Her first novel, *Skinwalkers*, is a Pathfinder Tales adventure. An avid gamer and gardener, she lives in Portland, Oregon, with her very understanding family. Follow her on Twitter @wnwagner.

PAUL BOEHMER, PODCAST PRODUCER

Paul Boehmer attended his first Shakespearean play while in high school; he knew then that he was destined to become the classically trained actor he is today. Graduating with a Masters Degree, Paul was cast as Hamlet by the very stage actor who inspired his career path. A nod from the Universe he'd chosen aright! Paul has worked on Broadway and extensively in Regional Theatre; coinciding with another of his passions, science fiction, Paul has been cast in various roles in many episodes of *Star Trek*. Paul's love of literature and learning led him by nature to his work as a narrator for Books on Tape, his latest endeavour. Paul is married to the love of his life, Offir, and they live in Los Angeles with their two midnight-rambling tomcats, Dread and David.

CECIL BALDWIN, PODCAST HOST

Cecil Baldwin is the narrator of the hit podcast *Welcome To Night Vale*. He is an active ensemble member of the New York Neo-Futurists, creating original work for the long-running show *Too Much Light Makes The Baby Go Blind*. Cecil has also performed at The Shakespeare Theatre DC, Studio Theatre (including the world premier production of Neil Labute's *Autobahn*), The Kennedy Center, The National Players, LaMaMa E.T.C., Emerging Artists Theatre, The Assembly, Rorschach Theatre and at the Upright Citizens Brigade. Film credits include The Fool in *Lear* with Paul Sorvino, *Open Cam,* and sundry national commercials.

ARLEY SORG, ASSISTANT EDITOR

Arley Sorg grew up in England, Hawaii and Colorado. He went to Pitzer College and studied Asian Religions. He lives in Oakland, and most often writes in local coffee shops. He has a number of short stories out at various markets and is hammering out a novel. A 2014 Odyssey Writing Workshop graduate, he works at *Locus Magazine*. He's soldering together a novel, has thrown a few short stories into orbit, and hopes to launch more.

PATRICIA PACE, ASSISTANT EDITOR

Patricia Pace is one of those badass librarians. You know the kind, with the books and the hair and the technology and all the know-how. She can fish, play the clarinet, identify a compound sentence, and do macrame. She's an asexual who likes whiskey and she has cool tattoos. (See, that was a compound sentence right there.) She looks after a library, her dogs, her family, her podfics, and at least one wayward fiddler.

SANDRA ODELL,
ASSISTANT & AUTHOR SPOTLIGHTS EDITOR

Sandra Odell is a forty-seven-year old, happily married mother of two, an avid reader, compulsive writer, and rabid chocoholic. Her work has appeared in such venues as *Jim Baen's UNIVERSE, Daily Science Fiction, Crossed Genres, Pseudopod,* and *The Drabblecast*. She is hard at work plotting her second novel or world domination. Whichever comes first.

JILL SEIDENSTEIN, SPOTLIGHT INTERVIEWER

Jill Seidenstein contains multitudes. She is a librarian, writer, yogini, traveler, and photographer. She enjoys tea in the coffee-obsessed city of Seattle. You can find her nattering about all of these things on Twitter as @outseide.

RAHUL KANAKIA, SPOTLIGHT INTERVIEWER

Rahul Kanakia's first book, a contemporary young adult novel called *Enter Title Here*, is coming out from Disney-Hyperion in August '16. Additionally, his stories have appeared or are forthcoming in *Clarkesworld*, *The Indiana Review*, *Apex*, and *Nature*. He holds an M.F.A. in Creative Writing from Johns Hopkins and a B.A. in Economics from Stanford, and he used to work in the field of international development. Originally from Washington, D.C., Rahul now lives in Berkeley. If you want to know more you can visit his blog at blotter-paper.com or follow him on Twitter at twitter.com/rahkan.

ROBYN LUPO, SPOTLIGHT INTERVIEWER
Robyn Lupo has been known to lurk around Southwestern Ontario, complaining about the weather. She helped destroy flash-sized science fiction in 2013 and hopes to wreck poetry for decent people everywhere soon.

C. BEDFORD, ILLUSTRATOR
Born and raised in Queens, NYC. Bedford has also spent time in the country side of North Carolina and suburbs of Pennsylvania before their great migration to the UK. Drawn to the androgynous male, Bedford often tries to paint varying features of men they believe are present but rarely portrayed. They do their best to capture qualities of masculine people we are told they don't possess or not allowed to have in order to maintain masculinity. C. Bedford hopes to return to and finish their comic Andro☆! and to continue trying to make awesome art.

PAIGE BRADDOCK, ILLUSTRATOR
Paige Braddock is the Creative Director at Charles M. Schulz's Studio in California. Braddock is the creator of the long running, Eisner nominated series, Jane's World, and co-creator of The Martian Confederacy. Recently she released a new graphic novel for kids titled *Stinky Cecil*. She worked as an illustrator for The Chicago Tribune and The Atlanta Constitution, before accepting her current position. More about her work can be found at PB9.com.

ISABEL COLLIER, ILLUSTRATOR
Isabel "Talin" Collier has been working as a character designer and concept artist for two decades now, primarily designing miniature figures to be used in tabletop games. When not engaged in that, she does music, puppetry, acting, and just about every other creative thing in the world, shamelessly squandering her degree in Fine Arts. Her other mutant abilities include the ability to converse with dogs.

ODERA IGBOKWE, ILLUSTRATOR

Odera Igbokwe is a graduate of Rhode Island School of Design, where they earned their BFA in Illustration. At Brown University, Odera studied movement-theater and west African dance with New Works/World Traditions. As an illustrator, Odera loves to explore storytelling through character archetypes, afro-diasporic mythologies, movement, and magical girl transformation sequences. Some of Odera's recent projects include work with Gallery 1988, Fantasy Flight Games, DΔWN, and the personal collections for Beyoncé Knowles, Solange Knowles, and Oumou Sangare. Follow Odera by checking out odera-igbokwe.com or odera.tumblr.com.

ELIZABETH LEGGETT,
ART DIRECTOR, COVER ARTIST, & ILLUSTRATOR

Elizabeth Leggett has illustrated for Lethe Press, Spectrum22, ArtOrder's INSPIRED, Infected By Art Vol 3, Quillrunner Publishing, Quiet Thunder Publishing, Little Springs Design, S.J. Tucker, and private collectors. She was cover artist and art director for *Lightspeed's* special issues Women Destroy Fantasy! and Queers Destroy Science Fiction!. In 2013, she published a full 78 card tarot and successfully Kickstarted the project. In 2015, she was nominated for a Hugo Award in the Fan Artist category. She has her fingers crossed!

STEEN, ILLUSTRATOR

Steen is a transplant illustrator who lives and works out of Queens, NY. She is a graduate of the School of Visual Arts, with a degree in illustration. In addition to her ink work, she enjoys succulent gardening, bird watching, and reading. More of her work can be found at steendraws.com or steendraws.tumblr.com.

ORION ZANGARA, ILLUSTRATOR

Orion Zangara is an illustrator, comic book artist, and aspiring author who lives in the Washington, D.C. metro area. He is a graduate of The Kubert School, an art trade school with a concentration in sequential art, founded by his grandfather, Joe Kubert. He hopes to someday create dark fantasy tales in both pictures and prose. And he finds it very strange describing himself in the third person. Visit his website at orionzangara.com.

ADDITIONAL STAFF

We made every effort to involve queer production staff whenever possible, but, as with the Women Destroy projects, we involved some allies on the production side of things. (Note: Copy Editing, though it has "Editing" right in the name, is actually a production job.)

Publisher
John Joseph Adams (ally)

Audio Editors
Jim Freund (ally)
Jack Kincaid (ally)

Copy Editors
Amanda Vail
Gabriella Stalker
Sonya Taaffe
Wendy N. Wagner

Proofreaders
Andy Sima (ally)
Anthony R. Cardno
Melissa V. Hofelich (ally)
Hannah Huber (ally)
Rachael K. Jones (ally)
Zoe Kaplan
Kevin McNeil (ally)
Lianna Palkovick (ally)

Submissions Readers
Lisa N. Morton
Merav Hoffman
Robyn Lupo

Book Production & Layout
Michael Lee (ally)

Cover Design
Henry Lien

Crowdfunding Logo Design
Julia Sevin

THE APOCALYPSE TRIPTYCH

EDITED BY JOHN JOSEPH ADAMS AND HUGH HOWEY

BEFORE THE APOCALYPSE	DURING THE APOCALYPSE	AFTER THE APOCALYPSE
MARCH 2014	SEPTEMBER 2014	MAY 2015
Trade Paperback ($17.95)	Trade Paperback ($17.95)	Trade Paperback ($17.95)
Ebook ($4.99)	Ebook ($6.99)	Ebook ($6.99)
Audiobook ($24.95)	Audiobook ($24.95)	Audiobook ($24.95)
ISBN: 978-1495471179	ISBN: 978-1497484375	ISBN: 978-1497484405

FEATURING ALL-NEW, NEVER-BEFORE-PUBLISHED STORIES BY

Charlie Jane Anders	Tobias S. Buckell	Sarah Langan	Leife Shallcross
Megan Arkenberg	Tananarive Due	Ken Liu	Scott Sigler
Chris Avellone	Jamie Ford	Jonathan Maberry	Carrie Vaughn
Paolo Bacigalupi	Mira Grant	Matthew Mather	Robin Wasserman
Elizabeth Bear	Hugh Howey	Jack McDevitt	David Wellington
Annie Bellet	Jake Kerr	Seanan McGuire	Daniel H. Wilson
Desirina Boskovich	Nancy Kress	Will McIntosh	Ben H. Winters

Coming in August 2015

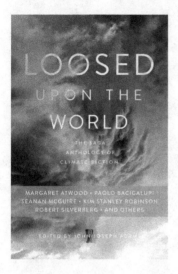

Saga Press

hardcover / $24.00 / 978-1481453073

trade paperback / $16.99 / 978-1481450300

ebook / $11.99

johnjosephadams.com/loosed

LOOSED UPON THE WORLD
edited by John Joseph Adams

This is the definitive collection of climate fiction from John Joseph Adams, the acclaimed editor of *The Best American Science Fiction & Fantasy* and *Wastelands*. These provocative stories explore our present and speculate about all of our tomorrows through terrifying struggle, and hope.

Join the bestselling authors Margaret Atwood, Paolo Bacigalupi, Nancy Kress, Kim Stanley Robinson, Jim Shepard, and over twenty others as they presciently explore the greatest threat to our future. This is a collection that will challenge readers to look at the world they live in as if for the first time.

PRESS START TO PLAY
edited by Daniel H. Wilson
& John Joseph Adams

You are standing in a room filled with books, faced with a difficult decision. Suddenly, one with a distinctive cover catches your eye. It is a groundbreaking anthology of short stories from award-winning writers and game-industry titans who have embarked on a quest to explore what happens when video games and science fiction collide.

From text-based adventures to first-person shooters, dungeon crawlers to horror games, these twenty-six stories play with our notion of what video games can be—and what they can become.

Vintage Books

trade paperback / $15.95 / 978-1101873304

ebook / $7.99

johnjosephadams.com/press-start